PEOPLE OF THE FIRE

In a parched and unforgiving land, a small band of pioneers battled for the future of a people:

Little Dancer—The young Dreamer whose awesome powers would change the course of history.

White Calf—The ancient medicine woman who taught Little Dancer how to harness his Dreams.

Elk Charm—The girl who won Little Dancer's heart, but feared she would lose him to his destiny.

Heavy Beaver—The false Dreamer who brutalized his people in his unquenchable thirst for power.

Two Smokes—The outcast tormented by forbidden love; his gentleness concealed an inner strength.

Tanager—The young woman warrior whose courage defended a Dreamer's vision.

FIRE DANCER

Fire filled the world, roaring like thunder mated to wind. Yellow-red, raging, it burned up from below, beating at him in loud fury. Crackling and snapping, the fire engulfed him. He blinked against the painful heat, trying to raise his arms in an effort to shield his face from the searing. The fire mocked him, walls of flame moving in retaliation, wavering this way and that in a frightening dance.

"We're One." Words formed in the roaring thunder of the endless flames. "All the world is One. We're all a Dream. Be with me . . . Dance with me."

He clamped his eyes shut, futilely shaking his head in denial.

"Free yourself, boy," the voice whispered. "Dance with me. Become One with me. Trust yourself. Forget your fear . . ."

Enflamed by the force of a shattering prophecy, a young man summoned the power of a time of fire to forge a new hope for his people. This is the true saga of the heroic ancestors of America's native peoples. This is the thrilling epic of the

PEOPLE OF THE FIRE

ATLANTIC

LAURENTIDE
ICE SHEET

CORDILLERAN
ICE SHEET

PACIFIC

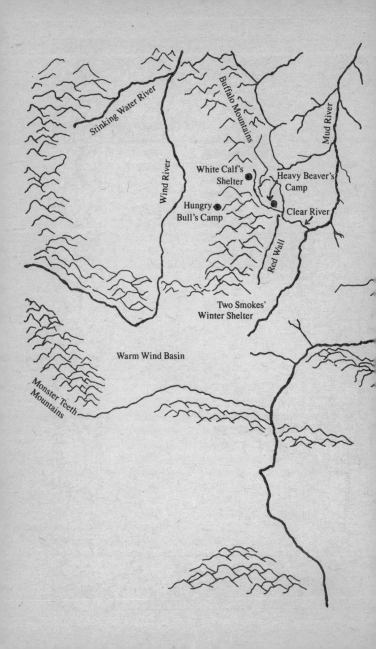

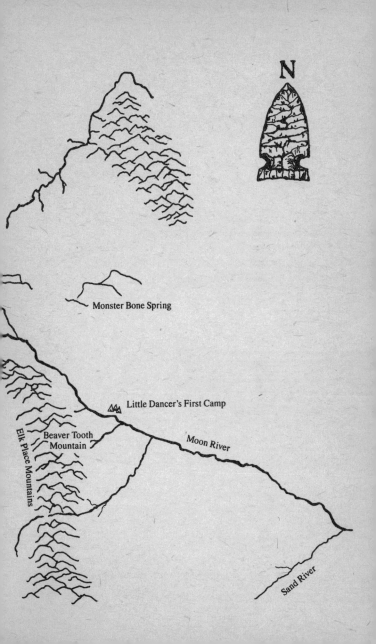

W. Michael Gear and Kathleen O'Neal Gear

People of the Fire

TOR

A TOM DOHERTY ASSOCIATES BOOK
NEW YORK

**To Gaydell and Roy and the rest of
the Backpocket Ranch Collier Clan,
who urged us to go for it!**

PEOPLE OF THE FIRE

A Tor Book
Published by Tom Doherty Associates, Inc.
49 West 24th Street
New York, NY 10010

Cover art by Royo

ISBN: 0-812-50739-8

First edition: January 1991

Printed in the United States of America

0 9 8 7 6 5 4 3 2 1

ACKNOWLEDGMENTS

This series on our nation's prehistory wouldn't be possible without the contributions of the following people: Michael Seidman cooked up the idea of doing a series of novels on North American prehistory, written by archaeologists, during his days as Executive Editor of Tor Books. Tappan King, who edited this manuscript, did a bang-up job on the line-edit and flagged the rough spots for revision. Ray Leicht, Wyoming State Archaeologist with the Bureau of Land Management, provided information and encouragement. Marv and Patricia Hatcher, Principal Investigators of Pronghorn Anthropological Associates, helped with the photocopying of stacks of archaeological reports gathered from across the West. Dr. George Frison, of the University of Wyoming, deserves our deepest gratitude for publishing so many of his observations on hunting techniques and Paleo-Indian weaponry, and for sharing his personal thoughts on the Mountain Archaic. Phyllis Boardman and the Torrey Lake Ranch deserve thanks for access to petroglyphs. Jo Hubbard eased the way. Walter Williams's *The Spirit and the Flesh* proved invaluable for information on berdache after Dale Walker turned us on to the book. Jim Miller and John Albanese receive special mention for their study and interpretation of Holocene geology. (See, we remembered all those lectures in the test pits!) Katherine Cook and Katherine Perry read the manuscript and provided helpful comments. Burt and Rose Crow of the Ramshorn Inn kept Guinness on hand for us when we needed a place to brainstorm plot. Irene Keinert and Justin Bridges of Wind River Knives photographed archaeological resources. Finally, we'd like to acknowledge our dirt-archaeologist colleagues for all the years of bull sessions over a beer or the crackling of a campfire. You know who you are. If you see your pet idea here, you've made a difference.

FOREWORD

From the time of the first human incursions into the Western Hemisphere, a thriving big-game-hunting tradition known as Paleo-Indian flourished through most of North America. Highly efficient, these human predators—in addition to climatic change and possible epizootic diseases—accelerated the extinction of animals such as the mammoth, giant sloth, horse, and camel. Through it all, humans, and their prey, adapted to the gradually warming climate until roughly eight thousand years ago. From the geological record, a dramatic climatic upheaval occurred: the Altithermal. A series of droughts baked North America, lowering regional water tables as much as twenty feet. Vegetation zones shifted, topsoil eroded, drainage channels ate deeply into the earth. The tree line climbed ever higher on the mountains. The huge lakes of the Great Basin vanished to leave salt flats and desert in Utah and Nevada. Giant dune fields spawned from destabilized parent material and drifted to cover parts of Montana, Wyoming, and Nebraska, while wind-borne loess settled over the American Midwest. Stricken with drought, the lush grasses on grazing land deteriorated; the buffalo herds declined in number. In this period of hardship people starved, bands of hunters fissioning, moving, warring—ever in search of elusive herds of game animals. Yet, from the seeds of these hard times came the birth of a new North American culture.

Introduction

"Jesus! I didn't know it would be so dusty." The blond man's shovel banged hollowly on rock as he tried to scoop it full. Muscles bulged as he straightened and threw his shovelful of dirt into the gray-headed man's sifter screen. The contraption rested on two wobbly legs and consisted of a shallow box with quarter-inch hardware cloth held across the bottom by metal strapping.

The screen made a *shish-shishing* sound, pebbles and rocks clattering across the mesh.

"Yeah, pretty dusty. That's the way it is in these rock shelters like this." A pause. "Nothing but them chips in this one. Keep digging."

The older man pulled a red handkerchief from his pocket and wiped at his nose. He wore an old checked shirt, and blue jeans hung from lean hips. While he waited he pulled a cigarette from his pocket, using a lighter to get it going.

With a practiced eye, he looked around the shelter, gauging the extent of it. "Bet there's ten feet of fill in this."

The blond might have been in his late twenties, tanned, with rippling muscles in his arms and back. He stood hip-deep in an irregular hole he'd pounded and hacked through the rocky soil at the back of the limestone overhang. Shirtless, he, too, wore Levi's, held up by a western-style tooled-leather belt. A can of chewing tobacco had worn a round circle in his back pocket.

"Sure is dusty. And there's all this charcoal."

"Injun fires, Pete, my boy! Injun fires! You look at the roof of this thing, now, and you'll see all that soot. That's how you know. And there's giant wild rye growing in front.

Injuns ate that stuff and it growed here when they dropped the seeds.''

The young man threw up another shovelful and used the spade to scrape off the wall, collecting another load to throw up. He banged the shovel and a large flat slab of wall rock cracked off.

"Burt? You're sure we won't get in trouble for this?''

"Naw!'' The older man hawked and spat into the back dirt at his feet. "Hells bells, I been digging for arrowheads for years. Nobody ever bothered me none.'' He gestured around before he clawed through the dirt. With a flip of his arms, he emptied his screen. "Clear up here? Forest Service don't drive that two-track very often. And we're back off the road.''

"So, like, what happens if they catch us?'' Pete muscled the heavy slab of rock up out of the hole and paused to wipe at the sweat beading on his forehead.

"Tell us to go away—and that it's against the law, probably. They got more important things to worry about . . . like selling trees to make money and fighting all them forest fires burning around. They ain't gonna bust us. Makes 'em look too bad. Like they're picking on the citizens. And I go to church of a Sunday.''

Burt caught another shovel load of dirt, sifting it in back-and-forth motions. A grin split his long face. "Hey! Lookee here. Bone bead. See how they polished it?''

He dropped the find into a sack. "Yep, you keep working these places, and you'll have a wall full of arrowheads pretty quick. Most of the ones out laying around, they been picked up.''

"Huh.'' The blond moved, squinting at the flat slab of rock he'd muscled out. He wiped at it, cleaning out the grooves, then looked at the wall. "Look at this. Something pecked in the wall. Looks like a spiral . . . but I busted it in half.''

"Spiral, huh?'' The gray-headed man bent and squinted. "Never seen one of them. Mostly it's critters and such. Too bad it broke in two. Otherwise we could take chisels and cut it out. Make a neat rock for someone's fireplace. Might be able to glue it or some such. We'll bring a chisel next time.

See if we can whack the other half out. If it busts again, well, hell, that's the way the cookie crumbles, huh?''

"And the Forest Service doesn't care about that?"

"Naw. And even if they did, what we're doing is small change. So we make a couple hundred bucks selling arrowheads? There's guys in Utah making thirty thousand for an Anasazi bowl.''

"Bet they bust them good.''

"Yeah, maybe. But then I remember a couple of years back, some fellas found a mummy up in the rocks south of here. You know, all stiff like and dried out. Sorta like them Egyptian kinds. The boys got drunk one night, tied a rope around its neck, and left it dangling from a telephone pole. All they got was a couple hundred dollars in fines and probation.''

"Hell! I get more than that for getting in a fight in the bar!''

The older man grinned, exposing brown teeth. "See, kid, nothing to it.''

They worked for a while longer, the young man shoveling dirt up to the old, listening to the *shish-shish* of the screen.

"So, like, don't the geologists get pissed off when they find these sites all dug up?''

"Archaeologists.''

"Huh?''

"That's archaeologists. Not geologists. And yeah, they bitch and moan. But who listens to them? They got lots of laws on the books, but after the shit they pull in Washington these days, who the hell cares about a bunch of dead Indians?''

"Whoa! A keeper!'' The old man pulled a white chert projectile point from the screen, holding it up to the light, cleaning the dirt off with his thumb.

"What kind?'' Pete asked when he finally got to see. He held the point up, a glint in his eyes.

"Looks like one of them Medicine Lodge Creek points. Probably eight thousand years old. Might be worth, oh, seventy-five or eighty dollars.''

"Wow!'' Pete's grin didn't fade as he fingered the stone. "Hey, I ain't selling this one. That's my first!''

"Yeah, you ought to keep it." Burt shook his head. "Damn stupid government! Got laws against everything anymore. So many they don't care. Down on the reservation, the fool Injuns squawk. But then, Injuns always squawk. Say we're foolin' with their ancestors. Hell, most of 'em don't know who their daddy is."

"So this is a pretty good site?"

"Yep, this's a good one. We ought to be able to dig here for quite a while. Got money in this one. I can feel it. Like knowing when you go into a bar that you're gonna get laid." Burt winked, a happy leer on his face.

"I'll tell Louise on you."

"Hell you will. You'll find your nuts handed to you on a platter, too."

Pete chuckled. " 'Course an old duffer like you ain't about to get it up just any old night either."

He resumed his digging, the shovel ringing off the rocks. The shadow in the rock shelter increased as Burt had to move his screen from the growing pile of back dirt.

"Whoops!" Pete stepped back. "Got a bone. Damn near cut it in two with the shovel!"

Burt came to look over his shoulder. "Burial? Or just a buffalo leg?"

"Kinda thin for buffalo, ain't it?" He moved back to let the more experienced eye of his mentor judge.

"Ah, that's human, all right. I seen enough of them. That ought to just pull right out of there. That's a shinbone."

Pete pulled, nothing happened. He looked up. "There ain't any haunts that go with this, is there?"

"Who you been talking to? Naw. You been going to too many of them creepy movies. Hell, shovel that dirt out up above there where the thigh would be. That's it."

Pete attacked the rubble, shovel blade ringing. He worked, tongue stuck out, undercutting the wall. He scraped the last of the dirt back, pulling on the bone. He jerked at the loud snap, rolling back on the dirt, holding up his trophy.

"Holy shit! Look at that, the knee's plumb growed together! Must've been a cripple. Too bad I busted the thighbone in two."

"Yeah, they didn't have much in the way of doctors back

then. Why, just think, maybe that's Geronimo's busted knee you got there!''

Pete grinned. "Shit! And you're full of it. Looks like it's almost dark. I gotta date with Lorena tonight. Might get lucky like you'll never see again. Give me a hand out of here.''

"Yep, s'pose we otta get going. You gonna keep that leg?''

"Damn right. Make a hell of a thing to talk about next time I throw a party at my place. Maybe so I'll file a groove here where I busted it off and use it for a cigarette holder. That otta show ol' Dink a thing or two.''

"All right, but I get the skull when we get it. There's money in skulls. I'll take the leg and stuff if you can carry that spiral you busted in two.''

Pete looked up at the sunset, gaudy and blood red. "Sure is dry anymore. Like the world's changing. All that drought in the farm states. Must be that damned greenhouse thing. Yellowstone burned up and now Washington and Oregon. Guess that'll keep the Forest Service off our backs for a while.''

"Bullshit. There ain't no goddamn 'greenhouse effect.' You'll see." Burt spat into the grass. "Government just tells you that to keep you scared.''

It took two trips to get artifacts and equipment down to the pickup.

Pete grinned and popped the top off a hot beer, handing it to Burt. Then he opened one for himself, climbing into the driver's seat. The big V-8 roared to life.

The old man looked back. "Too bad about that spiral getting busted.''

"You sure there ain't any bad luck in that? Some hoodoo Injun magic or something?''

"Hell no, that's just silly superstition. What harm could it do?" Burt paused, sucking on his beer. "Yep, that's a big shelter up there. We'll be able to dig for years in that one. Completely clean it out. Good money. I can just feel it!''

BOOK ONE

The Harrowing
of the Child

"To Power, time means nothing. Everything belongs to the Spiral—be it the path of the universe, the rotation of the Starweb itself, or the path of Father Sun across the sky.

"And where does Power come from? Like the storms, it comes from earth, and sky, and water, and the Power of Father Sun, and the Wise One Above—the Creator. Of all the sources of Power we know, the Wolf Bundle is most Powerful on earth. Once, back when First Man—the Wolf Dreamer— led the People from the First World to this one, the Wolf Bundle was made. Born of a Dream, it suckled itself from the minds of the People. Because the People believed in it, it grew in strength . . . warmed by as many hands as held it so reverently . . . powered by the spirit breathed into it from a thousand lungs; it is our soul, our Power as humans.

"The People carried it protected in the sacred wolf hide. They guarded it from rain and snow and dust. Men and women were born under its Power . . . or died with it in their arms. Sometimes it soaked up the blood of those who died to protect it from desecration or sacrilege. Part of their souls joined with the Wolf Bundle, as did the spirit of the rocks and trees and animals and the People themselves. Nothing on earth is more sacred than the Wolf Bundle. It's the Power . . . the Dream that gives the People life.

"That's what brought me to you. The Power of the Wolf Bundle. I don't know why. I don't know how. But the Circles are turning and the earth is changing. Something is trying to unravel the Starweb woven by the Wise One Above. The Circles . . . always the Circles, and time doesn't mean much to Power. Who knows how long we have left?

"I learned this in a Dream. There, in the Dream, in the

vision, I talked to the Wolf Bundle and heard the voice of First Man. So I followed . . . I came here to you . . . and the Wolf Bundle.''

—White Calf to Cut Feather

Prologue

Pain twisted the old man's belly—the sensation that of a keenly flaked chert knife cutting his soul loose from his back-bone. How long now? How long until it severed the tenuous threads of life?

Cut Feather tried to settle his aching back in a comfortable position. Inside the lodge, the heat seemed to intensify, stifling, raising a sweat sheen on his ancient wrinkled skin. He rolled the bottom of the lodge cover up, allowing the hot breeze to blow through, using the cover for a sunshade; it didn't help much.

He blinked against the constant gnawing pain, lifting his hands to look at the knobby bones under the crinkled thin leather of his skin. Old, so old. His hair gleamed white, braids worn ever shorter where they framed his withered face. His eyelids had sunk around the orbits, leaving hollows that gathered the shadows cast upon his soul.

I look like a winterkill carcass in spring—dried out, shrunk over brittle bone. Not enough of me left for the maggots to chew.

About him, the final remnants of his long life lay ready for inspection—all but the sacred Wolf Bundle, its place suspiciously empty on the little willow tripod. Beyond the door hanging, dogs yipped and growled. The soft voices of the Red Hand band, his people, carried in the dry air. Even here, high in the mountains, continued drought burned the land. How long since rain? Drought led to war.

Buffalo had become scarce in the wide plains to the east, so the Short Buffalo People had come here, seeking the herds that grazed the high meadows where the peaks scoured the clouds for what rain they could glean. The Short Buffalo People wanted to call this land theirs. The two peoples could not coexist. The plains hunters wanted only meat, disdaining the roots and pine nuts beloved by the Red Hand. Plains hunters used special Power to ambush buffalo—from which they obtained robes, hides for shelters, and all their food, even roasting the entrails. Their language made no sense, like the clucking of a grouse. Worse, they spat upon the Red Hand as eaters of plants.

The Red Hand had repeatedly driven the Short Buffalo People back into the basins and river bottoms to the south and east. Only the elk knew the mountains as well as the Red Hand. In the mountains, he who controlled the trails controlled the country. In the process of ambushing Short Buffalo People, the Red Hand had earned a new name: *Anit'ah*. That's what they were called in the Short Buffalo People's tongue. "Enemy."

Cut Feather stared thoughtfully at the smoke-browned hides overhead, knowing the shapes of each of the slender lodgepoles he'd trimmed by hand, knowing each stitch Clear Water had sewn so carefully. A fly buzzed behind the lodge where he'd relieved himself. Time for the camp to move again, time to allow the Sun Father to cleanse the wastes of the Red Hand. All part of the Circles, even flies and beetles had to eat. Circles like the ones he'd pecked so laboriously into the rock panels in imitation of the constant Dance of the Wise One Above who watched from the Starweb.

Only this time, I won't be going. Here, this is the end. The last camp for Cut Feather. It's a good place . . . a place to die high on the mountain where the soul is free to rise to the stars and meet the Wise One.

As if it heard, the knotted pain in his belly tightened, stealing his strength and breath, trying to twist his soul from his body. His body continued to waste, thinner and thinner except for the hard lump he could feel when he pressed under his ribs on the right side. The lump got bigger, and he grew less.

And I am left to the final Dream. . . .

Smiling wearily, he remembered Clear Water's face, the glow of youth in her full cheeks. She'd been the true Spirit Woman. She'd been the one who paused, eyes suddenly vacant, to tell him about the Wolf Man who whispered in her ear.

He'd listened . . . always listened, and told the People what to do. They'd never suspected the Power had come from his daughter. Never suspected Clear Water's counsel guided him. She'd seen, and now she'd gone, fleeing her man, Blood Bear. She'd left quietly in the night, accompanied by the odd berdache, Two Smokes, who watched the plants, picking the grasses and chewing the stems.

Angry shouts outside gave him the bit of warning he'd hoped to have. The rasping swish of moccasins in the grass allowed him that final instant to compose himself as a strong hand ripped the hanging aside.

"Where is she, old man?"

Cut Feather smiled up into Blood Bear's smoldering features. His son-in-law's strong face had flushed, dark eyes fired. Muscular, hotheaded, Blood Bear had always been trouble. In the short time he'd been married to Clear Water, he'd beaten her more than once. People had turned their heads at sounds of violent coupling in the lodge at night, shamed by her whimpers of pain.

He'd been helpless—an old Spirit Man without power. Clear Water had no other relatives to protest her treatment, to seek justice. And Blood Bear had no fear of a Spirit Man's threats.

"She's gone."

Blood Bear leaned forward, black eyes burning. "I know that, you simple old fool. *Where* did she go?"

Cut Feather reached for the gourd, half-full of water, extending it. "Come, sit. You are a guest in my lodge. Drink and—"

Blood Bear smashed the gourd away, spattering water about the worn hides, soaking the sacred bundles. *"Where, old man?"*

Cut Feather winced at the mess, blinking as he looked up. "You know, Blood Bear, you're not doing yourself any good. Shouting at me just undercuts your position. I'm dying and everybody knows it. Rage has stolen even your cunning."

"I'll—"

"Hush and hear me out. You're a laughingstock. Your wife ran away with another man. The People—"

A hard hand clamped on his throat. The heat of Blood Bear's breath warmed his skin as those burning eyes searched his. "What man, Cut Feather? Speak quickly, or never speak again."

The reflection of death watched from Blood Bear's flushed features.

"Let . . . go," Cut Feather croaked over his protruded tongue. Blood Bear relaxed his powerful fingers ever so slightly.

"Who?"

"Two Smokes."

"He's berdache! A man who loves other men! Why would she run off with . . . with *him*?"

Cut Feather tried to swallow without success. Instead, his saliva escaped the side of his mouth, trickling down his cheek and over Blood Bear's iron fingers.

"Why? Curse you!"

"You still don't understand?" Cut Feather closed his eyes, savoring the feeling of Blood Bear's choking grasp. Could he still enjoy memories when his ghost rose to the Wise One Above? Or did the soul evaporate like the physical body, eaten by this and that, rotted away?

The grip on his throat released entirely. "Tell me."

"She Dreamed it. That's why she went to you in the first place. The very sight of you disgusted her. Did you know that?" He looked up, not surprised at the arrogant disbelief in Blood Bear's eyes. "Yes, she thought you were no more than a surly camp dog."

"For a camp dog, she came willingly, old man. She saw I would lead the Red Hand People, saw I—"

"Fool! It was a Spirit Dream. I don't know the half of it. A man doesn't guess about Spirit Power. It has its own reasons for things. She Dreamed . . . and the Dream told her you must father the child. As soon as her bleeding missed, she and Two Smokes left. No. Don't threaten. I don't know where she went, or why, or what Two Smokes' part in it is, either. But he's a good person. Maybe she needs him to care for the baby. Maybe she needs his help for some other reason. He's berdache. There's Spirit Power in that."

"I think you know where she is. You tell me, old man. *Tell me!*"

"Think all you want. It's a new experience for you, I'm sure."

The blow caught him by surprise, the slap loud in the confines of the lodge. The power of it snapped Cut Feather's head sideways, bright flashes dancing behind his ancient eyes.

"Sure," Cut Feather grunted through the pain. "You can kill lots of Short Buffalo People and strut. You can even kill me. But you're ruined here. Finished. Out there, they're listening, hearing your rage. You would be leader of the Red Hand . . . but can people follow a man who can't keep his wife and child from a berdache? Can they follow a man who'll kill a dying old man in rage? No . . . Clear Water and I, we've broken you."

The corners of Blood Bear's lips twitched and jumped as he struggled to control himself. For that instant of time, Cut Feather knew true fear.

"Where is the Bundle . . . the Wolf Bundle?"

"She took it."

"That belonged to the People!"

"It was Spirit Power . . . something in the Dream."

"I'll find her. I'll find *my* child. You hear me? I swear on the Wolf Bundle she stole. *I'll find my child!*"

"The child? Or is it the Wolf Bundle? I think you could care less about the child. I'm dying. I have no more to say."

Under Blood Bear's taut cheeks, the muscles jumped violently, the sound of his grating molars audible. "Then die, *old man!*"

Blood Bear turned, hesitated, and kicked Cut Feather in the stomach. "There, that won't kill you. But you'll know how I feel."

And he was gone, bursting out into the light beyond.

Cut Feather grunted as he doubled over, knotting pain burning in his belly. He felt it pull as he straightened, a rush of warmth deep within. A queer tingling followed as he began to feel bloated and light-headed.

He barely realized when he fell over. Only it seemed that

faces peered sideways at him. The hides under his cold cheek felt wet, soaked, as if someone had spilled water on them. A dizziness swirled around him as people crowded in, seeking to help, asking questions he could barely hear.

"The Wolf Bundle?" A cry pierced the haze in his mind. *"We can't live without the Wolf Bundle!"*

But Clear Water had taken it. Spirit Dream . . . Clear Water knew what she was doing. His thoughts slipped away like smoke into a night sky. Fading. Fading. Grayness.

"Looks like you were wrong again, Blood Bear. You killed me despite yourself." And he chuckled.

The haze dimmed and floated around him, like tufted clouds on a mountaintop. His soul drifted, sinking into a calming warmth. Then he began to rise, upward, above his crumpled body.

Are you coming? a soft voice asked.

"Who? Who called?"

They call me Wolf Dreamer . . . the Sun Man . . . a new way lies before you now. A new way . . .

What must come, will. Human souls flow like the currents of a river—often angry, thrashing white, boiling and mad against the resistant rock that blocks the way. At other times human souls move peacefully, slow and lazy, barely rippling the surface of the tepid water they wind through. Then, depending on the time of year, they flow encased in blue-white ice, locked in a secret darkness.

Around the Wolf Bundle, souls gather, unaware of the rapids around this last bend.

"You must be patient," the voice of the Wolf Dreamer whispers through the mists.

"I know," the Wolf Bundle answers.

Chapter 1 🐃

The lodge trapped the heat of the night, warm and muggy despite the rustling dry wind shivering the smoke-browned hide cover. The cover had been drawn down tight, firmly pegged to the hard clay in order to form a seal so that none of the malicious Spirit Powers might wiggle beneath to steal in and find a home. The People did that during a birthing. Newborn children had no soul, and into that warm haven any manner of evil could creep. To further ward off harmful powers, sagebrush—the lifegiver—had been piled around, the purposely bruised leaves adding a rich pungency to the desiccating air.

From where the boy crouched outside in the darkness, a frayed seam had come unraveled enough to allow a peephole view of the interior.

A single fire of punky cottonwood smoldered and smoked, adding to the stifling heat in the lodge and giving light in the midst of so dark and windy a night. The warm, steamy air issuing from inside puffed on the boy's eye. It brought the odors of tanned hide, smoke, and sage to his nose. Mixed with it were other smells of sweat, wood, and fear. The delicately bitter taint of herbs wafted out as he watched.

Dancing Doe cried out where she lay naked on sweat-soaked robes. The smooth planes of her young face twisted and contorted as her belly contracted, seeking to force the child within from the safe confines of her womb. Between her breasts lay a natal bundle, a figure in the shape of Turtle—the magical animal that never sickened. Turtle brought health and luck. He disappeared with the coming of the winter gales, crawling down into the Earth Mother, returning when Father Sun brought spring and life to the world. The fetish on Dancing Doe's breast had been constructed of finely sewn antelope hide and stuffed with sage, bits of twigs, feathers, and other sorts of Power.

On her belly, a series of designs had been drawn to center the Spirit Power of birth. The most important, a bright yellow stripe, had been painted down from the natal bundle between her full breasts to end in a point in the mat of her black pubic hair. The Path of Light, it would lead the child on its way to the world.

The boy stared, feeling the Power of the women's chant within. Though he feared discovery, he couldn't force himself away from the fascinating events. He knew his mother would punish him—and Two Smokes would no doubt even now be looking for him, beginning to worry about his absence from his sleeping robes.

A night of heat, a night of pain. Across the mound of Dancing Doe's swollen belly, two women—one young, one old—looked at each other, worry etching their tension-worn faces.

The old woman's gray hair glinted in the light. Patterns of wrinkles were cast into a tracery of shadows across her withered face. The set of her mouth had gone grim as she continued her vigil over the struggling woman. Back curved from age, she hunched, upper body bared and sweaty in the heat. Long-dry breasts hung low and flat over the folds of her stomach. Lines of scars puckered the wrinkled skin of her shoulders, mute evidence of the number of times she'd offered bits of herself to the Spirit World. The people called her Chokecherry, after the bittersweet plant that grew in the high lands.

The boy watched as his mother, Sage Root, crouched to help, her anxious eyes on Dancing Doe's fevered body. He knew that strained look. Worry marked the faces of all the People. Lines, like arroyos on the land, etched deep into their faces. But the helpless concern his mother betrayed frightened him. When Dancing Doe cried again, his gut tightened like sun-dried sinew.

Poor Dancing Doe. Her husband, Long Runner, had gone to hunt the foothills of the Buffalo Mountains. He'd never returned.

Chokecherry took a breath, reaching into a neatly sewn

sack to withdraw damp sage and sprinkle it on the red eyes of coals. The perfume of life roiled up on a mist of steam.

She chanted softly in a singsong, "Come, little one. Come to walk in life and bless the land and sun and plants and animals. Come to join us on the path to the Starweb which leads to all good things. Hear our song. Hear our joy. Come, little one. Come into this world and make us smile."

Dancing Doe grunted again, tensing the muscles of her powerful brown legs. She sucked a frantic breath, exhaling sharply, eyes clamped tight, teeth bared in a rictus of effort. Beads of sweat traced irregular paths down her trembling flesh.

Sage Root gripped Dancing Doe's fingers in her own. "Easy. Breathe easy. It won't be long now."

Dancing Doe relaxed as the spasms passed. She gasped and looked up at the old woman, who continued chanting. "It doesn't always take so long. Chokecherry, is it all right? Am I dying?"

The old woman finished the litany and lifted a shoulder, smiling. "I've borne children more difficult than this. It's your first time. Those muscles have to be stretched and they don't know how yet. Nothing's torn. All that's come out is water—washing you, you see, making the way clean. That's all." She looked across, laughing reassuringly. "Just like Sage Root. She kept me and Horn Core up for almost a whole day."

Sage Root smiled wistfully. "I remember. But my son was born strong."

Only when Dancing Doe closed her eyes and nodded did Sage Root's expression tighten. Tension hung in the air like winter mist, reflected in the set of her features and in Chokecherry's burning eyes. It drifted from the rent in the lodge to settle like a water-heavy green hide on the boy's shoulders.

Chokecherry resumed singing under her breath, taking another handful of sage leaves from the pouch and sprinkling it over the fire to fill the lodge with a clinging steamy odor.

Dancing Doe cried out, anguish palpable as her belly tightened.

"Should we call Heavy Beaver?" Sage Root's hard eyes leveled on Chokecherry's.

From where he sat outside, the boy winced. Heavy Beaver, the Spirit Dreamer of the People, brought that kind of reaction. In his head, a voice whispered, *"No."*

Like a shadow in the night, he eased back, parting the piled sagebrush with careful fingers and creeping from his peephole. Free of the brush, he sprinted across the camp on light feet, heedless of the barking dogs. Before him, on the packed clay, the lodges huddled, squat, the bottoms rolled up over the peeled poles to allow the night breeze to blow through and cool the occupants where they slept on grass-padded bedding. Here and there, the sanguine eye of a dying fire cast a sunrise sheen on boiling pouches hanging from tripods, black orbs of hearthstones dotting the glowing coals.

Cottonwoods rose against the night sky, silhouetted black; the ghostly image of clouds could be vaguely discerned against the exposed patches of stars. In the trees, an owl hooted cautiously.

"Wolf Bundle," the voice in his head whispered.

Before he reached the lodge, he recognized Two Smokes' figure hobbling across the camp. No one walked like Two Smokes. "Two Smokes?" He changed course, trotting up.

"There you are! I've been half-sick worrying about you. Here your father is gone to hunt, your mother is—"

"I need you. I think we need the Wolf Bundle."

"The Wolf Bundle?" Two Smokes cocked his head, the familiar curious expression hidden by the shades of night. Tone softening and reserved, he asked in his Anit'ah-accented voice, "Why do *we* need the Wolf Bundle, Little Dancer?"

He hesitated. "I just . . . well, a voice told me."

"A voice? The one that speaks in your head?"

"Yes. Please, bring the Bundle," he pleaded. "Dancing Doe's baby isn't coming. Mother and Chokecherry are worried. Dancing Doe is afraid she'll die. And Chokecherry didn't say it, but I could *feel.* You know, what she didn't say. The look in her eyes. I thought the Wolf Bundle . . ."

"You thought right. Come. Let's see what we can do."

Two Smokes pivoted on his good leg, heading off in his

wobbling stride for their lodge, the fringed skirts of his dress swaying in time to his off-balanced pace.

The berdache had always been an enigma to Little Dancer's mind. No other man among the People wore a dress. In response to his childish questions, Two Smokes had smiled wistfully and replied that he was berdache—between the worlds. A woman in a man's body.

The berdache had lived with the People for as long as Little Dancer could remember, always staying in their lodge—a strange silent man who'd come to them from the Anit'ah. Patiently he endured, despite the jokes and gibes and the open ridicule of the People. Alone and aloof, Two Smokes helped Little Dancer's mother with chores, scraping hides, cooking stew, accepting the duties a second wife would.

Little Dancer's father, Hungry Bull, the greatest hunter among the People, remained civil to Two Smokes, his innate disapproval tempered by some other veiled concern the boy had never been able to penetrate. Mystery surrounded the berdache like the swirl of smoke from a rain-wet fire.

Not that Little Dancer cared. For all his eight summers, Two Smokes remained his best friend, listening intently when Little Dancer told him of the voices he often heard. When his mother or father scolded him, he ran to Two Smokes like other children ran to their grandparents.

"So you were hiding around the birthing lodge?"

Little Dancer stiffened. "I . . ."

"You know, men should never get close to a birthing lodge. That's a place for women. What if you change the Power?"

Shamed, Little Dancer dropped his gaze to the ghostly clay they trod, heart sinking in his chest. "I'm not a man. I'm just a boy. I'm not a man until I'm named and have proven myself."

"And you didn't think that even a boy might make a difference?"

"The voice didn't tell me I would. When I'm around Power, I usually know."

"Indeed?"

Into the stretching silence, Little Dancer added, "It's a feeling. Like . . . well, the silence before thunder. Only longer. Just a feeling, that's all. And sometimes the voice."

He stopped before his family's lodge, waiting as Two Smokes ducked inside, hearing the shuffling as the berdache carefully unwrapped the Wolf Bundle from the heavy parfleche that kept it safe.

Ducking through the low doorway, Two Smokes cradled the Bundle so carefully wrapped in a beautifully tanned wolf hide. The pelt gleamed gray in the faint starlight.

"If you don't believe me, why did you come for the Bundle?" He pointed at the furry gray mass Two Smokes pressed to his heart. But the berdache simply brushed past, heading for the birthing lodge.

"Well? Why did you?"

The sigh from Two Smokes' breath lingered. "One day, Little Dancer, I'll tell you."

"But I want to know now. I can't see why—"

"You've seen the eagles nesting on the high cliffs. You've climbed up to look down on the newly hatched chicks."

"Uh-huh, and Eagle's a Power bird. I could feel that. I know what newly hatched chicks look like, all fuzzy and—"

"Would you push one of those fuzzy chicks out of the nest? Simply because he's an eagle, would you expect him to fly because of it? Because of the Power in him?"

"I . . . No."

"Then don't push yourself out of the nest until your feathers are ready to support you."

Perplexed and confused, Little Dancer tried to make sense of it. *Does that mean I, too, have Power?* The question dazzled him, a warm glow forming under his heart. For the briefest moment, a tingling thread seemed to wind between him and the Bundle tucked so tightly against Two Smokes' heart. The pattern snapped as neatly as a sage twig underfoot as Dancing Doe's miserable cry penetrated the walls of the birthing lodge.

"Wait out here—and out of sight, if you please." Then in a louder voice: "Sage Root? It's Two Smokes. I have something to help."

But Little Dancer had already raced for his peephole, ducking through the sage, hunching over the little opening.

He could see his mother's anxious look at Chokecherry. In

a subdued voice she said, "He's berdache. He knows a great deal. Among his own people—"

"I know." Chokecherry stroked her chin. "The Anit'ah say the berdache have Spirit Power. Myself, yes, I believe it." She raised her voice. "Come, Two Smokes." Then quietly, "By the Blessing Power, we could use any help we could get . . . besides Heavy Beaver."

Two Smokes ducked into the dimly lit lodge, the Bundle still pressed to his heart. "If you would, let me use the Wolf Bundle." He extended it reverently, a plea in his gentle eyes.

"The Wolf Bundle?" Chokecherry cocked her head, still fingering her sagging chin. "Yes . . . perhaps."

Dancing Doe looked up, a new fright in her eyes as she saw Two Smokes. "No! Not a man. Not here where—"

"Shhh!" Sage Root soothed. "He knows Power."

"I want Heavy Beaver!" The fear in her eyes deepened.

"I'm berdache," Two Smokes appealed. "I've done this before."

"Trust him," Chokecherry urged.

Dancing Doe didn't have time to respond; another contraction racked her. Chokecherry nodded curtly to the berdache and backed to allow him room.

Two Smokes settled next to the whimpering woman, careful fingers undoing the wolf hide. He laid the hide out as a protective mat to keep the sacred bundle from contact with the earth. As he began to chant in the melodious tones of the Anit'ah, Little Dancer leaned forward, eye pressed to the peephole to see.

From the outside, the Wolf Bundle didn't look like much, only a skin bag tightly bound and painted a deep red along the pointed end. The top had been left white, traced by lines that resembled veins. *A heart!* That's what it was, a heart fetish!

Two Smokes took sage from the pouch he carried, dipped it in water where it hung from a tripod, and sprinkled it into the fire. Behind him, Chokecherry and Sage Root exchanged nervous glances.

"Here, this needs to be made into tea." He extended a hand containing cleaned phlox. "She must drink some, the rest will be rubbed on her. Sage Root, wash her down there where the baby will come.''

Then he lifted the Wolf Bundle up to the smoke hole, singing in the language of the Anit'ah, eyes closed, face serene.

From where he sat, Little Dancer watched, and a sudden giddiness swelled within, raising his soul to the haunting tones. The familiar feeling of Power wrapped around him.

Reeling, he barely noticed when Two Smokes touched the Bundle to Dancing Doe's perspiring forehead. The woman quieted, breathing easier. Two Smokes then touched the Bundle to her heart, just above the turtle effigy, then to her protruding navel and again to the swell of her pubis above the point of the yellow stripe.

Dancing Doe gasped, this time in relief.

The tea finished, Sage Root filled a buffalo-horn spoon, placing it to the woman's lips. Dancing Doe drank, and grimaced.

Resting the Wolf Bundle on the protective hide, Two Smokes dipped his hands in the steaming water pouch, now full of tea. ''This is the way my people have taught me. The phlox tea soothes the flesh.''

Hands dripping, he began to massage her heavy belly. At Two Smokes' nod, Sage Root copied his motions, working down. Dancing Doe bit off a cry as another contraction pressed through her.

''Easy now,'' Two Smokes cautioned, his fingers probing the woman's shuddering body. ''The pressure must be just so. Too much and the insides can tear. Bleeding can't always be stopped.''

''We tried massage,'' Chokecherry added. ''It didn't seem to work.''

Two Smokes nodded, eyes going to the Wolf Bundle. ''Perhaps this will.'' With that, he reached for the Bundle and touched it to Dancing Doe's navel where it protruded like a knob.

Dancing Doe cried out, another contraction wrenching her.

''There.'' Chokecherry nodded, crawling to get between Dancing Doe's legs. She positioned herself. ''We've got fluid. A little bit of blood.''

Two Smokes held the Bundle in place, eyes closed, still singing in his lilting tone.

"Child's coming," Chokecherry added.

Craning his head to see, Little Dancer didn't hear the soft steps. He jerked as the flap lifted and Heavy Beaver ducked in, caught sight of Two Smokes and the Wolf Bundle, and stopped dead.

Shock registered for only a moment before a dull rage filled his black eyes and rearranged the planes of his flat face.

"So, *this* is what's happening?"

Sage Root shot a look over her shoulder, a flickering of fright in her eyes. "The baby is coming."

Two Smokes didn't break stride in his chant.

"A little more," Chokecherry coaxed, hands placed.

Where he crouched outside, the blackness twirled with the Power. Heavy Beaver! He could feel it, a subtle whiff of anger and hatred. The effect stung him like a sulfur breeze on a green meadow, grasses and flowers wilting and smothering. The Wolf Bundle remained a powerful brilliance in the miasma.

"Ah-ha! Bear down!" Chokecherry cried, reaching where Little Dancer couldn't see. "That's it."

Dancing Doe shuddered as her belly flattened and Chokecherry lifted the infant, streaked and wet in her hands. The squalling cry of new life filled the lodge.

Two Smokes inhaled deeply and dropped his head, pulling the Wolf Bundle back to his breast, stroking it reverently as he whispered a prayer of thanks under his breath.

"It's a girl," Sage Root whispered, looking furtively toward Heavy Beaver.

"Why am I not surprised?" Heavy Beaver loomed, crouched under the low spread of the shelter. The look in his eyes tickled a cold shiver down Little Dancer's spine.

"Another girl? And born under the influence of malignant Spirit Power?" Heavy Beaver crossed his arms. "A wondrous gift to the People."

Dancing Doe worked her mouth dryly, too spent to do anything but stare with fright-wide eyes at the Spirit Dreamer.

In his accented speech, Two Smokes said softly, "The Wolf Bundle isn't evil. It's—"

"Just what I'd expect from Anit'ah—and from something the likes of you. What *are* you? A woman in a man's body like you claim? Surely a curse if I've ever heard one. And yet you'd pollute the birthing lodge?"

Two Smokes closed his eyes, expression pained.

"Leave him alone." Sage Root turned where she rested on her heels. "The Wolf Bundle freed the child."

"Another girl. A mouth to feed while men go hungry."

"So *you* say!" Sage Root colored. "You can't keep blaming starvation on women. We're the People! Why have you turned your hatred against us? What's your purpose? To drive the People apart? Then you're succeeding! We're not animals."

"Oh? And you think the Wise One Above hasn't—"

"I think your Dreams are false."

Stunned silence filled the lodge as Sage Root realized what she'd said.

Where he crouched in the night, Little Dancer started, gasping. Immediately eyes went his direction.

"Who?" Heavy Beaver wondered. "Another pollution?" He reached for the flap, and in that instant, Little Dancer jumped to his feet, vaulted the sage, and sped into the darkness.

Heart pounding, he crept around a lodge, hearing old Two Elks snoring softly. On silent feet, he circled, drawing near as Heavy Beaver reentered the lodge.

"Someone fast—or some *thing*. Tell me now that this Wolf Bundle isn't evil." The words carried as Little Dancer dropped on his belly to wiggle up next to a cottonwood bole. The flap hadn't fallen back in place so he could see inside.

"It's not evil. It's the soul of—" Two Smokes stopped lamely.

"The Anit'ah?" Heavy Beaver probed, looming over the berdache.

"The Power works for all people, Spirit Man. You, of all men, should know that . . . . Wait! *What are you doing?*"

Heavy Beaver ripped the Bundle from Two Smokes' grasp, stepping back to avoid clawing fingers. He ducked out as Two Smokes scrambled behind. With a vile curse, he threw the Bundle into the night. In the half-light of the fire, Little

Dancer caught the horror on Two Smokes' stricken face. In that moment, he felt the berdache's soul cry. Two Smokes' face masked a mind-rending terror as he reached a futile hand toward the night.

A soft plop sounded in the beaten grass beyond the camp. At that moment, Little Dancer's soul twisted, a wretched sickness welling in his gut. He vomited before he could fight the urge.

As if from a distance, he heard Two Smokes' horrified shout.

Voices of people awakened by Heavy Beaver's curse called back and forth, unsure of themselves. Some of the younger men rushed out of their lodges, searching the darkness for Anit'ah, seeking the cause of the disturbance. The babble rose on the night, men and women grabbing robes before hurrying out.

Lifting his head, Little Dancer wiped at his mouth, terror eating at his insides. Two Smokes stared up where he'd stopped on all fours, disbelief in his eyes. People gaped, seeing Heavy Beaver's bulk silhouetted in the birthing lodge's fire.

"The infant must be destroyed." Heavy Beaver turned, looking into the lodge. "Do you hear, Dancing Doe? This is your doing . . . all of you. The People are already polluted by foulness. They are polluted by women turning men's medicine against them. This . . . this infant is polluted by Anit'ah witchcraft and whatever vile spirit of the night lurked outside the lodge when it was born. I condemn all of you as unclean!"

"No!" Dancing Doe cried from inside. "Not my child. Not my baby!"

"Kill it!" Heavy Beaver roared. "It's *your* pollution."

Sage Root ducked through the lodge entrance, standing up before him. "I wonder just where the pollution lies? I don't feel polluted at all . . . except in your presence!"

"Don't!" Chokecherry grabbed Sage Root's arm, pulling her back. "He's a Spirit Dreamer. Apologize."

Little Dancer saw his mother start, anger draining from her tensed body. "I . . . forgive me."

Heavy Beaver's face worked, a curious mix of enjoyment

and vindication. "The child must be destroyed." At that he turned, lifting a foot and kicking Two Smokes down on his face in the dirt before striding off into the night.

A hushed mumble of voices rose from the spectators.

Stunned, Little Dancer shivered and blinked at the scene. Two Smokes raised his head, firelight tracing the tears streaking his face.

The wind had stopped, the air going heavy and stifling. In the sudden silence, Dancing Doe's baby wailed.

In White Calf's rock shelter high in the Buffalo Mountains, the Dream settled like morning dew lying lightly on her sleep. Like frost patterns, the Dream wove into her mind, tightening its hold on her soul. Beyond, the stars continued the circle of the sky, oblivious to the silent shelter in the mountainside so far below. Coyotes yipped and chorused as they harried the carcass of a freshly killed elk calf. Unnoticed, owls drifted over the meadow on silent wings while mice rustled the umbel-richening grasses for growing seed.

The night world lived as White Calf Dreamed. . . .

In a land of glare, she walked, one tired step after another—the ancient ritual of travel. A wind, hot as the draft radiating from ember-cradled cooking stones, puffed at her face, desiccating her thin flesh. About her, the slumbering anima of the land waited, restless, drying, and dying.

"Didn't used to be like this." She grimaced at the rasping of her voice. *The old stories talk of water, of buffalo so plentiful a strong man could cast his dart in any direction and kill. The old stories talk of grass up to a man's waist. And now? Springs my grandfather's grandfather drank from are no more than muddy seeps. Only the old ones know. Only the keepers of the legends.*

But the legends are changing. People are changing. Even place names are changing. Everything . . . changing . . .

The old familiar ache stitched and throbbed in the joint of her right hip. Down deep inside the muscles of her age-worn legs, cramps of fatigue gnawed like big black ants in the infested heart of a deadfall pine. The hurt in her feet had grown, expanding, encompassing. Arches flat and complaining, she padded across the hot clay, toes stinging as burning, eburnating joints swelled.

"Too damn old for this," she muttered. "Ought to have a fancy lodge . . . strong sons and daughters to bring me meat. Ought to be free to sit around and talk and make jokes. Tell the old stories so they're remembered. Watch the young men and women act foolish trying to impress each other. That's what."

Except the vision had come. While she prayed and fasted on the high peaks of the Buffalo Mountains, something had happened to her. Four days she'd been without food or water, chilled by the cool night air, desiccated by the rays of the spring sun; she'd shivered and purged her soul.

Naked, she'd sat on the high point, seeking the source of the call that had driven her all her life. Each time she had retreated, tried living like a human, the call had returned, imperative, driving her to abandon each of her husbands and the children they'd sired off her. Each time she'd returned to the high places to seek the source of Power.

So she had gone again, until, on the fourth day, a man's image had formed in the clouds, his features lit by the blinding rays of the sun. A handsome man, tall, his Power had sung in silence, dwarfing the clouds, a presence of warmth and sunlight.

She'd watched in awe as he smiled at her, an arm rising to point southeast toward the plains where her native peoples had lived since the time of the First Man. As quickly as it had come, the image faded to be replaced by that of Wolf, eyes glowing yellow as sunbeams pierced the clouds.

She'd blinked then, heart racing in her chest, staring up in wonder at the puffy white formations of a giant thunderhead. Weakened and shaken, she'd climbed down, found her clothes, and eaten before setting off on the journey.

"Wolf Dreamer," she mumbled. "He brought me here.

She took a deep breath, shaking her head and slowing to a stop. Her tongue smacked, sticky in her dry mouth as she squinted into the white glare of the beating sun.

An old woman alone in the vastness and heat, she stood, back stooped from the tumpline holding a bulky pack on the fulcrum of her hips. She peered around in all directions, catching her breath. The distant bluffs shimmered like a Spirit Dream—jagged outlines wavering. Even the blue vault of sky above had dulled, faded and parched. Outside of the restless whisper of the bone-drying breeze, only a grasshopper clicked to the emptiness. Even the birdsong had stilled during the heat of the day.

The spirit of the land smelled of heat, of prostration. The odor of dust tingled pungently in her nostrils.

Years of sun had seared her face into a shriveled husk of burnt sienna. Each pain, hunger, sorrow, and triumph of her long life lay etched, mapped in the maze-work of wrinkles that draped from her broad-cheeked skull. Eyes, knowing and powerful, burned from behind the sagging folds of brown skin. An undershot jaw betrayed the loss of all but a few of her wear-polished yellow incisors. Gray wisps of hair strayed from her short braids.

Her chest rose and fell as she hawked the thirst-spit from her throat and spat onto the gray-white clay. Fingers of hot breeze pulled at her, tugging at the few fringes remaining on the grease-stained dress, fluttering the tatters, rumpling the seat worn so shiny thin under her gaunt buttocks. Around her shoulders, a section of buffalo gut looped, the curve hanging over her hip, taut with tepid water. She found the end, lifting the gut until she could trickle a stream of moisture between thin brown lips.

She made a smacking sound, eyes always on the irregular horizon where it danced and wavered in silvery patterns.

"But then I made my choice years ago, didn't I?" She chuckled: the sound of sagebrush on leather. She shifted the pack on her back, easing the tumpline where it pulled at her forehead. Wearily she took up the march again. Beneath her tattered moccasins, bristly grass crunched—autumn brown even though the season had barely passed late spring.

To her right, a jagged arroyo cut the valley floor—a cracked wound in the dry breast of earth. The scaly sides of the vertical walls had patterned in desiccating fractures where the buried soils split, furred with exposed red roots. An impassable barrier, the gash dropped the height of two tall men to the gravel-traced channel bottom hidden in the noonday shadows. Across the dry flood plain to her left, rose a series of gray-white and buff buttes, sucked dry by the power of Father Sun.

"Maggot crawling luck," she grunted, coming to a stop. Before her, a confluence yawned, another sheer-walled tributary meeting the main channel. She walked nearer to stare down into the gash. Once, in a time long past, she would have slung her pack across, taken a run and vaulted the narrow chasm. Now she could only sigh, and go the long way around on her ancient, rickety bones.

The hard white earth reflected, rolling heat over her as Father Sun burned balefully down. The more she sweated, the quicker the wind drank her moisture away.

"Ah!" She blinked in the glare, staring at the headland forming out of the shimmering air. A line of sandstone slabs jutted from the ridge top like awkward vertebrae to cast fragile shadows down the sagebrush-dotted slope. "I know where I am. Monster Bone Springs is up there. Ought to make it by evening. Used to be good water there."

Back bent to her burden, she shuffled on.

Nearer the jutting ridge, she had to detour around other drainages sliced into the plain. Scrubby grass had receded to greasewood, some deflated until roots gripped tenuously at resistant hummocks of soil.

"Don't remember greasewood in here. Don't remember the arroyos so deep either. Changing . . . world's changing . . ." She shook her head, muttering to herself, trusting her antique body to jump one of the narrow gashes.

"Too old to be wandering around like a kid on a Dream search. Too old for this."

The sun had slanted to the west, her shadow lengthening as she plodded wearily along the tributary's path. Before her, the rounded profiles of the ridges rose against the brassy sky.

She stopped, aware of a difference. No, no matter how long it had been, she would have remembered. The effect might have been the same if the Monster Children had incised the slopes when they battled for the world, cutting long parallel grooves down the soil in intricate patterns around the sagebrush. The hillside was washing away, turning to badlands as the plants that had once held the soils dried in the drought.

She cocked her head, looking at the washed ground she walked on, noting the way the soil looked, how the pebbles remained on the surface.

"Used to be grassy," she remembered, running an appraising gaze over the eroded slopes. Here, the greasewood in the flats looked to be strangling, partially buried by the soils eroding down the side of the hill.

She sniffed at her dry nose and hurried on. "Gonna be dark soon. Better get to Monster Bone Springs and make a camp. Get a good night's sleep for once."

Shadows lengthened, stark in the washed skeletons of long dry rivulets on the slopes around her. Looking closer, she could see much of the sagebrush on the rounded hills had died to become nothing more than fuzzy-looking gray skeletons. The dark arroyo remained a defiant obstacle beside her. Step after step, she entered the jaws of the canyon, plodding along the bottom, trying to remember how far it was to Monster Bone Springs as the worn, rounded hills rose about her.

She crabbed up the slope a ways to avoid the thick net of giant sage—and the ticks that would be waiting on the leaf tips—and turned the final bend, remembering the line of sandstone dipping down along the slopes to Monster Bone Springs. There, at the bottom, a thick stand of giant sagebrush waited, its blue-green color that of silvered spruce needles in the crystal afternoon light.

She exhaled slowly, taking one last sip from her gut water sack, and ambled forward on trembling legs. Monster Bone Springs lay before her, an ancient camping place of her People. Here, they'd killed the last of the huge beasts now known as monsters. From the legends, the animals had had two tails, one in front, one in back. And she'd seen the teeth, long, curved, taller than a man.

Here, she'd prowled around the eroded fire pits, seen the cracked bones, picked up the long stone dart points with fluted bases. Now it all seemed to be washed away. Faint stains of charcoal marked the old hearths, eroded soils slightly oxidized from the long-vanished fires. Flecks of charcoal had washed toward the arroyo. Fractured reddened fire stones had broken in irregular shapes to be scattered like scavenger-gnawed bone and kicked about. Even the thick concentrations of stone flakes—chipped waste from tool manufacturing—had washed away.

The shelter had been hidden from view. At first, she'd thought it another buff sandstone boulder. But as she neared she could see the flattened conical shape of the lodge nestled in the sagebrush. A shabby-looking thing, it barely looked big enough to keep two people from the rain—if it were ever to rain.

She slowed, biting her lip. Who? Anymore, that question could be worth a person's life. Even hers. Not everyone knew who she was in these days of hunger and thirst.

"No one lives forever," she grumbled. "Just feels that way sometimes." She pushed on, looking curiously for the Monster Bones despite her wariness. One stuck out of the ground at an angle back in the sagebrush. The end—as big around as a strong man's thigh—had splintered, drying like the rest of the world. Long flakes of bone lay scattered about in the dark-gray sage duff. A few more faint stains of charcoal blackened the soil, a slight reddish tinge of oxidation around them. These you could almost see the shape of. Fire hearths. Old, so old . . . and almost gone.

The world was changing.

"Hello!" she hollered through cupped hands. "Who's there?"

Nothing moved. Something, a feeling, a wrongness, drifted through her thoughts like a bat in the night.

In the stillness, an infant cried.

The Dream wrenched her back again. White Calf started, blinking her eyes into the night gloom of her rock shelter. Her gut lurched, leaving her physically sick, as if something had been dislocated. She fought the need to vomit. Stillness settled on the night. What had happened? The feeling of sickness reeked of abused Power. But whose? Where?

Mouth dry, she reached for her water skin and sipped. Sitting up, she rubbed her old legs, feeling the night cramp of age-knotted muscles. Eight years had passed since Power had led her to the child and the berdache. What had gone wrong now?

Looking out through the hangings on her shelter, she traced the familiar outline of the peaks against the skyline. She searched the dark patterns of the clouds as the moon broke the eastern horizon again.

She stiffened as the moonbeams sliced the clouds, seeing him again. Moonlight played lightly over the mounded white. The young man of her Spirit Dreams formed out of the billowing cumulus. Half man, half wolf, the image spun from the clouds appeared to point off to the southeast—toward the land of her people.

In shock from Heavy Beaver's desecration, the Wolf Bundle vibrated, wailing its anguish into the clefts and curves of time. The voices of the thousands who had touched it in awe and left part of their souls within the bindings whimpered and moaned.

The Power pulsated, remembering the defilement, withdrawing from the world of men, sucking down into a smoldering kernel of being.

"Remember, the Spiral . . . Circles within circles, joined, yet never touching. The time hasn't come yet. But it will . . . it will. . . ."

And the Wolf Bundle waited.

Chapter 2 🐃

"You don't have to do this." Sage Root met Dancing Doe's eyes as she ducked from the birthing lodge, the infant cuddled to her chest. Dancing Doe shot a surreptitious look to where Heavy Beaver stood before his lodge with arms crossed on his broad chest. Sunlight revealed him as a middle-aged man, thick through the body and short. No hint of the thoughts inside could be seen on his wide heavy-jowled face. His nose, too, looked mashed and flat against his splayed cheekbones. A deep scar ran diagonally across his high broad forehead—legacy of an Anit'ah war dart.

"There isn't enough food," Dancing Doe whispered miserably, wincing at the tenderness in her hips as she straightened in the slanting light of morning.

"I say, don't do it. Something will happen." The angry knot in Sage Root's stomach growled. Nothing much remained of the last kill, only some thin strips of dried meat—enough for another meal or two. Some roots had been collected, enough for stew. Already women had gone out to beat the brush, look for rabbit or gopher holes close enough to the river that water could be diverted to flood them and flush a meal. Still, to kill a child . . .

Dancing Doe's mouth tightened. "My baby . . . it's a girl." Her gaze slipped to Heavy Beaver where he stood. "He knows."

"It's *your* decision! He can't make you kill your own—"

"Please." Dancing Doe's plea wrenched Sage Root's heart. "I know what you're trying to do, but until Long Runner comes back . . . Well, I don't want trouble."

"I'll stand by you. Give you what's left of my dried meat," Sage Root promised, knowing full well that Long Runner had been killed by Anit'ah. "Listen, we can't keep killing the girl children." Sage Root placed a hand on Dancing Doe's shoulder. "Trust me. How would you feel if you killed your baby and Hungry Bull, or someone from one of the other parties, came trotting in saying they'd surrounded a herd, killed enough for all?"

Dancing Doe bit her lip, haunted eyes still fastened on Heavy Beaver, his presence like a miasma. "And then what? How long until the next kill? No. It's all hazy, but I remember him saying I had to. It's for all the People. This one"— she indicated the infant—"doesn't have a soul yet. It isn't named. It's only an animal."

Sage Root closed her eyes, hearing the certainty in Dancing Doe's voice. "It's your . . ." *last link to Long Runner.* But she couldn't say that, couldn't force herself to add to Dancing Doe's misery.

Frantic, Dancing Doe's eyes darted. "You've done enough. You . . . and your berdache!"

At the sting in her voice, Sage Root's resistance crumbled. "We were just—"

"Please. Let me pass, Sage Root. The quicker this is done, the easier it will be."

Standing aside, she watched woodenly as Dancing Doe walked up the trail to the hilltop, a lonely dejected figure. Sage Root flinched as Dancing Doe raised the child overhead and slammed it down on the deflated river cobbles. The wind carried the sound of impact away.

Heavy Beaver, expressionless, turned and entered his lodge. People stared empty-eyed at the bowed figure on the ridge top.

"What have we become?" Sage Root whispered under her breath.

"Hungry." Chokecherry appeared mysteriously at her elbow. "So, she did it?"

"She didn't want to face Heavy Beaver."

Chokecherry nodded, eyes narrowing. "He's killing his own people, and no one knows any better. It's the times, the lack of rain. Our people are falling apart faster than our worn-out lodges." She spat in acid emphasis. "You heard him last night. Then he got her again just after sunrise. He made it sound as if every misfortune the People have suffered was her fault. Told her if she hadn't gotten pregnant, maybe Long Runner wouldn't have gone to hunt in Anit'ah lands. Asked her whose meat she expected to get to feed her baby. 'Which mouth will you rob?' Those were his words."

Sage Root ground her teeth, tears of frustration and anger forcing past her hot eyes. "Horn Core never said things like that."

Chokecherry nodded curtly, staring up at the sagging figure standing on the ridge top. "Keep that in mind, girl. The People are dying off one by one. Heavy Beaver has decreed that infant girls aren't necessary for the survival of the band. He blames the drought and the lack of game on us. Look around. See any luster in the People's eyes these days? Like smoke from an old fire, we're fading away."

Chokecherry pushed past, smacking her lips as she hobbled toward her weathered, smoke-stained lodge.

Sage Root took one last look toward the place where Dancing Doe stood hunched on the ridge. Even from here, she could see her shoulders rising and falling in grief. As she turned to leave, her eyes locked with Heavy Beaver's where he sat in the shadowed depths of his lodge. The Spirit Dreamer's eyes gleamed in promise.

"Like smoke from an old fire," she repeated numbly under her breath.

Little Dancer watched as Heavy Beaver walked out of camp. The man strolled lazily away from the lodges and up from Moon River toward the sagebrush-studded slopes leading to the upland terraces.

"He'll Dream up there. Call the buffalo," Two Elks said to no one in particular. The old man lounged in front of his lodge, ancient hands working a piece of chert into a fine dart point. He smiled happily up at the sun. "Good man, Heavy Beaver. He chased the ghost away last night. He purifies the People."

Ghost? I was that ghost, old man. Some Spirit Dreamer. Little Dancer turned his eyes away, seeing his mother use sticks to pick rocks from the cooking fire. She dropped them into the suspended pouch to boil stew made of some of the last remaining shreds of sun-dried meat. After that, all they had left would be the hides from which they'd made moccasins and lodge covers. Starvation food.

Little Dancer walked slowly toward the lodge, gut growling. Glancing up into the trees, he remembered the thrill of hunting for birds' eggs. Now the nests had been robbed for two days' walk up and down the river. Still, Heavy Beaver didn't move the camp to new grounds. Instead, he promised to call the buffalo—and killed babies.

The horror of it would last. The hollow place inside ate at him, and he wondered what hurt more: hunger, or the feeling he'd had when Heavy Beaver threw the Wolf Bundle into the darkness. Nothing would be the same again.

He squatted next to the lodge, peeking under the cover to see Two Smokes' stricken face as he cuddled the Wolf Bundle. A person with soul death might look like that, slack, listless, horrified at the future.

"Take a horn and dip some broth out," his mother urged, breaking into his thoughts.

He did so, amazed at the watering of his mouth. Curiously, he eyed the lodge cover, remembering the bitter taste from winter when they'd practically starved before his father, Hungry Bull, had led the hunters to kill a small herd of buffalo. Already reports had come in that the cows seen had few calves with them.

"What are you thinking?"

He looked up at her, noting the deeper worry in her eyes. "That Heavy Beaver will kill the People. We should leave."

She said nothing as she reached for a second horn and dipped it into the broth. "Take this to the berdache."

He did so, careful to spill none as he crawled inside. Two Smokes didn't even look up. Little Dancer laid the warm liquid next to him.

As he crawled back out, his mother said, "You know Heavy Beaver doesn't like us. What did you expect to prove last night?"

He dropped his eyes, absently pulling on his fingers.

"That *was* you, wasn't it?"

He remained silent.

"A boy doesn't get dirt all over his shirt like that unless he's crawling around. Did you ever stop to think of the effect you might have on Power?"

"No. But the voice didn't—"

"I don't want to hear about voices. Dancing Doe could have died last night. The baby could have . . ." She sighed, the sound of it like a tearing of the soul. "Well, never mind."

"The Power was right."

He could feel her eyes boring into him.

"And you know of Power, little boy?"

His mouth had gone dry. "I felt it. I felt the Wolf Bundle. Two Smokes' Power worked. It freed the baby. I felt that."

He could feel her sharpened gaze. "And what else did you feel?"

He swallowed hard, heart beginning to race. "I felt Heavy

Beaver. He's a bad man. Wrong. And then, when he threw the Wolf Bundle . . .''

"Yes?"

"I got . . . sick."

"You don't look so good now." She handed him another bowl. "Stop pouting like that."

Hearing the listless tone in her voice, he looked up. The look she gave him frightened.

She ran her fingers through her long hair, eyes drifting to where Heavy Beaver climbed the slopes. "After you drink your soup, you'd better go and sleep some. It helps, slows the hunger."

He nodded, lifting the horn and drinking, feeling the tightness in his belly.

A man living without his people didn't live well—a problem Blood Bear considered as he stared down at the remains of his moccasins. Idly he fingered the hole where the ball of his foot had worn though the sole. The buffalo-hide jacket hanging from his shoulders looked tattered, mangy where the hair had begun to slip. Poor tanning on his part: he didn't understand how hair could be set in the curing process.

A man alone could only pack what he and his dog could carry. Over the last couple of years a kill meant feast. A credible hunter in the beginning, he'd honed those skills until he passed through the sage as quietly as an owl's shadow. Despite that, a lone man couldn't organize a trap, couldn't drive, or utilize the benefits of numbers of hunters in a surround. Rather, he had to creep cautiously forward, employing every benefit of terrain, wind, and cover to his greatest benefit. The years taught him the cunning use of ambush and stealth.

In spite of it all, his ribs stood out. The muscles of his frame remained perpetually gaunt. The growl in his belly might be assuaged by a gorging feast after a kill, but within days the carcass would be down to stripped bone. Starvation followed him, hovering like a phantom over his shoulder. He crushed bones for the marrow and boiled the grease from the fragments. This he skimmed from the top of the water before he drank it, spitting out the sharp chips.

From where he sat on the ridge top, staring out over the vast basin of the Mud River, he could look back at the Buffalo Mountains and remember the warm, friendly lodges of his people. In his heart, an emptiness beat in tune with each breath.

He'd led the party of warriors after Clear Water. Throughout the fruitless chase, the reserve in their eyes haunted him. At night, they'd whisper among themselves, demoralized by the theft of the Wolf Bundle. Each man's expression reflected the thoughts within: The Wolf Bundle has left the Red Hand. This man who leads us chased it away. This man, this Blood Bear, killed the Spirit Man. *He* broke the Power of the People.

Of course they had failed to find Clear Water and Two Smokes. Their hearts had lost the fire. One by one, his party melted away into the night to return to the camps, telling of failure, of defeat. When Clear Water left, she'd taken the soul of the Red Hand with her.

"I'll find it," he promised. "One day, I will find the Wolf Bundle. And when I do, I'll return. Hear that, my people? I will return to the Red Hand . . . and bring back the soul Clear Water and Two Smokes took from us."

Until then, he would not go back. The thought of their eyes chilled him; the way they'd look at him couldn't be endured.

Raising his gaze to the endless blue vault of the sky, Blood Bear shook his head, standing, lifting his clenched fist overhead. Turning to face the blinding sun, he swore, "By my blood and soul, I ask you to honor my request. Give me the Wolf Bundle! Give me a sign . . . a way to find it! Do this, Wise One Above, and I shall humble myself before you. Hear me. Hear my plea. I would give my life for the Wolf Bundle. I would give everything dear to me!"

A stillness fell, the wind ceasing, sage thrashers going silent in the brush. Not even the call of a meadowlark intruded on the silence.

"Hear me!" Mouth working, he squinted up at the searing sun. From his pouch, he took his sharp chert knife. Crouching, he placed his left hand on a rounded quartzite cobble, looking down only long enough to center the sharp stone blade over the end joint of his little finger.

The sting of the knife gratified. The warm spurt of blood on the blade and hafting sent a shiver of excitement through his trembling body. He sawed through the tendons and ligaments, his face as hard as lightning-riven wood, severing the last bit of clinging skin.

Ignoring the pain, he plucked the bit of flesh from the blood-smeared rock and lifted it. "I offer of myself! With my flesh I bind myself to you! Take what you will of me, *but give me the Wolf Bundle!*"

With all his might, he threw the tip of his little finger up into the air, losing it in the burning glare of sun.

For a moment, he reeled, vision blurring. The glaring rays of the sun shimmered through the tears in his eyes to split the light into rainbow colors. For a moment, the image might have been a man, a man of light staring down at him, weighing his words. He blinked; the afterimage of the sun man burned darkly against his clamped eyelids. Trickles of water traced his cheeks as he opened his eyes, seeing only the too-radiant orb of the sun.

A puff of breeze cooled the tear tracks on his cheeks. A grasshopper clicked as it rose on the midday air. A bird warbled in the sage below him.

Had the Spirit World heard? After all his years of mocking, had anything happened? He heard and felt the spatter of blood on his moccasin top. Looking down, he stared dumbly at his throbbing finger.

Had anything happened? Or was it only in his mind?

Search as he might, he couldn't find the severed tip of his finger.

Pain . . . pain . . . *pain . . .*

Two Smokes hadn't felt so wretched and hurt since that day so long ago. Eight long summers had passed since he and Clear Water had fled Blood Bear and the Red Hand People. Now his soul shriveled as if burned in fire.

Across the lodge, Little Dancer slept, the muffled sounds coming from his lips echoing tortured dreams. Yes, he knew. Born under the Wolf Bundle, Little Dancer understood the horror of what had happened. His mother's Power lived strong in him, almost a throbbing presence that constantly sought relief.

"And I made a promise on the Wolf Bundle," Two Smokes whispered.

In his hands, he stroked the holy bundle, wounded by the damage done to the sacred object in his care, frightened at the future retribution he knew lurked just over the horizon. He could feel it, powerful, heavy in the air like the coming of a storm.

His responsibility. He blinked wearily, remembering Dancing Doe as she dashed her child onto the rocky terrace top. A child saved, a child taken. Would that be all? Would the defiled Wolf Bundle ask something more? Some other terrible retribution for his failure?

Last time, it had been his leg—and Clear Water's life—claimed in payment for his incompetence.

He went back to that day eight summers ago, reliving the pain. . . .

Just a berdache and a Spirit Woman, they had no business trying to work a trap like that. Experienced hunters could read the bison, understand their ways. Clear Water had located the small herd. His idea had been to hem the beasts between the banks of the arroyo above where they fed.

The drive had been easy, like in the stories told by hunters. They'd pushed the animals gently, the buffalo always drifting beyond dart range until the walls of the valley rose around them.

Clear Water had looked across, excited eyes flashing, seeing the buffalo milling before the mouth of the arroyo. "Now!" she'd cried. "Rush them! Frighten them!"

And he'd charged the big beasts, afraid of the lances of sunlight glinting off their long black horns. Looking placid, almost stupid, they bawled and wheeled, those crowded against the wall of earth goring angrily at their neighbors. Flies had risen from the curls of rust hair to spiral in the swirling dust.

The lead cow had turned to face him, head lowered, and he'd jumped to the side in fear. Seeing him give way, the cow whirled with blinding speed, bolting for the hole to freedom.

He opened his eyes, looking miserably over at Little Dancer. From the soiled Wolf Bundle on his lap, his hand lifted, as if to reach for the boy.

His inexperience had killed the only woman he'd ever loved.

Two Smokes remembered lying there in soul-searing pain. He'd tried to swallow, his tongue swollen and dry. He shut his eyes tight against the burning agony in his leg. Despite his thirst, sweat beaded to trickle hot and salty down his face. Whimpering at the attempt, he'd tried to move again, digging his trembling fingers into the gray silt of the arroyo bottom. The effort sent burning spears through his mangled leg. The cry tore from his throat like a thing alive and he collapsed limp on the arid soil, lungs heaving as he gasped. The rich smell of the earth clung musty and rich in his nostrils. Crumbly ground cushioned his sweat-damp cheek.

The infant. Got to get back to the infant!

Against the gritty feeling, Two Smokes stared at the sorted gravels in the main channel—beaten and pocked now from the milling feet of mad buffalo.

"My fault," he groaned. "What did *I* know about trapping buffalo?" *And without me, the child will die . . . alone . . . hungry. Maybe a coyote will come first, poking its long nose down into the bundle, baring teeth to . . . No, don't think it. I'll make it back. I've got to. I'm all he has.*

". . . All he has." He hadn't been able to bear the thought of looking for Clear Water's body. Enough horror would remain without that. Teeth clamped hard, he'd braced himself, pulled with his arms, and almost vomited as he levered himself forward, the mangled leg dragging behind.

Head spinning, lungs heaving, he sucked air to still his racing heart.

"My fault."

In his mind he replayed the final moments—that last desperate instant when the buffalo charged over them, eyes rolling, silver streaks of saliva slung from the corners of their mouths. He felt rather than heard the thick hooves clawing, pounding for traction. Sunlight gleamed from clattering black horns as clearly as it had that long ago day. He could smell the dust swirling up around their curly-haired brown hides.

He would die with Clear Water's shriek echoing in his mind. He would rise to the Wise One Above, reliving her efforts to stem the rush, waving her robe to frighten the stampeding animals, seeing her danger too late, turning to run.

The image slowed, as if in Spirit Dream. Clear Water's legs seemed to stiffen, reactions sluggish so soon after giving birth. Then the buffalo calf, eyes glazed wide with fear, broke left, passing on Clear Water's far side, bawling its terror.

The huge cow planted a foot, dirt spraying as she spun, twisting at the sound of her calf. Dropping her head, hind quarters lowered, massive back feet planted, muscles rippling down her flanks, she'd pushed off, the long horn tip catching Clear Water in the small of the back.

Helplessly Two Smokes had watched as the enraged cow tossed her head. The horn tip ripped upward, splitting the skin under Clear Water's milk-rich breasts. His eyes met hers for a split second, a communication of terror and disbelief.

Frantic buffalo obscured the rest.

He remembered the sudden impact to his own body, clipped from behind as he turned to run. Then pain . . . and silence . . . and . . .

He recalled the way his vision had shimmered when he came to, a mirage dancing his sight away and out of focus. In the depths of his mind he could hear a baby crying; the pitiful wailing bruised his soul.

Gray mist rose around him, cooling the battering heat of the sun on his back, throbbing about him in time to the pain that touched his nerves like white-burning coals on skin.

How long had he lain there, floating up and down from consciousness? A vague image of night, of shivering and hurting, played briefly about his mind.

Then something had changed. His head had been moved. He knew it despite the lightning bolts of pain that racked him. Perhaps the Power hadn't been dead. He remembered . . .

Two Smokes groaned, trying to find himself in the waves of misery.

"Anit'ah?" He recognized the word. Enemy.

"Anit'ah, can you hear me?"

"I . . ." The croak of his voice scared him.

"Drink. Slow."

Warm fingers parted his cracked lips, working between his teeth to pry his jaws apart. A slight trickle of water traced over his tongue. Desperately he licked at the roof of his mouth. More water, enough to tease his throat, then he was drinking, reveling in the liquid.

He tried to turn over—pain staggered his mind.

"Hold still. Your leg. Very bad. Wait just a minute. Drink more."

This time he recognized the pressure against his lip. Buffalo-gut water bag. He sucked more of the precious fluid into his dying body.

"Now, let me see your leg."

He felt fingers lifting the hem of his berdache's dress. Fire flashed white as fingers prodded and he cried out. The dress lifted higher and he heard an intake of breath.

"You're a man? In a . . . Ah! Berdache!"

"Got to get back to camp," he whispered. "My fault. Got to save the child. Got . . . to . . ."

"Child is all right. I've got to do something with this leg. It'll hurt."

He screamed as the practiced fingers probed his flesh. The grayness wrapped around him again, dragging him down into darkness . . . away from the pain. . . .

She'd saved his leg. The old woman had healed him while he waited there at Monster Bone Springs. Later she'd gone, bringing back ranging hunters. They'd carried him here. Now he waited, and suffered, and wished for the high Buffalo Mountains where he'd grown up and found a place among a people who didn't treat him like an animal.

Carefully, Two Smokes lifted the Wolf Bundle, placing it next to his cheek, feeling nothing of the Power it had once held. Singing, he dropped sweetgrass onto the coals of the morning fire, passing the Bundle four times through the cleansing smoke and singing his devotion. With reverent care, he smoothed the scuffed sides of the Wolf Bundle and expertly wrapped it in the protective wolf skin.

Fingers like ice traced his back. Power had been abused. Who would suffer to restore the circles? Power always proved so unpredictable. Offended, it might strike anywhere.

Anxiously he looked over at the boy.

With subtle tendrils, the Wolf Bundle reached out, twining itself around Heavy Beaver's soul. Like morning mist, it explored the texture of the man's spirit. Like the Starweb across the heavens, it wound around the sleeping man. Imperceptibly, the net began to close, tightening around Heavy Beaver's life.

Wolf Dreamer whispered from the stars. "The time hasn't come yet. He still serves our purpose."

"He seeks to drive human beings from the world around them. He would divide the world. If he has his way, men will become more important than earth, sun, animals—even women."

"The time hasn't come. Our plant has only sent up shoots."

"The boy may not be strong enough. He may be the Trickster." The Wolf Bundle hesitated. "This Heavy Beaver is evil."

"Trust in the Circles."

"It would be so easy to kill him now, disperse his soul into the rocks and mold, and send it flying with the wind-borne dust."

"And you yourself would alter the Spirals. Trust the harmony, trust the way of the Wise One."

Reluctantly, the Power of the Wolf Bundle unwound from around Heavy Beaver's soul.

Chapter 3

White Calf walked slowly down the trail. Countless elk, mountain sheep, and buffalo had beaten the path. Here and there a deadfall had blocked the trail, causing her to work her way around on brittle legs to find the main thread of the path again.

Animals thought differently than humans, and the game trails led from one meadow to another; or to shelter in the thick timber; or perhaps a place where water might be found. Human beings traveled in straighter lines.

She contemplated the problem and decided a lesson could be learned from it. Which were the brighter, the People, who traveled long distances and wanted long straight trails over the shortest route, or animals who traveled by the day, suffering only to meet their needs?

She stopped where the trail slanted down the thickly timbered slope. A pine squirrel chattered at her. She looked up to see the beast, crouched, tail tight over its back.

"Chug-chug yourself," she growled.

The squirrel promptly jumped a couple of branches higher in the fir and stamped its back feet, clucking and chirring at her.

White Calf scratched behind her ear, resettled her heavy pack, and sighed. Where a spry elk could sprint up and down a trail like this, aging women must tred a different path.

The scent of fir hung thick in her nose, as she promptly set off along the ridge crest. Not for four years had she followed this route to the divide that would take her into the basin. In that time, the Wise One Above alone knew what changes had been wrought. It might be a long trip.

From the place where she lay in the shadows, Tanager watched the old woman, wondering who she was. The witch,

White Calf? A brief flutter of anxiety seized her eight-year-old soul. What evil might come of watching a witch?

Tanager froze, not even reaching to pull the wild strands of hair back from her face. Smudged and soiled, she remained motionless. She'd learned well despite her age. While watching animals, a person shouldn't move. Elk, for instance, saw everything; they were almost magical in their abilities to see, smell, and hear. And once, she'd been forced to stay still as the dead when a grizzly bear had prowled to within feet of her. Only the breeze had saved her that time, blowing the bear's sour scent into her nose.

But then, Tanager had always known she was special. The games of the other girls had no appeal for her. Something had always drawn her to the timber, to skip gracefully along the polished trunks of the deadfall and climb around in the rocks where a fall would have meant instant death.

No amount of scolding by her mother could keep her home. Not when the trees and animals called to her.

She wrinkled her nose as the old woman disappeared. Who'd believe she'd seen a witch? Surely not Cricket or Elk Charm. With no more noise than a stalking bobcat, Tanager backed out from her hiding place and shot down the trail toward camp, running as only Tanager could.

Little Dancer curled into a ball, hoping his sleep would ease the cramps in his stomach. The string of uneasy dreams wound deeper into his mind.

Memories of what he'd seen replayed in his head. He'd never forget the sight of Dancing Doe's baby being smashed onto the hard cobbles of the ridge to flop and quiver and at last lie still. From where he'd hidden in the sagebrush, he'd seen the tortured expression on Dancing Doe's face. Above it all, Heavy Beaver's smile hovered, mocking.

The image shifted. Little Dancer's gut twisted at the sound of the hollow plop as the Wolf Bundle landed on unresisting ground.

"No!" he cried, remembering the sucking emptiness that had pulled at his young soul.

"The People are dying," came a voice. "Like smoke from a distant fire, we're drifting away, becoming less and less."

An old woman walked down out of the trees, hobbling with the aid of a walking stick. A tumpline secured an awkward pack low on her back while breezes tugged her gray braids this way and that. As she looked at Little Dancer, her deep-set dark eyes glowed with Power.

Shifting again, he danced and whirled, the world spinning below him. A man threw something at the sky, his face contorted as if by anger. A sudden light blinded him painfully.

He felt the hunger, like waves lapping the cobbles of Moon River. Pangs of want washed around him, bearing him on the current, twisting around, gurgling.

"Stop it! *Stop!*" He cried out; the knot in his belly grew, encompassing all the People. Pangs of hunger, like tendrils, reached out to touch the men who waited on butte tops; it tickled their bellies as they searched for fresh tracks. He ached for all the People, feeling the wasting of their bodies, the energy draining from their flesh.

"Feed us. Feed me," he whimpered into the dream. The cramping of his stomach tightened as the last of the thin stew entered his blood.

We come. Remember this day . . . for we are you.

He started at the nearness of the voice. A curious hazy sensation sent him drifting. A taste lay on his tongue, that of sage, usually so bitter, now almost sweet. He bawled in fright, unable to form words. Frightened, he ran on light legs. The view of the world around him expanded, oddly flat, but vividly clear.

He ran, realizing he did so on four nimble legs. Creatures, antelope, stood with rump patches flashing white at his alarm. A doe stood alert and chirped to him. Without thought he turned to race for her and the security she meant to him.

We come, the voice repeated. *We come.*

He shivered, torn from the body he inhabited. Dazed, he struggled against the pressure on his shoulder, kicking. He screamed, hearing his human voice loud in his own ears.

"Little Dancer, wake up! It's a bad dream. Wake up!"

He blinked, clearing his filmy eyes to stare at his robes piled before his nose, half-afraid of what he'd find. His mother stared down at him, concern in her tense face.

"It's a dream. That's all. A bad dream," she told him, running a soothing hand down his shoulder.

With an effort like walking through deep wet snow, he cleared his thoughts.

"Are you all right?"

He shook his head, the misty image of the antelope fawn clouding his reality. "No. Not a bad dream. We are one."

Sage Root cocked her head. "I know. I've been having nightmares, too. After last night you're—"

"*No.*" He looked over at where Two Smokes slept, the parfleche containing the Wolf Bundle tight against his chest. "We're one. The antelope heard. They're coming. To the river . . . coming . . ."

She stared at him, frown lines deepening in the smooth skin of her brow.

"I mean it. I saw. In the dream." He sat up, feeling the awe of it all. "I just can't . . . can't . . ."

"Explain?" She lifted an eyebrow, thoughtful as she stared out the lodge entrance. Avoiding his eyes?

"I got scared. But it wasn't bad. Not like Heavy Beaver would say. Not evil. Not bad. I swear. It was . . ." He frowned, perplexed, looking for the words. "One. Not different."

"Coming to the river? In the dream, which way was the sun?"

He thought about it. "There. West."

"And the antelope were moving which way?"

If the sun had been west, to the right, they'd be going . . . "South."

She hunched over, supporting her chin with a fist. "*If* the Dream was real—a Spirit Dream. *If* the time is now, then . . ." She chewed at her lip for a moment, fingering her long gleaming braids. "The old antelope trap is only a short walk from here."

"Heavy Beaver will get real mad if you trap antelope."

Under her breath, as if to herself, she said, "It's only a little boy's dream. Not a Spirit Dream. But what's left besides hope?" She took a deep breath, nodding slowly to herself. When she turned toward him, resignation hunched her shoulders. "We're all hungry. He can Curse us on full stomachs."

She said it flippantly. But the fear lurked in her eyes like a coyote in the night.

Blood Bear saw the Trader first. He walked easily up the buffalo trail along the valley bottom. He wore a brightly painted shirt, back bent to a pack secured by a thick, ornately beaded tumpline. In one hand he carried a long stick that rose to a hoop decorated in gaily dyed feathers—the staff of a Trader. A line of dogs followed, tails wagging, heads down, and panting as they bore saddle packs of their own.

Blood Bear approached the man warily. Despite the heavy pack on his shoulders and the string of pack dogs, he might still be an enemy.

"Ho-yeh!" the man called in the universal pidgin of travelers who came in peace.

"Ho-yeh," Blood Bear repeated. But the shafts of his darts felt smooth on his fingers where they rested in the atlatl, ready to be cast.

The man made the sign for "who?"

Blood Bear lifted his hand, palm out, fingers widespread. Then he pointed to the red hand he'd painted on his worn shirt.

"Red Hand," the man called, and smiled. "I am Three Rattles. From the White Crane People north of the Big River. Once, in my great-grandfather's day, Red Hand and White Crane Peoples were the same. Languages not so different."

"No. Language not so different." A relief, he wouldn't have to use sign language, with all its problems. Traders came and went, using a signing technique, when needed, to barter their goods. Traders had special Power. Everyone knew that and accepted them. No good came from killing or robbing a Trader. Doing so biased the Power the Traders claimed as their own, turning it against the murderer or thief.

Without the Traders, blue stones couldn't come from the far south. Olivella, dentalium, and oyster shells from the western ocean wouldn't be traded for special beads. Beautiful tool stones of chert and obsidian, elk ivories, dried delicacies like buffalo tongue or finely crafted robes could not leave his own area for that of the River Peoples in the east.

But the Traders did more than bring goods a people couldn't

find where they lived. They carried news of the land and animals. The Traders brought information about wars and different bands of people. Although Blood Bear had never been there, he knew of the oceans to the west and south from the Traders' tales. He'd never met a member of the Thunder People in the far south, but he knew they shaved the sides of their heads, scalp locks hanging far down their backs in a single braid. The Father Fish People, he'd been told, lived many tens of days of journey to the southeast and ate mostly fish because they didn't have buffalo. He'd learned of many people through the stories of the Traders.

Three Rattles hunched his back, slipping out of the tumpline, letting the heavy pack slide to the ground while the dogs came up to nose Blood Bear's own animal. At the first growl, he cuffed his beast, ordering it away.

"Been a long journey," Three Rattles told him, pointing far to the south. "Not good down there. Been a lot of raiding. Buffalo aren't doing good. Most of the people are camped along the rivers—mostly running mud now. Then there's places south of Moon River where the dirt blows so bad you can't see. I crossed places where sand drifts across the earth like snow in the winter. Nothing growing there. Nothing to eat. Got to carry rations. Each time I go, the dunes get bigger." He paused. "What's news here?"

Blood Bear shrugged. "The same. The People want rain."

Three Rattles looked Blood Bear up and down. "You been out by yourself." The unspoken question remained.

Blood Bear bridled and forced himself to sigh. "I won't go back until I find something."

"You're Blood Bear."

"I'm Blood Bear. I didn't know my fame had spread."

Three Rattles laughed, squatting down on his haunches. "Got some special stuff here. Dried fish from the south ocean. Not much left, only a taste or two. Share?" He reached up with some brownish-looking flaky stuff.

Blood Bear took the small piece offered and bit into it. He couldn't quite decide if he liked the curiously oily taste. The fish had been too long in the pack; a slightly rancid aftertaste remained in his mouth.

"Not buffalo," said the Trader, " but still food."

Blood Bear squatted. "You wouldn't have heard of a woman traveling south, would you? Among the Red Hand she was known as Clear Water. She left my people eight summers ago with a berdache."

Three Rattles nodded. "I heard. You've been looking that long?"

Blood Bear stared out over the baked flats. Only the greasewood looked green. Casually, he lifted a shoulder.

"No, I've heard nothing of a woman from the Red Hand. Me, I've been up and down. I like going along the mountains clear south to the wet lands. I go south for a year. Then I go north for a year to spend time with the White Crane and see my relatives. After the winter, the voice calls and I go south. In the four trips I've made, I never heard of this woman. That still leaves a lot of places to look, east and west and north."

"She had something that belonged to the Red Hand."

"The Wolf Bundle."

Blood Bear's heart skipped. "Then you know."

"I know. I know something else, too. You may not have had to go so far in your searches. Last spring I camped with a Short Buffalo People band where Moon River and Sand River join into one. I heard jokes about a berdache who eats grass. That was last spring, so I don't know how far to trust the strength of those stories. You know, information, like sinew, gets old and cracks and falls apart with age."

Blood Bear frowned into the distance. "Two Smokes used to collect grasses. He'd chew them sometimes, but mostly he put them in his pack."

"This could be him. The berdache they laughed about picked grasses. They said he had a sacred bundle with him. The other thing I remember is that he limped. Buffalo ran over his leg or something."

"Remember the band he was with?" Blood Bear's heart seemed to boom like a pot drum at Blessing. He struggled to keep himself still, fighting the urge to fidget and rock on his heels.

"Heavy Beaver's. They normally range on Moon River. Raid the Red Hand every so often. But then I guess you raid back."

"We haven't raided much in the last few years. The spirit

of the . . . Well, we just haven't raided.'' But if this berdache was Two Smokes, that would change.

''You know, that's why the Red Hand and the White Crane split so long ago. It was a fight over the Wolf Bundle. I don't know all about it, but it's old. Very old. We still have legends about it.''

Blood Bear stood. ''Heavy Beaver's band. They camp on Moon River.''

He helped Three Rattles with his pack, handing the man his Trader's staff. ''I don't have anything to trade now. But maybe someday I will.''

Three Rattles' face broke into an enigmatic smile. ''Good luck, Blood Bear. I hope to trade with you someday. I'll want something back for my fish.''

Blood Bear lowered an eyebrow, thoughts on the crippled berdache and Moon River. ''You'll have it.'' With a wave, Three Rattles was off.

For long moments Blood Bear watched the Trader and his dogs heading north. He checked his bearings; the High Mountains lay directly east. Moon River didn't lie all that far to the north. All he had to do was reach the river and find the Short Buffalo People camp of this Heavy Beaver.

It wouldn't take him long. Not now.

The Wolf Bundle floated in the boy's Dream. Perhaps he was the one.

From the shimmering of the Spirals, Wolf Dreamer's voice warned, ''Be careful. Too much of a taste of Power at so young an age, and he could go the way of Heavy Beaver. He's only a child.''

The Wolf Bundle pulled back, disengaging. The Wolf Dreamer had been right. It must wait, abide by the great Spiral of the universe. Time remained meaningless. Now existed, as it always had . . . and always would.

But another ''now'' would come . . . if the child proved strong enough.

Chapter 4 🐃

Kowwww! The cry lingered on the still air.

Sage Root wiggled the stick that held high a thin flag of white hide. She crouched behind a prairie-dog mound, keeping low, face screened by a clump of sage she'd twisted from the ground. Despite their ability to outrun the wind, antelope had limits. Those, she hoped to prey on today.

For the moment, she couldn't think of Little Dancer's Dream—or what it meant. The antelope had come, just as the boy insisted they would.

Her body lay in the sunlight, as sinuous as a powerful snake. Her rich thick hair glistened a deep lustrous black. Her work dress clung tightly to her sweat-damp body, accenting the full curve of her hip, stretched by the taut muscles of her buttocks, and the powerful lines of her legs. Broad-shouldered and narrow-waisted, she drew men's gazes. Even the old men watched as she passed, eyes lighting at the approach of such a healthy, sensual female. Despite the two children she'd born Hungry Bull, her belly remained flat, her breasts full and high.

Across the sage-strewn drainage, the antelope buck pranced, turning sideways to stare at her. The doe continued to walk ever closer, head lowered cautiously, curiosity obsessing her. The rest of the herd watched, some following the doe, others pausing to nibble at sage.

Come on, you've all got to follow. You've just got to!

In her head, Sage Root hummed the antelope song, fearing to Sing it out loud, fearing her Power wasn't great enough to meet the needs of the People. The memory of her son's gaunt face hovered in her mind. If only they could trap the antelope. If only Hungry Bull would come back, singing and dancing the news of a buffalo trap. If only it would rain. If . . . If . . .

And the threat of Heavy Beaver continued to loom, glaring and threatening, even in her imagination. Bad days, he'd said. Bad days indeed.

Sage Root jerked the stick again, causing the snow-white prairie-dog hide to flutter.

Kowwww! the doe called as she stepped cautiously over bunches of gnarled sage. Not far now. The wing walls of the laboriously constructed trap spread to either side. If they came only a couple of lengths closer, she could whistle the call to spring the trap.

Sage Root let the doe peer at the waving bit of hide for a moment and wiggled the stick again, distracting her from looking back at the buck. Then the doe came trotting forward, the rest following along, the buck, as usual, waiting for all the does and new fawns to take the lead.

She chewed her lip, sawing it back and forth between strong white teeth. Almost . . . just a little farther. The wind teased the bit of white hide, dancing and waggling it lazily.

Khowwwww! The doe called again, others echoing their curiosity.

The antelope bands were still small this time of year. The does had just fawned, scattering to conduct their birthing in secret, dropping twin fawns in thick sage to hide them from coyotes, wolves, and eagles until the young could suckle enough of their mothers' strength to run like the wind. Finally, the herd had begun to come together again, the mothers seeking the protection of more eyes and ears.

The buck passed the brush clumps marking the boundaries of the trap. The lead doe had come so close, ears up, walking nervously. So far, she hadn't signaled with the white patch of her rump, hadn't barked the retreat call. To either side, the wing walls of the trap stretched.

Sage Root—heart beginning to hammer—wet full red lips and filled her lungs. Her whistle shrilled in the wind, a perfect imitation of a bull elk's bugle.

The doe jumped and scampered, head back, trotting nervously. And from the sheltered pits dug at the end of the wing walls, the women and children of the tribe exploded, screaming, yelling, racing to close the gap.

The lead doe flashed her white rump patch in alarm, trying to slip to the side, finding a solid wall of woven sagebrush. She quivered, dancing sideways on lightning feet; the herd followed in panic.

Sage Root waited, fists clenched, heart pulsing in her chest as the antelopes' escape route was cut off. Behind the milling herd, the women and children closed in. Shouting and singing, they now advanced, pushing the antelope into the bottleneck of the trap. The lead doe turned, finding only one avenue of escape, and charged down the narrow runway into the arroyo. As the antelope pounded past, Sage Root thrilled to the sight of their flying bodies. She gripped her weapons firmly, a thrill like orgasm pulsing through her.

In the dust of their passage, Sage Root scrambled to her feet, racing after them, her long black hair flying in the pell-mell rush of the chase. She stood at the narrow end of the chute leading into the arroyo, knowing the antelope had to come back this way—that they'd entered a dead end from which they couldn't escape.

She waited, holding a long dart like a thrusting spear in case the antelope came racing back.

"We did it!" Fire At Night appeared at her shoulder, a stocky boy of fifteen, fast and agile despite his bulky body. His chest heaved as he panted, darts ready in his hand. He'd hesitated at first, daunted by Heavy Beaver's warnings about women hunting. Now he seemed to have forgotten his reservations.

"You can hold this end? Maybe keep Throws Rocks here? If they get out, we're all going to be hungry."

"We'll do it. It's a thing to Sing of."

She grinned at him, slapping his shoulder, before climbing up the side of the trap, onto the eroded terrace, running to where the antelope piled up, with barely enough room to turn, starting back down the narrow passage.

As they raced back, Sage Root nocked a dart, balancing, letting it fly with all the power in her supple body. True to the mark, the dart caught the lead doe full in the body, completely transfixing her. She stumbled and went down. The herd piled into her kicking body. Fawns bawled anguish and fear. Antelope scrambled, panting hard, hooves pounding. A curling pall of dust rose as Sage Root nocked another dart and speared the next doe that passed. About her, others appeared, whooping and yelling as they hurled darts down into the narrow confines that trapped the antelope. One or two panicked animals scrambled over the carnage, running a gauntlet of darts back down the arroyo.

Out of darts, Sage Root grinned at the kicking pile of dying animals. Dust streaked her face and hair, a song of joy in her heart. From where she'd left it earlier, she picked up a hide sack full of her butchering tools.

For the time being, no more infants had to die as Dancing Doe's had. No more pangs of hunger would pull at the People in the night. For the moment, they would eat. To fix the old trap had been a gamble, the work done in secrecy lest someone tell. Chokecherry's sobering reminders of Heavy Beaver's power lurked like hungry weasels in her mind. She couldn't shake his promise of retaliation that night of Dancing Doe's difficult delivery.

"Hey, you first!" Makes Fun called, offering her the honor of the first meat. "You put this together."

She flushed slightly at the compliment. Yes, she'd defied Heavy Beaver, taken the risk to make this happen when she'd seen the antelope winding down toward the river. The old trap had been so close to the route the antelope would take back to the uplands that the opportunity couldn't be wasted. She'd argued passionately, aided by the hunger in the eyes of the children. Uneasy at first, the People had followed.

Sage Root smiled back at Black Crow's wife and jumped down the dusty bank. Before her, the lead doe panted, a froth of blood bubbling around her nostrils. The fletched end of the dart shuddered with each dying breath.

Sage Root knelt over the dying doe, reaching out to stroke her head. "Forgive me, Mother. It is the way of things that men—like antelope—must eat. Bless your meat to our use. May your soul run like the wind to Dance among the stars." The thrashing doe relaxed, the deep pools of brown eyes meeting hers, as if admitting the reality of the Starweb, woven by the Wise One Above.

Sage Root lifted the heavy hammerstone. With the skill of long practice, she slammed it down on the doe's brain. An echo sounded in her mind, the memory of a newborn infant's skull popping on the hot rocks.

Then the work began in earnest, amid songs, jokes, and toothy smiles. The People gutted and sliced and packed meat from the trap. Hungry mouths consumed the livers on the spot, offering first-meat rites to friends and helpers, heedless of the red that dribbled down bobbing chins. Blood smeared strong brown arms and legs as quarters were handed up for the old women to cut into strips. In the shadowed arroyo, the hollow crunch of chopper stones on bone, mixed with laughter, filled the air.

"Get them strips off," old Chokecherry directed. "Weather this hot, you got to strip the meat quick. Get it laid out on the sage. You don't, more maggots'll eat it than People!"

Sage Root arched her back to soothe the ache of bending over. A grit of dust ground in her teeth, a fulfilling taste of blood and fresh liver on the back of her tongue.

"How many did we get?" She wiped at the perspiration on her face, streaking her beautiful features with red smudges.

"About three tens of fingers. Throws Rocks and Fire At Night didn't let a single one escape."

With her hammerstone, Sage Root split a pelvis, splaying the legs to expose the meat. Using a sharp flake, she cut the tendons and skin, severing the sacrum with her hammerstone, cutting the hide underneath. She lifted the last of her animals to eager hands above, leaving only bloody gray silt under the litter of white and brown antelope hair. Grabbing a blood-encrusted hand, she scrambled up the gritty side of the arroyo, squinting in the bright light of the afternoon sun.

About her, sagebrush had turned red under the weight of long strips of meat drying in the sun. Here and there children romped and played, waving hands, shooing flies from the wet meat.

"See? You didn't believe me, but I knew they'd come. I sat up on the hill, feeling them."

She turned, smiling, seeing Little Dancer where he pranced

and waved a sagebrush branch over a bloody bush. "Look! Food! Food for everyone!"

"Hey! Watch it. Watch where you wave that. You're knocking the meat off. Get sand in it, and *you* eat it."

Sobered, he dropped his gaze, face lining as he turned his attention to keeping the flies away.

She laughed to herself, a fullness in her heart. Yes, food for everyone. They'd all eat. And maybe, just maybe, Hungry Bull and Three Toes and Black Crow might have made a trap. Or possibly one of the other parties who'd gone out from the Moon River in various directions to hunt had found a herd.

She shaded her eyes, looking southwest toward the cool spikes of the mountains. The snow line had been higher than she'd ever seen this last winter. Down by the main camp, the river could be waded, water never coming higher than her knees. Even the cottonwoods looked dusty, the new leaves a darker green. Through it all, the wind continued to blow out of the southwest, hot, dry, sucking any moisture left from the prostrate dust.

"Sage Root?"

She turned at the cautious call, seeing Meadowlark gesturing down the drainage. Three people picked their way through the sage. She didn't need to squint to know Heavy Beaver's lumbering walk.

"I think it's a good time to leave . . . go hide under the bones in the arroyo," Makes Fun observed dryly.

"No. Just keep doing what you're doing." Sage Root straightened, a queasiness in her gut. "I'll go talk to him before he gets here. Keeps the rest of you out of it that way."

"Careful," Chokecherry warned from the side. "Don't antagonize him. You saw what happened the other night. Don't get him mad, girl. Don't do anything to make him Curse you. You know what he's saying about the women as it is."

"I know." Her throat constricted, premonition choking her. With iron nerve, she forced herself to walk steadily toward him. Old Two Elks came second in line, a nervous set to his sagging shoulders. Heavy Beaver's wife, Red Chert, walked last, eyes downcast in her round face. Her petulant lips pressed tightly together in a pouting expression.

Heavy Beaver stopped, pulling himself up, and stared at her through expressionless eyes.

"It's good to see you back, Heavy Beaver. You had good Dreaming?"

He tilted his head slightly, a distaste forming in the set of his wide brown lips. "Dreaming isn't your concern, woman. Looking behind you, I'm starting to wonder what is."

The crawling feeling in her stomach went ill. "Feeding the People should be everyone's concern. Don't look at me like that. You're Two Stones moiety. I'm Wolf Heart. I'm under no kin obligations to even be polite. But I will . . . since you Sing and Dream for the People. For that I respect you."

A slight curl of smile ghosted at his lips, but his gaze remained hard, cutting like freshly struck chert. "I'm glad you're an obedient daughter of the People, woman. If your piety is so great, what have you done here? Hmm? Could it be that you've killed brother antelope? Ah, yes, I suppose so. And the ritual? Did you Sing that? Dance it like Antelope Above likes it Danced?" His expression tightened. "Or perhaps you didn't. Perhaps you fouled the ritual . . . offended Antelope Above like Buffalo has been offended. What then, *woman of the People*? Who will feed us all if the animal spirits have risen to the Wise One Above, and told him to stop Rain Man from Dancing water from the clouds? What *have* you done?"

She crossed her arms, meeting his hot glare, refusing to cave in to the feeling of terror. "I fed my people. I told the antelope mother what I did. She knows. I—"

"And I suppose you're bleeding on top of it all? Menstrual blood? On a hunt? If there's trouble these days, you always seem to be at the bottom of it."

At the memory of Dancing Doe's infanticide, she bristled. "As if it was any of *your* business, I'm not. My moon passed two weeks ago. You should know, Heavy Beaver, you seem to keep good track of when each woman enters the bleeding lodge. Part of your Dreamer's responsibility? Or something else?"

Watch it! You're getting mad. You know what happens when you get out of control. She swallowed hard, trying to still the fires of injustice tugging at her gut.

He actually forced a smile onto his lips. "Times are changing, Sage Root. Oh, I know your lineage. I know the sort of woman your mother was. Passionate . . . like you. That's where you get it, I suppose. Your father never stood up to her, never taught you the manners to make you a polite woman, dutiful. Then you couldn't wait to rut with Hungry Bull—the name fits him. You've never—''

"Because I wouldn't bed you?" She arched an eyebrow, instantly regretting it, exhaling. "Never mind. It was long ago. You wouldn't have wanted me for a second wife anyway." *And that's one of the biggest lies I've ever told. Look at you, even now, practically drooling. And* you *talk to the Spirit World?*

Red Chert had stood through it all, eyes downcast as always. Stolid of expression, she waited, the wind tugging at her long black braids. A small dumpy woman, she'd never born Heavy Beaver a son—yet she bled like any other woman, taking her time in the menstrual hut. Ever quiet and docile, she never even laughed at the crude jokes the women told. She spoke rarely and then only of the essentials.

The realization settled in Sage Root's mind. *How terrible to be the object of so much sympathy. What a wretched life that would be. Imagine having a husband you never laughed with, never hugged, or coupled frantically with, or fought with. Imagine living all your life like a wounded puppy. Where would the purpose be?*

"Indeed, you'd have made a very poor second wife." Heavy Beaver's words sank into her thoughts. "And I'll hope you haven't ruined the People forever with this little display of yours."

The anger broke loose.

Despite the warning voice in her head, she jabbed a finger into his breastbone. It all came out, spurred by the fear eating at her gut. She had to strike back, she just had to—or it was all lost. "And where are the buffalo you've been Singing to for so long? Do I see the hills black with their bodies? All that Singing, Heavy Beaver? All that time the People have been giving you the best of what little remained so you could spend time in the Dream without worries about your fat belly going gaunt? Maybe you haven't listened past the sound of your own voice. The *children* of the People are *crying*!

"And what have we got? Rain? You see any of that this spring? No, all we get are *your* accusations that *women* are spoiling the world, killing the People! There wouldn't *be* any People if it wasn't for everyone doing what they can. *Including* women! Have you seen Dancing Doe recently? Have you seen the misery in her eyes every time she thinks about what you made her do?"

"You push too far, Sage Root." He said it so softly, she almost missed it in her tirade. The chill of fear, overly damped by anger, reasserted itself. She swallowed hard. This fool could Curse her. And he had every reason after she'd ridiculed him that night he'd tried to take her. Ridicule wasted a man, ate at him . . . and Heavy Beaver didn't forget.

"Yes, you understand." He lifted his chin, studying her through lowered lashes. "Perhaps you do too much—take on too much. You would divide the People when they must pull together, Dance and Sing and apologize to the Spirit World Above for so many transgressions. In you, I see only arrogance, and pride. So much pride. Is that because of your beauty? Because of your husband? Do you think you're better than the rest of the People?"

She bit her tongue to still the hot response.

"Remember," his smooth voice grated, "the Wise One Above led men up from under the ground and into this world. A being who crawled out of the earth like mole shouldn't be too proud."

"I stand on my own under Father Sun as you do, shaman."

"But I Dream the Powers, woman. And I think you're too proud. Go ahead, eat your meat. I refuse to touch it, to foul my lips with your sacrilege. We'll see where your impudence and arrogant pride get you in the end."

He pushed past her, raising his arms and shouting for all to hear: "Antelope Above! I see what the woman has done to you! I see the insult to your children! I see the defiling of my brothers! Know that I, Heavy Beaver, refuse to taste, eat . . . or even *smell* of this violation! I declare this meat to be putrid and fouled by a defiler of You . . . and my people."

And with that, he whirled, a gleam of triumph in his black

eyes as he shoved her aside and strode down the trail back toward the camp.

In stunned silence, Sage Root stared, disbelieving, unable to comprehend that he'd act to waste a good kill, a clean kill, defiling the meat in the very mouths of the People.

Like a great hand from above, a darkness descended on her soul.

Hungry Bull froze, half a breath caught in his lungs. The amber grass rustled again and went quiet as the thief moved in the gray light. He cocked his head to listen, tightening the grip on his weapon. The feeling of the smooth wood, balanced so perfectly in his knotted fist, reassured him.

The morning birds had begun to chirp. A light breeze puffed against his skin, dampening the excitement of the stalk. Still in shadow, the sage loomed purple blue in the predawn light. Not much time left now. The thief would escape, his night's raid left unpunished.

Grass whispered as Hungry Bull's quarry shifted position. Close, so close, just there, on the other side of the sage. Hungry Bull tested the balance of the trimmed wood in his hand, feeling the heft, waiting to dispatch his enemy.

Life and death, the old dance continued. Even here, in the deep sagebrush, the greatest game played out. This game, Hungry Bull played very well. Few matched his skill with weapons or cunning ambushes. His quarry retreated ahead of him.

Hungry Bull took the rest of the breath, feeling his heart pound harder in his chest as his air-starved lungs began to labor. Using all his craft, he slowly lifted his foot, drifting it silently forward, placing it between dry clumps of grass, delicately resettling his weight to the ball of his foot.

Ahead of him, the grass crackled and went still.

Hungry Bull studied each pattern of the shadows, searching for the outline of the raider. Tension hung in the air, straining at him, speeding his heart. He throttled the urge to charge forward, to match wits with his quarry. Killing took patience. Revenge would be all the better if the thief never knew his danger.

He eased another step forward, careful eyes on the spiky

uplifted arms of the sagebrush around him. The muscles in his leg trembled slightly as he shifted his balance, peering into the hollows where the brush thinned.

The thief stopped, raising, poised to flee, head cocked to listen while sharp brown eyes glinted in the graying light.

Hungry Bull froze again, tense as a green willow stalk.

The thief hesitated nervously, as if warned by some sixth sense.

He's going to bolt! Hungry Bull, not quite as balanced as he wanted to be, struck. Trained muscles flexed smoothly, arm hissing forward as he released his weapon. One chance only. Hungry Bull put body and soul behind the throw, knowing a miss would allow the quarry a clean escape.

The hardwood stick, curved into an L shape, warbled slightly in the air, and caught the thief low, tumbling him in a heap.

"Got you!" Hungry Bull yipped and vaulted the sagebrush in pursuit.

To his surprise, the thief pulled himself up and scrambled into the denser mat of sagebrush and grass.

Perplexed, Hungry Bull bent down, studying the tracks through narrowed eyes. "Huh! Must have been just a little off. Broke a leg."

Growling, he bent over a sagebrush, grasping the stiff gray branches and twisting them round and round until the root parted with a soil-muffled pop. Satisfied, he picked up his throwing stick, slipping it behind the buffalo-hide belt he wore, and took up the scuffed track of the thief. Using the uprooted plant for a flail, he smacked clumps of sagebrush, poking here and there, seeking to flush his wounded prey.

"All right, where'd you go? Look, you can't get away. You've got a broken leg. Come on out. Better I eat you than some tick-infested coyote."

Hungry Bull bent down, peering into a thick shock of grass, seeing a gleaming brown eye staring back in the breaking light of morning. The pink tip of nose quivered, a wealth of silvered whiskers shivering.

Hungry Bull jabbed his bush at the hole, satisfied to see a hobbling streak of brown shoot out the other side.

He jumped the sagebrush, charging after the wounded

creature, sprinting a zigzagging course through the unresisting brush. The quarry shot to the left. Hungry Bull planted a foot, leaping after him—only to step on a curled chunk of dried sage stem that leapt up as if alive to trip him. Bull slammed down, catching sight of his quarry disappearing. Frantic, he scrambled after him on hands and knees, spitting a curse as he stuck his hand in a clump of brown-spined prickly pear.

Getting his feet under him, he lunged, grasping for the thief's body, missing. Again he pelted after the small brown and white shape, sage crackling and snapping before his charge, scenting the air with its tangy aroma.

They'd crossed most of the drainage bottom now, closing on the gentle slope that led up to the rounded ridge top. If the thief got to the rocks up there, got to a hole, it would be all over.

Hungry Bull slid to a stop. "Lost you!" He cocked his head, sensitive ears tuned for the soft rustling. A meadowlark trilled, followed by a robin calling in crisp melody to greet Father Sun.

There! Bull jumped for the sound of scurrying feet. The thief had doubled back, making a wide circle as Bull crashed down on him. Again the mad scramble continued, the thief belying his broken leg as he slipped through the small spaces. Bull—condemned by size—had to pound through by dint of brute force.

As the thief shot across an open space, Bull launched himself again, slapping belly-down on the dust.

Roaring rage, Hungry Bull got a foot braced and lurched again, his grasping fingers slipping off the creature's back as he planted his other hand in a wicked patch of cactus. Bellowing from the sting and cursing the extraordinary luck of his wounded prey, Hungry Bull went momentarily berserk, diving headfirst into the thicket of sage, barely aware of the scratches it tore in his cheek.

Worming after the scrambling fugitive, he slapped at him, finally got a grip on his tail, and pulled. The captive clawed frantically at the loose dirt as Hungry Bull dragged him back.

"Got you!" he howled in victory.

Hungry Bull stood, grinning, his prey dangling by a brown-

and-white tail, front legs outstretched, broken hind leg limp. Under the sleek buff-brown coat, lungs labored, whiskers trembling. The smooth white underbelly gleamed like snow in the sun, in contrast to pink-padded feet.

Bull lifted him up to stare into the frightened black eyes. "You ate the last of my jerky. What you didn't eat, you pissed and shit on. To make matters worse, you chewed the thong of my atlatl in two! It takes time to make an atlatl just so . . . get the right Spirit Power into it."

The whiskers continued to quiver, the beady eyes bright with terror and hurt.

"So what I'm going to do," Bull continued, "is get even. Tonight, we're going to eat *you* for dinner. Get you back for our jerky, huh?"

He winced at the sting of the cactus spikes in his flesh and grabbed the beast about the chest, ready to break its neck.

Undaunted, the scrambling captive sank long white teeth into the web of skin between Bull's thumb and forefinger. He howled in pain and surprise, slamming the creature to the ground. Again, Trickster Coyote made a fool of him, providing a soft tussock of grass for the thief to land in. Like a shot, it bolted into the sage.

Bull stared stupidly at his hand for a second, realized what had just happened, and thundered his anger as he crashed after his vanishing quarry.

The threads of the Starweb had begun to tighten. The Wolf Bundle had watched as the world changed. Part of it had cried out as the last of the mammoth died under the hunter's darts. The way of the Spirals permeated everything, reaching from the roots of the winter-dormant plants to the shining glitter of a fly's buzzing wings. How odd that the last mammoth had been an orphaned calf. When the Wise One Above created the universe, he made everything balance, pain and ecstasy, birth and rot, heat and cold.

Now the Circles were coming full again. Wolf Dreamer waited, watching from his Dream. Something new would be spun into the Starweb . . . or its new Dreamer might fail where Wolf Dreamer had succeeded. It did not matter. If this Circle of the Spiral would be famine, the next might be feast.

Chapter 5 🐃

As the morning sun threaded yellow beams into the canyons, Hungry Bull trotted along a deer trail that wound through the thick sage in the canyon bottom. As his legs pumped, he bit cactus spines one by one from the palm of his hand, spitting them away.

To either side, the eroded hillsides rose in gentle slopes dotted with sage and occasional bitter brush. This buffalo hunt had turned into another debacle. Occasional chips had been located—all of them years dry, beetle-riddled and gray white from sun bleaching. Where were the buffalo? As he trotted down the trail, a limp brown-and-white body dangled and jerked from his swelling right hand.

He could count off a finger for each day since he'd left Sage Root and camp and add another three toes to the list. Never had the animals been so few, so far between. And if the faces of the People had looked gaunt when they left—

"Hey, you!" The cry hung on the still morning air.

Bull slowed to a stop, looking around warily as he tried to pin the location of the call. Cautiously he slipped his atlatl from where it hung on his belt. He pulled a long dart from the quiver over his back. Practiced fingers nocked the dart in the hooked end of his spear thrower. The atlatl added leverage, acting like an extension of his arm, allowing a man to catapult a dart three times as far as he could throw a spear by hand. He missed the chewed-away rawhide loops that had secured his fingers to the polished shaft.

"Who is it?" he shouted.

"Here!"

This time he caught the direction of the voice. Looking up along the ridge, he squinted against the brilliance of the sun.

He shaded his eyes with the flat of his hand; the body of his morning victim bounced limply in the process.

A hunched figure stood silhouetted by the morning rays. Hunched? Indeed, the way Trickster Coyote could do when the urge came on him to take human form. In an attempt to fool men, he sometimes came looking like an old hunchbacked woman, or so Heavy Bull had heard. The only way to tell was to pull up his skirts and look for a penis and testicles. Trickster Coyote couldn't change that—wouldn't. He was too proud of his man parts.

Already unsettled, Bull stepped off the trail, wary, climbing carefully, eyes searching the surroundings. Just as he'd trapped the little thief, so could he, too, be trapped in the endless game of life and death. Where they waited in hunting camp, Three Toes and Black Crow would never know the difference—if they hadn't already been caught.

"Here I am, already assuming it's an Anit'ah war party," Bull told himself. "The voice called in the tongue of the People." He bit his lip, seeing the figure above more clearly now. Silhouetted against the light, it waited, ominous, balanced on skinny legs, body bulky. Chill fingers of premonition tickled along Bull's backbone.

This isn't good. What did Heavy Beaver say? A Curse is loose on the land? Heavy Beaver says we've offended Buffalo Above and He's taken His children away, caused the rains to cease falling, made everything harder for Father Sun's people.

And this? Is this Trickster Coyote? Or some worse spirit? A wandering ghost? Something to take me and kill me?

By Buffalo Above's bouncing balls! It did look like Trickster! A cold shiver closed on Bull's heart. At the same time, some hidden memory tripped in his mind.

"I don't like Spirit Power. I don't have any use for that stuff. Just trouble . . . that's all." His heart had begun to thud and he stopped, swallowing hard as he stared at the sun-silhouetted apparition.

Wary now, ready to run, he stared around, looking for ghost sign, for a hint of evil—as if he knew what *that* might look like. That inner sense of trouble kept pricking at him like the cactus spines still in his hand.

Nerving himself, he called, "Trickster? That you? Coyote?"

A cackling laugh rolled down from above, almost irritating in the obvious enjoyment communicated.

"Coyote? *Me?*" The silhouetted figure slapped a thin arm against its side with an audible pop. "Hah! *That's* what they're teaching you kids these days? Horn Core gotten a little crazy in his old age, or what?"

Horn Core's dead! Smoke and fire! Is this some spirit joke? He swallowed hard, beginning to back away, ticklings of fear running through him like tiny ant legs.

"Oh, come on," the silhouette called, gesturing. "I'm not wandering all the way down there. I've walked too far for that. I need your help. Eh? What's this? Going to run?" The voice cackled hysterically. "I'm going to walk into a village of the People and tell them how one of their brave young men turned and bolted from me like brother jackrabbit from a wolf? Ha-ha, I can hardly wait!"

Slightly shamed, Hungry Bull continued to pick his way up the slope, searching his memories of the elders to place the voice. Against the light of the morning sun, he couldn't identify who it was. Chokecherry? Not fat enough to be her. Sleeping Fir? Too tall. Walkalot Woman? Maybe, but the figure on the hill didn't look right. Still, something about her . . .

"Or Coyote trying to trick me." But Coyote usually did that during visions and Dreams. Sometimes, disguised as a hunchbacked old woman, he'd lull a pretty young girl to sleep. Then his penis would sneak out and impregnate her and she'd never know.

One of the Dog Crow Clan? If so, she was awfully far west. From this angle, he could make out her form. The hunchback look came from the pack she carried. The face might have been beautiful once, broad-cheeked and full. Indeed, even through the sucked-dry look of age, she still bore the trace of proud beauty. And he couldn't shake the feeling he knew her.

But who is *she?*

He reached the ridge top, carefully looking around, still uncertain if he'd walked into the middle of an Anit'ah trap—

uncertain about a lot of things. Wind-polished cobbles, scraggly sage, and wispy clumps of wheatgrass met his eyes, all stroked by the caress of the morning breeze. But no warriors waited to ambush him.

The old woman cocked her head, watching as he looked over the crest of the ridge, casting about suspiciously.

"At least you're not entirely a fool." She winced in the sunlight, as if at a hidden pain, and walked forward.

Warily, he waited, palms sweating where he held the dart ready to cast. He knew he'd seen her before. But Coyote could trick a man that way. Take the face of a dead person— or maybe even a live one, for all he knew. From the look of her tattered dress, the gauntness of her flesh, she might have been a childless widow woman with no one to look out for her. Then he met her eyes and his soul froze.

"Who are you?" he whispered, the firm grip of the atlatl reassuring. The wood fairly pulsed with the spirit he'd breathed into it at Blessing. *And what good is a crafted dart against a ghost? If only he'd had Heavy Beaver Sing Ghost Medicine into his . . . but he hadn't.*

"You don't know me?" She cocked her head; a glitter of amusement animated her black eyes. "If you're who I think you are, boy, you've aged well. Handsome."

He half started. She called him "boy"! "I am Hungry Bull, son of Seven Foxes and Bright Cloud. My grandfather was—"

"Yes, yes, I know you. Knew your father. Know of him, I should say. Knew your grandfather, Big Fox, well." A saucy gleam filled her eye as she looked him up and down. "Knew him well, indeed. The ways of the wind lead us round and round, don't they? What a person starts always comes back . . . somehow, someway. The Vision was right. It was time to come."

Visions? He squinted, slightly irritated, still unsure. A man never knew what the demons might do to him. Could she be some spirit? If so, good or evil?

Close now, unsure, his heart beat like a stone maul on green wood. Swallowing hard, he set himself, terribly afraid. Quick as lightning under a thunderhead, he flicked the point of his dart down and jerked her skirts up.

"What?" she screamed, jumping back, arms flailing for balance, hindered by her walking stick.

In the melee, he ducked, looking under her skirt. A woman.

Only quick reflexes saved him as the walking stick descended in an arc. Crabbing sideways, he rolled under the blow as the stick whistled over his head.

"Hey! *Don't kill me!*" He scrambled sideways, the walking stick whacking the cobbles on the spot he'd just been. Before she could recover, he got his feet braced and scampered back.

"Waaaa!" The war cry tore past her old lips as she charged after him.

"Wait!" he called, racing away from her. "I was just checking!"

Her old body wasn't up to the chase. The pack—still on her back—slowed her even more. Panting and wheezing, she glared at him, walking stick raised high as strangled sounds gurgled in her throat.

"Coyote disguises himself as a woman!" Hungry Bull pleaded.

She started forward again, intent on cracking his skull.

"What would *you* think?" He backpedaled out of her reach, hands raised.

Lungs laboring, she slowed, jaw thrust forward.

"I'm *sorry!*" He gulped a breath. "I'm just a hunter. All I know about Coyote is what Spirit Dreamers tell me."

"You ever . . . seen Coyote . . . look like an . . . old woman?"

"No!"

"Then why—"

"Because he *might!* And if he wants to trick someone, it can be someone besides me! I got enough troubles!"

At the stricken look on his face, the old woman stopped herself short of the next attack and laughed, breaking into a coughing fit in the process.

"Okay," she admitted between lung-racking hacks, "I believe you."

Hungry Bull took a deep breath. "Good. Who are you?"

She sniffed, reshuffling her burden. "My first human name

was Green Willow." She chuckled, gesturing at the country around them. "Shows you how long ago *that* was. You're Hungry Bull? Supposed to be quite a hunter, I hear tell."

He swallowed hard. "I'm the best among my people."

She glanced at the trophy dangling limply from his left hand. "Well, if a bushy-tailed packrat's all you got . . . I wouldn't want to be one of your people." Her critical eye took in the scratches and scuffing of his clothing. "And it looks like quite a chase. Was that you I heard bashing through the sage like a Monster in rut? All that for a packrat?"

He bristled, straightening, heat rising in his face, ready to lash out in anger—but caution held him. In the old stories, proud young men like him got in trouble doing that. The Wise One Above turned them into frogs and snakes and worms and such.

And there was that look in her eye—a Spirit Power look—like she could see his soul inside, like she knew so very, very much more than he. And he knew her. He was sure of it.

"Green Willow? Are you . . . I mean, are you real . . . in this world, I mean?" His throat had gone dry. What would an old woman be doing up here?

She grinned wickedly, exposing worn yellow teeth. "As real as you. And judging from your recent behavior, a whole lot brighter."

He flushed, lowering his eyes in shame.

"Where were you going when I saw you down there? A camp of the People around here someplace?"

He swallowed, pointing with darts to the southwest. "Four days' walk. Down along the Moon River. Three of us, Black Crow and Three Toes, and me, we came to hunt. I tried circling to the north."

"Haven't had much luck, huh?" She shook her head, hawking to spit onto the cobbles. "Well, I've seen buffalo sign. One bunch, nervous and spooky. That was up above the hogbacks." She pointed over her shoulder.

"That's not that far. Only a half day's walk." He paused. "You came from *there*? That's getting too close to the An-it'ah."

"They leave me alone. Where's your hunting camp?"

He pointed back to the east.

"Hmm. And the People are south?" She rubbed her chin. "Tell you what. You go get your friends. Meet me at Monster Bone Springs tonight."

"Monster Bone . . . Why there? I mean, that's a Power place where the Hero Twins came and killed the Monsters and ate them. You mean, you . . ." Words failed as he backed a step.

"Hah!" She snorted, dry humor curling her lips. "So the stories go, huh? Hero Twins? *Men* killed the Monsters. Just like we kill buffalo." She paused, looking sadly at the rocky ground before her. "Oh, I don't know why it bothers me. Changing . . . everything's changing, turning, making itself into something different."

Hungry Bull waited, nervous. "We're told not to go there. That spirits like the Trickster will take our soul."

She pinned his eyes with hers. "Indeed? And I suppose that same lunatic tells you to look up women's skirts? Who tells you such things?"

Wincing at her taunting, he told her, "Heavy Beaver, he Dreams—"

"I remember him as nothing more than a sullen kid. What happened? He get touched by more than bad humor?"

"He's a powerful—"

"Maybe. Or he's fooled everyone into thinking he is. I'll wait and see. Usually you can see Power in a child. See it in their eyes, the way they move. Where's Horn Core?"

"Dead."

She gave him a steely look, lips pinching. "When?"

"Maybe three years now. No one knows why. He broke his leg and it grew together . . . but it never stopped hurting. Then it swelled up, poisoned from the inside, like happens sometimes. Heavy Beaver said it was because Horn Core called on bad spirits. And that's why Buffalo Above is punishing us . . . keeping Rain Man away. Horn Core never had the right Power to keep him—"

"Dung and flies, boy! Horn Core was a Dreamer in the old sense of the Power. Heavy Beaver? He's like a child who would hunt buffalo with twigs."

"No! I mean, never say things like that. Heavy Beaver will Sing a Curse over you . . . make the evil ghosts come and—"

"That tapeworm? Curse me?" She cackled happily again. "That'll be the day!" Then she paused, another thought striking her. "I see . . . it's all starting to make sense now. Curious how the Power of the Dreaming works. Curious . . ." She lost her line of thought, eyes going vacant as she stared out into space, seeing something far beyond Hungry Bull and the sun-washed ridge top.

"Who *are* you? I've seen you before someplace."

"Huh?" She started, vision focusing again. "I told you, they called me—"

"Who are you now?"

She smiled wistfully at him, raising an eyebrow to recrease the wrinkles in her forehead. "Met you in your lodge one night. Sage Root had just lost a child. Boy child as I recall. I needed a mother, a healthy woman with milk to give. No wonder you don't remember. That night, you were pretty upset. You hardly noticed me."

Breath caught in his throat. "*White Calf!* They said you—"

"Rose into the sky on a whirlwind." She grunted. "I know. Unlike ravens who chatter all the time about important things, men like to carry on with a lot of nonsense."

He gaped.

"The boy's doing all right?"

He nodded, still undone, remembering that night, remembering the grief in Sage Root's eyes as she cuddled her dead child. Then, out of the dark, came Horn Core and the old woman, a bundle wrapped in her arms. A gift, she'd said. A child given by the Spirits for one taken.

His concern then hadn't been for old women out of the night, but for Sage Root. So he'd taken his dead son from her arms, replacing it with the living. Awed, he'd watched as Sage Root's breast accepted the child. And when he'd turned back, White Calf had gone. No one could find her in camp that next day.

Before he left to start his own band, Elk Whistle told him about White Calf and the wounded berdache. She'd found Elk Whistle out hunting in these same hills, taking him to Monster Bone Springs, where the child and the wounded berdache had been.

Horn Core had filled in more details, talking of White Calf's Power, of how she lived high in the Buffalo Mountains, making magic. Other than that, little was known of her, at least, little that people would talk about.

She smacked her lips, shaking her head. "Enough of this. What I need you to do is get on to your hunting camp. Pick up your friends and I'll meet you at Monster Bone Springs. I'll have your packrat stewed by the time you get there. Then we can all hear the exploits of your hunt."

He nodded, mind wheeling.

"You gonna be there?"

"Y-yes."

White Calf lifted the packrat to stare thoughtfully into its dull eyes. "Best hunter among the People, huh? Looks like you sat on it!"

Without thinking, he admitted, "I did. It was going to get away again."

Three Toes whistled as he flaked a new point from a finely prepared translucent brown chert. From Knife River, far to the north, he'd traded for the superb material. With skilled hands, he scrubbed the edges of the tool on coarse sandstone grooved from years of such use. Testing the rounded edge with a thumb, he nodded and pulled a use-polished deer-antler baton from his pouch.

Still whistling, he sat back on his rock and began striking broad thinning flakes from the chert. Patterning his strokes with the skill of a master, he caught each flake as it came free, letting it drop with the delicate clinking chime of perfect stonework. Among the People, no one made better points. When Three Toes worked stone, his soul went into the crafting, permeating the very rock.

He sat before a smoldering sagebrush fire, a pile of jackrabbit bones still blackening in the center of the stone-filled hearth. Two packs and a brush shelter lay at the peripheries of the camp. Here and there, cratered stipples in the soil marked spots where they'd twisted sage out of the ground for the fire. Sagebrush made a wonderful fire. From the moment it was placed on the coals, it virtually torched, flames leaping for the sky in a roar. Then the fine laminar structure of the hard dense wood collapsed and the coals burned for days. When stones were dropped on top to absorb and radiate the heat, a man could cook on such a fire for a long time, or roast meat, or pile a hand's thickness of dirt over the whole and sleep warm—even in the coldest of weather.

Three Toes paused to wipe sweat from his high forehead and look up at the point where Black Crow sat. He stopped short, missing the dark silhouette of Black Crow's figure against the sky. Game? Studying the slope, he finally spotted his friend winding down through the scrubby sage.

Returning to his whistling, Three Toes used his coarse sandstone to scrub the brittle edge off the long lanceolate point to make a platform. When the platform looked right, he wrapped his point in thick buffalo hide and pulled his elk brow-tine punch from the pouch. Placing the punch tip just so on the platform, he began pressing long thin flakes from the point to create the final edge and shape.

To the *snap-snap* of his flaking, his whistle mocked the meadowlarks and redwing blackbirds. He warbled like the finches and trilled like robins, eliciting responses from within the tall sage that clustered around the drainage under the terrace where they camped.

"Hungry Bull's coming," Black Crow called from the slope, his presence announced by cascading gravel and cobbles. "He's in a hurry."

Tongue sticking out the side of his mouth, Three Toes pressured a tiny flake from the fragile tip, leaving a razor-sharp edge. That done, he looked up.

"In a hurry? Maybe he found something?"

Black Crow trotted in his loose-limbed, swinging stride that made it look like all his joints were unhooked. Tall and lanky, he had lived about twenty-five winters. His face, like the rest of his body, had been stretched out of shape. His ugliest feature consisted of his long fleshy crooked nose. People joked that it looked like a long turd slapped haphazardly on his face. The other incongruity—considering Black Crow was the finest scout among the people—came from the slight sag of belly, with protruding navel, in an otherwise whip-thin body.

Black Crow walked to where the water skin hung in the

shade of a particularly stubborn sagebrush that had repeatedly resisted their attempts to twist it out.

"We better hope so. Tracks make thin soup. I mean, there's nothing but dust and last year's buffalo sign."

"See anything else that looks like we could eat it?"

"Just tweety little birds—the ones you like to sound like. And I thought I saw some antelope out in the basin."

"Can't figure it. I mean, look out there. No water in the basin. Grass is brown and dead. You look around at the sky and all you see are those stringy little strands of thin clouds way up. How long's it been since it rained, huh? And no snow last winter." As he spoke, Three Toes resumed his careful pressure flaking, rolling the punch slightly in his hand as he finished the edge of the tool.

"Too long." Black Crow gulped water. "You know, if this keeps up, we're going to be living off packrats and mice. Think you can manage to Sing for a jackrabbit surround?"

"Ever hear this?" Three Toes lifted an eyebrow and reached into his pouch. Black Crow leaned down, curious, as Three Toes lifted a carved bone tube to his lips and blew.

Whhhaaaaahh! the sound carried on the still air.

"Pretty good, huh?" Three Toes grinned happily.

"So you can sound like a dying jackrabbit. That's important? It'd be better if you could smell like a buffalo cow in heat!"

Three Toes went back to his work, lifting a shoulder in a shrug. "You'd be surprised. Coyotes, skunks, badgers, weasels, wolves, lots of things come to a dying-rabbit call."

"Great! The answer to hunger in the camps. We can eat skunks and badgers. Wolf is sacred and must never be eaten, and coyote tastes like . . . like . . . Well, I've *never* been *that* hungry."

Three Toes frowned at his point, lifting it to the light, squinting along the flake-rippled surface, peering closely for any flaws he might have missed, for any cracks he'd made in the manufacture.

"I don't know. Them jackrabbits, they can get pretty mean sometimes, turn around in a trap and charge you."

Black Crow settled on his haunches, fingers clasped before him. "And you're worried? Remember the buffalo trap up on

Red Water Creek? Remember when that big bull ran over Black Bird and charged down snorting and blowing snot all over? I've never seen a man go over the corral as fast as you did! People're still laughing about the way you landed face-first in the—"

"Hey! Look! I'm alive and in one piece. Black Bird still can't breathe right after that bull stepped on his chest and broke all them ribs."

"Yeah, but you'd have saved yourself a lot of grief if you hadn't landed facefirst in the—"

"Okay! So buffalo get scared. They make those runny piles when they get scared!"

Black Crow grinned, dark eyes twinkling. "Let's see if my mind serves me. Seems to me, that wasn't the only runny pile—"

"I get scared, too!"

They both stood as Hungry Bull came trotting in, deep chest rising and falling as he slowed to a stop, grinning uncertainly.

"Well?" Black Crow and Three Toes cried at once.

Walking forward, Hungry Bull puffed and shook his head. "No game. But . . . I guess we're in trouble."

"Why don't I like the way he says that?" Three Toes grunted, half to himself.

"What kind of trouble? Anit'ah?"

Hungry Bull shook himself, as if to clear his thoughts, and walked to the gut water sack. He lifted it to his lips, draining a hand's section. Dragging a forearm over his mouth, he turned. "Not Anit'ah. You've heard of White Calf? It all happened this morning. . . ." And the story unfolded.

"Monster Bone Springs?" Black Crow wondered, from where he squatted on his haunches. "White Calf, the witch, wants us to meet her at Monster Bone Springs at dark?"

Three Toes scratched at the back of his head, staring skeptically at Hungry Bull. *He's always been sane before this. Not only that, he hates the idea of fooling around with Spirit Power. He even denies he has bad dreams at night!*

"I guess I've got to go. You don't have to. I guess I should have just done that in the beginning. Just gone with her. I mean . . . well, you might get ghost-sick or something. I don't know. I don't *like* spirit stuff.''

Black Crow had been frowning into the thin patterns of smoke rising from the fire pit. "And if we just run? Maybe Heavy Beaver could . . .''

"I don't think so.'' Hungry Bull's features had fallen. "She didn't seem the least bit worried about him.''

"If she's been that close to you, she's got a hold of our soul,'' Three Toes decided. "Maybe inhaled part of your breath or something.''

"*What?* Inhaled my—''

"*How do I know?* I don't know how witches steal souls!''

"Hey! Quiet! You two are making each other crazy,'' Black Crow called from the fire. He cocked his head, staring up at Hungry Bull. "You know that Green Willow and your grandfather, Big Fox, were married, don't you?''

Hungry Bull started, color draining. "Married?'' He swallowed hard. "You mean . . .''

"That's *just* what I mean. Red Moon—the woman you called Grandmother—she came later. Green Willow bore your father, Seven Foxes. There was trouble and she left the People. Left your grandfather, Big Fox, with the child.''

"How do you know all this?''

Black Crow's features pinched; he shrugged self-consciously. "Not all families like to remember things . . . especially things they think are embarrassing. Big Fox never told your father. He never told you. People are polite. They don't mention what your family doesn't want told.''

"She's my . . . No.''

Black Crow tilted his head, sharp eyes on Hungry Bull. "Yes. She's your grandmother. And I think we'd better go to Monster Bone Springs and see what she wants of us.''

Hungry Bull lifted his hands, shaking his head. "Not now, not after what you've just—''

"Hungry Bull,'' Black Crow reminded sternly, "she's not the kind of woman you want mad at you. According to the stories, she killed a woman who . . . Well, she killed her, that's all. The stories say she did it by looking at her. On the fourth day, the woman was dead. Green Willow left in shame, in the night.''

Hungry Bull cast pleading eyes toward Three Toes.

What do I do? What do I say? He cleared his throat. "But Black Crow, if we just leave, maybe—"

"She knows us," Black Crow added firmly. "Hungry Bull gave her our names. She's looking for a camp of the People. Like it or not, we're in this."

The words were twisted from him like a rabbit from its hole. "Then we don't have very long to make it to Monster Bone Springs, do we?"

Chapter 6

Snaps Horn laughed and danced away as Tanager chased him through the fir trees. Elk Charm ran along behind, shrieking her joy. It didn't matter that Snaps Horn was older, no one ran like Tanager.

The game had started with dart and hoop, where a willow hoop laced with thongs was rolled along the ground and the children cast sticks at it. The winner was the one who could pin the hoop the most times with thrown darts. Tanager, of course, had won, until Snaps Horn's patience cracked like a chert cobble in a fire. He'd turned and thrown his dart at Tanager.

Nimble on her feet, she'd dodged, grinning as she readied her own throw. Knowing her aim was deadly, Snaps Horn had fled.

Now she closed on him, feeling the power of her young legs. She planted her feet suddenly, putting all the strength of her supple body into the throw. Her dart, made of whittled willow, flew straight, catching Snaps Horn full in the back.

Snaps Horn howled at the pain and ignominy.

Thus repaid, Tanager shrieked her victory to the air.

She saw him turn, saw the anger in his eyes, the rage twisting his face. She almost flattened Elk Charm as she burst past her, weaving around the trees. But no one could run like Tanager. She yipped her happiness into the still mountain air. Let him run himself to the stumbles. No man—not even Snaps Horn—would catch her.

In the twilight, Sage Root walked, an ache pulsing through her. She looked up at the darkening indigo skies, eyes searching, as if solace lay there beyond her reach. Here, in the interim between night and day, Father Sun had vanished and the Starweb remained obscured in the half-light.

In her loneliness, she wished desperately for Hungry Bull's strong arms. But he spent this night far to the north hunting, seeking to do what she had done here. This dilemma, this problem of the meat, she faced alone.

What to do? She stopped, fists clenched at her sides as the evening breeze bobbed the dry grasses. Each heartbeat sounded a dull thud, hollow against her chest. Fear tickled her insides while an ill feeling weighted her stomach.

Heavy Beaver's power outmatched her—left her looking foolish and futile. How could a lone woman stand against a shaman? How could she prove she had acted correctly?

"I can't stand against him," she whispered. *And if I do, I'm ruined. My son will be suspect. And Hungry Bull? What of him? He'll be devastated, humiliated. For the first time, I'll force him to beat me. He'll have to protect his honor.* The very thought of the pain in his eyes left her soul cringing. *I can't act alone!*

And she remembered the desperation in Dancing Doe's eyes. Poor Dancing Doe, who sat alone, refusing to eat, staring into the distance in her head hour after hour.

Will I end up like that? Heavy Beaver didn't bear any festering anger against Dancing Doe. But he did against her.

The chill of evening settled over her as the stillness grew. The first flickerings of the Starweb twinkled on the eastern horizon. "Why is this happening?" she pleaded to the rising stars. "All I did was feed my people!"

The wind tugged at her fringed sleeve, threading soothing fingers through her hair, tickling her cheek.

Below her, in the deeper shadow cast by the ridge, a wealth of rich antelope meat lay drying on the sagebrush. In the night, coyotes wailed and yipped, held at bay by the odor of human urine and the soft movements of the old women who guarded the meat. Here and there along the arroyo, fires blinked amber eyes at the night. In the glow, people sat huddled, gesturing as they wondered, argued, and tried to make sense of the day. From where she stood, their conversations whispered, no more than a murmur.

Uneasy premonition hung heavily over the kill site, like blue smoke from winter fires on a crisp morning. Sage Root swallowed hard. The ghosts of the slain antelope hovered in the chilling air around her. A tingle ran through her as her people looked up from below, watching, the power of their scrutiny raising the hair at the nape of her neck.

Everyone waited . . . on her.

Gravel crunched under a light foot. Sagebrush rasped on tanned moccasins as a woman climbed from below. Sage Root steeled herself, knowing the decision loomed over her. Why did the responsibility *have* to be hers?

"What are you going to do?" Chokecherry asked, puffing up the last bit of slope, stopping, pressing wrinkled hands to the small of her back as she straightened and winced. Joints crackled in the stillness. The old woman cocked her head, staring across the darkened hollow and the knots of worried people.

Sage Root sighed, picking at the long-dried blood caking her fingers. "I don't know. They're afraid. He Cursed the meat."

Chokecherry grunted noncommittally.

"I know I didn't offend the antelope. I just *know* it! I looked into the doe's eyes. Our souls locked and she understood. I *saw*! I know the antelope don't begrudge the meat. *I* felt the rightness of the song as I Sang in my head."

Chokecherry nodded, a quick birdlike motion. "Then the meat's clean."

"But what about Heavy Beaver's Curse?"

Chokecherry smacked thin lips over toothless gums. "What about it?" She hesitated uneasily. "I think he's out to get you one way or another."

She nodded, soul frost settling around her miserable heart.

"I can't win, can I? There isn't a way out of this that won't waste the antelope, or offend Heavy Beaver."

"No."

"But what can I do? Tell me what to—"

"I can't. It's on your shoulders, girl."

Sage Root stepped closer, peering at the old woman's night-shadowed face. "I—I'm not a Spirit Dreamer. I'm just . . . me."

Chokecherry nodded. "Just you. And this is your decision. You killed the antelope. Heavy Beaver took it as an opportunity to destroy you. He—"

"We're *starving*! I refuse to look at the hunger in my boy's face! I refuse to watch his ribs sticking out, his limbs wasting! Look into the eyes of the children, Chokecherry! Look at them! I lost two babies. *Two!* I'm not about to lose this one. Heavy Beaver's got us killing our own children if they're born female! How do you think Dancing Doe will ever live with herself? *We're dying!*"

The old woman stood before her tirade, unflinching. "And Heavy Beaver's Dreamed a new way—"

"You don't believe what he says about women—that we're a pollution, that it's our fault the buffalo have become ever more scarce."

"He's a Spirit Dreamer."

"You've known a lot of people with Power."

"Yes, I have." Chokecherry laughed—a hollow brittle sound. "I think I know what he is. But you're avoiding the problem. What are you going to do about the meat down there? You going to eat it? Going to feed your son? Set an example?"

"I don't—"

"Dung and flies, girl! You're in the middle of it! Don't you understand yet? You're the one who has to lead now. It's your responsibility to take this by the horns and twist the People into acting . . . making a decision. Now, the meat's down there and all the People are waiting to see what you do."

"I didn't want this. I didn't want any of—"

"Well, it's yours. Quit whining and live with it. Life happens to people. Now, accept it and get on with it. What are you going to do? We need a leader. Maybe you're it."

"And if I challenge Heavy Beaver? If he Curses me? I mean I . . . He could kill me."

Chokecherry crossed her arms. In a soft voice she asked, "You believe that? You really believe he could kill you?"

Sage Root reeled at the implications, reading the old woman's challenge in her defiant posture. "He's a shaman, a . . ." She stopped herself, remembering Heavy Beaver as she'd always known him. "You don't think he could, do you?"

Chokecherry shrugged age-thin shoulders. "He might." A pause. "If *you* believe he can. But it's up to you. I don't know much about how Power works, but I know that you can defend yourself against it. I know that you can fight back. I also know that you can submit—and die—if that's your belief. What *do* you believe? You know Heavy Beaver. You know what sort of man he is. You grew up with him. Do you really believe Power came to him, just like that, when Horn Core died?" She snapped her fingers in emphasis.

Sage Root caught a handful of her hair, twisting it around into a thick rope, feeling the pull against the back of her scalp. "I only started to take him seriously when he began seeking visions."

"Uh-huh."

Sage Root frowned into the night sky, the reassuring flickers of stars beginning to fill the Starweb. "But he wouldn't get Spirit Power if he didn't deserve it, would he?"

Chokecherry placed a hand on her arm. "I don't know what to think. I don't know what's happening, why the game is going away, but Heavy Beaver's always been a little strange. I've watched him grow up as an adult watches a child develop. I don't know. His mother always protected him. She ran over his father like a buffalo tramples grass. She kept the boy from life, from play with the others. She never let him run with the pack. She always fought his battles for him. You know what happened to Heavy Beaver's father? He left. Took what was on his back and moved out of the lodge. Last I heard he'd finally died over east somewhere in Two Stones' band."

"He's not a puppy."

"Men and dogs are the same. Beat one, and it gets mean. Keep one from the pack and it never quite fits in. Never has a place with the others."

"You think he's . . ."

"Not right in the head?" Chokecherry spread her arms wide. "How should I know? Girl, we've lost so much, maybe we've lost our way to Spirit Power. Horn Core always worried that he didn't really understand. But he tried with all his heart. He gave all of himself, but he told me once that he didn't have the fire in his soul—and it worried him. A person with Spirit Power can Dance with fire, can Sing the stars."

Sage Root tilted her head. "Can you conceive of Heavy Beaver Dancing with fire?"

Chokecherry chuckled at the image it conjured in her mind. "Hardly." Then she sobered. "But the People are waiting."

"So are the antelope. I . . . can almost . . ."

"Yes?"

Confused, Sage Root tried to clear her roiled mind. "I don't know. I can just feel them. That's all. Hovering around. Waiting."

"An angry feeling?"

"No. Just . . . well, it's not clear."

"Then you had better choose. Will you eat the meat? Will you defy Heavy Beaver? You're not alone in your dislike for him. Don't look at me like that. Think about it. It's the young people who flock to Heavy Beaver. He preaches a new way— says if we do as he says, it'll all be better. He calls for us to separate ourselves from the old ways, to follow his path and change things. Sage Root, listen to the old people. We're the ones who remember. So many have split off—Two Stones, Elk Whistle, Seven Suns—all left to form bands of their own. We'll be like smoke on the wind in the end, drifted so far apart, we'll disappear. Is that what you want?"

"Why does it have to be me to stand up and—"

"Mother?"

The voice startled her. She turned, seeing Little Dancer approaching uneasily. 'Yes, little one.''

"Can we keep the meat? The antelope are all waiting. They're uneasy. I'm hungry again. I wish you could feel it like I do."

For the briefest moment, she sensed his want. The gnawing hunger in his small body became hers. She staggered at the impact. What to do? Fear of Heavy Beaver balanced with the pangs of want, of a full stomach.

And if Heavy Beaver Cursed her? *I'm just a woman. How can I stand against him?*

A presence lingered, expectant. Nervously, she scanned the sky, searching for the source. A shiver traced her spine as her son's eyes burned up at her. She struggled with her thoughts, and everything in the world seemed to go still, all of it waiting on her.

"We'll keep the meat, son. It would be more offensive to waste the animals than to heed Heavy Beaver's words." *Hungry Bull, forgive me. My dearest love, please, forgive me for what I'm about to do. But I swear, I'll never watch another of my children starve. I've lost two boys, not another. Never again!*

Chokecherry sighed, her relief almost tangible.

Sage Root blinked up at the stars, aware of a change, but her son surprised her again.

"Mother? The antelope are leaving. They were worried. You made them feel better."

"The antelope?"

"Yes, Mother. Didn't you hear them talking to you?"

Sage Root shot a quick look at Chokecherry, wishing she could see the old woman's face as she stared down at Little Dancer. The old woman had bent, peering intently in the darkness.

"No, son. I didn't."

Her soul felt dislocated, the sensation almost sickening. Heavy Beaver couldn't ignore this. How could she ever resist? What could she do to save herself?

Heavy Beaver leaned against his willow backrest, smoking red willow bark in his straight clay pipe. Before him, the fire smoldered crimson in the darkness of the sweat lodge. Looking up, he could see nothing but the faint outline of the low roof. He placed his hand in the water pouch and cast droplets onto the hot stones beside him. His skin prickled as heat and steam rose.

Hot, so very hot.

"Heavy Beaver?" a young man called from outside. "I have just come from the antelope kill site. Sage Root has ordered everyone to fetch parfleches. She will keep the meat and feed her family. Chokecherry and Makes Fun are Singing her praises."

Heavy Beaver smiled to himself, nodding in the dim light. "Very well. She has chosen. Thank you."

Beyond the walls of the sweat lodge, he could hear the young man's step's receding.

To his surprise, the thought of destroying her hurt slightly. After all these years, she'd finally let her pride force her into his hands. One never knew where Power would lead. No matter.

"Foolish to sweat in weather like this. But you see, it cleanses. Clears the confusions out of our souls. Now I must go and prepare myself."

Straight Wood shot a quick look his direction, nodding.

Heavy Beaver crawled out, the dry air sucking up his sweat.

He walked up to his lodge and ducked in. Red Chert started, looking bashfully at him, lowering her eyes. She sat on the woman's side of the lodge, stripped to the waist. Her long black hair clung to her damp flesh, curled slightly where it matted on her flushed skin.

Through lowered lids, he studied her, seeing the sweat beaded on her cheeks, trickling down between her full breasts. Of all the women, Red Chert remained fat. He saw to that. No one could call Heavy Beaver a fool. In his youth, he'd overheard a conversation between Chokecherry and White Foot—who had later left with Elk Whistle's bunch after a fight over leadership. Chokecherry had stated matter-of-factly that full-bodied women conceived better than skinny ones. Chokecherry had believed that women who were worked too hard, or starved too thin, didn't take when a man planted his seed. Besides which, a Spirit Dreamer ought to have a plump wife. To do otherwise would hint that he wasn't capable as a Dreamer or Singer. A man of Power should have the trappings to accent his skills.

Heavy Beaver pulled at the last of his pipe, enjoying the bitter bite of the chopped willow bark. Despite the heat and

Red Chert's half-naked body opposite him, he couldn't shake the thought of Sage Root. He remembered her standing between him and the kill site that afternoon, defiant, eyes flashing. The image hung before him, so clear he could almost reach out and touch her, trace the curves of her hips, finger the full breasts pushing against the thin hide of her antelope dress.

Better than she herself, he'd known she'd chose the meat—and, thereby, her downfall as well.

She turned me down. She ridiculed me when I tried to Sing her into my sleeping robes. She laughed in my face!

For as long as he could remember, Sage Root had obsessed him. As a young girl, her eyes and mischievous smile had beguiled him. Her limber body gave her preeminence in games and dancing. How many nights had he watched, enraptured, as her skipping, flying feet had come magically alive to the cadence of the Singers and the drums while she whirled and bobbed tirelessly. None danced as gracefully as Sage Root.

Then had come her first menstruation. In the ceremony which made her a woman, Sage Root had been transformed into a most wondrous beauty. Men paid court to her constantly, Singing to her parents' lodge from the shelter of the night, bearing her gifts, seeking to waylay her in the brush as she ran her errands and did chores.

Heavy Beaver had given it his best, the desire in his young heart driving him to the point of ambushing her. He'd almost forced her that night. The burning fever had filled his heart when she turned him down. A man who raped a woman paid dearly. The People paraded the culprit to the center of the camp, stripped him, and sawed his manhood from his body with a dull quartzite flake.

If he didn't bleed to death—a rarity—the women continued to cut him until he did. Only that sober reminder had kept him from fulfilling himself that night so long ago. And, by stale buffalo urine, she'd have been better off for it.

He closed his eyes, imagining himself as he threw her to the ground. With all his weight and strength, he bore her down, staring into her flashing eyes, seeing her hair cascading across the ground in a coal-black web. Her enraged face would redden with the heat of anger, her beautiful mouth gritted.

Pinning her hands above her head so she couldn't scratch him, he would reach down, lifting the hem of her dress, pulling it high so he could run his hands down her muscular legs, feel her calf-tender skin against his. He'd lose himself in the soft swell of her breasts and tease the nipples hard while she fought him.

When she realized the futility of her situation, he would lower himself, wedging a hard knee between her thighs, opening her to him. Through it all, he'd stare into her midnight-black eyes, enjoying her final defeat.

The fire popped and hissed, bringing him back to his lodge. He filled his lungs, exhaling slowly to still the tension in his tight body. Opening his eyes, he looked over at Red Chert.

"Your bleeding will come with the moon?"

"Yes."

He nodded to himself, figuring. He had at least five days before he needed to worry about her polluting him. He pushed Red Chert onto her back, suddenly awkward fingers undoing the belt at her waist. Eyes clamped tightly shut, he relived the fantasy until he spasmed and groaned with release.

He gasped deeply, rolling to the side, feeling sweat run as he flopped limply on his back. Red Chert's eyes remained fixed on the smoke hole overhead, no expression on her placid face.

Heavy Beaver ran a hand over his wet visage, wiping the perspiration away. He'd finished this time. As long as he could fix Sage Root in his mind, he could finish. If he opened his eyes, or if he let himself remember Red Chert under him, his manhood fled, leaving him limp and powerless. This time, he'd held on to the vision, held on to Sage Root. Perhaps, just maybe, this time he'd finally planted his child. Perhaps now he'd be whole—prove himself a true man.

And Sage Root had defied him openly. Tomorrow, first thing, he'd Curse her before them all.

Sparks, like living things, spiraled up to the night sky, twisting, dancing a pattern of glowing yellow orange against the soft velvet of the night.

Across from White Calf, Hungry Bull, Three Toes, and Black Crow squatted, tense features accented by the flickers of firelight. They stared at her, uncertain, nervous. Three frightened young men. She chuckled in dry amusement.

"You all look like you're afraid I'll hop over this fire and eat you."

Black Crow swallowed, throat bobbing. "I heard stories about you. Chokecherry said you weren't all human—that you could change into an owl at night and fly up to the stars. They said you could talk to animals, talk to . . ."

"Ghosts?" she supplied when he couldn't finish. Wearily, she took a deep sigh, stretching her knotted legs out, looking down to where the fire glowed. "No, I don't talk to ghosts . . . but I wish I could."

Her words hit them like cold wind. They waited, muscles tightening under smooth skin, eyes gleaming uneasily, hands propped to lever themselves up if they needed to flee in a hurry.

"Oh, stop that! What's the matter? You think the whole world is filled with evil? Who's spreading this dung-filled idea? Look at you! Three strong young men sitting here, scared to death of one thin old woman." She shook her head in disgust as they lowered their eyes. Dropping her voice, she added, "Look around you. See the plants? The stars? The very dirt? Hear the nighthawk and the owl? Feel the wind? None of this is bad. Life isn't bad . . . nor are ghosts. You think a man's soul changes just because he dies and rises to the stars?"

She cataloged their silent faces.

"You see, the question you have to ask is *why*? Why would a man's soul change after he dies?

"If you talk to ghosts—"

"I don't!"

"But you said—"

"I said I *would* if I could." She rocked to ease her aching hip. "Yeah, I'd like to know what's on the other side. The old legends say it's like a Dreaming. All is one, and one is all. I'd like to know. That's what. Am I scared of what I might learn? Of course. Learning things always scares you. Learning is like walking on sand. You never know about the footing . . . when it might shift under your feet and leave you off balance. But if you don't walk, you don't get anywhere, don't see anything new. You'd be better to sit in your lodge, screened from the world by that thin hide, and starve to death.''

Hungry Bull frowned, a perplexed look on his handsome features. Three Toes sucked at his lower lip while Black Crow scratched at the back of his head.

"Now, get your sleep. We'll start for the People tomorrow.''

Rolled in his sleeping robe, Hungry Bull stared up at the sky, wide awake. Why couldn't he believe the old woman? Premonitions of danger and trouble stirred that sixth sense common to hunters. Mouth dry, he looked over at where the old woman lay breathing easily.

A shiver sliced its way up Hungry Bull's spine. Spirits ran loose on the land, Dancing for souls.

Blood Bear walked down the long hills from the uplands south of the Moon River. To his right, slightly behind him, the tall peak of the Beaver Tooth caught the morning sun. Before him the river curled and wound through the broad floodplain. Even here the grasses crunched underfoot. No rain had fallen in this parched land.

Before him lay the river—and a choice. East or west?

High above, an eagle sailed in the thermals, its path ever westward. Since his early childhood, he'd heard of the Power of eagles. Very well, he'd go west. One way suited him as well as another. Besides, a person never knew. That moment of insanity he'd had might have worked after all. At the thought, a curious tingle burned in the scarring stump of his little finger.

Blood Bear turned his steps as he reached the hard silt of the floodplain. West. After all these long weary years of wandering, maybe luck had turned in his favor.

How wonderful it would be not only to recover the Wolf Bundle, but to kill the berdache—and perhaps beat his wife before him into the camps of the Red Hand as a reminder of how she'd disgraced him so long ago. No one would forget

Blood Bear after that. And as punishment for harboring his runaway wife, he'd wage a new war on the Short Buffalo People. Considering what he'd seen of the plains peoples, none had the spirit to stand before the Red Hand.

The Wolf Bundle flexed its Power. It seethed, remembering Heavy Beaver's hard hands, the malignant hate in his mind as he heaved the bundle into the night. Anger whirled and swelled within it.

In the camp, men, women, and children slept, minds tormented by nightmares of violence and rage. Heavy Beaver whimpered in his Dreams, feeling as if a black fog suffocated him.

The Wolf Bundle waited.

Chapter 7

Little Dancer woke in the night, chilled by the dew that condensed on the leaves around him. The hide he lay on had softened with the moisture. He shivered and sat up, instinctively looking for his mother first and the stars second. Perhaps an hour remained until the false dawn—or so he judged. Learning to tell time by the stars took practice. They changed so with the seasons.

He rubbed a knuckle in his eye, but couldn't see Mother anywhere. Among the shadows, the sage still bowed under the weight of the meat. Two Smokes lay on the other side of the fire. The bedding the berdache had brought for his mother remained folded, hair side in, against the brush.

Little Dancer shivered again, made uneasy by more than the nippy cold in his limbs. The night seemed to hover anxiously, like the voices of the antelope that had called to his mother.

He stood, clutching up his robe, and paced the few steps

to the sullen glow of last night's fire. Two Smokes lay with his head under a bent arm. The soft breathing of the berdache came as a relief to Little Dancer. Not since the Wolf Bundle had been abused had Two Smokes slept easily. Little Dancer squatted over the fire, pulling his hide around like a tent over the coals. Warmth rose around him, caressing, bringing life back to his stiff limbs, driving the chill out. A pungent tang of smoke filled his nostrils.

From the darkness, a nighthawk's cry sounded. Insects clicked and chirred in the sage. Like a winter frost, tension drifted in the air, closing down, icing the soul the same way the morning dew had chilled his bones and flesh.

Where was Mother? The heat grew uncomfortably around his bottom. He stood, starting back toward the place he'd lain earlier, hesitating, crossing instead to settle himself next to the berdache.

That's when he saw the wolf. A big black animal padded out between the sage. Like a spirit, the creature stopped, keen yellow eyes catching the glint of the low fire.

Little Dancer swallowed hard, staring around to see why none of the dogs reacted. The beasts lay asleep, unaware of the intruder in their realm.

Looking back, he met the wolf's eyes, sharing a feeling of promise. Then, like a denizen of the imagination, the huge animal ghosted into the darkness.

Two Smokes jerked as Little Dancer curled next to him.

"Little Dancer? Are you all right?"

"Scared. I saw a wolf. Big and black. It looked at me."

Two Smokes reached to lay an arm over the boy, hugging him close. "Don't worry."

"I've heard talk. While I was out in the bushes, I overheard Walkalot Woman and Sleeping Fir. People say Heavy Beaver will Curse my mother. What does that mean? What will happen? Little children say they Curse each other . . . and sometimes rocks, and snakes, and scorpions. But when a Spirit Dreamer Curses, it's different, isn't it?"

"It's different."

"What will happen to us if Heavy Beaver Curses my mother?"

"You'll be fine. He probably won't Curse her anyway."
Two Smokes added an Anit'ah phrase. "Sun rises, sun sets."

"You mean that we can't change what will happen? Like
the sunrise?"

"Your Anit'ah gets better all the time."

"Because you make me talk it." Little Dancer frowned
into the night. "Two Smokes?"

"Yes, little one?"

"You don't like it here, do you?"

"What do you mean? I'm fed. I have a warm lodge. Your
mother and father are kind. I have you to wake me up in the
middle of the—"

"But I've heard that sometimes . . . well, the men hurt
you." The boy felt his friend tense, but he plunged on. "And
people make jokes about you and what you do with your
private places. I've seen the other children teasing and making fun of you because you wear a dress. That all hurts,
doesn't it?"

"Shouldn't you be sleeping now? It was a long day and
you're probably—"

"That's a way of not answering a question, isn't it? Asking
another question?"

"I suppose."

"But you wish you were back with the Anit'ah, don't
you?"

Two Smokes swallowed loudly. "Yes."

"Why don't you go? I think things are pretty bad here.
I've heard the Anit'ah still have buffalo up in the mountains.
Maybe they don't have a Spirit Dreamer who Curses nice
people like my mother. And you wouldn't get ridiculed. And
men wouldn't catch you out gathering your plants and throw
you down and lift your skirts to—"

"Shh! You sleep now. Tomorrow is going to be a long day
and—"

"Two Smokes? Isn't that another way to keep from answering? Trying to make me think of other things?"

Silence stretched. Finally, the berdache said softly, "Once
long ago, I made a mistake—and a promise. I swore something on the Wolf Bundle."

"What did you do? It wasn't something bad. You're a good person. What did you swear?"

"You know better than that. You don't tell about promises and Power, not lightly. Maybe, someday, if you're good, I'll tell you. In the meantime, I can't leave you, not for a while anyway. And yes, Little Dancer, I would rather be with the Anit'ah. They understand and value the Power of a berdache. They don't blame me that I would love a man instead of a woman. To them a berdache is good, someone to bring luck."

"But why does a berdache happen?"

Two Smokes shrugged in his robes. "I don't know. Maybe a man's seed plants differently in a woman's womb. Maybe Power touches the soul—Blesses it—as it comes to seek a home in a newborn baby. You know that men and women think differently. Berdache are in between . . . different—not man or woman. Just berdache. Between the worlds, yet separate. Only these Short Buffalo People don't accept me as a human being. To them, I'm something else—a monster to be feared."

"Maybe we should all run away to the Anit'ah?"

"Your father wouldn't like that. Your mother wouldn't want to go either. They've made war with the Anit'ah. Your grandfather and grandmother were killed by Anit'ah. Do you think Hungry Bull or Sage Root would want to go live with people who'd done that? You know how they scowl when I teach you the Anit'ah language. Among the Red Hand, they might feel worse than I feel here. Do you want that?"

"Why do you teach me Anit'ah? And all the stories about First Man who brought all the people up from under the world? Do you think I'll be Anit'ah one day?"

The long silence stretched again before Two Smokes whispered, "Maybe it's my way of keeping it alive. Maybe I'm paying for my mistakes. Sleep now."

Little Dancer's mind rushed with questions. What about the Anit'ah? What about his mother? And Heavy Beaver? If the Spirit Dreamer Cursed his mother, what would happen? Could she really die?

He began to dwell on that, knowing Two Smokes didn't want to talk about it. A brooding dread grew in his gut. Heavy Beaver wouldn't kill his mother. Why should he? Sage

Root was loved by everyone. And Little Dancer loved her more than any person on earth. Thoughts whirled in his restless head. Fear lingered, tracing around his queasy stomach, shivering at the edges of his muscles. Anxiously, he blinked at the night.

He'd never forget the night Dancing Doe's baby was born. He'd never forget Heavy Beaver's look of disgust, of thinly veiled hatred for his mother. So long as the day and night danced across the skies, he'd *never* forgive the shaman for abusing the Wolf Bundle and kicking Two Smokes.

And if the Spirit Dreamer really did Curse Sage Root . . .

"Two Smokes?"

"Yes."

"If Heavy Beaver Curses my mother, I'll kill him."

"Hush. Little boys don't kill Spirit Men. They respect their elders. You don't want to fool with things, boy. You just want to behave. Hear me?"

"Yes." *But I'll kill him, Two Smokes. I won't forget what he did to you—to the Wolf Bundle. He'd just better not Curse my mother.*

Weary, so very weary. Sage Root stared at the long strips of meat she'd been turning every hour or so. Most had dried, shrinking in the hot sun, jerking in the dry sucking air. Ten antelope dried into a bundle a single woman could carry in a big pack. Chokecherry worked the other side of the brush with Meadowlark and Makes Fun. Others waited, slowly caving in to the power of hunger, fear of Heavy Beaver eroding as they watched the meat being packed.

Her nerves hadn't let her sleep despite her exhaustion. What had she done? How could she insult the antelope by turning her back and walking away? Hunger ate at her people. How could Heavy Beaver Curse the meat so callously? Didn't they have enough trouble?

Where is he? The worst part is waiting. She'd forced him, defied him openly. Mocked his power once again.

She straightened, squinting into the morning sun, searching the deep blue vault of the sky for any sign of rain. Overhead, small puffy clouds floated past, headed ever eastward, refusing to mass into a life-giving rain.

"Mother?"

She turned, seeing her son struggling under the weight of a water bag. His tongue stuck out the side of his mouth as he staggered forward.

"See, I brought the water. Hardly lost a drop!"

"You're becoming quite a man. Keep this up and we'll have to give a naming in another season or two. Are you ready for that? Ready to earn a real man's name?"

Merry eyes twinkled. "Really? You'd do that? I'm ready! It's all right to be called Little Dancer, but I'm big enough to earn a man's name."

She ruffled his hair, taking the water skin from his back, lifting it to suck down drafts of the tepid fluid. At least most of the mud had settled out. But then, the thirsty couldn't afford to be picky. The elders still talked of a time when the rivers ran clear as air, so a person could see the very bottom. Now silt from runoff gave the water a milky appearance—even late into autumn.

Thankfully, she wiped her lips.

"Do me a favor? Take this over to Chokecherry, then take whatever's left to everyone else until it's gone."

He grinned at her. "Sure. But maybe I could have some more? It was a long walk up here."

"Don't drink it all," she reminded him, reaching to turn the meat strips, squeezing the fatter ones to detect that mushy feeling of incomplete drying. Most were rock hard—testament to the aridity of the air.

"Mother?"

She looked back, seeing him watching her.

"Yes, son?"

"You can feel it. People are afraid. Is it Heavy Beaver? I heard in camp that he's going to Curse you today."

She stiffened, hiding her expression from him. "Yes, son, I suppose he will."

"That's why people are afraid? That's why you didn't sleep last night?"

"That's why. He also Cursed the meat. You heard him."

"But the antelope didn't mind. They told me so. I watched them last night. They don't like Heavy Beaver."

She made herself smile at him despite the emptiness in her

breast. "Then you listen to the antelope . . . always. Will you promise me?"

"Yes, Mother." His face puckered into a frown. "And if Heavy Beaver Curses you, what then?"

She swayed, uncertain what to tell him. She dropped to her knees to stare into his face. "I don't know. But whatever it is, you'll stay with your father. He'll see that nothing happens to you."

"But what of you?"

She shook her head, reaching to stroke his face. "I don't know. Chokecherry says he can't kill me if I believe he can't. But it's Spirit Power, and I don't know about how things like that work. I just don't understand. That's all."

"Why?" he cried desperately. "Why would he do it? The People need the meat and the antelope—"

"Shhh! Don't make a fuss. People are looking at you."

"But why? Does he hate everyone?"

Just women. Instead she said, "It's old trouble between him and me. Don't worry your little head about it. Everything will be fine. You'll see, things will work out."

He shook his head. "No, they won't. Heavy Beaver hurt the Wolf Bundle. Bad things are loose. I can feel them. Only the antelope were good." He nodded soberly, eyes wide as he stared into hers. "Why don't we leave? We could pack up and—"

"But our People are here. And where would we go? What if your father didn't want to leave?"

He lowered his eyes. "We could go . . . somewhere. Even the Anit'ah would be better than—"

"Hush. I don't ever want to hear you speak like that again. And if you do, I'll send Two Smokes away. You hear?" At his horrified look, she reached for him, holding him close, a tear creeping past her hot eyes. "I'm sorry. Don't listen to me. I'm scared, that's all."

"I know."

"It's just trouble, that's all. People do funny things."

"Because you didn't do what Heavy Beaver said?"

"That's right. People can't have everyone making their own rules—"

"But the antelope think you did right. They let you trap

them. They told me. Father wouldn't want you to hurt the antelope.''

''No, but he wasn't here.''

''Mother—''

''Hush, now. You think about what I said. And besides, you don't want everyone thirsty, do you? You've got a duty to the People, too. Your duty is to learn the ways of the People, to become a great hunter like your father. And for the moment, it's to see that Chokecherry doesn't die of thirst.''

''But, Mother—''

''March, youngster.'' She accented it with a pointed finger.

He filled his lungs to protest, disobedience in his small clouded face. Her lifted eyebrow overcame his reluctance; he turned, walking toward Chokecherry on uncertain legs.

Blessed Wise One Above, I never knew it would be this hard. She bit her lip until it hurt and bent back to turning the meat. A dead feeling already lay in her breast. How long now? How long before Heavy Beaver came? Couldn't he just get it over? The waiting ate at her like a thing alive.

Involuntarily, her eyes kept shifting to her son where he walked from person to person with the water bag.

Tears began to leak past her eyelids.

Never in all his young life had he felt so insignificant. Not even hunger hurt this bad. Little Dancer cried as he turned the meat the way his mother had showed him. People just looked away, shamed. He wiped at his eyes, feeling the worry hanging in the air like bad smoke. If Heavy Beaver made his mother leave, he'd go, too. He'd follow.

In his mind the presence of the antelope lingered like a familiar warmth on a chill winter day. To make them feel better, he picked a small piece of dried meat from the pungent sage and chewed it thoughtfully, thanking their spirits for the gift of life. To himself, he Sang as he'd heard adults do. The sun seemed suddenly brighter, a lightness cutting the dark in his soul. In his belly, the meat warmed him, spreading its power through his limbs.

Wouldn't Heavy Beaver feel the light? If Heavy Beaver

really Dreamed with the Spirits, he had to know the meat was all right. He had to know Antelope Above approved. He just had to! His thoughts always came back to the Spirit Dreamer.

Shivers played up and down his thin body as he recalled the fear in his mother's eyes. If his mother . . . A cold wind of fright rose up from the depths to terrify him. What could he do? Where would he go? If only he could save his mother.

People pulled hard strips of meat from the sagebrush and packed them into unfolded parfleches. Even the thick pieces that felt mushy in the middle had a hard crust on the outside. Flies couldn't lay eggs that would turn into maggots. But the coyotes could still come to steal pieces.

Feeling the urge, he walked to the edge of the kill site and lifted his flap to urinate. People had to do that to keep coyotes off. Ravens, on the other hand, paid no attention to markings and had to be run off or they'd steal a kill blind. Worst of all was when they crapped on the carcasses. The runny white droppings had to be carefully cut off. But then, given a choice, he'd take ravens over Heavy Beaver any day.

"Heavy Beaver!" He looked down at where his water spattered the dry earth. "Take that, Heavy Beaver! That's what you're worth."

A dark shadow loomed over him. Startled, Little Dancer looked up into the Spirit Dreamer's half-lidded eyes. His voice choked in his throat. He just stared, paralyzed, while his penis pointed straight at Heavy Beaver.

"A greeting? Too much of your mother in you, boy. We'll see about that one of these days. I promise you, I won't forget."

A croak sounded from Little Dancer's throat. Then Heavy Beaver strode past, the malignancy of his shadow like a black hail cloud.

Fear pumped with each beat of his heart as he ran, hearing people going silent as Heavy Beaver walked straight up to where Sage Root stood.

A strange expression changed his mother's face. The normally healthy tones of her skin had washed pale. Knowing her as well as he did, Little Dancer could see the brightness in his mother's eyes. Carefully, he walked wide of Heavy

Beaver, circling to hold his mother's dress hem. A fear unlike anything he'd ever known obsessed him, left him numb and mindless.

"So." Heavy Beaver's voice almost caressed. "You've continued with your pollution?" A lazy smile bent his lips.

"I made my peace with the antelope." Mother sounded hoarse.

"You polluted it, woman!"

The People tensed, stepping back at the angry tones in Heavy Beaver's voice.

"So *you* say."

"Take back your actions, woman. It's your last chance. Beg, and perhaps I'll Sing for you. Show you're sorry for your ways and I'll do my best to cleanse your pollution from the Spirit World."

Where he clutched his mother's skirts, Little Dancer could feel her shiver, tension locking her muscles.

"I would still Sing to save you despite your—"

Horrified, Little Dancer heard Mother laugh.

Heavy Beaver jerked as if slapped.

Her laughter stung like a yucca lash. "You'd Sing for me? The woman who turned you down? I'll bet. What next? You want me to beg? Let you possess me? Ah, I can see it in your eyes. You're no Dreamer, no Singer. You're the pollution, Heavy Beaver. A pollution within the People! What no one would put up with in anyone else, we allow in you because you've convinced others that you Dream. You're nothing but a sick man with delusions. You disgust me. Not even dung beetles are more repulsive."

Around them, people clapped hands over their mouths, eyes shocked. As Little Dancer looked up into Heavy Beaver's livid face, his guts loosened and tears began to streak his face. This couldn't happen, it just couldn't.

"Then there is no way to save you from yourself, woman." Heavy Beaver nodded. "In four days, I shall Sing your soul from your body. Before my lodge, I shall place four sticks, one for each day. And when the fourth stick falls on the fourth day, you shall die."

At that his mother shuddered.

Heavy Beaver saw, and smiled, and turned on his heel, walking away in long paces.

Little Dancer stood stunned, suffocating in the oppressive silence. The terror in his mother's rigid body powered his own. His mother's hand rested on his head. Her frantic fingers tightened in his hair until it hurt. He didn't care. Horrified at the thought, he began to bawl unashamedly.

Blood Bear kept to the drainages, easing after the last of the women who walked down the ridge toward the camp below. Last of all went a woman, a boy, and another woman who limped on a bad . . . *Two Smokes!*

Blood Bear slipped down the narrow drainage, all the while keeping his upper body screened by sagebrush. Could the woman be Clear Water? He craned his neck, getting the right angle to see her face. Even over the distance and time, he'd know her perfect features. But while beautiful, this preoccupied woman couldn't be mistaken for Clear Water.

He squatted down, back propped against the arroyo wall. So, he'd found Two Smokes. A joyous relief surged up to warm the smile on his face. Of course, he'd have to see if the Wolf Bundle remained with the berdache. Or did Clear Water have it? Surely, the two must be close, maintaining some sort of contact. Life among the Short Buffalo People would be a trial for outsiders. Clear Water would want to talk about old times, to hear the old stories.

Carefully, Blood Bear scanned the ridge tops, searching for lookouts, seeing none. Where were all the men? Hunting, most likely, scouring the surrounding terrain in search of the dwindling herds.

"So much the better. I can get in and get out unnoticed." The perfect opportunity would present itself. With the amount of meat carried in, most of the People would stuff themselves. Tonight would be a feast. There'd be a little singing and maybe a dance until all hours. But tomorrow they'd be heavy, lethargic after the night. He could sneak close just before dawn—and slip into the lodge where Two Smokes stayed. There, he could wring the location of the Wolf Bundle from the berdache, kill him, and be on his way.

It had to be tonight. The longer he waited, the greater the

chance of discovery. You never knew when some child would be creeping around the sagebrush, or a woman would be out looking for rodents or roots with her digging stick.

Besides, Blood Bear had never done things by half measures. This raid the Short Buffalo People would remember for a long time.

"Heavy Beaver?"

The Spirit Dreamer placed his drum to the side, rubbing at the sweat that had formed on his face. He situated himself just so, all the amulets and trinkets he'd placed before him neatly arranged to look precisely powerful.

"Come in, Two Elks."

The old man groaned as he bent over and pushed the door flap aside. He blinked, long gray braids hanging to either side of his head as he looked around the interior. The light that silhouetted his ancient body glared in Heavy Beaver's eyes.

"So dark." Two Elks entered, moving to the right where the male guest was expected to sit.

"Careful. You don't want to step on my raven's foot."

Two Elks muttered to himself and kept to the rear near the lodge wall. His bones cracked as he seated himself and grunted.

Every hardship in Two Elks' six tens of years of life could be read in the age-lined map of his face. Toothless now, his jaw jutted under the overhanging hook of his fleshy nose. His eyes had shrunk in his head, the orbits hollow looking. A long-healed scar crossed his left cheek. The right eye still twinkled with life and intelligence while the left had gone milky white.

"So, you're going to kill young Sage Root?"

Heavy Beaver smiled humorlessly. "She defied me."

Two Elks nodded to himself, still blinking to adjust his good eye to the gloom. "I would talk you out of this."

"Why?"

"Because it's worrying the People. They're—"

"I want it to affect the People. Women like Sage Root have brought us to these present dire circumstances. The only way to change things back the way they were is to purify ourselves. It can't be done without examples set and sacrifices made. I've Dreamed it, heard it from the stars. Sage Root proves my point. She went out in violation of my orders. She spilled the blood of Antelope Above's brothers. She turned them against us. Now we'll have to starve for a while to purge her sins from the body of the People. I intend to make her pay."

"You'd do this? You'd kill a good woman just because she spurned you? What of her son . . . her husband?"

"What of them? Her husband is a wild and reckless man. He's failed to teach his wife respect for Spirit Dreamers. You've lived here. You know it's no secret that he never beats her, never punishes her for disobedience. No wonder his hunting has been so poor over the last couple of years. No wonder the Wise One Above took his children from him. What more proof do you need?"

Two Elks stared at the dead blackness of the fire pit. "Doesn't it bother you that he might kill you for Cursing his wife?"

Heavy Beaver grinned. "Do you seriously think he would? I know Hungry Bull. How many times have I seen him shy away from Spirit Power? How many times have I heard him say he wants nothing to do with Dreaming or visions? No, all I need to do is threaten his soul—as I did his wife's—and he'll melt away like last March's snow."

"And Sage Root? Is there no way you'd withdraw the Curse?"

Heavy Beaver locked eyes with the old man. "I would. If she came here and submitted herself to me. If she came and apologized and bound herself to me for a year to learn proper penance for taking on a man's responsibilities. I could make a special exception and take her to the sweat lodge, cleanse her through the heat. Then I could heal her soul, rebind it to her body."

"She'll never do that."

Heavy Beaver lifted a casual shoulder.

"I have come to ask you to stop. People have been coming to me saying, 'Go to Heavy Beaver. Tell him to stop this. There is no good coming from this Curse. Tell him to stop for the sake of the People.' They're afraid of what will come if you do this thing."

"They should be. I've come to teach them a new way. Over the last couple of months, I haven't seen much change in the way they live their lives. Sage Root, Makes Fun, Sleeping Fir, Bright Cloud, they all continue to laugh and tell me what to do. I hear them speak as if they were the equals of men when—"

"It is the way of the People."

"It is pollution!"

Two Elks filled his old lungs, shaking his head. "And you'd split the People again? Can't you Dream a way for us that doesn't turn us against ourselves? That's not too much to ask, is it? You're splitting the young from the old, the men from the women, like a quartzite chopper splits bone. We can't—"

"Then they'll learn. That's what I've been trying to teach them. It's time for a new way. I've heard the voices, talked with the stars. Women can no longer be allowed to dictate the ways of the People. It is an age for men. Look at the Anit'ah. Look how powerful they are. You don't hear of women in *their* councils, do you?"

"Well, no, but then I've never—"

"And among the Cut Hair People? What of them?"

"I've never been among the Cut Hair People, but the way we live, you can't trap buffalo unless women handle part of the surround. And who drives the jackrabbits and packrats? Who helps work the drive lines when—"

"And they can still do that. But they can no longer take part in the planning. That's the obligation of men. How would you feel if you were Buffalo Above? Hmm? Would you want your children killed by women who pollute the world by bleeding at the crotch once a month?"

Two Elks frowned into the gloom, a look of confusion on his face. "But the old ways—"

"Have let us down! Face it, Uncle. Look around you. The buffalo have gone. Rain Man no longer Dances water from the clouds. Why do you think that is? No, you don't have the answer. But I do. And I'll save the People if I have to destroy them in the process."

Silence stretched.

"Yes." Heavy Beaver sighed. "I know they will come to

fear me. I can't let that bother me. A Dreamer has to take what the Spirit World gives him. If I have to change the People through fear and Curse some along the way, the rest will be better for it in the end.''

"You believe that, don't you?"

Heavy Beaver lifted his spread hands. "I'm the one who's experienced the Dreams, Uncle. Do you expect me to spit in the face of Power to keep the elders happy? No, I've been told to teach a lesson. Sage Root will be my way to do it."

Two Elks closed his eyes. "Please, don't do this thing. If you kill her, you can't go back. I think you don't understand what it will do to your friends and relatives. Think about it, Nephew. Think long and hard and seriously about what another division will do to this camp. We're hanging on by a thread. Blood and cries of witchcraft won't make anything better. Not at all."

"I'm the Spirit Dreamer. I have my own duties to the People."

Two Elks levered himself up, teetering on old legs. "Then your mind is set on Sage Root's murder?"

"I have said everything. I only sorrow that you would call it murder when I act to save the People. You know my heart and soul, Uncle."

Two Elks nodded sadly and stepped across to the door flap, a weathered hand bracing his ancient body as he pushed the hanging aside and stepped into the light.

After he'd gone, Heavy Beaver noticed the old man had stepped on his raven's foot and crushed it.

"My way . . . or no way, Uncle." *Just like my mother said, old man. Just like she saw—and you didn't.*

Raising his voice to the chant, he began beating on his drum, matching the hollow beats to the pulsing of his own heart. They'd learn now. And, of course, Sage Root—no matter how scared—would never come begging to him.

"He knows nothing of Power. What he calls Dreams, he makes up in his head. I wonder why you allow him to make fools of the People. They've begun to accept the fact that this imaginative deceiver is a Dreamer."

Wolf Dreamer answered through the shimmering balance

of the Circles: "Human beings have their own wills and abilities to discern true Power from lies. Leave them to their ends. You and I, brother, must follow ours."

The Wolf Bundle considered. "Nevertheless, it would be so easy, simply a touch at the edge of his soul, and the balance of his life would be changed. A flutter of Power around his heart and none would be the wiser. Why should the People suffer? Where is the purpose in their agony?"

"I'm not interested in their agony. They can choose their way . . . as can Heavy Beaver. I have other commitments."

"The boy?"

"Of course." A pause. "If he lives. I may have made a mistake in calling White Calf."

"You always had a softness for old women."

"If I do, it's none of your concern."

"And you'd sacrifice the People for the boy? You'd allow so much suffering?"

"I have to. A deadly dart point isn't crafted from flawed stone."

Chapter 8 🐗

Chokecherry ducked out of her lodge and squinted up at the sun, resenting the heat that beat mercilessly down. Below the camp, even the cottonwoods looked limp where they grew out of the Moon River's banks. Leaves flickered lazily back and forth in the morning breeze. Moon River itself consisted of braided channels lacing through lenticular mud bars. The water barely rippled. Gray-white cobbles marked old beds—now nothing more than the bones of the river.

Along the sun-bleached bank stood Heavy Beaver's sweat lodge—banned to the women now. She lifted her lip at the sight.

To the southwest, Chokecherry could make out the tall

conical mountain called Beaver Tooth where it stuck up above the Elk Place Mountains that rimmed the western horizon. Might be cool up there. A good place to go—if only Heavy Beaver would move the camp.

The thought of him brought acid to her stomach. Curse the fool anyway, why did anyone . . . *the Curse!*

She turned, looking across the beaten soil to Heavy Beaver's lodge. There, standing tall in the light, stood four dark sticks, each thrust into the ground.

A cold chill churned Chokecherry's gut. "Dung and flies, girl. He's done it." Her taloned fingers knotted in the front of her calfskin dress, old and shabby now from long wear. Steeling herself, she walked across to Hungry Bull's lodge, rounding the curve to find Sage Root sitting in the door flap, staring wide-eyed at the sticks, her beautiful face blanched.

"What's this? Maggots in pus, girl! That's what he wants you to do."

Sage Root continued to stare, barely aware of her.

"Get up!" Chokecherry hissed. "Hear me? Get up!"

The boy peeked around from inside the lodge.

"Son, help your mother up. We've got to get her out of sight of those foul sticks of his." She took one of Sage Root's ice-cold hands, tugging, while the boy tugged at the other. Sage Root shook her head, clambered to her feet, and followed without fuss. Chokecherry led off toward the river.

"That's what he wants, girl. You're supposed to stare like that . . . to dwell on what's going to happen to you."

"He's . . . a Spirit Dreamer. What if he's right? What if—"

"Hush, now. That's just what he's trying to get you to think." Chokecherry led her down beside the dry banks of Moon River, stopping at the edge of one of the rills. Bending down, she drank of the cool water, filling her parched tissues.

"Come on, girl. Drink. Then I'm taking you and the boy to my lodge and fixing some of that antelope you trapped. And after that, we're going to have a long talk about Power and how it works." She shook her head. "Wish my fool sister were here for once."

She caught the awed stare in the boy's eyes. He beamed at her, eager to hear. What was it about him? Now his eyes had gone unfocused, staring out over the sere plains, absently following the flight of an eagle where the bird rose high on the thermals.

"Come on, let's go feed the two of you. You're both getting a little moon-eyed."

Blood Bear might have been a snake sunning himself. He waited, belly-down, in a thorny green mat of rosebushes. From where he lay, he could look out through a ground-squirrel run and right into the lodge occupied by the woman and Two Smokes. The rest of the camp sweltered in the late-afternoon heat. He could feel the tension. He could see it in the way they moved, in their uneasy glances and subdued conversation.

He'd found no chance to sneak into Two Smokes' lodge before dawn. When he'd crawled close, the woman had been sitting in the entrance, eyes fixed on the shaman's lodge across the way. She hadn't moved, hadn't left for any longer than it took to relieve herself behind the lodge.

Turning his head ever so slowly, Blood Bear studied each of the lodges, listening to the Spirit Man's odd chanting to the hollow beat of the drum. For a brief moment, he shivered, feeling the stub of his little finger. Of all the stupid things he'd ever done, that rankled the most deeply.

I don't believe in such foolishness as Power. It's all curious myth and legend. That's all.

At that point, an old woman walked around Two Smokes' lodge and, with the help of the boy, dragged the pretty woman to her feet, leading her away.

And if something's happening, perhaps I'd best move first. He raised his head slightly, checking each of the knots of people where they talked in the shade of their lodges, heads bobbing, all eyes on the Spirit Man's lodge and the curious sticks standing there. So long as the wind held and the dogs didn't get his scent, or someone didn't decide to use the rosebushes to relieve themselves, he'd be fine.

But a person never knew when a party of hunters might return, or when an accident might happen to disclose him.

In the shade of a lodge, one of the dogs shifted, sighed, and rolled on its side, legs out. As the dog's breathing deepened, the eyes closed.

A fly buzzed in the afternoon. The cottonwood leaves overhead barely rustled.

A stillness settled over the drowsy camp.

Sage Root bent to do Chokecherry's bidding even though her mind knotted with other preoccupations. She drank her fill of the gritty water, enjoying the mineral aftertaste for the first time. Around her, the world seemed so bright, so clear and warm—unlike the chill inside.

She ran a loving hand over her son's head, following Chokecherry as she led the way up the path. Sage Root blinked, trying to clear her oddly dulled mind. Her thoughts blurred, as if her head had been stuffed with fur—or the cottony seeds of milkweed. She couldn't think with as much clarity as before.

As she walked, she couldn't help but look to Heavy Beaver's lodge, seeing the sticks, feeling the malevolence of their presence. Something in her soul whimpered.

"Come on," Chokecherry insisted, gripping her by the hand and pulling her down and into the amber-lit insides of the lodge. "Sit."

She went where Chokecherry pointed, dropping herself onto a roll of elk hide, propping her back on one of the willow backrests. Little Dancer settled beside her, staring around, one hand tucked reassuringly in hers.

Chokecherry's lodge—like most of the People's—had a shabby look. Overhead the cover shaded from buff to gray to black with soot from so many fires. Peeled poles formed a base three paces across and rose to a tall man's height. A thicker center pole supported the whole, the tops of all sootblackened. Chokecherry set about rolling up the bottoms of the lodge to allow the breeze to blow through.

Here and there, parfleches lay about the perimeter and one of Chokecherry's old dogs stared at her from the side. A big beast, it carried most of Chokecherry's possessions when the band traveled to new camps. Even the dogs looked worn these days; their gaunt sides had gone slat-ribbed. The barking and howling normal to the village pack seemed subdued. But then, so many of the pups had been clunked in the head and thrown into stew that she couldn't blame them. The People had grown irritable. Fighting dogs pushed them past the tolerance point.

Chokecherry wiped her hands, satisfied with the fire. She bent to the fire pit, stirring the ashes, blowing a coal alive as she fed it shredded sagebrush bark, adding bits of cottonwood branch until she had a crackling blaze. Then she piled rocks to heat in the center, digging ornately carved spoon bowls out of a parfleche.

Another time, Sage Root might have stopped to marvel at the pieces. Each had been carved from the boss of a mountain-sheep-horn sheath. The rich mottled brown and tan had been polished with fine sand until it glistened. The forms of buffalo, elk, deer, and antelope had been most carefully engraved on the sides while hunters surrounded the whole, darts flying.

"Now, tell me. Did you sit there all night looking at those sticks?"

Sage Root closed her eyes, nodding. By the Hero Twins, she'd hated herself for it. Through the long hours of night, as the filling moon traced its way across the heavens, she'd watched, seeing the angle of the shadows cast by the sticks slowly creeping across the ground. The chill in her soul had grown, eating away at the very warmth of her body until she sat like ice, feeling each beat of her heart. Time had begun to drag, slowing, becoming less and less real. The world had changed subtly, becoming an eerie place.

Not even the gentle breathing of her son beside her had affected the chill.

"Sage Root, listen to me. You're doing this to yourself. Do you understand?" Chokecherry hunched over, staring into her eyes.

For a moment, Sage Root let herself surrender to those warm brown depths, let herself believe the sincerity she saw there. Chokecherry caught that flicker of acknowledgment and smiled warmly.

"Now, you've got to pull yourself together and think. Heavy Beaver wants you to stare at those sticks. He wants you to *feel* them in your very soul. If you let yourself do that, if you let yourself play into his hands, you'll will yourself to die."

"But he's a Spirit Dreamer."

"I don't believe that. And I don't think you do either. After you let your imagination play with your head all night, you're not sure. That's the part of you he's betting on, preying on—like some sort of parasite. Sage Root, look at me. He's got his claws into you. Are you going to let him wiggle in the rest of the way?"

She dropped her head in her hands, feeling her son's grip tightening on her skirt. "I don't know."

"The other night, you chose to eat the meat. You knew he'd do this, yet you still chose. Why?"

She ground her teeth. "Because I *had* to. It was the right thing. I don't know. I felt so strong. I thought I could stand up to him, that it would be all right."

"And then?"

"Then I came back to the lodge last night with a load of dried meat. And I looked over and saw the sticks and it all became real. He's going to kill me. He's always hated me. I felt the Power of that. Hate, I mean. It's a powerful thing—and it's all turned against me."

"He still can't kill you—unless you let him."

"But I—"

"You're as strong now as you were when you made the decision to eat the meat. You acted right then, why can't you accept that now? Why can't you walk out and stare him in the eye?"

She swallowed at the clinging dryness in her throat. "I didn't know how it would wear at me. I . . . I feel lost, Chokecherry. I don't know anymore."

The old woman took a deep breath, leaning back. "I see. That's it, isn't it? You don't know."

"What if he's right?"

Chokecherry rubbed her lined forehead. "That's the real problem. You've only got his word that he's a Spirit Dreamer. Blood and tears, woman, you've *got* to believe he's a liar! That's your only hope . . . the only hope for the People! What if you die? Huh? Think of it! If you kill yourself worrying about his foul sticks, what then? You think he'll be a better person for it? Or will he turn his Power on someone else?"

Horrified, Sage Root stared into Chokecherry's eyes.

"That's right. After you, who's next?"

"I didn't want this. All I wanted was to feed my child."

Chokecherry shook her head. "I know. But it's you. Maybe the spirits chose, huh?"

Sage Root winced, claimed by a sudden urge to cry. "Why is this happening?"

Chokecherry sighed, slapping helpless hands to her sides. "It's the drought. The fact that the People are splintering into so many little groups just to survive. I don't know. Everything started going wrong in my father's time. That's when the White Crane drove us south, drove us to come here. The Cut Hair People fought to keep this land—then one of their war chiefs captured a young girl, fell in love with her, and married her. He made peace—stopped the fighting with the understanding that we wouldn't go further south. He bound us by our honor. The Anit'ah keep the good hunting grounds in the Buffalo Mountains because they know the trails up there; and we got the Moon River so far as the confluence with the Sand River to the east. Only there isn't enough to feed us all. But once, ah, yes, once there were huge camps of the People stretching as far as the eye could see."

"You said you'd tell me about Spirit Power," Little Dancer said shyly from beside her.

Chokecherry laughed. "Yes, I did, didn't I? Well, what do you want to know?"

"Everything!"

"Everything?"

"Yes. I want to be a Spirit Dreamer when I grow up and get a name. Then Heavy Beaver will never bother Mother again."

Sage Root stifled a sudden unease. "Why, son? Why would you be a Spirit Dreamer?"

Her boy looked up defiantly. "Because then I could put sticks out and kill Heavy Beaver!"

Sage Root closed her eyes and shook her head. "No. You'll never do that. I forbid it."

She could feel Chokecherry's eyes on her. "Girl, if the boy—"

"I said, no! I don't want my son to ever make anyone feel the way I do now. Do you understand? This is . . . is evil!"

Chokecherry shifted uneasily, reaching for her hearth sticks. They were nothing more than two willow stems tied in the middle; she could separate the ends to make tongs with which to pick up boiling stones. This she now did, plucking the hot rocks from the center of the fire, dropping them sizzling and steaming into the stew bag where it hung from a tripod.

"Come on, girl. You're upset. You haven't eaten and you haven't slept. The mind gets funny when it's like that."

She shook her head, turning hollow eyes on Chokecherry as the old woman stirred the stew. "No. I don't want anything to do with Spirit Power. It's ruining my life. I won't have my son ruining others."

Chokecherry bit her lips, testing the temperature of the stew before she scooped bowls full. "You know, when there are so few of us, what are you going to do if your son—who hears antelope spirits talking in the night—is a *true* Dreamer? What are you going to do if he can Dance with fire and Sing the stars?"

Sage Root stared at her, mind fogged with disbelief. "Not *my* son. Not ever." *If Heavy Beaver doesn't kill me, that is.*

"Aieeeeah!" A scream rent the quiet air.

"What the . . ." Chokecherry ducked her head around the flap, looking to see what caused the commotion.

Sage Root ducked after her from the lodge. People hurried toward the bluff back of the camp. Caught in the rush, she followed, aware of Little Dancer clinging to her skirt.

A knot of bodies obscured her view as she passed the birthing lodge, empty now. A fist closed on her heart, a premonition of what was to come.

"Dancing Doe!" Makes Fun cried, bursting from the crowd. Her eyes locked with Sage Root's for the briefest second before she broke into tears and clawed at her face.

"Don't," Chokecherry warned, placing a restraining hand on her arm.

Sage Root twisted loose, stumbling forward to peer over Walkalot Woman's shoulder.

Dancing Doe lay facedown on the ground. Where black

blowflies circled it, the keen point of a hunting dart protruded from her back. The dart's shaft had snapped when it took her weight. The fletching stuck out from under the coagulated pool of red beneath her. Even in death, Dancing Doe's eyes reflected her misery. She stared up, anguished expression condemning as Sage Root wilted, sinking to her knees.

"She ran onto the dart," Two Elks declared uneasily, standing from where he'd inspected the body with his one good eye. "She knew Long Runner wouldn't come back. She died on his dart."

"Heavy Beaver Cursed her, too," someone whispered.

Sage Root gasped, losing control. She placed a hand to her mouth, sobs bubbling up from her lungs.

"The time has come to stop this," Two Elks mumbled to himself. "Bad things are loose. Horrible things." He stalked off for Heavy Beaver's lodge.

Sage Root didn't hear as the People bolted for their lodges and weapons. She hardly realized Little Dancer remained beside her, frightened hands clutched in her dress. She only stared, horrified, into her dead friend's accusing face as the flies walked across the drying eyes.

"You have your wish. I know you've disliked the Short Buffalo People. Now you will go back to the Red Hand." The Wolf Dreamer's shadowy voice betrayed wry amusement.

"The Red Hand fed my Power. These numb-brained buffalo chasers have no more sense than their ancestors who slaughtered the mammoth. I suppose they'll do the same with the buffalo? Kill them off to the last one and then starve themselves?"

"Unless I can change the Spiral."

The Wolf Bundle contemplated for a moment, then said, *"I hope you can. I miss the mammoth. Since the last one died, I've missed the majesty their souls added to the Circles."*

"Then conserve yourself, brother. When the time comes, if the boy lives, he'll need your Power. We must do this right. To change the Spiral of the Wise One Above isn't done lightly.

*The world is changing. The boy might make a difference . . .
if we don't kill him in the process.''*

Chapter 9

Two Smokes sat on the rotten trunk of a blown-down cottonwood, watching the strands of the Moon River wind ever
eastward. The restlessness in his bruised soul wouldn't let
him sleep. He'd left in the night to climb up on the terrace
and watch the coming of the new day. Despite the reddening
of the skies and brilliant fires of Father Sun, the chill in his
soul didn't ease.

For hours, he'd collected grass seeds, slowly picking the
green umbels apart, letting the chaff blow away on the dry
morning breeze and mashing the little seeds between his
teeth. Grass went to fruit early—except the seeds were so
small. Nevertheless, grass grew everywhere, even in drought
years like these. If only people didn't have to depend on
buffalo to eat the grass.

For years, he'd wondered at the process, picking grasses,
looking at them, eating the leaves and stems and seeds. The
truth of the matter couldn't be denied. The Wise One Above
had made man different from his buffalo children. People
couldn't eat grass and live. With great care Two Smokes had
dissected his own droppings, finding leaves and seeds and
stems undigested.

He simply couldn't shake the feeling that he'd missed
something. Grass was everywhere. Buffalo ate grass. Then
people ate buffalo—which weren't always everywhere. If people could only cut buffalo out of the process and eat the grass
themselves, no one need ever hunger again.

The blackness inside stole his chain of thought, leaving
him to shiver in the hot sunlight. Anxiously, he stared back
upriver toward where the camp waited in ominous silence.

Even the little sounds of people during the day didn't carry—as if the entire camp held its breath, waiting for Heavy Beaver to act.

"The People are lost," he whispered. "Heavy Beaver has destroyed them through his arrogance. No one abuses a sacred bundle. No one spits in the face of the Wise One Above and expects a long or happy life." *And I can't feel sorry for the Short Buffalo People. They've beaten me, mocked me. Their men have raped me. Their women laugh at me. No, I can't pity them in their destruction.*

Sage Root and Hungry Bull had been kind to him. As White Calf directed, they'd made him part of their family and shared their food and shelter. He'd done his share in return. His nimble fingers had worked the hides, fleshing, curing, graining, and sewing to make the tightest lodge covers and finest clothing. Despite their mockery, Short Buffalo People dropped their prejudices when they traded for furs tanned and sewn by Two Smokes.

And now they would take that frail security from him, too. Sage Root had been Cursed by their mediocre Spirit Man. He shook his head. Compared to White Calf, Cut Feather, or Clear Water, Heavy Beaver couldn't make smoke rise from a hot fire. And Sage Root would die without knowing the difference. He'd seen the fear, the resignation, in her eyes. She *believed* she would die. The single-minded stare at the witching sticks proved it.

"And what then for Two Smokes?" He blinked up at the sun, now high in the sky. "Stay and be beaten and raped? How long until they kill me, too? How long until they declare the Wolf Bundle to be evil and burn it?"

You promised. Little Dancer is your responsibility.

He swallowed hard, staring back upriver. Little Dancer's words echoed in his mind. "We could run away."

He stood up and unrolled his special pouch. One by one, he placed his grass stems into the special holes punched in the hide. Unrolled, the whole thing measured almost two arms in length. In it he had grasses from everywhere. Giant wild rye, wheatgrass, needleandthread grass, buffalo grass, steppe bluegrass, and more. He rolled the long strip of leather into a compact tube and slipped it behind his belt.

Hobbling along, he stared dully forward, knowing trouble waited. His crushed leg had begun to ache again. Not for years had it caused him so much torment.

As he walked, he scanned the sky, noticing the thin strips of cloud that arched across the vaulted expanse. How long since rain? Three months since the last sprinkle? Now even the shadow of a rain cloud would be a relief.

A faint cry carried from the camp, causing him to hitch along a little faster on his bad leg. The knee had never worked right after the buffalo had stepped on it. Better stiff, however, than maimed so badly he couldn't move—or had to be left behind to starve and die of exposure.

Nothing seemed amiss as he passed through the trees. The camp looked deserted. But no, a knot of people had collected behind the birthing lodge. A wail broke out, keening on the heavy stillness of the day.

Two Smokes winced, feeling the dread. What new misery had befallen them? His stomach twisted like a snake unable to shed its skin. He wavered, half wishing he could run.

At that moment, the sky seemed to darken, as if his vision blurred and grayed. Two Smokes shook his head, trying to free himself of the terrible fear that grasped at his heart. What could . . .

"The *Wolf Bundle!*" he cried, wheeling, stumping toward Sage Root's lodge.

Blood Bear tensed as the cries rang out from the other side of the camp; the stillness shattered. People scrambled to their feet, running to investigate. Even the sleeping dogs followed, curious about their masters' excitement.

The camp lay open before him.

Moving with all the sound of smoke over polished granite, Blood Bear darted forward, heart thudding in his chest. By his very audacity, honor would be his. This act, this daylight invasion of the Short Buffalo People, would bring him praise and stature as a cunning and powerful man.

Without hesitation, he ripped the lodge cover back and ducked inside. Three rolls of bedding lay before him. The one in front drew his attention. A compact parfleche lay on a grass mat behind the head of that first bed. The bag had been manufactured with outstanding skill. The seams had been stitched so tightly one could almost believe the bag waterproof. The perfectly tanned leather gleamed white, accenting the brilliant colors of the decoration. Effigies of Wolf, of the White Hide, and all the other myths of the Red Hand covered each side.

Almost trembling, Blood Bear dropped to his knees, darts clattering as he discarded them to fumble the laces open with thick fingers.

The inside contained a beautifully tanned wolf hide. This Blood Bear lifted free, unwrapping the silky skin to expose the Wolf Bundle, its sides somewhat scuffed, but familiar nonetheless.

"The spirit of the Red Hand!" he gasped. "I've won. No one will stand against me now. I am the leader of my people."

Trembling with excitement, he could barely control his hands as he swiftly repacked the parfleche. In a final gesture, he kicked ashes over the inside of the lodge, grabbing up a packful of dried meat and slinging it over his shoulder.

The Wolf Bundle pressed to his chest, he reached for his atlatl and darts and ducked through the door.

"Blood Bear!" the cry caught him off guard.

He turned with the speed of a trapped lynx. Instinctively, his right arm snapped back, ready to launch a deadly dart even before he recognized the anguished face of his victim: *Two Smokes!*

"Die, berdache!"

Two Smokes flopped to the side as Blood Bear threw all his weight behind the cast. Two Smokes would have died right there but for the cumbersome pack of dried antelope meat that bumped Blood Bear's elbow during the release. As Two Smokes screamed in terror, the dart hissed harmlessly over him to skewer the lodge behind.

"*Anit'ah!*" Two Smokes shrieked, crabbing away from Blood Bear as he settled a second dart in the hooked end of his atlatl.

Dung and flies! The whole band would be onto him now. For a split second, Blood Bear hesitated, shrugging the meat pack out of the way. Should he waste another dart on the berdache? Or would he need every last one to escape?

An old man, white-haired, with frightened eyes, rounded a lodge, pulling up short, mouth dropping open to scream.

Blood Bear aimed true, his dart catching the man full in the chest. Two Elks shuddered under the impact, a gagging sound in his throat. Old legs turned rubbery as he sank to his knees and tumbled sideways.

Looking back, he saw Two Smokes had disappeared. Shouts came boiling from the people now. Heart racing, Blood Bear leapt over a smoking fire pit. Hindered by the flopping weight, he discarded the heavy meat pack to bounce in the dust behind him. With the Wolf Bundle clamped to his chest, he dashed with all his might, bowling over a young man who stepped out in front of him.

A woman screamed. People called to each other in confusion as Blood Bear raced through camp. A dog appeared from somewhere to yip and snap at his heels. Blood Bear whirled only long enough to drive a dart into the beast's chest and rip it out. Then he was sprinting for the bluffs again.

Panting and gasping, he forced his driven body up the incline to the bluff above. He slowed, catching his second wind. Looking back, he saw no pursuers boiled after him. From his vantage he could see the People milling around the body of the old man, pointing at his skylined figure.

Grinning to himself, he hugged the Wolf Bundle close and began trotting across the broad terrace. Far to the northwest, the cool slopes of the Buffalo Mountains rose like a beacon.

The Wolf Bundle! Gone! The place of honor at the head of Two Smokes' smoldering bedding held the barest imprint of the parfleche in the hard dirt. The emptiness swelled into a gaping hole in Little Dancer's heart and soul. Blackness welled around the edges of his conscience. First Heavy Beaver's desecration—now this.

Little Dancer stared in through the door flap, head shaking slowly in his disbelief. The lodge, *his* lodge, the place where he'd always been safe from storm and cold and danger, lay before him, gutted, violated, and raped by the Anit'ah. Bedding smoked where coals burned through the hides.

"No. This isn't . . . can't be. . . ."

"Blood Bear," Two Smokes muttered in Anit'ah, where he ducked out of Three Toes' lodge, a long dart in his hand.

Little Dancer lowered himself to the ground, one hand grasping a lodgepole. All his strength gone, he simply stared at the wreckage of his lodge. He barely realized when Two Smokes settled next to him, the dart spinning in his fingers.

"After all these years, I wonder how he found me here. Even the People know he's been roaming the country. The Red Hand exiled him after I left with Clear Water and the Wolf Bundle."

"It's because of Heavy Beaver. He threw the Wolf Bundle into the dark that night. I felt it. The Power changed. The world's falling apart. Everything shifted. Maybe the Wolf Bundle wanted to go back where people would care for it."

"I cared for it. I loved it, kept it—"

"Heavy Beaver abused it. It couldn't trust you." As soon as he said it, he regretted the words. He looked up hesitantly to see tears creeping down Two Smokes' face. In sympathy, he reached a thin arm around the berdache's waist and hugged him tight. "It's not your fault, Two Smokes. It's not."

So faint he could barely hear, Two Smokes whispered, "Yes, it is. All my fault. From the very beginning."

The whisper of moccasins on dirt behind him made Little Dancer turn.

His mother stood there, hair out of place and blowing in straggles in the afternoon breeze. Her hollow eyes barely registered the mess. Heart pounding, he stared up at her. The expression on her face belonged to a stranger. She looked through him, hands clenching and releasing spasmodically. The corners of her lips quivered, as if she might speak. Then she turned, ducking listlessly into the lodge. Soundlessly she stamped out the smoldering coals, tears like silver in her eyes.

"Mother?" he whispered, fearing the wild look, afraid to call after her. He looked out past the milling People who stood over Two Elks' body.

Two sticks remained.

* * *

What a stroke of luck! The People milled in confusion and disbelief as they hovered around Two Elks' body. Heavy Beaver stepped out of his lodge, dressed in his finest.

"My people! I've heard from the Spirits. Even as we speak, the world is turning, waiting. What has been wrought this day? Dancing Doe has seen the error of her ways. The Anit'ah have reclaimed their evil that lay like a festering sore to ooze its pus into our society!"

He grinned at the horrified look on Two Smokes' face where he stared up. *Your day is coming, enemy freak! After Sage Root, I'll drive your polluting presence from the People.*

"This is our last warning!" Heavy Beaver thundered. "Two Elks, so wise, so warm, has paid with his life! The final choice is upon us. We must purify ourselves of the ancient evils! We must make a new way for ourselves, or the Spirit World will turn its back on us for good. The evil ones know themselves. Within days, the Power I call on will banish them from our midst!"

"Hear our Spirit Dreamer!" Throws Rocks shouted, lifting his fist to wave it while he danced. "Heavy Beaver brings us a new way! With his Power, the buffalo will return!"

Fire At Night whooped and jumped, prancing on light feet as he yipped his zeal.

"The rest of you," Heavy Beaver ordered, seeing Chokecherry start to open her mouth. "Two Elks is dead! Do none of you mourn the loss of this great man? Do you all just stand here? Go! Go out and find sage to clean his body! Bring your best to honor him."

"And the Anit'ah?" Sleeping Fir asked, staring around nervously. "Are there more?"

"Only one came to reclaim the cursed object." Heavy Beaver narrowed an eye at Two Smokes and the soiled child who clung to his side. Hatred filled the boy's eyes. Well, that could be beaten out of him. He was still young enough to train in the proper ways.

"What of Dancing Doe?" Chokecherry called as the people began to split up, walking somberly to their lodges, voices a soft mumble.

Heavy Beaver closed his eyes, adopting a pained expression. "I would have you, Chokecherry—and Sage Root—see to her. Take her up on the ridge behind the village. Surely with the help of the berdache and the boy, the two of you can get her up there.''

"And you'll Sing for her?"

"I think, sometimes, you don't believe I have Power. Why do you want me to Sing for her?"

Chokecherry didn't hesitate. "I'm thinking of her family. Most are with White Foot's band. They'd want someone to Sing for her."

He nodded. "I'll Sing." *And you'll see my Power within days, old woman!* "And maybe it will ease the pollution she brought to the People."

Chokecherry's eyes hardened. "You know, boy, I can't help but wonder where the real pollution lies."

He stiffened, staring angrily into the old woman's eyes. "Do you want me to Sing for her, or not? Your words make it very difficult."

Chokecherry bit off her retort and walked over to Sage Root's lodge, muttering under her breath. Heavy Beaver stood, arms crossed, seeing the startled look on Sage Root's face. Frantic eyes turned in his direction, reflecting a loathing for what he'd asked her to do. Chokecherry's arms waved in appeal and Sage Root finally nodded, getting to her feet.

Heavy Beaver watched as they proceeded behind the birthing lodge. Then, looking surreptitiously about, he slipped silently into Sage Root's lodge. From his pouch, he took dried leaves, crumbling them between his fingers and dropping them into the stew in her horn bowl.

Casting a quick glance about, Heavy Beaver slipped out and returned to his lodge. The datura would do what threats couldn't. Power worked many ways—especially in the victim's mind.

Chokecherry lowered herself next to Makes Fun where she painted white clay on a staked antelope hide. Above, on the edge of the terrace, Heavy Beaver chanted, shaking a rattle, as he Danced about Dancing Doe's body. At least the story would get back to Dancing Doe's relations that someone had cared. Chokecherry rubbed at the bloodstains where Dancing Doe's body had leaked on the hem of her dress.

"Nice painting. That's for Two Elks?"

Makes Fun nodded, stirring the pigment in the horn bowl. "His children all moved away with Two Stones' band. Who else would do it? A man as good and wise as he should rise to the Starweb looking his best. We can't have him meet the Wise One Above looking like a starving coyote."

"No. I have a beaded necklace. I'll get it for him."

"How's Sage Root?"

"Not well."

Makes Fun sighed and rubbed a forearm across her sweaty forehead. "You think it's serious?"

"Of course it's serious. Heavy Beaver's killing her. He's doing it by preying on her one weakness. She doesn't know anything about Power. She doesn't know if he's right or wrong. Once he's got her questioning herself, he's won half the battle.

"Worse, he's hung raven feathers off the tips of her lodge-poles. Sage Root saw them, and threw up. She tore them down, of course, but you should have seen her shaking. Her lodge was the only one messed up by the Anit'ah. It's all piling up in her mind."

Makes Fun puffed a heavy exhalation and rocked back on her haunches. "He's been Singing in there all day. My nerves are stretched to the point where I dragged my hides out here so I couldn't hear. What a day. Dancing Doe kills herself. An Anit'ah kills Two Elks and steals the berdache's sacred bundle. And through it all, Heavy Beaver keeps killing Sage Root." Empty-eyed, she stared at the far buttes, where they shimmered in the sun's mirage. "And I thought my sister was trouble."

"Everyone's nervous. That doesn't help, either." Choke-cherry settled herself, drawing her ancient knees up to her chest. "We've got to do something. If we don't, Heavy Beaver is going to destroy us."

"Us? I thought he was after Sage Root. She turned him down you know. Refused to bed him. He's—"

"Bah! That's only the excuse. Like sneaking into a buffalo herd under a hide, it's misdirection. True, he's been grousing about that for years. You can see it festering in his eyes every time he looks at her. You know, I even caught him one time.

He'd sneaked out after Hungry Bull and her, watching while they coupled outside of camp.''

"No!" Makes Fun clapped a hand to her mouth to hide astonishment. "That's . . . that's . . .''

"Rude? An understatement. But then, that's the sort of man he is. He killed Dancing Doe as surely as if he'd thrown the dart himself. And destroying Sage Root is another step. You want to live in a band he controls? Hmm? What about your children? How about your son, Mouse Runner? You want him growing up hearing Heavy Beaver's talk about how women are polluting the earth? You want your daughter growing up to marry a man who'd been raised to think that?''

Makes Fun braced hands on her knees, staring off across the valley of the Moon River. After a long moment, she asked, "What can we do to stop it? Black Crow's out hunting with Hungry Bull and Three Toes. I'm not sure what I can do.''

"Back me up.''

Makes Fun cocked her head, eyes worried. "Back *you* up? And if he Curses you, Chokecherry? You're my aunt. I don't—''

"Blood and dung! Listen to you. You're half knuckled under already! Think, girl! Heavy Beaver's just a thieving raven. He's found a bunch of mice head-sick from alkali water. Now he's hopping around, cawing and squawking to keep them confused. He's got his first mouse killed and eaten. The second is frightened and running in circles. Soon as Sage Root keels over, he'll get another one. And when it's all finished, the ways of the People will be gone forever. That's right. He's trying to remake the People to fit *his* image of what they ought to be. And me, I'm not going to play mouse for him! I'm going to remind him that he's nothing more than a scavenging raven.''

"Careful, Aunt." Makes Fun looked around. "If he hears you—''

"Bah! Let him! He's been a festering pain for too long. Now, you going to back me up, or not?''

"But Black Crow—''

Chokecherry grabbed her by the chin. "You listen to me.

If you back down, you'll find yourself with less standing than a dog. You want that? To be like a beast?''

"Black Crow wouldn't—"

"No, but Heavy Beaver would. He's got problems. His mother, for one. That boy's hated strong women all his life. Look at who he married! But I've been around long enough, buried enough husbands to tell you that after he's had a year or two to work on Black Crow, you'll be right down with the dogs as a pack animal and breeding bitch.''

Blood burning, Chokecherry hoisted herself to her feet, wincing as her knees cracked. "You think about that, sister's daughter. You think hard, because that's what Heavy Beaver's working for. Sage Root stood against him. If he breaks her . . . or kills her, there will be no stopping him. The People, for all that we've come unraveled in the last tens of seasons, will be no more.''

She stalked off, aware of Makes Fun's eyes burning into her back.

Tanager sat wrapped in a robe next to Elk Charm. The peaks rose tall, ghostly in the moonlight. Behind them, the camp of the Red Hand seemed quiet, peaceful. A dog barked until someone threw something at it. After a yip, nothing but the soft murmur of voices bothered the night.

"I hate being in trouble," Tanager complained.

"Well, if you'd stay home and help your mother with the chores, and maybe stop beating up the boys, maybe you wouldn't be in trouble all the time.''

Tanager lifted a shoulder, ears tuned to the sounds of the night. "I'll bet the elk calves are walking around. We could sneak off tomorrow morning and—"

"See!'' Elk Charm giggled. "How are you ever going to find a husband if you never stay in camp?''

Tanager looked across at her friend. "Why would I want a husband?''

"Husbands are a great help. You can't get pregnant without one. They lift heavy things like logs to make animal traps.''

"I don't need a trap. I sneaked up to within a foot of a deer once. I could have driven a dart right into her. And besides, babies are trouble. There's lots of things you can't do when you have a baby. You have to find someone to look after them when you go hunt. And then you have to give part of the kill to whoever looks after the baby.''

''Someday you'll be sneaking around out there and get caught by a Short Buffalo warrior and he'll eat you.''

''Be serious! If I can sneak up on a deer, where's the stupid Short Buffalo man who can catch me? You've heard the stories about how they stumble around in the trees. They don't know the trails. No one knows the trails like me.''

''Except Ramshorn and Never Sweat and Tall Fir and—''

''But I know most of them. And by the time I'm a full woman, I'll know them all. You watch.''

Elk Charm sat in silence for a moment, face puckered in a frown. ''Why are you like that? Why are you always trying to be different from everyone else?''

Tanager shrugged, genuinely baffled herself. ''I don't know. It's like something in the trees whispers to me. Maybe it's like when you go with your family to collect berries and you want to go home, to be back in your lodge where you know where you are. You know that feeling? It's just that I feel the same way about being out in timber and climbing the rocks.''

''You ought to be a boy.''

''Maybe, but I don't know any boys that run as fast as I do. And I've had Snaps Horn and Warm Wind try and follow me. They slip off the logs and break branches and trip a lot. Not only that, I can throw rocks straighter.''

''You can't outwrestle them.''

Tanager grinned. ''No, but if I trip them first, they can't catch me!''

Sage Root drank the last of the cold stew. She'd sent Little Dancer and Two Smokes up to eat with Chokecherry. She had no desire to cook anymore. She didn't want Two Smokes bustling around doing things that intruded on her thoughts. She didn't even care about the lumps of hard grease that floated in the tepid water.

Something black and ominous rose from Heavy Beaver's lodge. Sage Root gasped, clapping a hand to her mouth. She shook her head, blinking, feeling the icy chill in her soul. Peering fearfully up at the stars, she found no sign of the black thing. Raven's spirit? Had Heavy Beaver promised her to Raven Above in return for spiritual help?

She clamped her eyes shut, experiencing the reeling sensation of lost balance. She was passing through life as if it were a dream. Images shimmered and went glassy until she couldn't trust her eyesight. Sounds seemed to become disjointed. Voices whispered out of the air. Nothing seemed real except the cold in her soul, and fear.

"I'm not me anymore." And the chill ate at her, increasing with each beat of her heart. How could she deny his power when so many strange things happened? As the sun set, she'd seen the trunks of the trees waver and dance to the thump of Heavy Beaver's drum.

She shivered uncontrollably, stomach spasming. Not that, please, not again. Every time she'd eaten or drunk, her nervous stomach pumped it back up.

Sage Root sat in the rear of the lodge, fingers idly tracing the ruins of the bedroll where Hungry Bull had so tenderly held her. Here, in the confines of this very lodge, she'd borne her sons. Here, she'd nursed them all, hugged and loved them. Two of them had died in her lodge, their bodies cleaned and prepared to be taken and placed on a high ridge, where their souls could climb to the Starweb.

Here she'd laughed at Hungry Bull's stories, scolded him when he needed, and smiled her love into his warm brown eyes.

The lodge looked dingy and ragged, the skirts of the heavy hide cover tattered, rot-brittle around the edges. As the cover had disintegrated, so had the poles been worn away as they moved from camp to camp. What had once been a grand lodge, requiring ten dogs to transport, now could be carried by five. Like the rest of her life, even this, her home, hung frayed and stained.

A humming filled her ears with the sound of a million bumblebees. Groaning, she pounded at the side of her head. As quickly, the noise stopped, leaving a slight ring from the battering she'd given herself.

Heedless, she sat in the ashes of her life, fingers absently tracing the holes burned through her belongings.

She couldn't bear to look at the dirt out front. Horrified, she'd watched as Heavy Beaver had walked out and drawn a series of lines into the earth.

"I could save you." He'd looked at her through heavy half-lidded eyes and cocked his head. "You need only admit your guilt. Bind yourself to me for purification."

The cry of horror had strangled in her throat as she shook her head frantically.

He'd smiled, chanted some more, and walked away into the twilight.

Fear had pumped like sparks through her veins as she scrambled madly to wipe away the patterns of lines, scratching at the dirt until her fingernails bled. Then she'd huddled into a ball and sobbed until Little Dancer came to hold her. Two Smokes had picked her up and carried her inside. Now the two of them slept like a guard before the door.

Hungry Bull is far away. I'll be dead before he comes back. What then?

"Stop it," she whispered to herself. "Got to believe it's a lie. Heavy Beaver can't Dance fire. He can't Sing the stars. He's trying to scare me. That's all. Just trying to scare me."

And how do you know? the voice inside demanded. *How come your stomach doesn't work? Why do you ache all over? How come you hear things? See things that aren't there? Why do your muscles shake all the time? Why do you always feel so cold—even in the sun? You're dying. You can't fight his Power.*

The chill in her soul seemed to expand. Despite herself, the old stories recited in bits and fragments in the back of her mind. Tales from the Winter Counts, they told of witches who could steal a man's soul. They told of the Hero Twins who brought human beings up from underground and into this world. And when it was all done, one of the brothers hit the other on the head, his blood dripping to become red jasper. The other brother had risen to the sky, becoming one with Starweb since his people were safe from evil.

"Evil. And has that returned?" Numbly, she stared at the moonlight outside. Flickers of moonbeams bent and shimmered to break into a thousand spinning stars. Undone, Sage Root cowered and covered her head. She lay that way until her body began to float away from the earth, turning slowly in the air.

She gasped and jerked at the familiar shadows of her lodge. Blinking to clear her sight, she dug frantic fingers into the singed robes to reassure herself of the firm ground.

Somewhere the dogs where yipping and growling. Outside, Two Smokes and Little Dancer huddled together in sleep, their shadows speckled where the moonlight shot patterns through the cottonwood leaves overhead.

Her mother had told of ghosts that walked the winter nights, howling like the wind. Always restless, the ghosts would steal a little girl away if she wasn't good and obedient. So the story went. Later, she'd come to wonder. Now, when she was faced with soul death, perhaps Heavy Beaver had found a way to call a ghost to come steal her soul? And why not?

Straining her ears, she could hear him, chanting softly from the insides of his lodge, the faint thump of a drum like the beat of her heart. The hair on the back of her neck rose in a prickly sensation.

"I had to do it. I *had* to save the antelope—make it right for the People." She dropped her head into her hands. "I had to . . . that's all. I just couldn't do anything else." *And now I'll die for it.*

The faint thump of the drum echoed in her head. She shifted, reaching for the water skin and froze. Only one stick remained standing.

White Calf woke with a start. She blinked up at the moonlight. A call had stirred her soul, left it trembling and afraid. About her the night shifted, the feeling of unease slipping through the moonlight like a capricious spirit on dancing antelope feet.

She sat up, her old heart pumping the anxiety. Around the edges of her consciousness, the dream she'd had frayed and blew away like downy seeds from a thistle. What had it been about? Only the memory of haunted eyes and desperation remained.

She swallowed and stared up at the stars where they twin-kled through the masking moonlight.

Around her, Three Toes, Hungry Bull, and Black Crow slept soundly. The night air brought the subtle perfume of sagebrush and the rich mold of earth to her nose. Crickets chirred in the silence.

The fear descended.

White Calf shook her worn hide robe off.

"Come on. Get up."

Hungry Bull sat up, instinctively reaching for his darts. Three Toes blinked owlishly. Black Crow squinted in the moonlight, looking around in confusion as he rolled out of his bedding.

"What?" Three Toes asked. "It's the middle of the night."

White Calf was already rolling her hide. "I know. I only hope we're not too late."

"Too late for what?" Hungry Bull demanded.

"I don't know." White Calf laced her rolled hide to her pack, squatting to get the tumpline over her forehead.

"Hey! I mean . . ." But the old woman had already wad-dled off down the path that led to Moon River.

Gaping, Black Crow stared across at his friends, throat bobbing as he rubbed his round belly. "What now?"

"Got me," Three Toes mumbled, yawning, crawling from the shelter of his hides and starting to roll them up. "But I think we'd better find out."

You're the one who has to lead now, Chokecherry's words echoed in her head.

"I can't. I'm not strong enough." Heart like a lump of punky wood, she stared at the single stick standing before Heavy Beaver's lodge. By noon, that would be gone.

And if you're not? What then, Sage Root? If you let him kill you, what happens to your son . . . to Hungry Bull?

A whisper seemed to rise from above, Dancing Doe's voice calling. She strained to hear the words, wincing at the pain in her stomach.

"I didn't ask for this. I just wanted to raise my child, keep my husband happy. I didn't ask for any of this. All I wanted was to see my people fed. Now I've become some sort of monster. Dancing Doe killed herself because I tried to help. If I hadn't been there . . .'' She winced, closing her eyes to the pain as gray dawn shaded the outlines of the lodges.

She stood, stepping out to look around—and froze. The bundle hung from one of the soot-stained lodgepoles. Black raven feathers stuck out from a tightly packed leather pouch.

A sob choking in her throat, she pulled the thing loose. Unable to control her shaking fingers, she ripped the hide open and whimpered as a roll of maggots spilled out over her fingers.

Something dark fell and rolled to one side.

She strangled her cries, frantically wiping the maggots from her hands, shivering uncontrollably as she fought the urge to scream. Backing away, her stomach pumped again, having nothing left but sour bile. The black pad, still wiggling with white maggots, caught her eye. She recognized shredded sagebrush bark. A menstrual pad. Hers? Of course. It had to be. Heavy Beaver wouldn't have used it otherwise.

"A piece . . . of my soul," she choked. "He's got a piece of my soul." *He's won! I'm dying. I can feel it.*

She swallowed hard, lungs pulling at a knot of fear locking her windpipe. *What can I do? Where can I go? How can I save myself?*

Two dark shadows passed overhead, wings rasping in the air. *Ravens!*

Tears streaked her face. *He'll give my soul to the ravens. And then what? I'll never get to the Starweb. I'll never . . .* Dancing Doe's eyes stared up from the depths of her tortured memories. Dancing Doe had risen to the Starweb.

Sage Root's teeth chattered as a soul chill wrapped around her. How long did she have? How long until Heavy Beaver twisted her soul from her body?

Dawn. Her last sunrise. Numbly, she reached inside the lodge, finding her butchering kit—the one she'd used on the antelope. How fitting.

She turned, forcing her back straight, catching a glimpse of Sleeping Fir as she started out of her lodge, met her eyes, and ducked hurriedly back inside.

The chill in her soul deepened. Even her friends feared her now. Who would want to be seen talking to a Cursed woman?

One way or another, she was dead. She could let Heavy Beaver steal her soul through his Spirit Power, or free it herself.

With careful steps she avoided Little Dancer where he slept in Two Smokes' arms. Muffled whimpers escaped his lips. Perhaps he'd been too close to her and caught the edges of Heavy Beaver's Curse? Another mistake on her part.

She walked down to the river, following along the bank. Barely aware, she looked up at the graying skyline, listening to the trilling *tee-yee* melodies of the red-winged blackbirds as they sang in the thick brush back from the river. Below her, a great blue heron splashed and rose to wing, wary of her presence. Even the birds avoided her.

A suggestion of movement caught her attention. A huge black wolf stood on a rise, watching with knowing yellow eyes. Thick muscles rippled along the animal's lean body. The increasing light accented the sheen of its sleek coat. Another of Heavy Beaver's creatures? She tore her frightened gaze away.

A terrible loneliness crushed her. "Hungry Bull? Where are you? Come back to me. Don't let me face this alone."

"Why did you let Blood Bear steal me?"

The Wolf Dreamer's voice drifted from the illusion that surrounded the Wolf Bundle like a cloud. "He asked and gave of himself. Let us see what he does with Power now that he's wished it."

The Wolf Bundle tested the fringes of Blood Bear's mind. "I see no change. He's as much a fool as ever. He mocks what sober men consider with care."

"He has asked, and I have the piece he gave of himself. Am I one to deny a seeker?"

"You're not the one riding in his arms. Suppose I end up in the fire?"

"Not even Blood Bear is that stupid."

"But Bundles—and the Power in them—can be killed."

"Like Dreams . . . and Dreamers."

"The Watcher keeps his eye on the boy."

"And if this goes beyond the Watcher's ability?"

Chapter 10 🐂

A fight broke out between two of the camp dogs. Little Dancer woke. He could feel fear hovering around him. Like the stench of carrion, wrongness and evil rode on the morning air. He dug fists into his rheumy eyes to get them open. Beside him, Two Smokes groaned and yawned. Golden bars of yellow morning sunlight slanted under the rustling cottonwood leaves. Things looked bluish, tinged by the smoke from morning fires. Around them the camp stirred to life.

Little Dancer caught sight of Heavy Beaver's lodge, the ominous stick standing tall in the yellow light. Memories flashed back of the horrible yesterday, a collage of images of Dancing Doe's horrified expression of death, the panic in his mother's eyes as she saw the single stick, Blood Bear's raid, and the stunning loss of the Wolf Bundle. He remembered Two Elks' body where it lay on its side, the old man tucked in a fetal position around the violent dart that had drunk so deeply of his life.

Little Dancer rose frantically, stumbling to look about the wreckage inside the lodge. Empty. A premonition of ill spread within. He felt another's pangs of wretched anxiety filling him, familiar, yet alienated: alone.

"Mother?" He trotted around behind the lodge, peering into the brush to see if she had simply gone to relieve herself. No trace. *"Mother?"*

"Hush!" Sleeping Fir called from inside her lodge. "People are sleeping here."

"MOTHER!" His breath went short, a feeling squeezing his chest like a giant hand.

"Here," Two Smokes called. "Come take my hand and we'll go find her. No sense in alarming the whole camp."

The berdache smiled uneasily, eyes searching the quiet lodges.

Not quite placated, Little Dancer reached up and placed his hand in his friend's. "We'll find her?"

"We'll find her."

Together they searched, circling the perimeter of the camp, finding nothing. The trails had been used until the dust had been beaten into a fine powder. The only tracks consisted of blurred images.

A sudden flood of desperation caught Little Dancer completely unaware. The world seemed to slip sideways. Suddenly dizzy, he leaned forward, clutching his stomach. An urge to vomit convulsed his gut while his legs turned rubbery beneath him.

"Little Dancer? What's wrong? What's . . ."

An utterly hopeless feeling possessed him for a moment before final desperation took over. He could feel her, feel the movements of her hands as she took the cool stone and . . .

"No!" he choked before his stomach emptied into the trail. "No." He coughed at the stinging bile that had gone up the back of his nose and threatened his windpipe. *"No!"*

As quickly, the feeling of dislocation passed. Completely drained, he came to, staring at the vomit-splattered earth before him. An abyss, endless as the wind, opened inside him. Loss whirled about his mind. Disoriented, he struggled to find his breath, the feeling that of having been kicked in the chest.

". . . and take a deep breath. Just breathe easily. Don't be afraid. It's just the fear, the worry that's gotten to you." Two Smokes comforted from where he knelt beside him. Strong warm hands supported his wrenched body as he coughed again and raised his head. The world looked washed out, as if seen through a film of water. The colors didn't appear as bright. The air felt sluggish and half-alive. Even Father Sun's light had lost its fire, becoming pallid and weak.

"Mother! Come back. Come back to me!"

"Now, little one, we don't—"

"She's dead!" He fought to get his feet under him, Two Smokes supporting him as his balance wavered. The berdache stared down, a deep worry eating at him.

"She's probably just gone to—"

"No!" the boy bawled, eyes searching the trail frantically. "I *felt* her die! I *felt* her."

"Please, little one, don't go imagining all the—"

"Stop it! Stop it! She's dead! I know!"

"You're being crazy." The berdache stopped short, frozen by the look Little Dancer gave him.

Choking on tears, Little Dancer cried, "You know, don't you? I've seen it in your eyes. You know I feel things. I hear things most people don't. I heard the antelope at the kill site. I called them. *I* did that. In a Dream, Two Smokes. I called them in a Power Dream." Tears burned hot on his face, dribbling from his quivering chin. "And Heavy Beaver killed my mother. He drove the Wolf Bundle away. He killed Dancing Doe's baby . . . and then he killed her. He's evil. He's bad and wicked."

"Shhh!" Two Smokes went pale, dropping on his knee to stare into Little Dancer's eyes. "*Quiet*, little one. You're already in trouble. Heavy Beaver's a powerful man. He can do anything he wants and no one will say anything. You *must* hold your tongue. Will you? For me? You know he'll hurt me. He's just waiting for his time."

Little Dancer stared uncertainly at him while his mind reeled, feeling ill to the depths of his tormented soul. "I hate him. I'm going to kill him. Hear me, Heavy Beaver? *I'm going to kill you!*"

"Hush!" Two Smokes clamped a hand over his mouth, peering fearfully back the way they'd come. "Never say that. *Never.* Your life is a dart's cast away from dead as it is." Two Smokes swallowed hard, a trembling in his hands. "Promise me you won't say that again. *Promise me!* And then we'll go find your mother and I'll show you how silly your idea is that she's dead."

Little Dancer stared at him, anger and grief churning. Deliberately, he raised his arm, pointing. "She's over there."

"Then let's go see. And maybe on the way I can talk some sense into your little head." Two Smokes offered his hand.

Beyond caring, Little Dancer refused it and walked past with a miserable purpose. Tears continued to leak down his face. Periodically he stopped to drag a filthy sleeve across his eyes to clear his blurry vision.

Images of her formed in his mind. She smiled at him, speaking gently. In the firelight of a warm lodge, her face reflected love and concern. How many times had her gentle hands soothed him, healed his hurts? How many times had her expression lit as she told him a story, or watched as he ate the broth she gave him? When winter nights came again, whose warm hands would tuck the hides around his chin? Who would listen when he had a problem? A light had flickered out in his soul. Only blackness remained.

The old cottonwood had blown down years before. Seasons of rain and wind had scoured the bark from the underlying wood. Since then the bright plain's sun had bleached the smooth wood silver white. Where the heavy trunk forked into two thick branches, Sage Root had stopped. She lay propped there, cradled by the bones of the tree. Her head had fallen back, exposing her face to the morning sun. She looked tired and vulnerable. Beside her, her worn butchering bag lay open. On the ground, a black obsidian core lay canted to one side. Sunlight sparkled from the vitreous ripples where flakes had been driven off. A small quartzite hammerstone rested beside the core.

Flies already rose in a gossamer buzzing column over the rich wealth of her blood where it pooled in the skirts of her dress.

A hard hand clapped Little Dancer on the shoulder, trying to pull him back. "Go back to camp," Two Smokes ordered. "Now! You don't—"

"She cut her wrists, Two Smokes. I felt it. That's when I got sick. She cut her wrists and left me here all alone." The tears ran hot from his eyes again. "Why did she die? Why did she leave me here? I need her, Two Smokes. I need her to hold me."

"Let's go back now."

"It didn't hurt," Little Dancer mumbled, weeping. "Obsidian is so sharp. She just knocked off a flake and cut her wrists open. And she died. Two Smokes, why is the world so mean to us?"

The hand on his shoulder began to pull him inexorably back.

They'd stopped moving, Two Smokes holding him, crushing him tightly in a shared embrace. Together they cried, each adrift with nowhere to go. But nothing filled the aching void inside him.

He'd gone empty. So empty.

Heavy Beaver blinked awake. Through the smoke hole, he could see a blue patch of morning sky. He hadn't slept well. Like a wraith from the fog, his mother's ghost had lurked in the shadows of his dreams. Echoes of her voice tried to sort themselves out in his mind.

Why couldn't all women be as perfect as his mother had been? The endless longing filled him. He'd loved her like he'd never love another woman. All he'd ever had to do was cry out and she came running. When the other boys teased him, she'd driven them off with a stick. When he hurt himself, she'd come and cooed and soothed him. When his father had objected to her constant attention and tried to force him to go and play, she'd chased him off with vile threats. Against the troubles of the world, she'd stood unflinching. Of all the People, only she had understood his fears and needs. She had recognized his special talents and virtues even before he had. Once she'd pointed out his greatness, not even he could ignore it.

"You've been chosen, Heavy Beaver. That's why you're different. The spirits have singled you out for special things. That's why you don't fit. That's why the other boys tease you and play tricks. They're jealous. They can see how special you are—and they don't like it. That's the way of great men . . . always shunned by their inferiors. You'll see. You'll rise above them all one day."

If all women had those same intelligent and sensitive abilities to see clearly, the world would be a better place. He wouldn't have to fight so hard to put the People on the right path.

Even now, years after her death, he missed her with an open longing in his soul. He'd barely noticed the day she'd begun complaining of the shortness of breath. He'd been preoccupied with other things. Of course she'd always been there, strong, knowing what to do. The thought that she wouldn't be with him forever seemed impossible. The decision to marry Red Chert had been her idea. She'd seen to the arrangements with the girl's family—and the choice had been right.

"Red Chert's the girl for you, obedient. She won't try to suck you dry like most women. She's worthy of you, recognizes your talents without being jealous. You see, that's why Dancing Doe and Sage Root and the others don't bed you. They're worried, that's what. Around you, they couldn't control everything the way they do now. Have you seen them? Strutting around, shaking their hips and breasts to get a reaction. No, you couldn't live with a woman like that. She'd constantly be trying to hold you back. She'd have to live in your shadow forever, so she'd make you miserable because that's all that would be left for her. That and plots. You know how women are with plots. Always trying to cause trouble. Take that Chokecherry. Look at the way she tries to humiliate me in front of others. Always criticizing. You don't want a spiteful woman like that. You want one who sees you for who you are—like Red Chert."

Indeed, she'd been right. Red Chert had never challenged him. Instead, she'd seen his ability from the first. People had laughed, amused that he'd marry a woman no one else wanted, but that was their mistake. They didn't see as clearly as he. They didn't understand the real situation.

He smiled as he looked over to where Red Chert slept. If only he had his mother now. If only she could see his success.

The shortness of breath hadn't gone away. Day by day, she'd wasted. As time passed, and the inevitable loomed, he'd gone slightly crazy with worry and grief. Of course, that, too, couldn't be helped. All Spirit Dreamers got a little crazy at times. He hadn't known then that Dreams were making him so nervous. In her final days, his mother had told him.

"It's the Power, boy. That's why you've been so scared. It's Power coming to live inside you. That's why you've been mean to everyone. Power does that. Takes some getting used to. You'll be afraid in the future, but it's the Power. Trust it and use your head. That's why Power chose you. You're smarter than the rest. Think, boy. Use the Power.''

Like the patterns hot coals left in leather, the morning when he'd been awakened by Red Chert's soft intake of breath burned forever in his memory. The woman who'd borne him, cared for him, and seen his greatness lay dead, expression slack, eyes dull in the morning light.

His mother's death had almost killed him. Only the knowledge that he had Power had kept him sane through those first hard days. But no one recognized his Power. No one except his mother and Red Chert had seen and understood his abilities.

When he started to preach the pollution of the People, men and women scoffed. First came Horn Core's death, then the deepening drought, and they listened more carefully. The young men had begun to nod when he told them how women angered the spirits. One by one, they came to see how right he was. Each time he predicted trouble, it came true. Now everything he claimed had come to pass. Buffalo Above had taken his children away. The Rain Man no longer danced afternoon showers from the clouds. The Anit'ah couldn't be kept back. The People were suffocating in their own pollution.

Today the discipline his mother had instilled in him would bear fruit. He'd seen the look in Sage Root's eyes last night. Eaten by doubt, she'd been on the verge of collapse. Such a piece of luck that Dancing Doe had run onto Long Runner's dart. Until then, Sage Root might have withstood his machinations despite the datura. Peering through the slits in his lodge, he'd watched her go ashen and tear the raven feathers down. To have stolen the menstrual pad from the women's bleeding lodge had been fortuitous. Idly he wondered whose it had been. A chance gust of wind had carried it out where he could find it. Of course, he'd had to pick it up with sticks to keep from fouling himself. The whole idea of a woman bleeding once a month disgusted him. In all his memory, he couldn't remember his mother bleeding like that—but then, she'd been special.

He stretched and crawled across to peer through the slit

where he'd cut Red Chert's fine stitching of the lodge cover. The bundle no longer hung from the lodgepole. She'd found it.

Red Chert stirred where she lay on her robes and rolled over again, one arm flopping out. For a long moment, he gazed at her. How right his mother had been to choose her for him.

In his mind, he began composing the speech he'd give over Sage Root's body. He'd tell them how Antelope Above Danced across the sky with joy that the People had killed the defiler. People listened when he made up stories about his Dreams. He spent most of his time thinking them up. Then, when the days grew tedious, he'd walk up on the ridge tops and sit, and watch the sky, and think up new stories to tell them. Bit by bit, he'd learned the role. He knew now how to get that faraway look in his eyes, how to modulate his voice. They'd listen, eyes downcast, and accept.

Now only the old ones scoffed. The worse the drought got, the more skittish the animals, the better the People listened. Already the younger hunters had started to berate their wives and exclude them from the hunting councils. That had put most of the women in their places.

Some, like Hungry Bull, continued to ignore him—but Hungry Bull would learn to his dismay. A slight shiver ran down Heavy Beaver's back. How fortunate that that fiery young man had decided to go on a long hunt. One less barrier to overcome—not to mention the fear of a dart in the back. No telling how Hungry Bull might have reacted to his wife being Cursed. Now he'd return to an empty lodge. Everything would be finished.

And if Sage Root dug up some final resistance? Heavy Beaver chuckled to himself. He had the datura witching plant he'd obtained from the Trader Three Rattles. "A beautiful thing," he'd been told. "Grows in the far southern deserts west of the high mountains. The leaves are dark green, and in summer it has a large white flower that opens to the day. Dreamers down there use only small portions. Too much brings a chill to the soul—makes a person throw up and see and hear things." Heavy Beaver had used most of it in Sage

Root's stew. Distracted as she was, she'd eaten the whole thing. What he had left would finish her.

A slight pang stung his heart. Such a shame to waste so desirable a woman this way.

She stood in the way, however, and he *would* remake the People the way his mother would have wanted. In her image of purity and virtue, he'd chip away at them as a craftsman did a fine point. Then, when he'd purified them of pollution, they'd take what the Anit'ah kept them from. In his shadow, they'd claim the rich hunting grounds in the high meadows of the Buffalo Mountains.

Like a fire, his new way would sweep them up and burn a new path across the plains.

Other women, just as desirable—only obedient—would be his. Among all the People, he would choose.

He crawled over to his shirt, shrugging it on. Then he pulled on the fine calfskin breeches made by Sleeping Fir.

"Mother?" The cry lingered in the air outside.

Who? Ah yes, that little undisciplined pup of Sage Root's. He called out again. Someone yelled at him. Heavy Beaver's heart leapt as the boy's cries became more frantic.

By the time he ducked out of the lodge, the little brat had been silenced. Heavy Beaver caught a sight of the wretched Anit'ah leading the lad down one of the trails. A welling of wrath tightened around his heart. Today, once Sage Root had been removed as an obstacle, he could deal with the berdache. For years he'd accepted the irritating presence of a man in woman's clothing. He'd egged the young men into waylaying the Anit'ah, explaining that degrading rape could be permitted against a *thing* like Two Smokes.

Before the sun dipped below the western horizon, Two Smokes would be driven off—or dragged away with his brains bashed out. By tonight, the People would be clean of pollutions and defilements like that. What a blessing that the Anit'ah had stolen the Wolf Bundle and given him the perfect lever to use against the berdache. Heavy Beaver's only regret was being denied the glory of burning the witch-thing in the fire while he Sang and Danced to awe the People with his Power over the Anit'ah magic.

No wonder the buffalo had left them. His People had rotted

at the core like an old cottonwood. New strength must be breathed into them like a spring sapling.

On his way to relieve himself, Heavy Beaver stopped near Sage Root's lodge to see the bit of menstrual pad where the breeze had blown it into the brush. Drying maggots writhed in death where they lay scattered in the dust.

He chuckled softly to himself.

White Calf led the way down the long ridge. The pain in her hip nagged at her while her lungs labored. Too much hurry. Her old body couldn't take such a pace anymore.

Behind her, the three hunters trotted easily, chests hardly rising and falling. Ah, to be young again. Once she'd been able to race the wind, despite her woman's hips and muscles.

"There," Black Crow called, pointing in the growing light of morning. "That's where camp is. Where the river runs straight."

She grunted and turned her steps, but not before she'd caught the strained look in Hungry Bull's face. Did he feel it, too?

"Time's short," she growled. "Let's go."

"Short?" Hungry Bull asked, worry eating at his handsome features.

She paused for a moment. "Something in the wind. Spirit's loose. Has been for the last four days." She hesitated. "Listen. I don't know what's stewing in the boiling pouch, but the vision is calling. Whatever it is, *I want to handle it.*"

The men glanced back and forth, eyes expressing their growing unease.

Panic spread in Hungry Bull's gut. He'd felt it before—the sensation he experienced when he knew the buffalo would wheel and charge. Now a wrongness pulsed with his soul. Each moment passed with the urgency of blood falling drop by drop to spatter in the dust. Anxious, he started to rush ahead, only to have White Calf reach for him. Her taloned fingers sank into his flesh.

"Don't go balky on me now like some moonstruck buffalo calf in a lightning storm. This is Spirit Power. Understand? Let me worry about it."

Pulse racing, Hungry Bull licked his lips. "I've got to go. I can feel it. *I've got to go!*"

She pinned his eyes. "I want your promise. On your soul. *Let* me *handle it!*"

"On my soul.".He swallowed nervously. "I don't like messing with Spirit Power. I don't want anything to do with it. But we've got to go!"

She jerked a nod. "Good. Then trust me. I take your promise. On your soul."

White Calf wheeled, putting her old legs to work again. Under her feet, dried grasses crackled as if she broke tiny bones.

As they continued she muttered under her breath, "I hope we're not too late."

At that moment, an anguished cry pierced her mind like a thrown dart. She forced her tired legs to move faster, wincing at the spike of pain in her hip.

Little Dancer's limbs felt detached the way they did in a strange dream. The morning might have been imagined, unreal, something he couldn't really touch, or hear, or smell. He wasn't part of the sunlight or the earth underfoot. He existed separately from the air and the soul of the land. Two Smokes' arms around him might have been illusion but for the crushing pressure in his lungs. The tears had drained away to leave a hollow ache inside his ribs. He'd become no more than a husk with nothing within—like the thin hulls the berdache peeled from his grass seeds to blow away on the wind.

"We've got to take her back," Two Smokes whispered hoarsely.

The voice in Little Dancer's ears sounded distant. He didn't feel the berdache's arms drop away. He stared fixedly into eternity. Two Smokes pulled Sage Root's limp body from the cottonwood, struggling to prop it on the smooth wood so he could get a grip on the sagging flesh.

Little Dancer barely noticed the pain reflected in Two Smokes' face as his mother's weight fell on his crippled leg.

The berdache hunched his back and pulled to resettle the dangling burden.

He looked back at the crimson-stained log. There, behind it, he saw the black wolf. The animal stood motionless, ears raised, watching. A prickling of Power traced along the nape of Little Dancer's neck. His eyes locked with the beast's, joining, twining their souls.

No! I don't want this! Mother! Where are you? Little Dancer tore his eyes away and followed. Like a hammerstone on a hollow log, Two Smokes grunted each time his stiff leg took the load. The path back couldn't have been more than three long dart casts, but Two Smokes staggered by the time they entered the camp clearing.

A pain pierced Little Dancer's heart as Two Smokes reeled and let go of his mother. When her body hit the ground, it made a hollow thud and bounced like a freshly killed carcass dropped heedlessly by the hunter. Two Smokes collapsed next to her. His teeth sank deeply into his lower lip as his face contorted in response to the pain in his maimed leg.

Little Dancer stood mutely, eyes locked on his mother's body while Two Smokes ran anxious hands down his stiff leg. Sweat droplets caught the morning sun, shining like ice crystals as they traced his hot cheeks. The berdache's hair looked wet and sticky while sweat stained the finely worked leather of his dress where it clung to his back.

"Sage Root! She's dead!"

In the haze of his numb mind, Little Dancer didn't recognize the voice. He only vaguely noted the rushing of people as they came to stare. A tension began to build inside him as their whispered voices intruded on his empty mind. The rising murmur irritated him as it grated on his concentration. Didn't they understand? Couldn't they feel the hurt and grief?

"So the moment has come! Do any of you doubt me now?" Heavy Beaver pushed his way through the press to stand above Sage Root's body. The Spirit Dreamer raised his hands to the morning sky. His moon face flushed hot, alight with triumph.

"Let no one doubt the Power of my Dreaming. Look! Look before you, my people! See the cleansing of the pollution!

Look to the skies and see Antelope Above rejoicing in the justice meted out to the woman who defiled his children!''

Little Dancer stared up at the morning. He looked again, harder, seeing nothing but emptiness in the air where Heavy Beaver pointed. A fist clenched and turned in his stomach; wrongness soured the air around him. He'd heard the antelope, remembered the Oneness of the Dream. He'd shared the taste of sage in their mouths, frolicked and felt their worry. Now he felt nothing but the sense of being apart. When he looked at Heavy Beaver, he saw nothing, felt nothing but unease and a curious sense of being cheated.

"You lie!" he called out in his misery. "You see nothing but what's in your head. You don't know the Oneness. You can't feel the Power around you. You're a deceiver. A thief.''

A gasp from the People fanned the spark of anger kindled in Little Dancer's breast. In the nothingness, it burned brightly, seeking to strike out, to repay hurt with hurt and terror with terror.

Heavy Beaver wheeled, black eyes gloating as his lips parted. "From now on, boy, you'll live with me. You've been tainted by pollution. I can see it hiding in your soul. An evil lies within you. An evil which must be beaten, burned, and driven out if your soul is to be saved from Anit'ah sorcery.''

"No!" Two Smokes cried, raising himself up slowly, sweat popping from his tortured face. He got a foot under him, wincing at the pain as he started to stand and face the Spirit Dreamer. Heavy Beaver turned, kicking out to knock him flat.

"And you, *Anit'ah*! You're a worse pollution than anyone. You're a monster! You offend everything normal in the world. A man who loves men and dresses as a woman? You're a vile pustule! From this moment, I banish you for the evil you are. Get out! Get away from the People. Now! Leave us . . . and if you ever come back, it's to receive the cleansing death you deserve!''

Two Smokes shook his head, pulling his good leg under him, starting to rise again. "No, you don't understand the—''

He cried out in agony as Heavy Beaver kicked him in the maimed knee. The cry shivered Little Dancer's soul, loosening his intestines with the intensity of the suffering it communicated.

Little Dancer's sanity collapsed under a rush of hatred. Rabid, he flew at Heavy Beaver, clawing, shrieking, kicking with all the rage broken loose in his little body.

The frightened scream torn from Two Smokes' lips was for him, yet pain and grief spurred him as he screamed with rage and desperation. The man's heavy body defied him. A hand caught in his shirt, lifting, as he battered at invulnerable flesh. The world spun as he was thrown violently away.

The ground rose, whirling. When he smacked and bounced, lights blasted through his brain. His breath burst from heaving lungs. Pain—pulsing physical pain—seared his nerves. Fright strangled his breath in fevered lungs as his vision spun and little sparks played behind his eyes. A ringing filled his ears.

Two Smokes cried out again like a wounded rabbit twisted on a sharp stick.

"See? See what this pollution has done? See how he's turned that poor little boy into an animal? This is the evil we've inflicted on ourselves! We allowed the evil into our midst. And you ask why rain doesn't fall? Why the grass doesn't grow thick and green for buffalo? How could any worthy Spirit send game to a people who harbor an offense like this?"

A voice of assent rose from the People.

"Curse you, Heavy Beaver!" Chokecherry's old voice pierced the air. "Haven't you done enough? Now you'll add torture to—"

"*Silence, old woman!* You're part of this. Someone remove her. Take her away before she angers the Spirit Powers!"

Chokecherry cried out over a scuffling of feet.

As breath rushed back into his starved lungs, Little Dancer's vision clouded with unrestrained tears. He sobbed at the pain, at the futility and hurt. He sobbed at the injustice and violation. Most of all, he sobbed at his helplessness. Blood ran from his nose. Heavy Beaver had thrown him down so hard that everything hurt.

"So, you haven't left, berdache?" Heavy Beaver's voice

penetrated Little Dancer's mind like oil soaking into dry leather. "Then you've made your choice. Your evil ends here. Someone bring me a club. Today we'll all Sing the end of the pollution. Together, we'll Dance the lingering taint of the berdache away. With our voices united, we'll call the Spirit Powers to see how we've cleansed the People! Then the rains will come. Then the buffalo will return."

"Cleansed with my blood?" Two Smokes cried. "By murder?"

Little Dancer's heart froze. He swallowed his sobs, dragging his sleeve across his eyes to clear the swollen tears. Heavy Beaver loomed over Two Smokes, a flush of excitement reddening his flat features. Two Smokes huddled on the ground, slowly shaking his head in disbelief. His hands had raised, empty, beseeching.

Little Dancer pulled himself forward on abused muscles until he reached the entrance to his lodge. There, inside, the old familiar furnishings brought no solace.

Grinning and whooping, Fire At Night pushed through the crowd. In his right hand he waved a hafted maul back and forth like a trophy. The heavy hammer consisted of a pecked and shaped stone head. A thumb-thick green willow stick had been doubled over the head to act as a handle. Green rawhide had then been sewn over the whole and allowed to shrink tight to hold it all together.

Two Smokes began to shiver, eyes horror-locked on the maul Heavy Beaver took from Fire At Night. "No," he whispered. "Don't do this thing."

Heavy Beaver lifted the hammer high, offering it to the sky. "Today, Wise One Above, we cleanse ourselves to be worthy of your truth! See this act of humility! See the People once again turn their faces toward you and your path of light! Watch, Father Sun, as we drive this filth from among us!"

Two Smokes swallowed hard, looking for an escape. People ringed him, eyes bright as they pressed forward.

A whimper caught in Little Dancer's throat. Panicked, he looked around, seeing only the hides and cold fire pit and the empty space where the Wolf Bundle had once rested. There to the side lay Two Smokes' grass collection in its hide and . . .

"I call on you, Spirits Above! I call on you to watch!"

"No!" Two Smokes screamed, scrambling backward as Heavy Beaver charged forward, the hammer lifted high. A snarl of vindicated rage twisted the shaman's broad face.

Little Dancer reached with fear-charged fingers, closing them on the wood. He turned, screaming his fear, and rushed forward in one final desperate attempt.

Someone cried a warning. Heavy Beaver stopped, staring wide-eyed. He jumped back, feet tangling in his retreat. He started to fall just as Little Dancer drove Blood Bear's dart into his body.

The cry saved him serious injury. Heavy Beaver felt his feet snag. Arms flailing, he fell as the boy drove the dart at him.

By instinct, Heavy Beaver twisted away. Instead of slicing through his belly, the point bunched the leather of his shirt, ripping through as he pulled away. The razor edge of the stone slipped along under his clothing, stinging as it went.

"Get him! He's trying to kill me!" he screamed as he rolled away. The dart caught in the folds on his shirt. The shaft wrenched from the boy's grasp and tumbled him.

Fire At Night jumped forward, plucking the boy from the ground, shouting angrily as the child kicked him hard on the kneecap. A flailing fist caught the older boy on the cheek.

Snarling, Fire At Night slapped Little Dancer across the face. As the boy blinked, Fire At Night doubled a fist and punched him the belly. Little Dancer whimpered miserably and desisted.

Heavy Beaver exhaled relief. He'd lived. Collecting himself, he winced as the sting of the wound began to throb. Heavy Beaver got slowly to his feet, forcing his legs to stop trembling. His heart battered at his chest as he lifted his shirt to peer underneath.

A long gash bled freely where the dart had skipped across his ribs before fouling in the thick hide of his shirt.

Heavy Beaver's fear melted, to be replaced with a white-hot anger.

"You're *evil*, boy! You just tried to kill one of the People. I can't save you now. The taint from wicked Anit'ah Power goes too deep.'' He pulled a hand back and slapped the mewing boy. The cry he elicited warmed something deep inside him. He hit the boy again and again, happy with the marks he raised.

''Hold him. You, Throws Stones. Get his other arm. Too much of the berdache is in him. His soul is too fouled to save. Today we cleanse the People . . . all of the People.'' *And no one will doubt my Power!*

''By the First Man,'' Two Smokes shrieked. ''You can't kill him! *He's just a boy!*''

''Straight Wood, if the Anit'ah filth speaks again, kill him.'' Heavy Beaver smiled down at the berdache. ''Don't worry, your soul won't be far behind Little Dancer's. I meant what I said. Today I cleanse the People, no matter how much blood I have to let.''

Two Smokes clamped his eyes shut as Straight Wood took a position over him.

Heavy Beaver retrieved the hammer and swung it to test the balance. People stared in horror, some covering their mouths, others covering their eyes. No one spoke. No one stepped forward to stop him. His authority went unchallenged.

Little Dancer wailed as the two boys stretched his arms between them. Heady with victory, Heavy Beaver stared into the insolent child's fear-glazed eyes and raised the hammer high overhead, picking the spot on the boy's skull where he'd land the blow.

Hungry Bull's heart quaked. Not for years had he experienced this feeling of dread. Anxiously he stared ahead over White Calf's tottering figure where she led the way.

Smoke rose from the cottonwoods in a blue haze, just as it would from a normal camp.

Then a flight of ravens rose from a huddled shape on the terrace overlooking camp. Hungry Bull's gut twisted. Someone had died. No wonder he felt like catastrophe hovered above him, ready to fall and snuff his peace and happiness. Well, no matter, in a few moments he'd be in Sage Root's arms, hearing the news.

A tingle of anticipation warmed him. Once he was home, he'd be clear of all this. He could retreat to his lodge and let White Calf and Heavy Beaver worry about the Spirit Power and visions.

The image of Sage Root's happy eyes danced in his mind. She'd chide him about his misplaced worry. He could already imagine the feel of her warm arms around him, feel her happy body pressed to his as she laughed. With her long fingers, she'd pull the gleaming black hair from her eyes to stare up at him with joy. How his soul tingled when she smiled at him that way. All her love would reflect in the gentling of her eyes and the expectation in her lips.

Perhaps this time he'd stay home for a while. Let Black Crow and Three Toes and Travels Far do the hunting. Besides, young Fire At Night and Throws Rocks were old enough to be going on their first hunt.

White Calf's legs wobbled under her as they entered the trees. Would the old woman make it that far? She seemed on the verge of collapse. An old one shouldn't push herself like that. No wonder he felt nervous. If a Spirit Dreamer like White Calf keeled over and died on him, the Wise One Above alone knew what the consequences would be.

"I don't like Spirit Power," he told himself. "And I swear, I'll never get involved with it again after this." But then, he'd sworn that before—and trouble had come looking for him. What stories he'd have to tell Sage Root and Little Dancer.

A scream sounded from ahead. The anxiety in Hungry Bull's heart spasmed. The sound couldn't be anything but a man in pain. More cries tortured the air as they hurried forward, pressing White Calf.

They burst into the camp clearing to see a knot of people clustered before Hungry Bull's lodge.

Heavy Beaver stood in the center, blood streaming down his side. Fire At Night and Throws Rocks held a young boy by the arms, stretching him between them, feet off the ground in what had to be a painful position. Straight Wood stood over another figure—Two Smokes—angrily kicking the berdache in the crippled leg every time he tried to reach up for the boy who—

"Little Dancer!" The cry caught in Hungry Bull's throat as Heavy Beaver lifted a hammer high over his head.

Little Dancer squealed in fear as the shaman approached. Where they braced themselves to steady the struggling boy, Fire At Night and Throws Rocks looked eagerly at the lifted hammer.

"No!" The cry tore from Hungry Bull's throat.

"Enough!" White Calf shouted, catching Hungry Bull with one taloned hand as he tried to charge past. People turned to stare. Heavy Beaver stopped, mallet held high as his enraged face fixed on Hungry Bull and froze.

Hungry Bull struggled against the old woman's eagle-strong grip. "Let me handle this," she hissed, eyes burning of Power and locking with his.

Sage Root? *Where was Sage Root?*

"You promised on your soul, hunter. Don't break that promise now. Three Toes, Black Crow, see that he doesn't do anything stupid."

And at that, White Calf hurried forward, panting with effort. Hungry Bull followed, fear charging his taut muscles.

"Turn the boy loose!" her ancient voice cracked like a buffalo-hide whip. "Now!"

"White Calf!" Two Smokes cried.

"White Calf?" Heavy Beaver stood uncertainly, the heavy hammer still held ready. "The *witch!*"

"Turn the boy *loose!*" At her words, Fire At Night gulped and let the boy down. Throws Rocks held on for a moment more before he let go. Little Dancer ran screaming, jumping into Hungry Bull's arms to bawl uncontrollably. Hungry Bull hugged him tight, feeling his son's frantic need. He whispered gently to reassure him.

Two Smokes crawled from under Straight Wood's guard, dragging himself forward with his hands.

"Who *are* you?" Heavy Beaver demanded. "What new form of pollution are you? Why are you here?"

She turned on her heel, staring from face to face as the People watched, waiting, shocked by it all. "So." She shook her head, trying to catch her breath. "This is what the People have fallen to?"

"Why are you here, WITCH?" Heavy Beaver demanded, advancing toward her the hammer threatening.

"If you were a Dreamer, boy, you'd know." She met his eyes, stopping him in his tracks. "But you're not, are you? You haven't heard the child calling?" She jerked her head at Little Dancer. "You didn't hear his Dreams? You didn't know what you had, did you? Is that what this is all about? You're tormenting what you don't understand?" To them all, she shouted, "Is that it? Have you lost so much that you *don't see Power anymore*?"

A hushed intake of breath met her words.

White Calf spat her disgust.

"Get out!" Heavy Beaver cried, advancing again. "I declare you a pollution! Get your filth out of here!"

White Calf hunched, shaking her pack from her back, lifting her hands wide. "Or what? You'll Curse me?"

"I Curse you now, witch! By the fourth day your body will be—"

"Oh, shut up! You wouldn't know a Curse if it lifted its head from the grass and bit you on the ass. Where's this boy's mother?"

People had begun to back away. Now they left at a run, leaving a space open where a young woman lay sprawled on the ground before a dingy-looking lodge.

"Oh . . . no . . ." Hungry Bull stared, hugging the weeping Little Dancer to his chest. He knew. All of a sudden it came clear, his soul crying and screaming within him.

The rest seemed to blur as he charged forward, lifting her into his arms, tears blurring the reality of her pale flesh, the red-stained earth under her gaping wrists.

He lifted his face to the sun, blinking at the rush of pain. "Why? *How? WHO DID THIS?*"

White Calf barely shifted as Hungry Bull rushed past. To the two hunters, she added softly, "I think he needs your help now."

No one moved as Black Crow and Three Toes hurried after.

"I Curse you!" Heavy Beaver repeated. "By the sun above, I declare you unclean and evil."

"You declare nothing." She cocked her head. "So you killed Sage Root?"

"He drove her to it." Two Smokes cried, voice cracking. "Just like he did Dancing Doe. He abused the Wolf Bundle—threw it into the dirt and chased it away. It's gone."

White Calf gasped and placed a knotted fist to her breast. "O Blessed Wise One Above." She shook her head, mouth falling open as she stared into Heavy Beaver's triumphant eyes. "Do you *know* what you've done?"

"I've cleansed the People!"

"You ignorant, stupid *fool!*" She darted a hard finger at him. "That Wolf Bundle . . . that *sacred* bundle is the *legacy of the First Man!*"

Horrified, more and more people began to melt away.

Heavy Beaver stood uncertainly, mouth bobbing open and closed as a frown lined his head.

"Get me away from here, White Calf," Two Smokes pleaded from where he lay on the ground. "They're tainted, all of the them. You brought me here. Take me away. I can't do anything for them anymore."

She reached down, wary of Heavy Beaver and his hammer. "Can you stand?"

"Vile pollution!" Heavy Beaver growled, having recovered his courage. "Take him! Get out of here. All of you. *Get out!*"

She got Two Smokes up, every vertebra in her back crackling. He leaned against her, and she could feel his trembling muscles.

"You bet we're leaving," White Calf added. "Considering what you've unleashed, I wouldn't stay within five days' walk of this camp."

"You're the reason the People have come to this. You and your kind. You're the reason. *You've* offended the Spirit World. You've caused the Spirits Above to turn their faces from the People. And you can stand here before decent human beings with your arm around a misbegotten foulness like Two Smokes?" Heavy Beaver danced from foot to foot, pointing.

"You've made your way, Heavy Beaver. Let's see where it takes you."

Two Smokes stiffened and gasped, pointing.

"*No!*" White Calf ordered.

A glazed look filled Hungry Bull's eyes as he stood, a dart nocked in the hook of his atlatl. Heavy Beaver turned, caught sight of it, and backpedaled in horror.

"Hungry Bull! *Don't!*" White Calf snapped. "His time hasn't come! Curse you, Bull! You promised me on your soul! Don't do this or you'll let loose Power you can't conceive of!"

"Hungry Bull?" Three Toes called gently, stepping nervously in front of his friend. "Trust her. We promised. White Calf knows what she's doing."

"You're Cursed," Heavy Beaver spat angrily, face pale as he stared at the promise of death in Hungry Bull's eyes. "Cursed, I say!"

Makes Fun cried out, a hand to her mouth as she stared in horror at her husband, Black Crow. Meadowlark had rushed to hang on Three Toes' arm, eyes glazed with fear.

White Calf turned sad eyes on the Spirit Dreamer. "The only person you've Cursed, fool, is yourself—and those who follow you. You've degraded the Wolf Dreamer's Bundle. Think on that for a while."

"It is only an ancient myth," Heavy Beaver insisted. "I know, I Dream the new way."

"He killed Dancing Doe and Sage Root," someone said from the side. Mumblings of confusion came from all sides.

White Calf helped Two Smokes hobble forward until she stared into Hungry Bull's eyes. "Leave it be, hunter. I see your anger. I feel your pain. But this is out of your hands."

The keenness in Hungry Bull's eyes sharpened.

"I mean it. You never wanted to mess with Spirit Power. Don't do it. You're not ready for it. Heavy Beaver's made his claims. He's the one dealing with Powers he doesn't understand. Power takes care of its own. It's not your place to meddle."

Hungry Bull hesitated, the war within reflected in his obsidian eyes. The will to kill, to strike back, eroded into grief.

Chokecherry came sputtering from one of the lodges. She pulled up, startled by White Calf's presence. As if all her stamina had finally fled, her shoulders stooped. "Thank the Wise One."

"Black Crow, Three Toes. I'm not done with you." White Calf turned her attention to the two ashen-faced hunters. "Take Sage Root up on the bluff so I can Sing her soul to the Starweb tonight. There's nothing here for any of you anymore. Help Hungry Bull pack his things. Then you can pack your own. I don't think you want to stay here." She smiled ironically. "You're too tainted with Power for Heavy Beaver and all his bluster."

She turned, Two Smokes hobbling as she moved. Over her shoulder, she called, "Little Dancer? Follow along. You and I, we've got a lot to talk about."

Wide-eyed, lost and afraid, he hesitated. Chokecherry rushed forward, taking his hand. "Come on, boy. She only comes once in a while. Good things happen then."

White Calf lifted an eyebrow. Good things? Her sister had changed her tune over the long years. But then, Chokecherry didn't feel the tremors, the welling and flowing of Power around her. A shiver ran up White Calf's back.

Power moved on the land; forces had been let loose that White Calf could only wonder at. In the back of her mind, an abyss yawned and cold misty vapors lifted from the depths. No good would come of this day.

Tanager sat high on the rocks, looking out over the vast basin of the Moon River. To the north, the Mud River ran its snakelike course toward the Buffalo River that in turn met the Big River. Nevertheless, her eyes kept returning to the faint trace of the Moon River, no more than a shadow in the distance.

The rocky spire she'd climbed had been a challenge. Only men with a need to prove their courage would try such an ascent. Something she couldn't define had driven her to climb to this perch more suited to eagles and lightning strikes—some internal need. The slight handholds had been a challenge to her agility and balance, but she'd made it. A sheer cliff dropped off where her thin legs dangled. She'd found a desiccated bone when she reached the top. That she'd dropped, watching it fall away to shatter on the rocks so far below.

Wind pulled at her hair, tangling it into a knot. Its strong push tried to topple her into the depths. That lent a thrill to the sensation that she could fall so easily.

She stared out over the plains, studying each change in color until her eyes lost themselves in the distance.

The Short Buffalo People lived there. None had come to raid this season, but why did she feel so uneasy? Her premonitions were more than the chance of falling, as if her soul trembled within.

Tanager turned to climb down, catching movement on the outcrop across from her. The wolf stood, separated from her by a cleft in the rock, its front feet braced against the battering wind. For long moments they stared at each other, Tanager meeting that knowing yellow gaze. Then, like a flicker of shadow, the dark hunter disappeared, only the sensation of promise left behind.

BOOK TWO

The Forging of
the Youth

The Wolf Bundle complained into the wavering haze of the Spiral, "The sacred number of seasons has passed, and what has changed? I've helped bring the rains back. The buffalo calve with greater regularity. For my help I see Heavy Beaver growing stronger and stronger. His authority is consolidated. He unites the People under his standard and his new way.

"Meanwhile, among the Red Hand, Blood Bear proves just as much a fool. I am bandied about as a symbol of his authority. At the same time, his scorn is apparent in his deeds, if not his words. Within his lodge, I'm mocked. My Power is eroding. Is that your purpose? To kill me?"

The haunting voice of the Wolf Dreamer shivered out of the Spirals. "My purpose is the boy."

"My inclination is to pay Blood Bear back for his ways."

"Be patient. The boy grows."

"And so does Heavy Beaver's way. He's changing the Spirals. Too many People believe him. In the end, we cannot defeat an idea," the Wolf Bundle warned.

"There is a way. Remember the tripod. Without another leg, we'll topple in the dirt."

Chapter 11 ✋

The world behind the small band had vanished in a haze of gray. Gray everywhere—like the feelings in their hearts. Where could people go when the world had gone insane?

Underfoot, the damp ground grated, gravel crunching beneath the weary placing of each moccasined step. Silence lay heavy on the land; only a slight sighing rose from the timber in the canyons below. The sounds of their passage—the scuff of tanned hide on stone or brush, the muffled groan of leather straps, and the puffing of breath—accompanied them as they climbed. Chill moisture hung in the air, stinging their noses, clammy on exposed skin.

Three Toes looked up at the winding trail, nervous at the way the clouds packed so thickly around the people he led. A few wind-gnarled fir trees clung to the reddish-brown rock with knobby roots twisted into the Earth Mother's bones. How high were they? From here, he should have been able to see the whole of the basin, Moon River to the south and Mud River running north. The somber gray of the encompassing clouds masked everything, even seeking to blur the edges of a memory turned painful and cutting.

He and Black Crow had no way back, no trail to return to the People. Now and forever, they would be outcasts. Nothing remained for them, no sanctuary in a camp of the People. In an irregular line, they climbed, disjointed figures in the mist—people without place or context, travelers in the clouds.

Behind him, Makes Fun gasped for breath while she talked softly to her son.

And what if I can't find White Calf's camp? What if we run into an Anit'ah party up here? What if Hungry Bull's dead? Killed? Then what's left for us?

He continued along the irregular game trail tracing the ridge top. In the gritty soil he could see the tracks of bighorn, deer, and an occasional elk. Moist air drifted coolly against his hot cheeks. The damp skein of clouds pressed down to make the world unreal—a blessing and curse. The gray dampness hid their passage from Anit'ah eyes, and obscured the landmarks White Calf had told him about in such detail during their flight from Heavy Beaver those four years past.

Four years? The sacred number, the number of the First Man, of the directions and the Wise One Above. So much had changed in four years. Who could have guessed?

On the trail ahead of Three Toes, a shadow shifted in the mist and brought him back to the present. Instinctively, he tightened his grip on the handle of his atlatl, the dart shaft resting securely in his fingers. He squinted past the blotchy outlines of the conifers and stopped, dropping to a slight crouch.

As the faint ghost of breeze played with the gray fog, the glimpse solidified into Black Crow's lanky shape.

"See anything?" Three Toes asked mildly, unwilling to break the eerie silence.

Black Crow lifted a shoulder, his mashed-turd nose contorting as he sniffed the cool air. "No—unless you're interested in what the inside of a cloud looks like."

"About like this, huh?" He waved in a sweeping gesture.

"About." Black Crow shook his head. "I don't know how we'll find them up here. We could walk around for weeks."

"If we don't stumble into a camp of the Anit'ah in the meantime."

"There's that, all right. After that raid Heavy Beaver made on their camps last year, I don't think they'd smile at us and wave as we went by."

Three Toes nodded, hearing sighs of relief behind him as Meadowlark, his wife, bent down to help his youngest daughter with some problem. Makes Fun had sagged onto a rock. A haggard look lined her face as she stared anxiously up at her husband. Black Crow's oldest boy lifted his flap to urinate. His water spattered on the hard ground.

"Nothing Heavy Beaver ever does leads to any good. Raiding the Anit'ah will come back to haunt us in the end like geese through the seasons.''

A slight shiver played along Three Toes' spine. He smiled without humor. ''I kind of started to wonder if maybe this wasn't such a good idea.''

Black Crow propped hands on his lean hips, shifting uneasily on tired feet as he looked down the obscured trail they'd just traversed. ''What other choice did we have? What was left? The Cut Hair don't want anything to do with us. No matter where we go, we're moving into someone's hunting grounds and people are mad and hungry. It's not a good time for intruders.''

''And the Anit'ah hate us more than anyone,'' Three Toes reminded him, wishing he could recall his words uttered in council long months back. However, words, like the wind, couldn't be captured and brought back. All the People had gone crazy. Heavy Beaver's power had continued to grow, pulling together the splintered bands. Two Stones, Elk Whistle, White Foot, all had joined with Heavy Beaver, dancing his new Dance of Renewal. And when Seven Suns had decided to join with Heavy Beaver, Three Toes had stood, drawing all eyes toward him.

''I cannot be part of this. If you go to Heavy Beaver's camp, my wife and I will be Cursed. I know Heavy Beaver. I grew up with him. I know his hate. I'll leave the People before I'll share a camp with Heavy Beaver.''

He'd been outvoted.

''Remember, you can always come to my camp. I'll protect you. Feed you.'' White Calf's words echoed in his head as they had the day they'd parted company four years ago. *''Follow Clear River west through the red rock wall and take the Spirit Trail up the mountain. Stay to the south of the canyon and you'll find a trail. You'll know it by the rock piles. Follow that over the ridge top and you'll find my camp in the valley bottom beyond. You'll be safe there.''*

Three Toes sucked his lip. Safe? He'd bet his life, and that of his family and friends, on that illusive promise. Only how would they know the right trail in this dense fog? Up here in the land of the Anit'ah the clouds caught on the peaks, hiding everything.

A misty rain began to fall.

"It's getting colder."

Three Toes grunted. "All that time we wanted rain and we get it now."

"The whole world's gone crazy. Maybe the Wise One Above is tired of men." Black Crow lifted a bony shoulder in a shrug and rubbed his sagging belly. "Maybe the end of the world is coming like Heavy Beaver says."

Three Toes searched the somber grayness with anxious eyes. "I hope you're joking when you say that."

Fire filled the world, roaring like thunder mated to wind. Yellow red, raging, it burned up from below, beating at Little Dancer in loud fury. Crackling and snapping, the fire engulfed him. He blinked against the painful heat, trying to raise his arms in an effort to shield his face from the searing.

The fire mocked him, walls of flame moving in retaliation, wavering this way and that in a frightening dance. He tried to turn away, only to have flames swirl in a countermove, roaring and hissing to each of his movements. Little Dancer's breath caught in his throat. If he tried to breathe, the fire would dart in to char his lungs and consume his very soul.

"We're One." Words formed in the roaring thunder of the endless flames. *"All the world is One. We're all a Dream. Be with me . . . Dance with me. We're One . . . One. . . ."*

He clamped his eyes shut, futilely shaking his head in denial. Tears formed in his eyes, hissing and popping into steam as they started from his cheeks.

"No!" he screamed. *"No!"*

The pressure in his lungs burned as feverishly as the inferno outside.

"Free yourself, boy. Dance with me. Become One with me. Forget your fear. Trust yourself."

He jerked back as the flames twirled around him like some impossible whirlwind. As the winds drew him up, his flesh sizzled like fat dripped on white-ashed coals.

He squealed in fear—and snapped awake, heart battering at his ribs.

"Hey? You all right?" Two Smokes half started from his bedding, blinking owlishly.

"Dream. Just a dream." Little Dancer tried to catch his breath, blinking as he dug his fingers into the bedding. The touch of warm hide and the security of cool dirt below reassured him.

"What Dream?" White Calf demanded from behind.

Little Dancer bit his lip, lowering his eyes. "Nothing. Just a dream. Nothing."

"That so, boy?" He could hear the skepticism in her voice. She'd started again, picking at him, never letting him have a moment's peace.

"Just a dream." He stood up, the beautifully worked mountain-sheep hide falling to one side. He swallowed dryly, frightened by the sweat that soaked his clothing.

"A Dream about fire?"

How did she know?

"No. Just a dream about my mother." There, use the old defense. He didn't have anything else to stand against the old woman's constant questioning.

The roomy rock shelter consisted of a large cavity in the cliff side that measured fifteen paces across where the limestone had been water-hollowed in the distant past. The back wall curved around, lined with nooks and caches that held White Calf's medicines and Power bundles. A spiral had been pecked and subsequently painted on the wall above where White Calf slept. Packs containing dried meat and berries hung from pegs driven into the stone. Overhead, soot had formed a thick velvet covering that rounded the angles of the rock.

A half-body length from the rear wall where rodents weren't as likely to find them, rounded storage pits had been dug into the floor. The cysts had then been lined with closely fitted stones to at least hinder the insects and audacious packrats and ground squirrels from burrowing into the stored reserves. Topped with a thick sandstone slab, these were filled with limber pine nuts, rose hips, yampa, balsam and biscuit root, and dried sego-lily bulbs. Tanned robes, a couple of carved digging sticks, and a set of horn bowls had been placed neatly at the rear. The outside wall consisted of a series of poles braced vertically against the overhanging ceiling. Hide had been laced to these to block the evening chill and retard the strength of the breezes. Enough gaps along the rough rock allowed smoke to filter out at the top. Two fire pits had been excavated in the floor. One consisted of a deep, bell-shaped roasting pit, the other a shallow basin mounded full of rock to radiate the heat. A sandstone slab acted as a reflector for each of the fires.

All in all, the rock shelter made a snug home. Unlike the hide lodges he'd lived in as a youth, the shelter stayed warmer, radiating heat absorbed during the day until late at night. In summer, it remained cool. The shelter would have been perfect had it not been for White Calf's constant and irritating presence. This place belonged to her—and she dominated it in every respect. He couldn't help but wonder if her soul hadn't leached into the very rock along with the soot of her fires.

He turned to meet her burning eyes. If anything, she'd shrunk in the last couple of years. Now her hair glistened in the firelight as white as the deep-winter snow. Her face had evolved into a shriveled caricature, the flesh of her neck sagging like the wattle of a misbegotten turkey. She looked so frail a sneeze might have broken her like a stem of winter grass bent too far. At least, he could think so until he faced the shining challenge in her passionate eyes. Now they caught the ember-tinged light of the fires, gleaming of Power, seeing through him as if he were nothing more than morning smoke. The familiar tingle of premonition teased his uneasy gut.

"You can't hide from yourself forever, boy." Her words came at him softly, almost like drifting fog. "Deny your Power all you want—but you can't escape it like some hawk from a torn net. It's you, boy. You're the one."

He said nothing, resentment and frustration building.

"Why do you always deny me, boy?"

His mother's words echoed inside: *"I forbid it!"* The horror of her death lingered—as tangible in his mind as the hard earth under his physical self. Every time this argument reared, he could feel his mother's dark eyes staring down, watching him, a constant reminder of that hideous moment he'd felt her death, found her bloodless body.

"Why, boy?" White Calf persisted. "No matter what your mother said, you can't change your nature. You're a Dreamer

. . . it's in your eyes." A pause. "Look at me. Tell me you're not. And mean it when you say it."

He refused, biting back the seething anger her words always brought. He wanted to shout at her, revile her for the meddling old sage hen she was. How sweet it would be to spit in her face and tell her to leave him alone for once. What a precious reward it would be to strike back at her for the last years. For the moment, he dreamed of kicking her packs apart, reveled in the fantasy of throwing her prize possessions into the fire. What a joy it would be to stomp them into the coals as they caught fire and incinerated themselves to wispy ash. That would show her. That would teach her to leave him alone. He could pay her back for all the endless harassment and all the little games to bend him to her will.

Except, he never would. He had been born of the People. With the very milk from his mother's breast, he'd sucked up the manners of the Short Buffalo folk. The young never acted disrespectfully to the elders who had come before. No one would dare take such a liberty. No matter how she might goad him, twist him, and eat away at his resistance, he could never scorn her, or shout his anger. And that made the anger and frustration even worse.

"Boy, you've got to listen to the voices in your head. You got—"

"I'm going to find my father." Unable to look at her, familiar with the pained expression on Two Smokes' face, he ran for the door hanging and exploded out into the night.

"One of these days," Two Smokes said into the sudden quiet, "you will drive him too far. Chokecherry warned you before she died."

"She never understood my role."

"Maybe. But she knew this boy. I know this boy. White Calf, you can't keep pushing like this. You've alienated his father. Hungry Bull's lost himself . . . lost his way through life, and doesn't know what to do except stay away. He won't argue with you on account of the debt he owes you. He's afraid of Power. But when you badger the boy, it tears at him. It's another strand pulling apart between us. If you keep this up, you'll—"

"Yes, yes . . . I know."

"Do you?"

She looked at him, keen black eyes smoldering with a curious desperation. "I do. I just can't seem to reach Little Dancer."

"He'll find Power himself. He can't ignore it forever."

White Calf seemed to deflate as she sighed from the depths of her soul. She nodded absently. "Yes, old friend, I suppose. But I don't have much time. And there's so much he needs to learn."

Little Dancer trotted down the trail, keen eyes picking out the undulations and rocks in the darkness. The red flush of anger began to dissipate, leaving in its place a foreboding depression, thick and gloomy as the cloud cover over the night sky.

"Why don't they leave me alone?" He swung a half-hearted fist at a fir branch, oddly relieved by the action. He continued slashing at the tall grasses that had gone brown and brittle with the first frost. Already the air carried a promising tang of coming cold. A person could feel it; the subtle bite of winter cloaked itself in the crisp mornings, or hid in the gust of the afternoon breeze. Like a ghost, it waited, ready to slip out of the memories of summer and bear down on the land in full-fledged cold. Daylight had begun to dull the belly of the fall sky as Father Sun retreated to the southern trail across the heavens.

And what would this winter bring? More stifling days around the smoldering fire as White Calf retold the old stories? More of her constant harping, the endless questions and ceaseless picking comments about Power?

These days Hungry Bull stayed out of sight except during the coldest of weather when he might suffer frostbite. What good was a frostbitten hunter? If the flesh froze too severely, his father's only pleasure in life might be denied him. And if Hungry Bull lost that one solace of the hunt, he'd be as good as dead.

Hungry Bull had changed. That sparkle of fun had gone from him, leaving him dull. He wouldn't even meet White Calf's eyes. His spirit had fled someplace the day he'd walked in shock from Heavy Beaver's camp. Then, not even a year after they'd come to White Calf's, Chokecherry had died in her robes. Without her to share the past, no one understood him anymore.

What had happened to them? Once again Little Dancer asked himself the old worn-out question. From the day he'd Dreamed the antelope, everything had changed. Existence had turned inside out and lost itself in a tangle of hurt and confusion. Power had entered his life—*and it wouldn't leave.*

The Dreams continued to haunt him. The old woman was right. He could deny all he wanted, but that didn't change the truth. Like this night's Dancing fire, the Dreams spun around him with the power of Crafty Spider's Starweb, ensnaring him, holding him captive. Once he'd tried beating himself with a quartzite cobble, seeking to drive the visions from his head. Outside of swelling bruises and a wretched headache, he'd received a tongue-lashing from White Calf that ended in a fight that had ensnarled Two Smokes and his father for months until White Calf finally relented.

"Let him beat himself half to death!" she'd finally agreed. "That's fine with me." Then she'd hesitated for a brief moment before adding, "I'll bet Heavy Beaver would *love* to hear about that!"

And he'd never tried to harm himself thereafter. At the thought, the knowing, satisfied smile of Heavy Beaver would form sickly sweet in his memory.

With no pattern or hint, the Dreams would come on him. And the old woman never seemed to miss it. So what if she really *had* been his grandmother? She didn't have to watch him like that. At times he felt like a mouse scurrying under a coyote's nose. The huge jaws always gaped open, ready to snatch him up. He never knew when those heavy paws might pounce and smash him flat in the grass to leave him dazed and dying before being swallowed by something he didn't understand.

Two Smokes hadn't been any help either. He didn't talk much anymore—he'd never forgiven himself for the insult to the Wolf Bundle. Berdaches lived between the worlds. Not only did they function as the mediators between men and women, understanding each, they had been fashioned by the ways of Power so they could feel the spirit realm as well as the world. Two Smokes had felt the desecration of the Wolf Bundle to the bottom of his soul. The experience had left a hole, a lack of purpose in his life.

I'm just miserable, that's all. Mother? Why did you go away and leave me to this? Why did you give up? Where are you, Mother? Come back to me! Take me away!

Moving out from the mountain, Little Dancer could see the western horizon where the clouds had drifted east. Pinpoints of light from the exposed portions of the Starweb twinkled and danced. Overhead and to the east, the sky remained masked by cloud and darkness. He could imagine the blackness over Moon River and his old childhood haunts. Did Heavy Beaver look up this night, too? Did he stare at the same blotted heavens and wonder?

Little Dancer kicked at a low sagebrush, satisfied with the tangy odor as he bruised the seed-heavy stalks rising above the aqua leaves.

They'd made him a prisoner, keeping him like a child kept a baby bird in a stick cage. White Calf, the Power and Dreams, the Curses of Heavy Beaver, everything worked against him.

Viciously, he kicked at the sage, happy to hurt back for once. So much for Heavy Beaver. So much for Dreams and White Calf and everything else that left him miserable and harried. The anger rose again, relentless, burning. He struck out at the world, seeking to hurt it, to pay it back for the frustration he lived.

With a stick, he laid into the sagebrush, thrashing it as hot tears rolled down his cheek. He attacked a small fir tree with his flail, imagining it to be White Calf and Heavy Beaver rolled into one. He screamed as his muscles rolled under the attack. A cry of rage rose to his lips, fueling his assault.

The stick broke, cracking under the violence of his tantrum. He bent to pluck rocks, pelting the tree, watching the branches whip under the impact. He screamed his anger, exulting in the triumph flooding his charged body. Wild rage keened and sang in his veins.

Finally exhausted, he sagged, chest heaving, completely spent. A tremor scurried through the muscles of his arms and legs. In the passing fury, his mouth had gone dry and his throat burned. A welling pain began to throb in his torn fingers where he'd shredded the skin trying to lever rocks from the resistant dirt. The chill of the night-dark air began to seep into his sweat-flushed cheeks.

Around him the night waited, silent, patient, eternal, knowing the futility of young boys and their spells of impudent misbehavior.

Little Dancer blinked owlishly at the tree before him. His vented wrath didn't seem to have made an impact. The shadowy fir stood resolute; the veil of darkness obscured any scars he might have imparted on the supple branches. In defeat, he lowered his head, rubbing the back of his neck, aware of the quiet pressing down like a smothering robe.

Why won't they just leave me alone?

A shadow detached itself from the blackness.

Little Dancer gulped at the sudden shiver of fear, tensing.

The big black wolf might have been a dream image, so silently did it slip into the trees.

How long had the animal stalked him? How long had it watched? On rubbery legs he stood and retraced his way to the game trail. Exhausted and drained, he set his steps toward the meadow where he knew his father had started a buffalo trap.

Elk Charm huddled inside the wrap of her soft elk-hide robe, bending low to peer under the flap of the menstrual lodge toward the camp. The Red Hand always put the menstrual lodge uphill and downwind. First Man had told them to do it that way.

She wrinkled her young nose. For the life of her, she couldn't imagine why. Did the old men really think they could smell a woman's bleeding? She remembered sniffing the breeze surreptitiously to see once, and had only detected the more powerful odor of camp: smoke, feces, dog and human, and the faint tang of cured hide over the light scent of boiling foodstuffs and roasting roots.

She tensed as Blood Bear walked past the edge of camp, his black silhouette framed by the fires. The Keeper of the

Wolf Bundle paused for a moment, staring as if his eyes could make her out in the night-shadowed lodge.

For a long moment, she held her breath. Then he ducked into his lodge.

Had Tanager forgotten? Had she skipped out on some crazy adventure in the timber again?

Elk Charm exhaled wearily. Would her mother *never* come? The menstrual lodge confined her like a mountain sheep in a catch pen. If only Blood Bear didn't stalk the night, waiting. If only she didn't understand why he lurked in the darkness. Would it always be this way? Would each time be this terrible? Silently, she reminded herself that after all, this was her first time. That it had happened so soon had been a rude surprise for her.

At first, she couldn't understand what had gone wrong. When the cramps hit, she just knew it must have been the pine-nut patties she'd stolen from old Green Horn's grinding stone—that the old woman had cast some sort of enchantment to give young-girl thieves a bellyache. But Elk Charm should have known. The budding of her breasts should have been a clue. The broadening of her hips—which had become so pronounced in her shadow—hadn't prepared her. Not even the downy-dark tracery of pubic hair had warned her. When the blood first appeared, she'd almost panicked.

"It's your time," her mother, Rattling Hooves, had told her proudly. "My daughter's become a woman."

In utter spiritual chaos, Elk Charm had simply stared, mouth open, unable to speak. In all her life only the tragic death of her father had left her so off balance and devastated.

Ushered to the menstrual lodge in great ceremony, she'd spent four days under the shelter, alternately confused, ecstatic, bored, excited, or miserable. Then her mother and grandmother and most of the other women had come, plucked her eyebrows, and stripped her bare. With gaudy colors, they'd painted her body as all women had been painted since the First Man had shown them the way up from the First World and exposed them to the light of Father Sun. Her mother had dipped both hands in wet ocher and clapped them to her breasts, symbolically dedicating her future milk to the Red Hand. They had painted her face white with a blue circle on her right cheek to indicate the sky and a brown circle on her left to indicate the earth. Down from her breastbone, they had painted the yellow Path of Light to cross her navel and end on the rise of her pubis. Green Horn had used charcoal to draw arrows pointing up the insides of her thighs. "To lead these stupid young men to the right place, you see!" And she'd cackled to the immense delight of the other old women.

Flushed with embarrassment, Elk Charm had swallowed hard, certain the old hag knew just who had stolen her pine-nut patties.

Orange was painted in a big circle on the flat of her abdomen, a symbol of the morning sun and the new life it brought to the day just as her loins would bring new life to the Red Hand.

Through it all, she endured, knowing the ritual as every young girl somehow did. No one ever really discussed it openly; nevertheless, she had known from whispered conversations shared with her friends, Cricket and Tanager. Somehow, it hadn't seemed real until afterward. The old women had left, accompanied by her mother. They'd gone, singing and rattling their deer-hoof noisemakers. A new woman had come to the Red Hand.

Elk Charm had straightened to watch them go, feeling the difference in her life. The men had been waiting, laughing, singing, and clapping their hands as they danced along with the procession. Cricket and Tanager had observed from the edge of camp, wide-eyed, knowing their old easygoing relationship had changed. Elk Charm could no longer laugh and joke with them like a child, or play games like hoop and stick. She had to assume the duties of a woman—and she had no idea how women laughed, or what all their jokes meant.

A man would want her. That thought had possessed her, going through her thoughts like a cool breeze on a hot day. She'd been so preoccupied, she'd barely noticed at first.

One man didn't join the dancing. The Keeper of the Wolf Bundle simply looked on, stern face expressionless. Across the distance, she'd felt the anticipation in his eyes. Head up, alert, the consummate hunter had found prey.

He'd looked in her direction, smiling to himself, a gleam

in his eyes. The realization had hit her like a thrown rock. Her soul tightened and twisted in on itself: Blood Bear wanted to have her first!

Desperate, she'd sent Tanager for her mother, unwilling to elaborate on the reason why. Even as she'd struggled to explain, will-o'-the-wisp Tanager had slipped away into the night.

That afternoon, as singing and chants rose from the camp, she'd huddled under her robe. They'd expect her to leave the lodge tomorrow morning. What then? Blood Bear would lie in wait. How could she refuse him if he caught her outside the camp? What could she do? No one denied the Keeper of the Wolf Bundle. Blood Bear had returned the stolen heart and spirit of the Red Hand. He could take what he wanted.

She bent down to peer under the cover again, seeing a dark shadow detach itself from the camp to walk up the flat-trodden path. The familiar stride warmed some of the desperate chill within. Tanager *had* managed to slip into her stepfather's lodge and catch her mother's ear.

Soft-skinned moccasins whispered on the path, a swish of fringed hide brushed against skin as Rattling Hooves bent down.

"Hello, daughter. What's this I hear? You wanted to see me?"

"I need to talk."

Her mother chuckled in her throaty manner and ducked through the flap. She sighed as she sat down and rolled onto her side on the padded hide floor of the lodge. Relaxed, she kicked her legs out, leaning on one arm to stare across in the darkness.

"Worried about being a woman? Tanager wasn't any too specific."

Elk Charm swallowed hard, nodding in the blackness. The old familiarity they shared—that close link between a mother and daughter who'd suffered together—communicated more than words.

"Well, don't. There's not much you can do about it. I guess I made it, huh? Just be yourself. Wait and see, everything happens like it will happen. You don't need to be afraid of the future. Life just comes and you live it day by day.

Right now you're scared of what it will be like. When you've cleaned your first grandson's runny butt, you'll wonder where it all went.''

"It's not that." Her heart started to race.

"Oh?" Her mother's warm voice rose in question. "That's what worried me."

"It's . . . well, Blood Bear." The charcoal arrows Green Horn had drawn on her thighs itched in the darkness: a premonition?

Her mother sighed. "I see. He's been watching the lodge?"

"Ever since everyone left. He knows I'm ready. Only . . . Mother, not him. I don't . . . I mean . . ."

Her mother moved closer in the darkness, shifting. A warm arm settled around Elk Charm's shoulders. "I think I understand." Silence stretched. "Is it all men? Or just him?"

"Just him. I hoped it would be Snaps Horn. He's said some things—well, maybe even promised. I don't think he was teasing. I've seen him watching me. I wish it could be him. I really do. But other men, well, I can say no to them."

"That's right."

"But Blood Bear keeps the Wolf Bundle. No one says no to him. I can't . . . I won't let him touch me. I don't want what he does. He hurts women. I heard about what he did to Soft Spring Shower her first time. He made her bleed. That's not right. I don't want to hurt."

"Shhh! I know. If it were me, I wouldn't want to either. I got lucky. When I left the lodge, I had wonderful men to choose from."

"But I—"

"Hush, girl. I'm thinking."

Long moments passed. Elk Charm kept looking under the flap toward the camp. The evening fires had been lit in the lodges. The cone-shaped tops of the hide shelters glowed yellow brown, lit by the firelight within. She knew the scenes from experience. Inside, people sat, laughing, telling stories about Elk Charm's childhood, wondering who she'd marry in the end. Most of the tales began with, "Remember when Elk Charm was five? Remember when she . . ." and they'd go on.

Why did these cold fingers of dread trace through her soul

despite the celebration? Why did Blood Bear have to want *her*?

"White Calf."

"What?"

Her mother nodded slowly in the darkness. "That's the answer. I'm sending you to White Calf's. In the meantime maybe Blood Bear will forget you. Or maybe you'll find a man somewhere, eh?"

"But why would I go to White Calf's? I don't—"

"Where else would you be safe? Hmm? Fast Runner's? Blood Bear would just go there . . . and besides, your family is all here, so you wouldn't have an excuse. We've got to get you someplace that you'd be expected to go. White Calf's is perfect."

"Why would I be *expected* to go there?"

"Because I'll be busy. I'll—"

"But there are all those Short Buffalo People there! That hunter! He might—"

"Quit panicking. Not even a Short Buffalo hunter would bother you in White Calf's camp. You know better than that. Besides, the berdache, Two Smokes, will be there to guard you. Even now, after so long, people don't forget Cut Feather's murder. To Blood Bear, the berdache is a reminder of those days of disgrace. If there's one place Blood Bear won't go, it's White Calf's."

"But why would I go there? I mean, won't Blood Bear know that it's him that I'm hiding from? Won't he make it worse when I come back?"

"Didn't I teach you years ago to trust me?"

"Well . . . yes."

"Good, because you're going for medicine for your mother-in-law. Wet Rain is sick."

"She's sick? But I saw her just—"

"You know, I might have taught you to trust me, but you didn't get my brains, girl. Fortunately, Wet Rain's got plenty of her own. She'll act plenty sick for a couple of days. And your step-father hates Blood Bear about as much as anyone does. Old Cut Feather was One Cast's best friend, you know. He thought of him like a father. He'll play his part. I wouldn't

have married him after your father died if he hadn't had sense
. . . and cared for you, too.

"So here's what we'll do. I'll sneak back with a pack and
you leave tonight. You know the trail to White Calf's. Go
fast, girl. You can be halfway there by morning. If anyone
asks, I'll tell them you've gone to get medicine for Wet Rain's
stomach ache. I'll send word when it's safe to come back."

"And Blood Bear?"

"He'll believe it."

The stars hadn't passed a hand's breadth across the sky
when a dark figure slipped from the menstrual lodge.

Within moments, Rattling Hooves ducked out behind her
daughter. Thoughtfully she stared down the night-shadowed
trail. Elk Charm would be starting to realize what she'd un-
dertaken. Traveling alone through the middle of the night on
an unfamiliar trail would daunt all but the most courageous
of hunters. Elk Charm would brave the dark, and the possi-
bility of ghosts, and perhaps even a fall-hungry grizzly. Anything would be better than Blood Bear.

Rattling Hooves walked wearily down toward the lodge.
With Wet Rain playing sick, she'd have twice the chores to
do. The lot of a second wife could be considerably worse
than she got from One Cast and Wet Rain. Still, she'd always
felt like an interloper, intruding on their happiness. One Cast
and Wet Rain had never made her feel less than welcome,
but she couldn't shake the subtle feeling of intruding. She
would never share that intimacy they did. Some people just
fit together like that. One Cast and Wet Rain might have been
made as two pieces—male and female—of a unique whole.

Thinking about it, she experienced a pang of regret. She'd
loved like that once. If only he hadn't gone traveling in the
winter. The snow always became treacherous in spring. They
hadn't found his body until almost midsummer. And the hole
left by his death could never be filled.

She sent one last nervous look down the trail, heart-worried
about her daughter. What a terrible way to come into womanhood.

* * *

"Sometimes I wonder about your faith in the boy. He's wild, resentful."

"That's the strength of his father," Wolf Dreamer reminded him from within the translucent golden hues of the Spiral.

"I live with his father! Too much of his insolence has gone into the boy."

"Wolf Bundle, you yourself are created of disparate pieces. Each has its part in Power. Together we manipulated the Circles to get the boy. Did you complain then?"

"My Power wasn't leaking away then. I didn't experience the sensation of my own slow death. We've taken a terrible risk. I've seen the boy through the Watcher's eyes. You know we can't affect his will. He will be what he will be. And I see trouble."

"We never had any guarantees. The future is a murky place."

"He fights the Dreams. He'll fight us just as vigorously."

Silence . . .

Chapter 12 ✋

Behind the boy, a nameless terror stalked the ridge, the fetid odor of its breath—that of a carrion-feeding bear—warm on the back of his neck. He tried to look, tried to glance over his shoulder to see the horror, but his balance fled at every attempt, leaving him flailing his arms to keep his precarious footing.

Death followed, snapping at his heels. He could imagine the silver drool running in strands from the monster's teeth.

His only escape consisted of a dangerous path along a knife-edged ridge of sharp gray granite. Sheer walls fell off to either side, endless, dropping into a dizzying depth. Around him, the clouds scudded past, partially blotting the deep blue of the sky. Wind batted at him as he tried to keep his footing on the hazardous slope.

He jumped frantically from one rock to another, terror powering his leaps over infinity. There, ahead of him, his mother clung to the rock, blocking the way. She looked back at him with a sickening anguish in her face. Wind whipped her long black hair, partially obscuring her features as she blinked against the gale. Her fingers wove into the very rock, locking her in place.

"*Hurry!* It's too close. You've got to keep going, son." The wind ripped his mother's frantic cries away and hurled them into the vastness. "Go. Climb over me."

As he teetered, unwilling, her face grew ashen, her skin hard, turning to stone as he watched in horror.

"No!" he cried into the vastness. The whistling wind sought to knock him off. He could feel the thing behind him extend its neck and open its corrupt mouth to snap at him.

"Mother?" Desperate, he jumped, the rounded mass of her back taking his weight.

He could feel the presence of the nightmare thing behind him, looming up, reaching even as he scrambled to find footing on the rock that had once been his mother. As he changed his balance, the rock shifted, grating and vibrating.

Sobbing with fear, he looked down. The rock with his mother's face cascaded into the depths, debris falling to clatter against the cliff.

The unseen horror reached for him as he crabbed along the thin, friable rock. He jumped for a huge flat space that turned into Chokecherry's back as he landed. The old woman looked up at him, a crafty smile forming on her lips. But then she shifted, as if trying to pitch him off into the abyss.

Little Dancer braced his feet, grabbing for the ridge beyond. He caught a glimpse of Chokecherry's body solidifying into gray granite and plunging into the depths under his weight. His grip held as Chokecherry's rock crashed down the precipice in a shower of tumbling scree. Teeth chattering, he got his feet under him, pulling his body back onto the trail and grimacing as the rock cut into his flesh.

Breath catching in his throat, Little Dancer hurried forward, searching for footing on the treacherous edge, feeling the claws of death again at his back. A grating of crushed gravel sounded behind him as a huge weight bore down on the ridge.

Two Smokes looked up at him from underfoot, the berdache's face forming below him in the uneven granite. Even as he stared down in horror, his friend's eyes dimmed to stone, the rock shifting and crumbling beneath him. What had been Two Smokes rolled loose to plunge into the eternity below. Little Dancer threw himself ahead again, shivering with each gust of wind.

Looking down, he saw that his father now stared up at him, inevitably turning into stone. Little Dancer began to sob, forcing himself to scramble across the shifting rock, knowing even as it took his weight that this too would betray him.

The monstrous thing behind him leaned closer, the bulk of it obscuring the sun. Its breath choked the wind in his throat.

"I could save you," White Calf's voice called from somewhere ahead.

Little Dancer's heart pounded with fear as the rock that had been his father cracked loose and slid sickeningly sideways.

What to do?

Behind him, the horror laughed: *"Too late."* Heavy Beaver!

Little Dancer froze, fingers gripping tightly to the rock that had been his father. The horizon tilted, gravel pelting him as together they fell into the abyss.

"Fool!" White Calf cried.

Heavy Beaver cackled with glee.

Little Dancer's stomach rose into his throat. Nausea tickled the back of his tongue and left him dizzy. His father's terrified voice shrieked into the nothingness below. Wind howled past his ears, tearing at his clothes and burning the tears into his blurred eyes as the faraway rocks rushed up at them.

Falling . . . falling . . .

Little Dancer's eyes jerked open the second before he knew he hit bottom. A lurching jumped in his gut as he sucked a fevered breath into heaving lungs. He trembled as the after-images of the Dream faded to startled wakefulness.

He stared around the dawn-gray meadow and shivered with

the morning chill, seeing the faint, hoary trace of frost on the leaves. Here, at the edge of the timber, the plants still stood lush and green. A raven chattered and clacked in the trees behind him. Somewhere in the timber a loud pop sounded as a squirrel cut fir cones loose and dropped them onto the deadfall below.

Above, the sky remained shrouded in gray.

He sat up in a cascade of needles from where he'd burrowed into the duff beneath an old forest giant. Little Dancer stretched, a gnawing emptiness in his belly.

He crawled out and looked around, snaking fingers through his long hair to comb the brown needles free. Images from the Dream haunted him. Dully he braided his hair and started across the meadow. The night chill cramped his muscles and left him unsure on his feet.

A chickadee greeted the bracing morning while a squirrel chirred into crisp air before scrambling from one branch to another.

Crossing a timbered patch, he encountered a rocky upthrust ridge and looked over the edge. Below him the meadow narrowed, restricted by steep sandstone walls. A fence had been constructed of timber carefully placed for strength and height to run diagonally across the browning grass—Hungry Bull's drive line.

Sighing with relief, Little Dancer eased across the rocks, glancing quickly over his shoulder before starting down the slope. Even as he reached the level bottoms, a thin tendril of smoke rose from the trees.

He smiled and forced his wobbly legs forward in a trot.

Hungry Bill crouched before a small fire, the freshly killed carcass of a snowshoe hare wide-splayed and roasting on the hot rocks. With the canny eyes of the hunter, Hungry Bull had already seen him and raised a hand in greeting.

"Had to get away?"

Little Dancer nodded, coming to sit next to his father, sharing the moment of camaraderie. "Got lost last night. Didn't know I was this close."

For long moments they sat in silence.

"How's the trap coming?"

"Almost done, you can help me finish today. With the first

snow, there should be buffalo starting to move down from the high meadows. There's a herd up in the valley above us. They'll want to follow this trail. We should be able to get enough to keep through winter.'' He raised his eyes to the gray skies. ''We'll do fine if we make a kill and it freezes good and solid. That's the best way. Kill late like this and let it freeze. The meat'll keep all winter.''

They ate in silence, Little Dancer's mouth watering as he tore into the hot flesh of the rabbit.

When bones had been cracked and sucked empty of marrow, they were thrown into the fire to char into memory. They walked over to stare at the trap.

''You think this will hold buffalo?'' Little Dancer cocked his head skeptically.

Hungry Bull smiled, narrowing his eyes. ''Part of a hunter's success is to know more of the animals than they know of themselves.'' He pointed. ''You see how I placed the roots and branches? See how the sharp points are sticking out? There's a reason for that. Buffalo look stupid and half-asleep. But they're thinking all the time—as Two Smokes found out when he misjudged them at Monster Bone Springs. Even though they look sleepy and dumb, they're always ready, waiting . . . and lightning fast on their feet. They can whirl in a blink, despite how clumsy they look. They don't like to be forced against a wall, you see. And they have a thin hide that tears easily and they know it.

''So look at how I built this. A good hunter knows that the buffalo will bear away from the snags. He knows that they'll want to mill out there in the center, where they can see all around. The lead cow will take a minute to decide what to do when the way is blocked. That's why I placed the fence so. I'll want that moment of indecision to drive a dart into the lead cow.''

''And you'll be up on that ledge?'' Little Dancer pointed to a sandstone outcrop slightly above the kill area.

''You've got more hunter in you than I thought. That's just where I'll be. Not only does a hunter have to know his animals, he's got to know what he has to work with. That's why the shape is like it is. This trap could be worked by one person. With just the two of us it will work better. We'll need to start the drive and drift them down here. We don't want to panic them, just urge them down slowly. Then, when they wander into the trap, I've got to run up there to the point. Meanwhile, you're over behind that stump there. If they shy from my darts, they drift right into yours.''

"Until one panics and breaks down the fence."

"But by then . . . if we haven't panicked ourselves . . . we'll have killed, or seriously wounded, enough to keep us through the winter.''

"But you don't make a trap like this in spring."

Hungry Bull propped his hands on his hips. "Wouldn't work. Buffalo act differently in the spring. Cows have new calves. They're more wary, nervous, because the calves are vulnerable. Old bulls are on edge and acting protective. Strategies for taking animals have to change with the season. Doesn't matter how straight or far you can cast a dart if you don't know how to work the animals. You have to know how they change and think differently with the seasons, or you're going to starve—or eat plants all your life like the Anit'ah!''

Little Dancer lifted an eyebrow. They'd eaten a lot of plants recently, at Two Smokes' urging. He'd developed a liking for sego lily and biscuit root. In the fall, chokecherries and plums made a wonderful treat. Serviceberry had become one of his favorite meals.

"Buffalo are the most important thing in the world to you, aren't they?''

"Part of my soul is buffalo." Hungry Bull stared thoughtfully into the distance as they walked toward the trees. "It hurts to think that buffalo are so scarce. I remember the stories from when I was a boy. I remember my grandfather talking about the old days when a couple hundred would be killed at a time. Then the People were so numerous we could run a big kill. Everyone had a specific duty in the kill. The circles were complete then. Buffalo and the People were one. They fed us and we prayed for their souls to the Wise One Above. Our souls mixed with buffalo as theirs mixed with ours.''

"And here?''

"Here I'll manage to trap maybe ten or fifteen buffalo. More than enough to feed us, but not so many as my skill would permit if there were more buffalo up here." He hesitated. "Maybe that's the way it should be. A wise hunter takes only what he needs and a bit more for surplus in case something spoils too soon, or wolf or coyote or a grizzly gets into it."

Little Dancer grabbed the small end of a lodgepole his father indicated. He lifted and followed, staggering under the long pole. Straining, he got his end into the fence where his father indicated.

Did the past always outshine the future? Did life always have to get worse instead of better? It seemed that way. How many times had he overheard White Calf saying the world was changing? And if it kept getting worse, whatever would become of him? The images from the Dream ate at his peace. The people in his life had turned to unstable stone under his feet, seeking to drop him into the abyss. He caught himself staring uneasily at his father's broad back as they laid pole upon pole onto the fence.

Using a sharp chert flake he'd struck from a well-used core, Blood Bear absently shaved at a thumb-thick willow stalk. Under his practiced hands, the bark peeled in long curling strips to expose the white wood beneath. This piece would make a wonderful dart shaft. One end he would hollow and fletch to rest in the atlatl hook he'd laboriously carved from moose antler, traded from north of the Big River by Three Rattles. The other end would be countersunk to create a socket for a foreshaft made of hardwood like chokecherry or ash.

He walked as he whittled on the shaft, absently glancing up at the menstrual lodge. Elk Charm should have already made her way to One Cast's lodge. He'd been up since before dawn, waiting at the edge of camp. She should have come. And if he'd missed her, she should have had to excuse herself to the bushes by now. So where had she gone?

She'd always intrigued him. Despite her young age, the way she walked so straight and poised had caught his eye more than once over the last year or so. He'd watched with growing interest as her coming womanhood had become apparent. Of all the women, she and Tanager would be the most beautiful. Tanager would be the most passionate, proud, and stubborn—provided anyone could catch her long enough to bed her. Elk Charm, however, had a vulnerability that piqued his desire. She always had her chin just so, as if she were shyly aware of her beauty and charm. Her hips curved nicely over her thin, long legs. When she didn't wear her hair in a braid, it hung down below her waist in a blue-black wave that caught the sunlight and sent it gleaming into a thousand separate rays of light. Most of all, he enjoyed those dancing eyes of hers. Blood Bear, for all of his advancing age, would see those eyes shine for him.

He frowned slightly, sighting down the shaft of his new dart . . . and right into the menstrual lodge. Despite the morning shadows, he could tell no one sat within.

Perplexed, he wandered slowly up the path, eyes on the ground as he shaved a knot flush to the shaft. The long years of hunting and tracking stood him in good stead. Here Rattling Hooves had walked up the path and returned. As he neared the entrance, he found a fainter imprint half-scuffed in the dry grass. Elk Charm! It had to be.

Frowning slightly, he continued his perambulations, slowly circling the camp, checking for tracks. Curious. Usually a newly made woman finished her bleeding and came to camp surrounded in the glow of her bashful pride. Saucy Elk Charm should have done exactly that, basking in her glory at this most auspicious of occasions.

Another track. He whistled to himself, walking along, mind racing while he studiously worked on his dart shaft. Elk Charm had taken the trail south. No doubt of that.

He paused, staring down the trail, knowing the way it ran along the upper reaches of Clear River before it turned east to drop into the canyon and finally tumble out through the Red Wall and into the plains beyond where it ran into Mud River in the land of the Short Buffalo People.

So what was down there? Why would a freshly made woman miss all the celebrating in her honor? Why would she miss the chance to hear everyone compliment her and receive the gifts that would come her way?

Blood Bear sucked at his lip and backtracked to his lodge. He checked, as he always did, to see the Wolf Bundle on the tripod at the rear of the lodge. Silly thing. For all the time he'd been forced to listen to Cut Feather talk about the bundle's Power, he'd never experienced it. During the last four years since he'd walked into the main Red Hand camp, the Wolf Bundle held high over his head in triumph, he'd never felt the slightest tingle of Power.

"Cut Feather was a fool," he grumbled. "My people are as great a bunch of fools for believing such nonsense."

He reached over, thumping the Wolf Bundle with a thick forefinger. "Take that, Wolf Bundle. I found you and brought you back. Me, Blood Bear! And without any Power!" He lifted his lip and snorted. "And what good did you do the berdache? Huh? For all the time he had you, he's a cripple now, living on the charity of White Calf, an outcast Short Buffalo hunter, and *my* goodwill!" He shook his head. "Fool!"

He opened one of the packs laid against the rear wall and found what he'd been searching for, bringing forth a small pouch. He undid the knot at the top and poured out the contents: six beautiful elk ivories extracted from the upper jaws of young bulls.

He poured them back into the pouch and ducked out of his lodge, strolling lazily across the camp.

"Is anyone home in the lodge of One Cast?" he called pleasantly. "Blood Bear comes on this special morning with a gift for a new woman."

"Just a minute." He recognized Rattling Hooves and heard the shifting about inside. Too bad about her. If only he'd been around when her first husband stepped out on that unstable snow and triggered the avalanche that killed him. She would have been worthy of him. Not even a fool could wonder where her daughter came by her beauty and charm.

Rattling Hooves ducked through the flap. He caught the sleepless look in her eyes, noting the tight lines around her mouth.

"I would offer a gift to the daughter of One Cast. I hear she is a new woman among us."

Rattling Hooves smiled uneasily. "She'd be honored, but she's not here. It's Wet Rain. . . . Well, maybe she ate too much yesterday. In the middle of the night she woke up com-

plaining about her stomach. A fever and chills followed.''
Rattling Hooves ran a nervous hand through her hair, expression pinching with worry. ''I don't know. In the dark of
night, maybe I panicked. Anyhow, I sent Elk Charm off to
White Calf's for something to help her stomach.''

''I have the Wolf Bundle.'' He crossed his arms, considering. Elk Charm would be on the trail to White Calf's? She'd
be alone, anxious to try her womanhood out on the first man
to come along. ''I had planned to go hunting today. Perhaps
if I left the Wolf Bundle here, it might help. You must care
for it while I'm gone, however.''

A gleam grew in Rattling Hooves' eyes, her lips parting
slightly.

Blood Bear managed to keep his features under control.
Idiot woman; she, too, insisted on believing the old bag contained Power. Who knew, maybe that would work to his advantage in the future. And if Elk Charm delighted him as
much as he hoped she would, maybe that lure of power would
lead Rattling Hooves to favor a marriage?

''We'd appreciate that. We'll take very good care of it and
honor it the whole time it's within our lodge.''

He smiled, mind already on the trail to White Calf's.
''Good, I'll fetch it.''

He turned on his heel, walking rapidly for his lodge.

Snaps Horn waited quietly in the trees. Like the hunter he
was becoming, his outline could barely be distinguished.
Tanager moved carefully, testing her skill against his. She
slithered through the branches that hung down. Each foot she
placed just so, settling her weight around the dry twigs, balancing to keep from crackling the brown needles underfoot.

Snaps Horn shifted, moving slowly to crane his neck and
look down the trail. He started and froze.

Tanager hardly breathed. She could hear footsteps on the
trail. Warily, she noted how Snaps Horn tensed, sinking down
to obscure his form in the grass that veiled the fir. Who did
her friend hide from?

She caught a flicker of movement, and remained motionless as Blood Bear trotted past. From Snaps Horn's tensed

posture, she read his dislike. The silence stretched before Snaps Horn finally straightened.

Tanager resumed her stalking, moving to within easy reach before she shot hard fingers into Snaps Horn's ribs.

"*Got ya!*" And she raced away, while Snaps Horn cried in horror and whirled.

Bursting through the trees, she waited to see if he'd chase.

He exploded from the thrashing fir branches and slid to a stop, face a masterwork of convulsed anger.

"Don't! *Don't ever do that again!*" He stamped, gesturing, shaking with rage. But he wasn't going to chase. She could see that.

She cocked her head. "So, who you going to ambush?"

"None of your business, *girl!*"

"Ah! Elk Charm!"

His crimson features went bright.

Tanager grinned. "Well, you and Blood Bear are in the same fix. She's not here. She went down to the witch's."

Snaps Horn gaped. "But there's Short Buffalo People there."

"Uh-huh, but there's no Blood Bear. And no *you!*"

He bellowed and leapt for her. She danced away, ducking effortlessly under his grasping arms. Dashing away like the wind, her heart exalted. She had her chase!

Three Toes pulled at the long braid hanging over his left shoulder. The crawling feeling in his gut didn't diminish no matter how hard he pulled. He stood on an isolated outcrop of gray limestone thrust far enough up from the spine of the mountain to allow him to see over the surrounding wall of fir trees.

The crisp air carried a pungent tang of conifer and damp earth. High above, a golden eagle shifted on the ghostly thermals. An elk bugled shrilly and angrily somewhere to the west in the black timber.

Cloud-capped peaks rose to the north, a white dusting of snow visible below the punctured belly of the fluffy clouds. Between him and the peaks stretched an endless expanse of uplifted and rugged country swelling to rounded summits, broken ridges, and cracked-looking canyons—all of it carpeted with a thick mosaic of trees. Ancient burns made a patchwork of forest where lightning had caught the old growth with high fuel load during the drought.

He looked back to the south, grinding his molars. More broken country—but the peaks weren't as tall, and he couldn't see any snowfall there. A taller ridge rose to the west and obscured the view in that direction. Traveling east couldn't even be considered since an impassable jagged canyon had been gouged through the mountain's bones.

"Well?" Black Crow called up.

Three Toes filled his lungs full to bursting and exhaled slowly, savoring the feeling. "We're lost."

"Great!" Black Crow slapped angry hands to his sides. "And the Anit'ah know all the trails up here. That makes me feel just wonderful!"

Three Toes took another breath, wondering just how many more he'd get if they didn't find White Calf.

Little Dancer paused for a second to catch his breath and rest his quivering legs. To lessen the load on his hips and knees, he bent double, bracing his arms on his kneecaps to support the weight. His ankles didn't hurt, but everything else did.

The pack on his back had to weigh nearly as much as he did. The broad leather of the tumpline cut into the skin on his forehead—long since gone itchy and numb from lack of blood. Despite the weight, he couldn't help but smile.

His first buffalo! Under the guidance of his father, they'd worked the trap perfectly. Hungry Bull had known exactly what the buffalo would do. Together they'd cautiously pushed the animals down the valley and into the trap.

Sprinting to his controlling position, Hungry Bull had driven his first dart deep into the lead cow's side. His second dart penetrated a younger cow's rib cage. As the rest began milling, they'd stayed well clear of the sharp snags woven into the trap fence.

Little Dancer's chance came as a young cow backed away from the killing area, nostrils distended, head lowered as she grunted at the smell of blood. The shot had been perfect. From no more than ten paces, he'd driven his dart from slightly behind, through the diaphragm and into the lungs. The young cow had jumped, kicked out behind her, and puffed a frightened breath. Moaning, she'd trotted forward from the group—and fallen over to wheeze and bleed her life away on the red-matted grass.

One by one, they killed seven of the buffalo before the milling bunch crowded a crazed cow into the fence. She dropped her chin, goaded by the branches, and with one toss of her head, demolished most of the fence, goring one of her fellows in the process. In the melee that followed, all but the desperately wounded had fled down the valley, seeking the safety of the winter range below.

Little Dancer had stopped short then, feeling the awe of having killed so large a beast with his hand-crafted dart. Under White Calf's tutelage, he'd breathed Spirit Power into wood, stone, and binding. The act of knapping out the fine chert into finished points had left his fingers laced with cuts. Enough of his blood had grimed the razor-edged points to imbue them with soul and the power to kill.

Now it had all come full circle. He sucked the cool air into his lungs, too happy to care that his leg muscles burned from the added weight. He, Little Dancer, brought his first meat back to camp. In the joy of that occasion, even the prospect of facing White Calf didn't matter so much.

He steeled himself, and straightened, joints complaining. Blinking against the stress, he started the last couple of lengths to White Calf's rock shelter.

He didn't even hear his father's approach. "You all right?"

"I think my back's broken. I keep waiting to hear my bones crack and snap."

"You'll get used to it."

"Oh . . . sure, and I'll be two hands shorter!"

He swallowed against his dry throat and forced himself to stare at the comforting hollow of White Calf's shelter. Not far now, only a little while longer. Pace by burning pace he made it, gasping and wheezing up the last little rise, taking short quick steps.

"A little farther, that's all," his father's voice soothed.

He started across the trampled grass, all set to shout and drop the load—when the girl stepped out.

Girl? He stopped, blinking, lifting his head without thinking. Suddenly off balance, the load pulled him over backwards. His arms flailed futilely in the air. He yipped as he tumbled, the pack almost breaking his neck as he sat down too hard.

Lights flashed in his eyes, the world spinning. He barely felt his feet slam down hard in the dust.

He flushed at the girl's tinkling laughter.

"How does it feel?" Wolf Dreamer asked, the haze rippling with his voice.

"As if I were evaporating. Power dissipates. Blood Bear wastes. Every time he mocks, that which I am is less. At night, when he sleeps, I play with his life, knowing I could snuff him like a burning twig in the dirt."

"Things have changed. Blood Bear is the cause of it."

"The girl?"

Wolf Dreamer's voice gentled. "I am worried. We could lose the boy to love. I know the Power of it. I know how love can wind itself up in the Power and lead to disaster. Once, I, too, came close to disaster because of love."

"I may be diminished, but I could still reach out, remove the threat created by Elk Charm. She is nothing."

"You are angry; you always wish to strike out. I would . . . well, grant him time I never had. Perhaps she's a way to reach him. Overcome the damage Sage Root did. The Watcher will know."

"Don't hesitate too long, Wolf Dreamer. The way humans experience time works against us now. I feel that we're coming to the end . . . one way or another, and very soon."

Chapter 13 ✋

Life worked in a curious fashion, Blood Bear decided as he trotted along, wary eyes on the trees around him. He'd left in search of a wayward girl he hoped to fill with his child. Instead, he'd stumbled onto the tracks of Short Buffalo People in the heart of his domain. The sting of last year's raid still ate at him.

They'd come in the early morning as the sun grayed the eastern horizon. In the confusion that followed, Blood Bear had charged out, darts in hand, to see the Spirit Dreamer he'd observed the day he'd stolen the Wolf Bundle, singing and exhorting warriors to kill the Red Hand.

A smoldering anger refused to die as he thought about that day. Perhaps, had he remained, he could have rallied his people to fight back. Instead, his first thought had been that the Short Buffalo wanted to steal the Wolf Bundle back. If they had, they might have broken his hold on the Red Hand. To have lost the Bundle once was bad enough, but twice? Unthinkable!

So he'd grabbed up the Bundle and run. The Red Hand had not stayed to fight, seeing his own inglorious retreat. His warriors fled, too, lost heart at his flight, and broke under the attack, leaving the camp to the howling, dancing Short Buffalo People. They looted everything and burned what was left. A man and two women had been killed, darts catching them in the backs as they ran. Some children had been captured along with a couple of women.

Disaster, all in all.

Now he had another chance. Now he could lead the Red Hand in retaliation against their enemy. Of course, Elk Charm remained out on the trail somewhere, but if the Short Buffalo People didn't get her, she'd still be around for his pleasure when this other business had been brought to a successful conclusion.

He burst from the trees, heart leaping as he found the camp peacefully intact.

"Red Hand!" he called out, waving furiously. "Grab your weapons! The Short Buffalo People have come again! This time, let us surprise them!"

Within minutes, he was leading his hunters back down the trail. All that remained was to locate the tracks of the intruders, hunt them down, and kill every last one.

The fire crackled and popped, sending flickers of yellow light to play on the soot-thick ceiling of White Calf's shelter. The air swelled with the scent of roasting buffalo hump and boiling tongue mixed with dock, wild onion, cattail root, bee-plant leaves, and sego-lily root.

Little Dancer worked his sore shoulders, feeling the pinch of overtaxed joints. Tomorrow, every muscle in his body would be screaming. He looked over to where his father sat beside a rack of drying meat. Satisfaction filled Hungry Bull's face, animation from the success of the hunt momentarily replacing the sadness that normally filled his eyes. Two Smokes propped himself against the back wall, agile fingers working supple leather as he trimmed cured hide for moccasin soles to shape with a sharp chert flake. Elk Charm stood at the rear of the shelter, studying the hanging bundles and medicine bags. The firelight played in her shimmering hair. Little Dancer couldn't keep his eyes off the girl as she moved, graceful, like a deer in fresh snow. White Calf sat by the fire, fussing with the coals with a piece of firewood.

Little Dancer watched uneasily as White Calf bent forward, staring into the buffalo-gut paunch that hung from the juniper-wood tripod. "It could use another couple of stones. It's steaming, but we want to keep a good boil in it."

Elk Charm hurried to help and used the hearth sticks to grab another cobble from the glowing coals and drop it sizzling into the stew. Bright black eyes flashed in his direction as she replaced the sticks.

A curious feeling, a warm excitement, formed deep inside Little Dancer—and it heightened as their eyes met. The air between them might have been charged, so painfully could he feel her presence. What was it about her? Why couldn't he get her out of his mind?

He dropped his gaze, amazed to find himself awkwardly engrossed with his fumbling hands. Try as he might, he couldn't still his fingers. Every nerve in his body demanded he do something. He stood up, paced a couple of steps, and dropped to squat where he'd been in the beginning. From the corner of his eye, he glimpsed the girl's amused smile as she sought to avoid his glance.

The Red Hand had passed through and camped near White Calf's more than once over the years. On those instances, he'd played with the children. He'd even met Elk Charm a time or two. One time, he'd spent an afternoon with her and a couple of other children playing at stick and hoop, laughing and running. So why hadn't he noticed the tones of her skin, the way her hair gleamed in the light, or the mysterious depth in her dark eyes before? Now her every movement absorbed him, almost to the point of being painful. No matter how he tried to center his attention on other things, he couldn't help sneaking a glance at her, wishing she'd smile at him, talk to him.

For the moment, the girl had involved herself with a careful study of the spiral pecked into the rear wall. White Calf had daubed the lines with yellow from crushed balsam flowers.

Elk Charm reached up to touch it, her finger lingering on the stone before she looked at White Calf. "There are a lot of spirals like this pecked into the rocks on the north side of the mountains. I remember them from when I was a girl. We'd camped there to meet with the White Crane People. I think they were trading."

White Calf nodded. She'd been curiously reserved for once, her predatory gaze going first to the girl and then to him. He hated it when her eyes got that smoky, veiled look. Some worry preoccupied her, an uneasy premonition lurking in her mind. What had he done to stir her cranky soul this time?

As if the morning breeze had shifted to blow a clinging smoke away, Little Dancer realized it wasn't him, but Elk

Charm. White Calf didn't want Elk Charm around. He perked up. Why? What was it about her?

"You know about the Spiral?" White Calf asked, shifting her glance to Elk Charm.

"Just that it's Powerful. It's old, isn't it? Something from the time of the Monster Children and the Hero Twins?"

White Calf smiled wistfully, eyes going to the rock art. "Yes, child, it's old. The Spiral is as old as First Man. In the beginning, the Wise One Above made a world. Then he made animals and men. For a long time things were good. Then, like always, something came along to mess it up. It might have been the people. Maybe it was the animals, but somewhere, the One of creation got separated. Split apart. Everything started going in different directions. Humans came to believe they were the most important beings in the First World and they ceased to thank the animals and plants for giving themselves as food. Animals started to think they were the most important, and they left the people to starve, refusing to offer themselves to be killed. Like a flawed chert nodule struck with a hammerstone, it all shattered into different directions and nothing fit together anymore."

Elk Charm's face lit, enraptured as she stared at the spiral. Little Dancer watched her fingers trace the carving, a curious sense of premonition spreading in his breast.

"Seeing all the trouble, Wise One Above got disgusted with everything," White Calf continued, "and made a new world for himself. Turning himself into Crafty Spider, he spun the Starweb—the Second World. He figured that humans, in their physical bodies, couldn't get there and mess it up. Except he was wrong. No sooner had he finished the Second World than all the souls of people who'd died started to rise up and fill the Starweb. They became the stars we see in the sky."

"But that didn't fix the trouble on the First World. It just crowded the Starweb, right?" Elk Charm flashed a hopeful look at White Calf, hanging on each word.

The girl's interest overrode White Calf's suspicions and she launched into the story, animation in her old eyes. "Yes, things were still bad in the First World—everything all split up and men and animals all fussing and fighting. Wise One

Above thought about it and he saw a way he might be able to fix it. He created another world, the Third World, and filled it with spirits to help people when they asked for it. Wise One Above made Dreams so that spirits could talk from the Third World to people in the First. For a while things were better, but the First World still had bad things in it.''

"And is that where Dreamers come from?" Elk Charm asked.

"You know this story," White Calf chided. "Dreamers are the key to keeping things in balance. They make everything right again, and Dance along the Spiral."

"You're losing your place, old woman," Two Smokes called from the side. "Get on with the story."

White Calf shot him a withering glare. "Yes, well, about that time, the Hero Twins—First Man and his twin brother—were born in the First World. Something happened and their mother died and left the boys all alone. Wise One Above could feel the Power of a Dreamer, but which child would it be? He couldn't just let one die, because a Dreamer might be able to fix the First World and make it right again, so he called out and told Wolf—who is always smart and cunning—to go find the babies. Wolf found the little boys lying alongside a beach next to an ocean and raised them. First Man liked the day and lived in the light. His brother liked the darkness and hid and schemed.

"Meanwhile, Wise One Above decided that he'd start over and make a new world, a Fourth World. When he made it, he thought it was good. So he called to Wolf and told him to find all the good animals and bring them through an underground hole to the new world. Wolf did this and led all the animals into the Fourth World—this world we're in now—and saw how wonderful it was."

"Then what about First Man?" Little Dancer asked. "If Wolf only led animals, then First Man was still on the other side."

White Calf studied him for a moment, nodding. "That's right. First Man and his brother were on the other side of the hole between the worlds. But Wolf got lonely because he had to leave his two human children behind. So what he did, he Dreamed the Wolf Dream to First Man and gave him the

Wolf Bundle to use as a guide to bring the good people from the First World. First Man did this, leading the good people up from under the earth. Some say the hole was through ice. Others say it was through a tunnel in the sky, and sometimes it's told as being through rock, but no matter how, they came into this world.''

''But the bad brother followed?''

''Yes, First Man's brother followed him and brought evil with him.

''When First Man saw what had happened he hit his brother on the head and cut him open. The bad brother ran off into the night, bleeding. That's why, to this day, you can find red chert. That's where his blood went into the ground and turned to rock.''

''But that doesn't have anything to do with Spirals,'' Elk Charm pointed out.

White Calf clapped her hands, a big smile creasing her ancient face. Her eyes gleamed, fired by the enthusiasm of her audience. ''Ah! But it does! You see, after he'd killed his brother, First Man drew the Spiral to remind people that everything is One. He hoped that maybe that way he could keep the bad things from happening. So long as people remember that a spiral is a circle within a circle without end, they'll never forget the One. Never allow the world to fragment and break apart and become separated like happened in the First World. That's why we need a Dreamer, to Dance and keep the Spiral whole.''

''So that's why it's so Powerful? It reminds the People of the journey from the First World?'' Elk Charm's forehead lined as she inspected the Spiral.

White Calf nodded, a loose-lipped smile on her face. ''More than that, girl. The Spiral is the most powerful of *all* symbols. The Spiral is life. It's the whole of creation, everything within itself: unity. Beginning and end and the transition between. It's the circles within circles. The Oneness, the whole of Wise One Above right down to the smallest seed or bit of dust. Everything and nothing. One.''

''*One.*'' The call echoed in Little Dancer's head. For a brief instant, his vision shimmered and shifted. Slightly dizzy, he dropped his head down between his knees. When he pressed his eyes closed, afterimages of the Spiral burned on the backs of his eyelids, turning, spinning, encompassing his very soul. White Calf's reedy voice echoed in his mind: *"The whole of creation, everything within itself: unity."*

Too much work today, he lied to himself. *Should have carried a lighter pack. It's exhaustion. That's all.* He shook his head, as if to rid himself of the images spun by White Calf's story. When he lifted his head, White Calf had shifted, keen eyes missing no detail of his discomfort. He glared back, defensive.

The old woman sighed and mouthed her toothless gums as she sat down on her robe again. "So how long do you think you're here for?"

Elk Charm's eyes glowed with the magic of the old woman's story as she continued to stare at the big rock carving. "I don't know. Until my mother says Blood Bear has turned his mind to other things."

"Blood Bear?" Little Dancer frowned.

Two Smokes puffed at his pipe where he rested against a pack that had been propped along one wall. "It seems the leader of the Red Hand has developed an interest in Elk Charm since she's become a full woman. He would force himself on her."

"But rape—"

"It's different among the Red Hand." Two Smokes rubbed the back of his neck. "A man who forces a woman is ridiculed. What man wants it known that he isn't Powerful enough to win the woman he desires? Who wants to be a laughingstock? And, believe me, a forced woman would tell *everybody*! Men will exclude him from their company. Women will lift their skirts and tease him. Children will throw dung on him and urinate on his belongings. Who could live like that? The last man I know of who forced a woman was so shamed that he finally stripped himself naked and walked off into a winter blizzard to die rather than live like that."

"Then why would Blood Bear risk that?" Hungry Bull asked, looking up from inspecting his butchering tools.

Two Smokes lifted his hands wide. "Blood Bear is the Keeper of the Wolf Bundle. That gives him certain privileges. Elk Charm can tell any man no—any man but the Keeper of the Wolf Bundle. To deny the Keeper is to deny the Wolf Bundle. The Keeper and the Power are One. Do you see?''

''The Wolf Bundle.'' Little Dancer experienced a tug at his heart. He saw the tortured expression on Two Smokes' face. Until the day he died, the berdache would torment himself over the defiling and loss of the Wolf Bundle.

''It's not right,'' Hungry Bull insisted in his stilted Anit'ah speech. He lifted a mottled agate point up to study it. The rippled surface of the stone caught the firelight, gleaming like polished ice.

''Right or not,'' White Calf grumbled, resettling herself, ''the ways of the Red Hand are different from the ways of the Short Buffalo People. Not better, not worse, just different. Among the Red Hand, a woman doesn't normally marry until she's pregnant. The Red Hand place a great value on a woman's ability to bring life into the world. I remember the curious remarks when Clear Water went to Blood Bear. But then, she was a Spirit Woman.'' White Calf's eyes narrowed as she looked at Little Dancer. ''And I still haven't unraveled all the knots and twists in the weaving of her actions.''

Little Dancer dropped his gaze, pursing his lips. Two Smokes had finally told him about his real mother. Maybe it helped blunt the pain of Sage Root's death. Maybe it only made things worse.

''Blood Bear.'' Elk Charm shivered. ''He doesn't believe in Power.''

''Oh?'' White Calf snapped her head around.

Elk Charm bit her lip, looking suddenly ashamed.

''And how do you know this, newly made woman?''

Elk Charm swallowed hard, her glance darting about, looking for a means of escape. Seeing none, she sighed and explained, ''Tanager and I were hiding one day while Cricket was looking for us. We were back of Blood Bear's lodge. He was inside talking to himself and to the Wolf Bundle. I heard him thumping it with his finger and telling it how he didn't believe. We both got so scared we froze there. We didn't leave until hours later.''

Despite himself, Little Dancer gasped, staring at the girl in shock before his eyes were drawn to the Spiral; it seemed to twist and shimmer in the light, sucking him into the middle of the endless circles.

White Calf's face had hardened, a glint in her obsidian stare.

Two Smokes groaned under his breath, pained eyes focused somewhere only he could see. "But he cares for it? Keeps it safe anyway?"

"He guards it jealously." Elk Charm looked up uneasily.

"Of course he does," White Calf growled. "What would Blood Bear be without the Wolf Bundle? Remember how he was before he brought it back to the Red Hand?"

Two Smokes nodded miserably, hitching himself to his feet. Limping on his bad leg, he ducked out into the crisp night, the sound of his shuffling gait growing fainter in the darkness.

"Blood Bear will suffer in the end." Little Dancer shook his head, mesmerized by the Spiral. "He's a fool. I know, I felt the outrage that night. . . ." He started, suddenly realizing what he'd said. White Calf hadn't missed a word. One of the old woman's eyebrows lifted to crinkle the lines of her forehead.

"I didn't mean to hurt Two Smokes' feelings," Elk Charm apologized. "I didn't know he'd—"

"Hush, child." White Calf waved it away. "This stew's about done."

"Let's eat," Hungry Bull agreed. "Here we are, talking about all these terrible Power things. That's for Dreamers and Spirit Healers. Today we should celebrate. Little Dancer and I have made meat for the whole winter. We're forgetting that today my son is a man! He's killed his first buffalo. Maybe he's earned a man's name?"

A man's name? Little Dancer's heart leapt in his chest. Finally, after all these years?

"We could probably think up a name." White Calf frowned, chin propped on a withered arm. "Let's give it some thought. A man shouldn't be named just like that." She snapped her fingers in emphasis.

Elk Charm gave him an openly appraising look, a pensive anticipation in her eyes. Perhaps it was a trick of the light, but her cheeks seemed to redden.

He should have swelled up fit to burst himself open at the

ribs. He should have been jumping and hollering his joy, dancing and singing his adulthood. Instead he stood, stepping over to touch the deep grooves of the spiral. The stone felt warm and gritty under his fingertips. He couldn't forget the pain in Two Smokes' face, the words about the Wolf Bundle, and First Man, and Blood Bear. He could feel Elk Charm's presence as she came to stand beside him. White Calf's eyes burned into his back with the intensity of glowing coals. Power pulsed on the night.

Outside, beyond the hangings, a wolf howled anxiously.

Rattling Hooves trotted down the trail in the swinging gait of a woman used to traveling. To either side, the tightly growing firs stretched toward the cloud-mottled sky above. The first frost had passed. Humans and animals would have a reprieve before the real breath of winter blew down to lock the Buffalo Mountains in their white grip.

She slowed, climbing over a deadfall blocking the trail. Elk had already broken most of the branches, making it easier to swing her legs across. Her dress caught on a snag. With old familiarity, she broke it off with a loud snap and continued on down the trail to White Calf's.

So, it had all worked out sooner than she could have thought. Blood Bear had found sign of Short Buffalo People on his fruitless hunt for Elk Charm. Good luck had a way of cropping up periodically. Perhaps by the time the hunt for the raiders wound down, Elk Charm might have had enough men to dull Blood Bear's interest. Perhaps one might even have made an offer to marry her if she conceived. Many things could happen.

She filled her lungs happily, exhaling as she resumed her distance-eating gait down the game trail.

The track barely registered in the hardening mud of the trail. She slowed, stooping to inspect the track. No! They wouldn't be here. Not on this back trail so far from the buffalo tracks that led to the plains to the east.

Slowly she began to back away.

She didn't have time to draw a breath as a hard arm slipped around her. A muscular hand clapped over her mouth, cutting off her scream.

* * *

"I get the feeling White Calf doesn't want me here." Elk Charm tilted her head to watch Two Smokes' expression.

He rubbed at his brow, slapping at a fly that insisted on pestering him. They sat on the slope several dart casts south of the shelter, enjoying the golden sunshine. Even the sky reflected the peace of the day, stretching forever in an incredibly blue canopy that dazzled the eyes. Here and there a brilliantly white fluff of cloud coasted slowly, changing shape as it crossed the sky. A chipmunk paid them modest attention as it continued its routine of clipping the spikes from the sagebrush around them, nibbling off the tiny seeds until it filled cheek pouches to brimming and skittered off with a stiffly erect tail to cache them.

Elk Charm glanced skeptically at the pile of reddish-gray bark beside her. The hairy pile didn't seem to be getting any smaller. As they talked, they worked the long thin strips of juniper bark Two Smokes had laboriously stripped from the trees during the summer. Elk Charm's quick fingers spun them into a strand, rubbing it between her palms like a fire stick before twining the endless length. Two Smokes laced the strands back and forth and knotted them neatly, creating a section of net the height of a tall man.

Warm wind sighed through the weather-gnarled trees around them. The delightful sun warmed the rocks and shot through the fall-dried grasses in tawny colors. The late flowers turned yellow heads toward Father Sun's gentle caress.

"It's not you. Normally, White Calf would be talking your ear off trying to get you to learn all about the plants and things. She'd be telling you endlessly how to do this and that. It's Little Dancer she's worried about."

"He seems nice."

"That's what she's worried about."

Elk Charm's fingers slowed. She looked up at him frankly. "That he's nice?"

"No . . . it's that *you* think so."

"So?"

"So, he's a young man . . . as you're a young woman."

"That's bad?"

Two Smokes moved with the speed of a falcon, slapping at

the fly. He grinned, looking at the mashed body smeared on his palm. "Not bad for an old berdache, eh?" Then he got back to the subject. "Little Dancer has Power. White Calf worries that if he gets involved with a woman—namely you, since you're the only woman around here—he'll lose it."

"And she thinks he's interested in me?"

Two Smokes smiled wistfully. "He's interested. He just doesn't know it yet. You're interested in him. I watch you glancing back and forth, playing the games that lead to giggles and finally to the robes. You're a woman, freshly made in the manner of the Red Hand. It's our way that you lie with a man to prove your womanhood. You're curious, wondering what it's like."

"How do you know so much about women?"

"You'd ask a berdache?" Two Smokes laughed with genuine amusement. "We're the mediators, the ones who know the hearts both of men and women. We're half of each—and something different. Not men, not women. You know that—I'm made that way by Power.

"Oh, I remember what it's like. But things are a little different for a berdache. The man I loved was called Five Falls. I had gone as a youth to Cut Feather, of course, and asked him to proclaim me as berdache. I knew, even then, that I was berdache. I enjoyed the games of little girls and not the rough and tumble of the boys. One shouldn't fight what they are. To the body, it matters not what physical equipment we're blessed with, the drive for coupling is always there.

"Five Falls and I had been friends for a long time. To be berdache is never easy, even in a society like the Red Hand. Generally the trouble comes when you're a child before you—and others around you—have come to realize what you are. But Five Falls had always seemed to know. He was older by a couple of years, but he'd always taken care of me. When I was declared berdache, he took me for a second wife. He got great prestige for that, and we'd always cared for each other anyway. Fallen Aspen was his first wife. She didn't particularly like me, but then first wives can be jealous. It's not unknown," he added dryly.

"She bore his children and I was his lover. We were especially happy even if Fallen Aspen groused a lot. She had little to complain about. I did the work; she got the status."

Elk Charm nodded. "Five Falls died in a bad fall, didn't he? Hunting mountain goats, I heard."

Two Smokes stared into the distance. "Winter hunting takes great courage. I'd told him not to go. Just one of those feelings a person gets in his bones." He clapped callused hands to his knees. "Well, no matter. That was long ago. Clear Water became my friend after that. She, too, had problems with not fitting very well. We were drawn together."

"You shared a robe with her?" Elk Charm wondered.

Two Smokes nodded. "A time or two. I suppose the reason for that came from the Power. A berdache lives between Power and the world. Love comes in many ways, that's all—and spirit called us together. My real preference was always for men. But I lose my point. I've watched young people for years. I see the attraction between you and Little Dancer."

Elk Charm concentrated on the bark she worked, feeling the prickly stiffness of it between her palms as she rolled it back and forth. "He's got a look in his eyes that touches me inside. Like he's been hurt. It makes me . . . well . . ."

"Want to hold him? To help him? I know, that's the way of humans. We wish to ease each other's hurts. Is that your only reason?"

She smiled shyly. "I also think he wouldn't hurt me. After Blood Bear and the thought of what he'd . . ." She shook her head. "Oh, I don't know. I never thought it would be this complicated."

"He's just passed his thirteenth summer." Two Smokes raised an eyebrow.

She considered. "He seems older."

Two Smokes nodded. "Life hasn't been kind to him. I told you, Power walks with him. It fills his Dreams, and it's hurt him in the past. Now he seeks to avoid it. Only I . . . well, I wonder what his way will be in the end. A berdache is thought to be touched by difference. That Power hasn't treated me kindly through the years. The Short Buffalo People used to beat me. The men would rape me when they got the chance. To them I was a freak, an accident of nature they couldn't comprehend—and therefore dangerous. Some thought I'd ruin their children somehow, like a contagion.

"But Little Dancer, he's different. He has his mother's Power in him. Clear Water heard a voice, a voice she thought was from the First Man, the Wolf Dreamer. Look where it took her and what happened. That's why Power makes me nervous. I'm part of it; it rolls around me and through me. I'm the bridge—the communicator—between this world we live in and the Power. Power is why I am the way I am—but I don't see the reasons behind the things that happen. I don't know where it's going or what it's making of us. All I know is that Little Dancer is Powerful, and he's going to be an important man one day. You may take the word of a berdache on that."

An important man? She felt a curious excitement.

"Ah, interest, hmm?" Two Smokes scratched the back of his ear. "Perhaps I didn't do anyone any service. Listen, girl, and remember we're talking about Power. Little Dancer is the important one . . . the one Power is working on. Despite White Calf's worries, I think he can't avoid it. Someday, he must follow the Power.

"Heed me, Elk Charm. Power might make a man important, but it can also make him difficult to live with. Power tends to use people like a hunter uses his tools. A dart is made with great skill and effort. It is prepared, blessed, spirit is breathed into it. Then the hunter uses it. He makes his cast. That dart, so carefully crafted, is loosed to land we know not where. Perhaps it will strike a deer or an elk in the side, piercing its lungs and heart, bleeding the animal to death so that people can eat. Perhaps it will miss completely and smack a rock. The point will shatter, the wood will split, and there it will be left . . . forever."

She looked up at him, a hollow forming under her heart.

"Do you want to take that chance?" Two Smokes asked gently, a sympathetic warmth in his eyes.

She swallowed hard, unsure how to answer.

"Hey! Hungry Bull!"

Little Dancer looked up from the bloody buffalo quarter he bent over. Three Toes came skipping and jumping down through the meadow, arms held high, a joyous laughter split in the middle by loud whoops. Behind came Black Crow, a huge grin on his radiant face. Makes Fun followed with Meadowlark and the children. Another woman walked before Black Crow, her face anything but happy.

"Three Toes?" Hungry Bull straightened, shading his eyes with a blood-caked hand. "It's you!"

A melee resulted as Hungry Bull, Three Toes, Black Crow, and the rest shouted and danced and hugged and slapped each other on the back.

Little Dancer turned to the woman first, ignoring the babble of questions and laughter from the men. "You're not Short Buffalo People," he noted in Anit'ah.

"No. I'm not." Her hard eyes bored into his. Even in his youth, Little Dancer noted the handsome lines of her face. She added a little testily, "They caught me yesterday." A wry smile curled her lips. "Perhaps I'm getting older than I thought."

Little Dancer glanced sideways at the backslapping mob centered around his father. "They didn't hurt you."

She chuckled dryly. "Outside of my dignity, no."

"I am Little Dancer. I live at White Calf's camp with—"

"I know who you are. Is my daughter there? Her name is Elk Charm; she would have arrived a hand's full of days ago."

"She's there. She's fine. You're Rattling Hooves?"

She filled her lungs. "I'm Rattling Hooves." She looked over at where the knot of Short Buffalo People still danced and shouted questions in such confusion that no one could be heard. "I didn't know what was happening. The warriors could sign in Trader Signs for White Calf and ask directions. Since they didn't hurt me, I led them here. But you should know that Blood Bear has found their tracks and is following them with a war party."

Little Dancer's blood chilled.

"Father!" he called, waving to catch Hungry Bull's eye. Despite the festive nature of the occasion, the tension must have signaled him. Hungry Bull disengaged himself from Meadowlark's happy embrace and walked over, one arm around Three Toe's shoulder.

"Blood Bear is on his way here with a war party," Little Dancer explained in the tongue of the People. "This is Elk Charm's mother. Perhaps we should get back to the camp and see what White Calf has to say?" He looked up at Three Toes. "You've come for a visit?"

"To stay," Three Toes supplied uneasily. "Heavy Beaver . . . well, he's made it impossible for us among the People. He's become very powerful. White Calf was our only chance."

Hungry Bull's excitement faded like the shadow of a tiny cloud in an endless summer sky. "The Red Hand are still angry over the People's raid last year. The souls of the killed are still roaming unburied."

"I told you Heavy Beaver would haunt us," Three Toes reminded.

"He'll be worse before he's better," Black Crow growled.

In his stilted Anit'ah, Hungry Bull asked Rattling Hooves, "How long until Blood Bear comes here?"

She lifted an absent shoulder. "He's been after your friends for three days now. He'll be moving fast. Since I didn't know your friends' motives, I marked the trail for him in subtle ways."

"Then we'd better go." Little Dancer bent to pick up his butchering tools.

"What about all this meat?" Hungry Bull pointed to the half-butchered carcasses. "As warm as it is, it'll sour if we don't . . . The flies will . . ."

"And do you think Blood Bear will wait for us?" Three Toes asked nervously.

"Buffalo Above will understand," Little Dancer added. "He knows our hearts." *And I told that to my mother before she died for the sake of meat.* Chill ate at his soul. "Come on!" And he led the way down the trail to White Calf's at a trot.

Somehow, Rattling Hooves ended up running beside him. "Blood Bear will coming to White Calf's, following the Short Buffalo People," he said. "He'll find Elk Charm there."

She looked down at him, working her lips. "If we get there first, I can have her run. She can hide where he can't find her." A pause. "Why do you care, young man?"

The question left him unbalanced. Why did he? Why had she dominated his thoughts from the moment he'd seen her? "She's nice."

"Uh-huh?" Rattling Hooves managed to chuckle softly as she panted for breath. "You know, this is all getting complicated, Little Dancer. Short Buffalo People and Red Hand, all mixed up."

"White Calf will know what to do."

"She usually does."

And if she doesn't, what then? Little Dancer wondered. *Together, we've got four atlatls against how many Red Hand? And if we do fight and they don't wipe us out, what's left?*

He swallowed hard and ran with all his might.

What had Rattling Hooves been doing out on the trail in the first place? What could have possessed her to take a chance like that, knowing Short Buffalo People lurked in the area? Blood Bear glared ahead as he led his warriors down the trail. From the sign, the raiders were no more than a couple of hours ahead of them. With the children, they'd move more slowly. He'd have them before sunset.

Rattling Hooves had been headed toward White Calf's . . . obviously worried about her daughter. Still, a woman her age should have had more sense than to risk herself over a silly girl like that. Worse, Rattling Hooves had blithely run into the Short Buffalo People's ambush. Served her right for not being more careful.

As usual, the raiders didn't know the trail. They'd wandered around for days, climbing through black timber, struggling up and down ridges and skirting meadows, taking elk trails that led into the heaviest of timber and disappeared. Since they'd caught Rattling Hooves, the woman had led them straight away from the Red Hand—and straight for White Calf's. Now, what did *that* mean? White Calf, of course, had originally been Short Buffalo. She'd married into Red Hand, been a Spirit Woman for years, healing those who went to her for help.

A prickling lifted the hairs at the nape of his neck. Even though he didn't believe in Power, White Calf scared him. You couldn't tell what that crazy old witch might stir up.

People feared White Calf. If she said anything, word would get back to the camps and cause him no little bit of trouble.

He hugged the Wolf Bundle to his chest. This time he carried the Power and spirit of his people. Unlike the last time when his warriors vanished one by one into the night, he'd taken the silly little talisman that gave them heart and spirit. This time the Wolf Bundle led them, and his warriors would fight to the death to protect it from the Short Buffalo People who'd defiled it. With it, he could spur them to greater effort than they'd give otherwise.

Amazing how much strength can be taken from a mere trinket! And it's mine . . . all mine! He ignored the sudden throbbing in his little finger. Angrily he batted it against his muscular thigh, as if to swat the tingle out of it like that of a pinched nerve.

"Got to catch the raiders and kill them before they get there. That's the best," he whispered under his breath.

It wouldn't be long now.

As he thought it, the trail turned suddenly, leading down into a meadow. Ravens rose from the trees, cawing as their black wings rasped in the air.

Blood Bear pulled up, chest rising and falling as he caught his breath. Before him, the meadow was littered with half-butchered buffalo. Muttered conversation broke out behind him.

He walked to one of the carcasses, touching the exposed meat. "Skinned not more than an hour ago." He grinned at his warriors. "We've got them!"

"The Spiral shifts," the Wolf Bundle observed. "We are in serious danger. It can all come apart now. Free will is in play. So much for the Power of your Wolf Dream! I'm carried to the destruction of your Dreamer. I see my end. I can kill, save him, perhaps to renew me. The link is strong, but how will he react? If I wrap my tendrils into his heart, will he accept me? Or will he turn his back . . . listen to the voice of his dead mother where it echoes in his mind? I don't have much strength left. To kill, I must use all of myself. The boy doesn't know the way to Power. The Watcher isn't prepared, yet. We're not ready. Too soon . . . too soon . . ."

The Wolf Dreamer's voice conveyed worry. "Wait. Perhaps White Calf can save it. If not, we lose everything. If we act, we'll prove his mother's words. If we don't act . . ."

Chapter 14 ✋

What's going to happen? Three Toes wondered as they all were seated before White Calf's shelter.

Little Dancer watched. He could feel the tension, flashes of Dream images disrupting his concentration. Why? Why did he feel so worried? Thoughts not his own seemed to whisper at the edge of his consciousness.

The sun continued to beat down, friendly and warm, despite the anxiety reflected on each face and in the nervous postures that bespoke unease. A late grasshopper clicked in the still air, its sound rising and falling to the beat of its yellow and black wings.

White Calf hobbled out, braced on her old walking stick.

Little Dancer almost winced at the way she looked, ancient, frail, as if any rapid movement might cause her to snap and collapse. When had she grown so old? A tingle of guilt ate at his stomach.

"So, Heavy Beaver's driven you out?" Her scratchy voice wavered.

Old, so old. And if she dies? What then? What do I do? A sudden uncertainty gripped Little Dancer's heart. *Have I been right to fight her so?*

"He's gathering the People," Black Crow said unsteadily as he stood and faced White Calf. "He's begun a new way. He's teaching a Dance of Renewal and Blessing. Since he's become leader, the rains have come back, and with them the buffalo are a little more plentiful. It seems to the People that the more Power he gets, the better things are."

"Fools!" White Calf hissed. "All young fools. I've

watched all my life. You get these spells—a little wetter for a couple of years, but the world's changed slowly for as long as I . . . or the legends, can remember. Does water run in Monster Bone Springs? Is the Moon River up to its old banks running so deep a person can't wade?''

"No." Black Crow looked around uneasily.

"Then the drought's still with us. Some years it's wetter. Other years it'll be drying. We live in an age of fire, not water. When you see the water in Moon River run clear, you'll know the age of fire has passed. Meanwhile, the earth is being washed away. Have you seen any of the arroyos filling? No? They're still cutting into the earth? I thought so. People will be starving again soon. They'll be pushing the last of the buffalo into extinction like they did the monsters. Heavy Beaver's a fool.''

"He may be a fool, but he's a powerful one," Black Crow answered. "When Seven Suns' camp decided to go to his Blessing, we argued against it. We've had war with the Fire Buffalo People to the east. The Cut Hair People to the south are warring with Heavy Beaver. The old peace was broken when Heavy Beaver took warriors to raid the Cut Hair. Fire At Night and Throws Stones have become great warriors. They've taken parties of young men as far south as the lands of the Squash Rock People and killed their men. They've brought back women captives—all carrying their weight in dried meat, fine robes, and tool stone. Last spring, Throws Stones raided the White Crane People, killing many and burning one of their camps to the ground. The women, dogs, and children he brought back carried many wonderful things.''

"And these women? They don't make trouble?" White Calf wanted to know.

Meadowlark shook her head. "What woman would make trouble? If they refuse a man's orders, they're beaten. If they beat a man back, they're killed. Sometimes a woman who objects is Cursed by Heavy Beaver himself. And if a captive woman tries to escape to her people, she's hunted down like a wounded buffalo cow, and a dart is driven through her.'' Meadowlark lifted futile hands. "What good does it do to fight back? What's better? To live or to die? That's the choice—and the men believe it. Women among the Short Buffalo People live in terror.''

White Calf nodded thoughtfully in the silence that stretched. "So that's how he kept the People from vanishing like smoke. And I'll bet the captured women are kept pregnant? Their children are the new People?''

"Uh-huh." Makes Fun grimaced. "And I argued with Chokecherry when she said this could happen. Now, here I am, chased from my people by something—this madness— that I still can't believe is real.''

"The world's changing." White Calf wet her lips, spreading her hands wide, palms up to catch the sun. "Heavy Beaver wanted to make the People strong again. That happens when things go bad. You always find somebody's getting up dancing and singing about returning to the old ways, the ways of the fathers . . . as if they remembered what the old ways were really like. Heavy Beaver did that—and blood and spit take you if you remember different old ways than he does!''

"He's the Dreamer. It's worked." Three Toes glanced up from where he sat on a flat rock, a haggard look about him. "Not only that, but the Spirit Dreamers among the Cut Hair and the Fire Buffalo People are worried that Heavy Beaver's ideas will spread. Already angry young men are pointing fingers at the Short Buffalo, demanding revenge on them for the deaths and the stealing of their women. They're claiming that Heavy Beaver's way is better, more powerful; otherwise they wouldn't be defeated in battle like they are.''

"And it continues to sweep the plains?" White Calf turned her head, bright eyes on Little Dancer. "Then it will continue to grow, to wind up more and more peoples like spring-shed buffalo fur around a turned rosebush stem.''

"But if a war party could raid them back, defeat them in a battle, maybe—''

"Bah!" White Calf waved her hands at Hungry Bull's thought. "You're dealing with an idea, not a war party. It's what Heavy Beaver's teaching that's got to be stopped. You won't win by killing his young men in a big fight.''

"Then how?" Black Crow asked.

"Power." She whispered so softly they almost didn't hear. "He's got to be out-Dreamed. This is the Fire Time. Someone has to Dance with Fire . . . to hold the coals and be One with them. That's where the end comes. A new way has to be taught to everyone. The buffalo hunters are dying off. The world's changing, just like it did when the animals we call monsters were vanishing. Men hunted the big beasts to death—just like we're doing with the buffalo.''

White Calf looked around, taking in each face. "That's right. Heavy Beaver, with his way, will kill them all. His people will be desperate. Maybe the buffalo have to go after all, huh? Maybe that's what the Wise One Above has Dreamed for this Fourth World of his.'' She smacked her lips, keen eyes on Little Dancer, as if she spoke to him without regard to the others. "But then, maybe another way can be Dreamed for the People—a way that gives them other means to survive than to kill off buffalo in this age of Fire.''

"You can't live like the Red Hand in the plains," Hungry Bull insisted. "Sego lily, biscuit root, serviceberry, and things like that don't grow there. It's just grass and occasional buffalo berry along the drainages. And besides, the People wouldn't want to eat things like roots. They're buffalo people. They eat meat.''

"That's what has to be Dreamed.'' White Calf steepled her fingers. "And the only way it will change will be for a powerful Dreamer to go down there and change it.''

Little Dancer's throat went dry. *No! Oh, no you don't. Not this again. You can't make me. I'm not the one! On my mother's dead soul, I'm not the one. Power's wrong, it hurts people.*

And his mother's words echoed in his memory: *"I don't want my son to ever make anyone feel the way I do now."*

Slowly, he got to his feet, shaking his head, realizing that everyone was looking at him. He backed away, aware that his father had dropped his eyes and was fumbling at the dirt with a stick, drawing little lines and crossing them.

The Dream image of the rocky ridge shimmered in his mind, his father turning to stone below him. *Like all the others, he'll fail me in the end, leave me to plunge into the abyss.*

Little Dancer turned to run . . . and froze. Coming down the trail, Blood Bear led his band of Anit'ah warriors.

And worse, Elk Charm walked ashen-faced before him.

* * *

As Blood Bear broke into the clearing, Rattling Hooves jumped to her feet. She'd missed most of the conversation chattered back and forth in the Short Buffalo tongue. This she could understand. Blood Bear had captured her daughter.

She started forward only to end up on the point of Blood Bear's war dart. The keen-edged stone dimpled the hollow of her throat as she looked up into his smoldering eyes.

"What have you done, woman? Led Short Buffalo People through the lands of the Red Hand? Is this how you treat your people?"

"Let go of my daughter." She forced the words, aware that all he had to do was move his hand to slit her throat wide.

Elk Charm thrashed in his powerful grip. Behind, the warriors watched warily as the Short Buffalo People clustered behind White Calf.

"She's a woman now—and I have her. First, I think we'll kill these raiders . . . and keep their women as they kept ours last year. Then you and your daughter will come and live with me."

"Never!" Rattling Hooves managed through gritted teeth.

The anger in Blood Bear's eyes began to shine. "You're a beautiful woman, Rattling Hooves. Even at your age, you've managed to snare my interest. Normally, a man doesn't marry a women as well as her daughter."

"You wouldn't!" White Calf limped forward, leaning on her stick. "Among the Red Hand, that's incest! You'd be her father!"

"I make my own rules and Power. As I control the Wolf Bundle, I control the Red Hand."

"Stupid, ignorant *fool*! Not even the Wolf Bundle allows you to take the ways of the Red Hand into your . . . *Yah!*" White Calf's eyes went big as she started to raise her hands to protect herself.

Moving like lightning, Blood Bear shifted, his arm a blur as he pulled the dart back, pivoting on his heel. He thrust Elk Charm violently away. His atlatl whipped back, poised for that brief instant before the cast.

Rattling Hooves gasped a cry, aware even as she moved that she'd acted too late. She lurched forward, off balance, desperately clawing for him. Blood Bear threw his weight behind the cast.

She had trouble sorting it out later. Blood Bear had whooped in triumph as he released the dart. A shout. A clacking sound. And Hungry Bull leapt in from the side. The hunter stood braced, his atlatl gripped like a club. White Calf remained propped on her walking stick, eyes wide. She stared, first at the broken dart Hungry Bull had batted out of the air, and then at Blood Bear, where he fumbled for footing, trying to nock another dart.

"Hold it!" Rattling Hooves shouted, seeing the other warriors, muscular arms reaching back, stone-tipped darts glinting in the bright sun as their atlatls balanced. "What are we doing?" They hesitated for a moment while Hungry Bull turned his back, arms raised to stop the sudden advance of Three Toes, Black Crow, and Meadowlark, all with darts ready to cast.

"Insanity!" Elk Charm cried, running up to the warriors, pleading particularly to Snaps Horn. "What's happening?"

White Calf ambled forward, waving her hands. "Stop it! You fools!" She whirled, pointing a finger at Blood Bear. "So, you'd kill me before we could talk this out? And you call yourself a leader? You think *you* have the brains to keep the Wolf Bundle? Idiot!"

The warriors froze, looking back and forth uncertainly. From long experience, Rattling Hooves could see the change in Blood Bear's expression, instantly aware the situation had shifted. He lowered his nocked dart. The old cunning light glinted in his eyes as his brain raced.

"How did I know, old woman? How did I know you weren't plotting with these"—he indicated the Short Buffalo—"to raid our camp again? You keep strange company."

"Like Rattling Hooves?" White Calf demanded dryly. "You don't—"

"I don't *what*? My people have been killed! Raided by Short Buffalo People." He turned, chin up, glancing at his warriors through slitted eyes. "How do I know where the next raid might come from?"

"Surely not from an old woman who Dreamed and bore children for the Red Hand."

"Or from her?" Blood Bear indicated Rattling Hooves with his dart point. As quickly, Hungry Bull's atlatl knocked the point aside.

"Use your finger next time. It's polite," Hungry Bull insisted, meeting Blood Bear's burning anger with his own.

"This woman is one of *my* people. You take chances, hunter."

Hungry Bull barely nodded. "So do you." They bristled as they glared into each other's eyes.

Rattling Hooves shot Hungry Bull a quick glance. Why? Why did he intercede? He could be killed on her account.

"Enough!" White Calf bulled between the two men. "Put your darts down. There will be no killing here."

Uneasily, the warriors lowered their weapons.

"Old Woman, I'm the Keeper of the Wolf Bundle." Blood Bear half crouched, glaring anger and frustration.

White Calf met him eye to eye. "And you still haven't learned anything, have you? Remember when you killed Cut Feather? Eight years you spent wandering homeless for that. And now you want to kill me? You keep wishing for Power, and then you spit in its very face! You act like it doesn't exist without you."

The final resistance drained from Blood Bear's warriors. They shifted now, looking uneasily at each other, wetting lips, fingering their darts nervously. Only Snaps Horn stood firm, a grimness to his features as he shot searching looks at Elk Charm.

Blood Bear stiffened, a quiver eating at the corner of his lips. "Watch yourself, old woman. You push me too far."

"And I'll keep pushing, fool." She caught the end of his dart with her frail fingers, lifting the point to the hollow under her ribs. "Go ahead, push, Blood Bear. I've made it easy for you. But before you kill me, want to make a bet? Want to gamble on how long you'll have before you're wandering the plains again, hungry, in tatters, looking for a snake or a toad for a meal?"

He swallowed hard.

Heart thumping in her throat, Rattling Hooves reached

around and pushed the dart down with the flat of her hand. "I think that's enough for all of us."

Hungry Bull took the old woman by the shoulders. "Come, Grandmother. Come and sit and let us all talk this out. With Heavy Beaver making war in the plains, we can't have the Red Hand breaking into factions in the mountains. The whole world may die if we do."

White Calf looked up, realizing Hungry Bull had spoken in Anit'ah. "You've got a lot of sense, boy." She nodded, smacking her old gums. "A lot of sense."

Rattling Hooves exhaled slowly, seeing the quick smile Hungry Bull gave her. As she turned, she noticed Elk Charm stood behind Little Dancer. The boy looked pale, a dart nocked in his atlatl. The look Snaps Horn gave him would have melted ice.

Blood Bear pushed past them, stalking up to the rock wall and hanging the Wolf Bundle on a peg. Arrogantly, he seated himself on a tumbled boulder below it and braced his hands on his knees, looking around with a hard expression.

"Now then, who are these Short Buffalo People? What do they do here?"

"Where's Two Smokes?" White Calf asked Elk Charm.

"He's still working on his net. I came down for another armload of bark. By now he'll be on the way, figuring something happened."

"The berdache is still here fouling the air?" Blood Bear asked in irritation.

Several of the warriors, Ramshorn and Never Sweat among them, flinched at the sacrilege. Snaps Horn looked like a compressed willow stick—ready to strike out in any direction.

"He's part of my family," White Calf said testily. She hesitated, propping herself as she looked at the Wolf Bundle. "So the Power hasn't come back to it yet?"

Rattling Hooves caught the drawn expression on Little Dancer's face, still pale, the total of his concentration on the Wolf Bundle. His eyes glittered—an expression of tears barely held back. The boy took a step, then another, one hand outstretched, his mouth working wordlessly.

Blood Bear cocked his head, watching as the youth came

forward, step-by-step, a tear tracing his cheek. Oblivious, he reached for the Wolf Bundle.

Blood Bear's atlatl pushed his hand away.

Little Dancer came to, starting at the contact, staring down into Blood Bear's hot eyes.

"It's . . . cold," Little Dancer whispered. "You've made it cold. You don't smoke it in sweetgrass . . . don't care for it right. One day, it'll turn against you . . . just like it will against Heavy Beaver and everyone who doesn't respect it. You're strangling it."

The warriors shifted uneasily. They stared at Little Dancer and the Wolf Bundle, backing away a step at a time. Only Snaps Horn stood his ground, glittering eyes never leaving Little Dancer.

"And you're a heartbeat from dead, boy," Blood Bear's rejoinder came.

Rattling Hooves could hear Hungry Bull's teeth grind as he started forward. She reached for him, placing a hand on his shoulder, acting by instinct. Under her touch, she felt his bunched muscle barely restrained.

Hungry Bull glanced at her, worry in his eyes. She shook her head, knowing the anxiety he felt. No, Blood Bear wouldn't hurt the boy. She could feel it.

Little Dancer's hand fell, the pained look deepening. "You don't understand. It's waiting. It wants the right person to clean it, make it whole again. The Power's there, waiting for something . . . for someone. Feel the flames? Feel . . ."

He started to reach for it again, and again Blood Bear blocked him.

Rattling Hooves couldn't be sure what had happened. Maybe Blood Bear had hung the Bundle with some kink in the straps that suddenly loosened. Maybe the light made it appear to move. It seemed to jump, then patted softly on the rock.

Little Dancer staggered as if slapped and shook his head. He backed away, a dazed look in his eyes. "No," he whispered. "Not me. *I'm not the one!*"

Blood Bear cleared his throat, glad for the distraction. "And no one wishes to speak for these Short Buffalo People?"

"They've come to see White Calf." Rattling Hooves stepped forward. "From the moment they caught me on the trail, they've been considerate. I don't think they're here to make war."

Blood Bear studied her. A shiver danced up her spine on frozen prickly feet. *Like it or not,* she told herself, *your life is changed. How will you ever manage to live in the same camp with him? What will that do to One Cast and Wet Rain?*

"I'm glad to know you've become an expert on Short Buffalo People."

"They've come here because they can't go anyplace else," Hungry Bull added from the side, pronouncing the words thickly.

Blood Bear lifted a lip in a sneer. "I'm not finished with you, hunter."

"I'm here, Blood Bear." Hungry Bull stood easily, a slight smile on his face.

Rattling Hooves shot a quick glance in White Calf's direction. Where was she? This was her opportunity to . . . The old Spirit Woman seemed made of stone, gleaming eyes burning as she stared at Little Dancer. The boy had sagged to his knees, mouth open, while his gaze locked on the Wolf Bundle.

"White Calf?" Rattling Hooves reached for her, aware of the tension in the air. Black Crow's group shifted uneasily. The Red Hand waited, totally lost. Everything would turn on White Calf's words, and the old woman could only watch the boy, that burning interest in her eyes.

"*White Calf!*" she hissed, reaching to pluck at the old woman's sleeve.

"What?" The ancient eyes seemed to clear. She shook herself, as if to rid her mind of a dream. "Yes? What?"

Blood Bear reminded haughtily, "The Short Buffalo People . . . if you'd care to make some comment. If not, I'll solve this one way or another. Maybe you don't understand the forces at work here, old woman, but the future of the Red Hand is—"

"Fool!" she snapped, taking a step forward. "What do *you* know of the Powers at work? You think you're here because of Three Toes and Black Crow? Idiot! This is a turning

. . . a day just like the one when Heavy Beaver threw the Wolf Bundle into the dirt. Hah! And you're worried about a few Short Buffalo People?''

"But I—"

"Be quiet, Blood Bear. You're almost finished. Oh, you've some time yet. You'll be able to delude yourself a while longer and enjoy your status.'' She turned, cocking her head to stare at the nervous warriors of the Red Hand. "Go home. Trouble is coming, but it isn't here yet. Not this year. The storm's brewing out on the plains. You'll need to guard the trails . . . but not this winter. Go. Get on with you. Hungry Bull here killed some buffalo. Take what you can pack with you. My blessings on you.''

Ramshorn stared back and forth, desperately seeking a solution. Hanging Rock reached up, pulling Ramshorn back, and the rest faded, backing away. Snaps Horn stood resolute, and only Hanging Rock's unsubtle tug got him to move.

White Calf shooed them along, getting them moving before Blood Bear could figure out what had happened. But what had that look of frustration in Snaps Horn's eyes been for?

Blood Bear stood, filling his lungs to shout. White Calf banged him on the shin with her walking stick, causing him to jump, the order lost on the wind.

"What? You want to make a fool of yourself again?'' White Calf asked.

The anger flooded back. "Beware old woman! You're—"

"Bah!'' She spat at him. "You had one chance today. Hungry Bull took it from you. So long as you killed me with the first cast, you could have saved something, maybe changed the Circles and affected the world. But you've lost. Power's not with you, Blood Bear. You've done something I don't understand. You offended the Power so completely it's left you like an old blind bull run out of a buffalo herd.''

As he gaped at her, she shook her head. "I don't envy you. You're a tool whose life is past. Like an exhausted obsidian core. Only you've cut too many of the toolmaker's fingers to simply be left behind. Even being around you scares me—like standing on a high peak in a lightning storm. That kind of scared.''

"And what of the Short Buffalo People?" Rattling Hooves looked at the last of the Red Hand vanishing up the trail, the warriors happy to be going away from White Calf and the trouble brewing in her camp.

"They'll stay." White Calf sighed, as if deflating. "Not here. I can't handle so many people. But I know of a shelter down on the south slope of the mountains. Two Smokes can take them."

Rattling Hooves glanced at her daughter and then back at Blood Bear. He watched her, a threat in his eyes. At the look, her heart thumped dully. He'd make her . . . and Elk Charm, suffer for this day.

White Calf tapped her stick on the rock behind him. "You have anything else to say?"

Blood Bear gave her a wicked smile. "No, old woman. Not this time. But one day soon, you'll wish my dart had passed right through your heart."

White Calf laughed. For a brief instant, the years seemed to fall from her ancient body. "You'll never know what you've given me this day, Blood Bear. You'll never understand the depths of what you've let loose." She laughed again and clapped her hands together, almost dancing as she rocked back and forth.

Blood Bear straightened and lifted the Wolf Bundle from the rock behind him. Without a glance he turned and began running up the trail, legs pumping powerfully.

Rattling Hooves exhaled, feeling suddenly weak-kneed. A strong hand at her elbow led her to the rock where Blood Bear had sat. She looked up, seeing the concern in Hungry Bull's eyes.

"It's been a hard journey for you. Thank you for acting when you did. It took courage."

She blinked up at him. "Why did you stand up for me?"

He looked away, a pain stealing into his soft eyes. "You were brave. You spoke for my friends. Once, long ago, no one stood up for my . . . Well, I wouldn't see that happen again. I wouldn't have your husband feel what I did that day."

She spoke without thinking. "My husband's dead." She cocked her head, wondering what One Cast would think to hear that. But she knew. She'd always been outside the circle in One Cast's lodge.

He didn't give her a chance to clarify. "So's my wife. Killed by a man like Blood Bear."

Stunned, she studied his sober face. He smiled shyly, but the pain in his eyes touched her own, blending. Startled by her reaction, she forced her gaze away from his, wondering at the rapid beat of her heart.

Little Dancer stared up at the stars. The biting chill of the night ate into his bones. The crystal air burned in his lungs as his thoughts continued to whirl—dust in the wind. His world had come undone as if someone had pulled every peg from the lodge cover of his life. He felt open, exposed to the sight of things he couldn't even conceive. He tried to think, lost in the sensations of that afternoon.

The Wolf Bundle had burned his soul—the same as a boiling stone would his hands if he tried to pick it up without hearth sticks. He'd felt the longing, the Power, the *need* of the Wolf Bundle. He clamped his eyes shut at the memory. Power had played around him like the flickering light of an evening fire.

Images and memories shot through his mind in a jumble: *"Not my son . . ."* his mother's words continued to repeat. White Calf's powerful stare burned into him with an acid intensity. Heavy Beaver's cruel smile seeped through the pores of his thoughts, as if it were hot bear oil. Two Smokes cried out in misery. Elk Charm's body swayed, tempting. The deep pools of her eyes promised. He could feel the gentle touch of her hands, his body responding. . . .

Everything whirled away, tossed in the tempest of his disjointed mind. He fell into a Spiral, turning, never finding the center. Blood Bear's smug face mocked him, the danger of the deadly dart tip hovering over his life. The man's obsidian eyes pinned his soul, sending a shiver through his quivering guts.

Through it all, the Wolf Bundle called to him, the presence of it haunting, lingering in the air like the faint perfume of spring phlox. Fragile fingers of memory caressed his soul. The familiar touch of the Wolf Bundle reminded him of his childhood. That warmth, that wondrous proximity of Power, wrapped around him. He could almost believe himself in his bedding, his mother and father sleeping at the back of the lodge. If he reached up, he could touch the decorated parfleche, reach inside and feel the reassuring wolf hide that protected the bundle from harm.

Without thinking, he lifted his hand, fingers encountering nothing but the night sky. He raised his eyes, seeing the inky shadows of his grasping fingers. Above, only the Starweb stretched into the infinity of the night.

"The Wolf Bundle," he whispered hoarsely.

As if in answer, the weird howl of a wolf echoed from somewhere in the night. The cry rose, ascending the scale of his soul, sending shivers along his trembling muscles. A hole emptied in his being, part of him draining away to float like the eerie notes on the clear air.

Moonlight broke over the mountains, sending white bars of light shooting across the canyon to touch the sage with silver and strike gleaming sparks in the whispering dry grass. The ghostly silhouettes of black trees danced in the eerie light.

Little Dancer froze, looking to the west where the clouds piled high. A man looked at him, his image formed of the mounded clouds, moonlight shining from his eyes. The hair on the back of Little Dancer's neck rose, chill tickling his skin like a thousand insect feet.

"What . . . are . . . you?"

"Wolf Dream." The words might have formed of the air around him. *"The time will come. You're not ready yet. The Circles haven't turned."*

He swallowed, gaping into the darkness. "I'm not the one," he insisted, heart battering fear against his ribs.

Out of the faint sighing in the trees, his mother's words spun like strands of spiderweb torn loose on the morning breeze, *"I forbid it."*

Little Dancer winced, the power of the words engraved as deeply as the old petroglyphs above White Calf's camp.

"And your wish, boy?" The words uttered from a deeper throat, intense, undeniable.

He blinked, jumping as if physically touched. A shadow

shifted. The wolf stood silver black in the moonlight, huge, almost the size of a four-point mule deer. It watched him, yellow eyes piercing his wounded soul.

"I . . ." The words caught in his throat.

"You know the Watcher," the voice continued. *"He's followed you. You are tied."*

The huge animal stepped closer, head lowering as the mouth dropped open. Bright moonlight shimmered off the long white teeth like sunlight through ice.

Fear coursed through Little Dancer in electric patterns. Frozen, he could do no more than stare.

Wolf stopped a hand's length away.

"The Spiral has almost come around. The Circles are changing—the balance shifting. The ability to Dream it back is yours. The Power lies in you, Fire Dancer. You needn't choose yet. You have time to learn about life . . . about what it means to be. One day, you'll be called. In the meantime, live . . . and learn. When the Dreams burn in your mind until you can think of nothing else, seek out White Calf. She understands now. She'll listen . . . and teach."

The man-shaped clouds flickered from within, illuminated by flashes of lightning. The man's features glowed eerily white, watching, pensive, brooding.

Little Dancer gasped and looked, tearing his eyes away from the Watcher, for the briefest instant. When he glanced back, the animal had disappeared into the night, only the grasses waving to indicate its passage. With trembling fingers, he reached to feel the crushed stems, almost detecting a warmth through his fingertips.

The dull rumble of thunder rolled across the mountains, the voice of Power unrestrained. Little Dancer swallowed hard and turned toward the towering clouds; the looming thunderhead had changed form. Where the man had watched, the head now resembled that of a huge wolf. Another low growl of thunder echoed across the canyons.

For long moments he sat paralyzed. Beat by beat, his heart counted the long moments as the thunder rumbled away for an eternity and took his soul with it.

"Late for thunder."

Little Dancer yipped and jumped.

"Scared you?" Two Smokes asked as he hobbled down from the elk trail and settled himself. Behind him, Elk Charm moved like a shadow. "Power's loose tonight. You can feel it. You know, like that silent calm before a violent storm."

His heart continued to beat like a pot drum.

"You all right?"

"The wolf, the Watcher . . . did you see it? Huge . . . black . . . ."

Two Smokes cocked his head. "No wolf ran by us. But Power's been around. Skin prickles. When you sniff, you smell the scent of it."

Little Dancer dropped his head onto his knees, breathing hard. A sudden trembling took control of his quivering muscles.

Two Smokes talked on, feigning unconcern. "White Calf wanted us to come find you. I'm supposed to lead Three Toes and his people to a camp I know. You can go or stay here. The decision is yours. It's been a busy day for everyone. Hungry Bull is going. I think he wants some time with his friends, time to be with his people."

Little Dancer tried to still the racing of his heart.

"I'm betting Rattling Hooves will go with him," Two Smokes continued. "I guess she doesn't have much to go back to among the Red Hand for the time being. Blood Bear would make her miserable. White Calf thinks it would be a good thing if she went to tell the People how the Red Hand live."

Little Dancer chewed the inside of his cheeks. "I won't stay here."

Two Smokes nodded, expression hidden by the shadows. "I think she expects as much."

He peered uneasily at his old friend. "She didn't order me to stay?"

Two Smokes slowly shook his head. "I don't understand it, but she almost insisted that you . . . and Elk Charm, go. She just smiled, rocking back and forth, looking . . . well, I'd call it satisfied."

Little Dancer frowned into the night. His nerves bunched like those of a ground squirrel when hawk's shadow passed through the grass. Too much had happened too quickly. In the roil of his mind, nothing made sense. He couldn't think. Life twisted around him in a rush, out of control, tumbling head over heels before he could think about it.

"And she didn't even argue for me to stay? Demand I talk to her about Dreams?"

"No. She says you're in other hands than hers now. She says your way has been set."

Little Dancer plucked at a stem of grass, twirling it in his fingers. "You've known her for a long time, Two Smokes. What do you think she's after?"

The berdache shrugged. "She thought she could teach you things that might make a difference when you finally meet Heavy Beaver. She thought she could—"

"I'm not going to meet Heavy Beaver. I'm *not* her Dreamer."

Two Smokes paused for a moment. When he spoke, it was with great deliberation. "I think, my friend, that she knows that. I think that whatever happened today, she saw that you're not her Dreamer."

"Oh?"

Two Smokes swallowed, the sound loud in the silence of the night. "I think . . ."

"Go on. We've been together for too many years for you to try and wiggle out of it like a snake from a pouch."

Two Smokes laughed under his breath, the expression without humor. "I suppose so. Then maybe you should know that she whispered something to herself." He hesitated, expression pensive. "The words she whispered when she thought no one could hear were, 'He's not mine. Fool that I am. He's always belonged to Wolf.' "

Stricken, he looked back at the clouds. Fingers like ice played along his spine.

"We have him." The thousand souls of the Wolf Bundle stirred wearily, worry alleviated.

"For the moment," Wolf Dreamer agreed. *"He's torn. Drawn at the same time he's repulsed. He still denies."*

"This is the chance. Renew me. Let me add my Power. Let me adjust the Spirals—"

"Not yet," the Wolf Dreamer rebuked through the golden

haze of the illuminated Spirals. "You live in the Now. Look beyond. What we have gained with Little Dancer we have lost with Heavy Beaver. He plans to move on the Red Hand. As his authority consolidates, he looks to the mountains."

"You gambled that the rains would lessen his need!"

"I didn't understand his driving hunger for domination."

"What else have you misjudged? Things become more precarious. Another mistake . . ."

Chapter 15 ✋

Packs lay ready in the pink morning light. Blue wreaths of smoke rose from the shelter hangings to trace up the irregular gray wall of the limestone cliff. Chill lay heavy on the ground, breath condensing as people attended to last-minute preparations.

Little Dancer stood to one side, watching, curiously detached. Sleep hadn't come. Mostly he'd lain awake, tortured by fragments of Dreams when he did doze off. Once more his world had changed—and he didn't know how, or why.

White Calf ducked out of the flap and walked painfully across to where he stood. She seemed to huddle over her walking stick, eyes on the dirt before him.

She worked her toothless gums and looked up, meeting his eyes. The previous day seemed to have aged her even more.

"I was wrong," she said gently. "I thought you were my responsibility." She shook her head slightly, eyes never leaving his. "I knew you had so much to learn. I didn't think I had much time left. You see? I thought I might die before I could teach you."

Of everything she could say, he hadn't expected this. Words wouldn't come.

She looked up at the Starweb above and laughed. "He's the one, the Sun Man, the Wolf Dreamer. He'll train you, Little

Dancer." She laughed brittlely, half turning away to glance at the others. "Foolish of me, boy. But then, that's the way of humans. We tend toward pride, toward thinking we're more than we are. No wonder we messed up the First World."

"I don't understand."

She sniffed in the cool air. "I didn't either. I thought my part was greater than it was. Huh! Took seeing the vision yesterday. It all came clear. Oh, I had my part, all right. I was the key to your conception and safety. You know your real mother was Clear Water—my daughter. I bore Hungry Bull's father, to spawn him, to marry Sage Root, to care for you. I was called to take you from Heavy Beaver at just the right moment. I was here to provide a safe haven for you to grow in. I have another couple of things to do, but they'll come in time."

He reached out for her, surprised at the ache in his heart. "I'll be back."

She nodded. "Oh, we'll see each other again. I think by the time winter's about over, you'll appear at my hearth. We're still tied, boy. But remember this. It's the Spirals that are the most important of all—more important than those you love, or even yourself. He'll guide you to them. They're the places of Power where his Dreams are strongest."

"I don't understand what you mean. The spirals?"

She pointed to her shelter. "Like the one back of the fire pit in the shelter. The ones pecked into the rock. The old ones in the high places."

"Circles within Circles."

"That's the world, boy. That's all of the Wise One Above's creation."

"Will you be all right here? I mean Blood Bear might come back."

She waved it away. "I'll be fine. Oh, I've seen a bit of the future. Blood Bear won't bother me. I've got enough food laid in and there's firewood aplenty around here." She cocked her head, sighing. "It was always the Power, you see. That's what you've got to remember about White Calf. I left Big Fox and my son, Seven Foxes, to chase the Power to the high places. Then, when I established myself here, I met Cut Feather. Power brought us together—in more ways than one."

She scratched back of her ear, and he could see the memories spinning in her head. "We lost ourselves for a while. He and I, that is. Something about love and coupling under the robes that lessens the way Power works within you. Lessens the thirst for Dreaming. Ah, he was good! One passion to weaken another. Coupling does that, rushes your head with delight and leaves you floating like a dream. But human love weakens the Power. I bore him Clear Water, and another child. That one was stillborn. Maybe I should have understood then, but it took a while longer. Cut Feather understood. He let me go . . . took care of your mother.

"It was always the high places." She clucked to herself. "Power's stronger there. Like firelight will draw a moth to its death, so the Power drew me. It sucks you up, possesses you, and you lose yourself in the wonder of touching that other place."

She hesitated, lost in some private vision in her mind.

"I think they're about ready." He pointed to where Two Smokes had picked up the bulky pack and his net. Now the berdache waited. The others stood around, talking in the quiet manner of people about to embark into the unknown.

She didn't seem to hear, still sailing like an eagle on the currents of her mind.

"I guess I just didn't understand. I wish I could have done better for you. I wish I could have been your Dreamer."

She didn't seem lucid, those ancient eyes still unfocused as she whispered, ". . . No, not a Dreamer. A Dancer. *Fire Dancer.*"

His muscles tightened. The Cloud Man had called him that. What did it mean? "Take care. We'll be back to see you soon."

She stood, staring fixedly at the infinite point in her mind only she could see.

Awkward, not knowing what else to do, he walked past her, finding his pack next to the shelter where he'd left it.

"Is she all right?" Elk Charm asked, coming to stand beside him.

"I . . . I think so."

"She's fine. I've seen her like this before." Two Smokes turned on his good heel. "Maybe she wants it this way. Wants us to leave while she's in a vision."

Hobbling along, Two Smokes started down the trail.

Little Dancer looked back, catching one last glimpse of the old woman, still propped on her walking stick like a patient heron, infinity in her clouded old eyes.

Little Dancer sat on an outcrop of sandstone where it rose like a monster's backbone above the ridge. From the vantage point, he could look out to the east and the coming of the night. The land lay mottled, shadowed in lavender and buff where broken ridges extended their lengths to the north and south. Timbered patches looked somber, bluish green in the failing light. Yellow stripes of mudstone interbedded with gray and white shales. Beyond, the tan of the grasslands humped and rolled into the cloud-shadowed vastness of the plains, drifting away, leading the eye into an endless horizon of charcoal and blue until it merged with the indistinct haze of the cloud-packed sky.

Heavy Beaver waited out there, somewhere, his flat features knowing and powerful. That superior smile—so familiar to Little Dancer's memory—lay lazily on those full lips. The scar from the Anit'ah war dart dimpled his broad forehead. Those smoky eyes looked placid, hiding the intent of the wicked heart and mind within.

Little Dancer clamped his eyes shut and shook his head slowly. "They don't need a boy with bad dreams. They need a hero—like the First Man."

Below him, the ridge dropped off in a steep slope spotted with sage and rabbitbrush, yellow flowers still fading on the latter. Angular blocks of sandstone broken from the rim scattered the slope. Gray-capped rosy finches flitted through the sage on agile wings. An insect chirred in the silence. The dried grasses rustled uneasily under the promise of the cool wind.

The autumn of the soul stretched before him.

Gravel crunched under a hesitant foot. He turned, watching Elk Charm climb gracefully up the dun-colored rock, easing to sit next to him where she could share the view.

"Lost in your head again?"

He smiled nervously, looking down at where his callused hands gripped the gritty sandstone. "I guess."

She shifted, wrapping long legs under her, and propped herself with a bracing arm. The western breeze teased the rich raven tones of her long hair. "Two Smokes says it's the Power in you. Do you feel it? The Power, I mean?"

He tried to make an answer that wouldn't betray too much—and failed to find the words. "I don't know. I guess. I . . . I don't know."

"What's it like?"

He shot her a quick look, noting the concern in her eyes. "Scary."

"You're very brave."

"I don't feel that way."

She shrugged, dress rasping as she sought a more comfortable position. "I guess it's because people do what they have to do to stay alive. I wonder about me. A handful of days ago I was happy, playing with Cricket and Tanager and full of laughter and games. Now I'm here because the world changed. I became a woman and Blood Bear wanted me. Now I'm mixed up in the middle of it."

"Are you afraid because of that?"

She raised her head, meeting his searching gaze. "Yes." A ghost of a smile hovered at the edge of her lips. "But I'll take my chances. I guess I don't . . . well, I don't wonder about Power the way you do. I think it just happens and I accept it."

"I wish it was that easy."

She cocked her head. "Maybe you make it hard?"

"Maybe."

A silence stretched while he enjoyed the closeness. How long since he'd had anyone he could simply talk to? If the Dream of the ridge top repeated itself, would Elk Charm turn into rock and try to topple him into the chasm below?

"I think my mother and Hungry Bull are going to sleep together."

Her simple statement shocked him. He turned to stare, suddenly adrift again, seeking some secure footing from which to deal with this new revelation.

"But he . . ." *Mother? Could he forget Sage Root? Just like that?*

As if she understood, she asked, "How long has he been

alone? Almost five years, isn't it? He looks like he's a very lonely man."

He swallowed and forced his attention off to the east, out over the huge basin where Heavy Beaver now controlled the Short Buffalo People. "Yes," he replied dully. "A long time." And Hungry Bull lived alone, probably more alone than he did. Would it be so terrible? Would it be a betrayal of the dead if he slept with Rattling Hooves, who smiled warmly and had laughter dancing in her gentle eyes?

"You look unhappy."

He shook his head, still wondering what he felt. "I don't know. No, not unhappy. Just . . . lost. Like I don't understand anything anymore. So much is happening and I'm . . ."

"Confused?"

He nodded, glancing at her. "Every time I start to feel like I know where I am, it all changes again."

She stared at him, a slight frown on her face. "Can I help?"

"I don't know." Then sourly: "You may not want to. I seem to bring trouble wherever I go. Do you know the story of my real mother, Clear Water?"

She gasped, staring at him with wide eyes. "That's who you are? The story's told among the Red Hand. That she had the baby and was killed. That Two Smokes was crippled and the child died. That White Calf came too late and only Two Smokes was alive."

"Well, that's not what they tell me. And no one tells me who my father really was." He propped his chin. "That's funny, don't you think?"

She bit her lip, staring off into the distance as the evening rushed toward them. "You don't know? Really?"

"No. Two Smokes wouldn't tell me."

"Blood Bear."

He stiffened. "Blood Bear? My . . ." He shook his head at the impossibility of it. "No. That can't be. Impossible."

She avoided his eyes, turning her attention to her suddenly nervous hands. "I don't know. He was married to Clear Water. Something about a Dream of hers. Then she left the Red Hand with Two Smokes. Blood Bear killed his father-in-law, Cut Feather."

"Who White Calf had been married to." His understanding drifted away again, leaving him frustrated and uncertain. "I don't . . . Why isn't this simple? Why does it always seem to be caught up in circles without ending?" He swallowed hard, soul tracing the pattern, understanding White Calf's words.

"What's wrong? You've gone pale."

"Blood and dung," he whispered hoarsely. "It never stops, does it?"

"I don't understand." She shook his hand, the touch warm against his. "Little Dancer? Are you all right? Look at me."

Absently, he turned his head, seeing the anxious light in her eyes. Her hand tightened on his. He smiled weakly.

"It's all right. Really, it is." But his soul drifted like smoke, twisting and without form, homeless, to blow here and there on the wind.

"You feel cold," she told him, snuggling closer.

A sick feeling formed in the pit of his stomach. Was that part of the Power? That he constantly be upset, left reeling and off balance? Of course, he didn't *know* for a fact that Blood Bear really was his father. Two Smokes would know—if he'd tell. Or else it all might remain hidden, another layer, another circle within a circle to spring at him when least expected.

Desperate, he hugged Elk Charm close, laying his cheek on her head, enjoying the reality of her physical presence. The fragrance of her hair filled his nostrils. A new stirring rose within him, one associated only with Dreams.

He pushed her back so he could stare into her worried eyes. She studied him anxiously.

"I don't know myself anymore."

She nodded slightly. "Could I help?"

Something about love and coupling under the robes that lessens the way Power works within you. A man and woman joining like that, it dilutes the call of the Power. Makes you less susceptible to the thirst for Dreaming.

He stared into her kind eyes. "Have you ever . . ."

She smiled inquisitively. "Go on."

"You're a woman."

"You want to couple with me?" She looked away into the

distance, a slight flush rising in her cheeks. "If your father marries my mother . . ." She swallowed hard. "What would . . . I mean, is that incest?"

He gave her a sober stare. "Hungry Bull isn't my father. My mother was Clear Water. You say my father was . . . was Blood Bear."

She chewed her lip for a moment before she burst into happy laughter. "Of course! And he's not even of my clan! We're free, Little Dancer. I've been worried about it for days, but we're free!"

"Then you'll let me?"

"According to my people, a man is made when he kills his first big game. You killed buffalo."

He nodded, wishing his heart hadn't started to pound again.

"You've never coupled with a woman before?"

He shook his head.

"White Calf didn't want me around you. She thought I might affect your Power."

"I know."

"Is that why you want to couple with me?"

He grinned nervously. "Maybe a little. Then, too, I Dreamed of you in the night—of what it's like."

"And we've coupled?"

He nodded.

"And planted seed?"

He nodded again.

She smiled to herself. "Among our cousins, the White Crane People, it's said that a Dream like that twines souls together. That if the people involved don't couple in life, that it makes the soul sick with longing, and eventually you'll die."

"I get this warm feeling inside every time I look at you."

She giggled, pulling him to his feet. "Come on. Let's go down in the trees. I think I'm ready to be a woman in all ways. And I certainly don't want to take the chance of your soul sickening."

She didn't let go of his hand as they clambered off the rock and made their way into the limber pine.

* * *

Tanager enjoyed being right. She stepped out in the trail, blocking Snaps Horn. "Quite a pack. You going on a hunt?"

He started, lifting his arms in frustration. "You know, one of these days you're going to scare someone and they're going to drive a dart right through you."

"Want to bet?" She crossed her arms and grinned. "You couldn't hit me with a dart if you wanted to. I may not be as strong as you, but I'm quicker."

He worked his mouth, shaking his head. "Maybe. All right, I'm going on a hunt."

She narrowed her eyes at the grim look he got.

"And now let me by. What I'm doing is none of your business."

She nodded, a flutter of worry building. "It's Elk Charm, isn't it? You're going after her."

"Maybe."

"It's not like you, answering short like that. You're planning something else, too."

"What if I am?"

"You're in love with Elk Charm?"

He kicked at the dirt in the trail. "What if I am?"

Tanager studied him curiously. "You've been angry ever since you got back. You and Blood Bear."

"Leave him out of this."

"That's who you remind me of. Is that how you want to be? Like him?"

Anger burst. "Look! You're always poking around in my affairs. I put up with it because we're friends. But no more. I'm going to go get Elk Charm away from that Short Buffalo boy and that's it! You hear? Now get out of here!"

He shouldered by her, trembling with rage.

Tanager stared at his broad back as he left at a trot. Short Buffalo boy? The one who lived with the witch?

Tanager squinted after him, pulling at her hair. She nodded to herself. A burning anger she'd never seen before had been goading him, something dangerous and deadly. If Snaps Horn caught the Short Buffalo boy, he'd kill him. Elk Charm might be widowed before she got married.

* * *

Two Smokes watched from where he sat in the shade. They had stretched out every hide they had under the limber pine. Now Hungry Bull, Three Toes, and Black Crow whacked the branches with long poles, flailing. From the shivering limbs, a wealth of pine nuts and needles cascaded onto the hides.

"Does that look like all of it?" Hungry Bull called out to Rattling Hooves.

"Enough for this one," she called back, scrambling on hands and knees over the hides, checking the size and quality of the harvest.

How many winters had passed since he'd heard that spirit in Hungry Bull's voice? How long since he'd seen the light of laughter in those pained brown eyes?

"Two Smokes?"

He craned his neck to find Little Dancer picking his way down the rocks from where he and Elk Charm had been hunting for packrat middens in the rimrock above.

"Yes."

Little Dancer came to squat next to him, hands locked in his lap, watching the men and women picking through the hides, lifting the edges to pour the harvest into a skin bag.

"Blood Bear is my real father, isn't he?"

Two Smokes froze in midgesture. Stunned, he looked over at the boy. "Where did you hear that?" Little Dancer's wry smile didn't reassure him.

"One of the problems of living with Red Hand people is that they know the history. Clear Water married Blood Bear. When her bleeding missed, she left with you for the plains."

"Yes, that's the way it was." He felt old.

"Then Blood Bear is my father?"

"He is." Two Smokes winced at the censure in Little Dancer's voice.

"Why didn't you tell me before? You're the berdache, the man who lives between the worlds. A berdache understands and mediates. He knows both sides." A pause. "And you *didn't* tell me."

Two Smokes looked over, seeing this young man who had once trusted him so thoroughly. "Would it have done you any good? Would it have made things easier for Hungry Bull?"

Little Dancer sniffed, vision drifting to where Hungry Bull laughed and prodded Three Toes in the ribs over some gibe. "No. But . . ."

"But you hate to find out from someone else."

"It's like . . . well . . ."

"Like you've been cheated somehow. Like the Trader took a dozen finely tanned robes and left you with a pack of rotten jerky."

Little Dancer grabbed his knees in the circle of his arms and leaned back, sitting down. "That's how it is."

Two Smokes exhaled softly, resettling his game leg. "That's how it is, all right. But I didn't know what else to do. Now that you've met Blood Bear, you know another reason I, for one, never told you." Two Smokes shook his head. "I heard tell that when he left, all he could talk about was his 'stolen' child. How he'd get his child back. Curious, isn't it, that all he took was the Wolf Bundle? He never asked about you. He assumed the stories were true that you were dead.

"Then, that day he raided Heavy Beaver's camp, he had a chance to kill me—but the Wolf Bundle was more important than killing the man who'd run off with his wife."

"You were berdache."

"I was berdache . . . but I slept with Clear Water. Oh, yes. Don't look at me like that. I loved her. I don't know, maybe I loved her as a man would love a woman. Maybe I loved her as one woman to another. That doesn't matter. All that counts is that I loved her. After Five Falls died, I thought I'd never love again."

"Love's a funny thing."

Two Smokes grunted. "You want to tell me? I suppose you're literally on fire inside, hardly waiting for the opportunity to sneak away into the bushes to pump Elk Charm full of your semen?"

He got a hot look in return.

"Oh, come on, Little Dancer, you're not exactly fooling anyone. Three Toes and Black Crow laugh behind their hands. Meadowlark and Makes Fun wonder quietly among themselves if you aren't too young to understand what you're meddling with—but that's the Short Buffalo People's beliefs at work again. And Hungry Bull is so lost in Rattling Hooves' embrace he could care less.''

''And what do you think?''

Two Smokes waved at a buzzing fly, seeking to grab it out of the air. ''I think you're old beyond your years. I think I know what White Calf saw . . . why she stopped worrying about Elk Charm and let you go.''

''And what was that?''

''That you can't help yourself.'' He met the young man's hot gaze, and shrugged. ''You asked what I thought. I told you.''

''I guess I did,'' Little Dancer relented. ''But she's so . . . I don't know. Thoughts of her fill my life. She's easy to be with.'' He plucked a rock from the ground and sent it sailing off into the rabbitbrush. ''I don't have to worry around her.''

Below them, the rest of the band began moving the pile of hides to another tree, spreading them around to catch what they could knock loose.

''And you think if you bury yourself so thoroughly in Elk Charm, the problem of the Dreams, of the voices and Power, will go away like a water puddle on a hot day?''

''That would be nice,'' he admitted.

Two Smokes snorted a laugh. ''If only it could be so easy.''

They sat for a moment in silence, watching the men beat the branches on the new tree, nuts, cones, and needles raining down on the hides below.

''Why didn't you ever go back to the Red Hand? You told me once that maybe someday you'd tell me.''

Two Smokes considered. ''I swore on the Wolf Bundle that I'd take care of you.''

He smiled, remembering that day in the hot sun. He'd been holding the infant while White Calf did something, went looking for food or some such. And he'd sworn to care for the infant—unaware he'd done so on the Wolf Bundle until too late.

''Was it worth it?'' Little Dancer wanted to know.

Two Smokes remembered all the suffering, the insults, the pain of being raped by callous men, his arms and legs held while they brutally took him from behind. Their laughter at his debasement echoed hollowly. He remembered the pain from the beatings goaded by Heavy Beaver and the final days when the Wolf Bundle was defiled. He relived the time of Sage Root's Curse up to the moment that White Calf had come. And since then? Had anything been easier?

"Yes," he reflected. "Because for a while, I got to feel the Power." It had always been there, warm, extending its glow to him day after day—until Heavy Beaver had offended the Bundle almost beyond repair. For those memories, an entire life of horror could be endured.

"Me, I'm glad I'm shut of it."

The words stung him. "Don't say that."

"Well, I am." Little Dancer braced himself, crossing his legs at the ankles. "I've found what I'm looking for. Here"— he waved at the peaceful valley—"is everything we need. Food. Protection. Here I'll watch my family grow. Heavy Beaver's far away in the plains to the east. Blood Bear's in the high country. What reason would they have to come bother us? No, I'm through with Power and all the trouble and circles and . . . and . . . I'm just through with it."

Two Smokes smiled ironically. "The problem with Power is that you never know." *We will see, boy. We will see!* Then he changed the subject. "And speaking of this woman of yours, are you letting her do all the hunting for packrats?"

"We found a couple of nests up there. She wanted to look a little further."

"Then you'd better take your fire sticks up. You know how to do this?"

Little Dancer gave him a skeptical look. "What's difficult? I make a fire and we set the midden to burning. When the packrat runs out, we bash him with a club."

"But you have to be very, very fast."

Little Dancer grinned. "I'm like lightning. And Elk Charm, she's even quicker."

With that, he jumped to his feet and strolled over to his pack. As Little Dancer fished for his fire sticks, Two Smokes whispered to himself, "I hope you're right, little friend."

He watched Little Dancer start back up the slope, a smart, proud young man who thought he could handle anything.

* * *

Young men jumped, their greased bodies catching the fire-light that accented the swell of muscles and body paint. The bonfire in the middle of the camp snapped and popped, sending spirals of sparks high into the midnight sky. Beyond the illuminated confines of the camp, the grandeur of the Starweb could be easily seen—but not here, not where so much light filled the air.

Around the circle of lodges, women watched, some chanting with the Singer, some just looking on, faces impassive. They stood, mute, buffalo robes pulled tightly over their shoulders. Women of every size and build stood there—tall, short, some thin, others fat—the spoils of his renewal of the People.

Heavy Beaver sat on a white buffalo robe, each of his seven wives behind him. Two Stones, Elk Whistle, and Seven Suns sat watching to either side and slightly to the rear. Before him, planted in the ground, stood a long pole decorated with raven feathers and antelope-hoof rattles: his insignia. It went where his lodge went. Among the Cut Hair, the Fire Buffalo People, and the White Crane, that standard had brought fear.

This celebration, this night of Blessing, marked the reunification of the People under Heavy Beaver's leadership. He smiled happily up into the darkness, imagining his mother's severe face. *I did this, Mother. You were right, like always. All it took was discipline—and desperate people in need of what you taught me. When my young men had nothing left to lose but their lives, they managed wonders. All I had to do was Dream the new way. Mother, you saw so well.*

That flow of pride welled up in him. The whirling leap of the dancers reflected the ecstatic gyrations within his own breast. Through his vision, he'd re-formed the People. Against bands of warriors sent to stop him, his young men had always prevailed, believing themselves invincible. Among peoples who had never seriously warred, Heavy Beaver had sent fanatics willing to kill to the last man. Against his berserk young martyrs, no one could provide more than a token resistance.

The beat of the pot drum, and the rising and falling of the chant, swept him away. This night throbbed of life for him. What he watched was a celebration of his mother's vision and his implementation of it. If only she could see, tell him. . . .

You saw this, Mother. You're the real leader. I only used the strength you taught me. He cocked his head slightly. If he let his imagination drift a little, he could make out his mother's voice in the chanting of the Singers. The cadence of the booming pot drum might have been her very heart, speaking to him.

"You've done very well," Seven Suns admitted from the side. "I never would have believed this many of us would ever be in one place again."

The gruff old voice wrecked his concentration. The urge to rebuke the old man surged, hung for a moment, and ebbed as a cool wind of reason scattered his anger. Seven Suns needed to be won yet. *That's right, son. Take your time. Use your senses and win him over completely. Then you can put him in his rightful place.*

That's what she would have said.

Heavy Beaver spread his hands wide, head back, serenity on the flat features of his face. "We're the new hunters of the buffalo lands. Like the very wolves, we prowl and take what we need. But it's more than the mindless courage of our young men. You see that warrior there? The tall one, painted in blue with the antelope headdress?"

"The one dancing closest to the fire?"

"That's him. His name is Two Blue Moons. He's the oldest son of the Cut Hair People's chief, Fat Dog. He came to me. He offered himself to the new Dreamer. I have a great deal of faith in him. When he leads a war party, his very presence drives our young men to seek to outdo him. Rarely does he let them. But the important thing is the daring, the cunning in warfare that such behavior develops."

"Is that all, though?" Seven Suns leaned forward, gesturing with his hand. "Life must have more to it than war and the ability to demoralize enemies."

"Must it?" Heavy Beaver lifted an eyebrow. "Look around you. Once we were in rags, starving, always moving and dying, trying to find fewer and fewer buffalo."

"We had some good years. Rain came. The herds began to grow, the calf crop—"

"And now the rains might fail again." Heavy Beaver yawned, letting his soul sway to the beat of the drum and the rising keen of the Singers. Where was his mother's voice? There, hanging just at the edge of consciousness. ''And if it does, Seven Suns, we'll not stay bound by the old agreement to hunt only the lands drained by the Moon River. Indeed, we can hunt south to the Sand River, to the Big River in the north. We can hunt where the game are, and no one will stop us. No, we hunt more than buffalo. We hunt people. If we can't find buffalo to kill for hides, we'll take them from those who do.''

''And if others become—''

''They won't. They can't.'' *Mother won't let them. She takes care of us, you doddering old fool! You knew her. You should have recognized her talents then.*

Seven Suns shook his head slowly. ''You sound very sure of yourself, Heavy Beaver.''

The Spirit Dreamer smiled and waved a hand. ''I am. I've Dreamed the new way . . . and it's as the spirits told me. It's a new age, a new kind of life. We've cleaned the pollution from the People.''

''And what comes next?''

''To purify others as well. I don't intend on letting the Cut Hair, or the Fire Buffalo, or the White Crane ever challenge us again. Their power must be broken, enough of their women taken to ensure marriage and economic ties with our bands.'' A flush of certainty, like the rising of the morning sun, warmed him. That *was* the way. He could almost feel it in the very air.

''And the Red Hand? How do you plan to tame the wild men of the mountains?''

Heavy Beaver chuckled to himself. ''Oh, they'll fall. For the moment, the only advantage they have is that they know the country up there. They can ambush us at will. The key is to plan ahead. When we have enough supplies laid in, and enough warriors trained for it, we'll go up there and root them all out.''

Seven Suns frowned, sucking at his lower lip. ''There are some of my elders who—''

''Forget them. This isn't an age for the old men and old women to spout stories about First Man or the Hero Twins. Here, in this new world, we're making a new way. I'm the legend of the new world, Seven Suns. My mother had this vision. She foresaw this future. She had Power running in her veins like blood. I'm just living it for her."

The image he'd conjured possessed him. In his reverie, the pot drum reflected the beat of her heart. She had *become* the People. He cocked his head, listening again to the chant, seeking her words. They hovered at the edge of his understanding. If only he could break that last barrier and comprehend.

"What is it?" Seven Suns asked.

Heavy Beaver ignored him, lost, trying to unravel the secret of his mother's words.

"The water has ceased to run in Monster Bone Springs. As my Power weakens, so does that of the world. Even the sagebrush is wasting. Can't you do something?" The Wolf Bundle called up into the spinning golden haze, its plea sending shivers along the silver silken way of the Spirals.

Wolf Dreamer's voice came hazily from the Spirals. "We have reached our limits for the moment. We must wait, hope."

"And watch a world die?"

Chapter 16 ✋

Hungry Bull helped Two Smokes down a steep place, looking around the new shelter. The old berdache led them down a twisting trail as a gentle dusting of snow settled about them, whitening shoulders, heads, and packs. A scattering of juniper mixed with limber pine along the drainages while the south-facing slopes had a gray look from bitterbrush, currants, and serviceberry. Deer tracks had stippled the trail they walked.

Across from them, the opposite side of the canyon looked cool and somber as the conical tips of fir rose dark green above snarled black timber. At the crest, however, broad meadows appeared to stretch up into the grayish haze of falling snowflakes and cloud.

"Elk winter up there," Two Smokes said, gesturing toward the high meadows. "Good place to hunt in the deep cold."

"Good camp all around," Rattling Hooves agreed. "Doesn't look like anyone camped here for a long time."

"Maybe." Two Smokes shrugged. "Last time I stayed here was as a young man. Five Falls came here with his cousin and we spent the winter. The camp was pretty good, but the mice and packrats almost drove us crazy that year."

"But did you come this late?" Rattling Hooves asked, twisting her body under the tumpline so she could see him.

"Earlier." Two Smokes pointed up the canyon. "But we did the hard work then. We built a sheep trap up there. I don't think it would take much to fix it up. We've got the new net Elk Charm and I have been working on. Once we kill some bighorns, we'll have hides and meat for a while until the elk come down. Perhaps Hungry Bull, here, and Three Toes and Black Crow can kill a deer or two. From those hides we can make snares for elk."

"Whoa!" Black Crow cried. He'd been listening with his head cocked, trying to pick up the Anit'ah words. "Did he say *snare* an elk?"

Hungry Bull chuckled. "Hunting here is different. Come, let's find this rock shelter." He winked at Rattling Hooves. "Maybe you can teach me how to snare elk and hunt sheep?"

She grinned at him before returning her concentration to the trail. "I think you'll learn. But come on, it's starting to get dark. Better to be off this loose slope before we can't see our feet."

Tall stands of giant wild rye—brown under the hand of winter—hid the mouth of the rock overhang. The place looked to be ten paces in length and Hungry Bull found it extended back another three paces once he'd pushed through the screen of grass. In the failing light he could barely make out the litter of a large packrat nest in the back corner where the floor met the rock.

"You could be right about the packrats."

"What we don't drive off, I'll eat." Rattling Hooves sighed

as she swung the pack off her back and rubbed her arms. "Hey, great hunter of the Short Buffalo People, why don't you make us a fire?"

Three Toes helped Two Smokes up the slope and into the dark shelter. The rest straggled in one by one, sighing, shivering, and puffing in the cold as they shed packs here and there.

"So this is home?" Black Crow called as he reached up to rap knuckles on the stone. He shook his head slowly.

From where he dug around in his pack for fire sticks, Hungry Bull looked up. "Worried?"

Black Crow led Makes Fun by the hand, his three children staring around owlishly. "Worried?" Black Crow cocked his head, watching as Hungry Bull's quick fingers placed the charred sharpened end of the small stick in the friction hole of the base piece. Puffing foggy breath, he began spinning the sticks as Black Crow added, "No, we're not worried. Everything's just new, is all. We're . . . well, we don't feel like we fit here. Like the world's different, you know?"

Hungry Bull nodded, glad for the blood he pumped through chilled arms. "I felt that way when we left Heavy Beaver's camp—but Sage Root had just been killed. I followed along like a soul without a body."

Rustling grass marked the arrival of Elk Charm and Little Dancer. Some private joke had them laughing with the buoyancy of youth, despite the cold and fatigue of the long journey.

Makes Fun's teeth had begun to chatter from the cold, before the spinning fire stick coaxed a faint thread of smoke from the tinder. Despite chill-stiffened fingers, Hungry Bull grinned as he got a red glow.

"Got a place for this?" he asked Black Crow.

The latter immediately reached into his pack, drawing forth a twist of dried ricegrass stems and shredded bark, all partially charred. Makes Fun reached for the packrat nest, pulling long-dried lengths of sagebrush and duff from the mass. Somewhere back in the rock, a faint thumping could be heard as the frightened rodent stamped with a nervous back foot.

"And there's worse coming," Makes Fun promised the little creature.

Hungry Bull scooped his glowing tinder into Black Crow's grass twist and blew cautiously. The ember gleamed, a bright red eye. Smoke rose in a thin trail. A dance of flame gave birth and greedily devoured the twist. One by one, they fed bits of twigs and sticks, adding bigger pieces until they had a crackling blaze.

"Hey, look at that!" Three Toes pointed at the sloping back wall of the shelter. A long section of sandstone had broken loose, the top of it barely protruding from the floor, so long ago had it happened. In the meantime, the flat panel created by the roof fall had been smoke-blackened and soot-encrusted, but not so much that a person couldn't make out the figures pecked into the rock.

A large spiral dominated the panel. Three Toes stepped closer, rubbing at the side to clean the rock. "Blood and dung," he whispered. "A monster! Look! Look how well this is done. There's the humped back, the big teeth, and the tail thing growing out of the snout!" He scrubbed at the wall with his hand, wiping more of the soot away, and stopped cold, peering at the figure he'd uncovered.

A man with a dart stood to one side, obviously in the act of casting his deadly weapon into the monster's side.

"White Calf always said that people killed the monsters like we do the buffalo." Hungry Bull reached over the huddle of children clustered around the fire with hands out to the warmth. He snagged a burning brand and stuffed it into the side of the packrat's nest.

His smile beamed up at Rattling Hooves. "I don't like packrats, they chew things in the night. They also lead to trouble with Spirit Power. I was doing just fine until a packrat chewed my atlatl once."

She slapped his shoulder. "That nest ought to make enough coals for a day or two. I'll smack them when they run out this side."

She positioned herself across one of the runways with her walking stick raised. Elk Charm took the other side as fire crackled into the nest.

Three Toes shook his head, attention glued to the rock carvings as Black Crow came to stand next to him.

"I don't know how long those have been there." Two

Smokes settled himself on an angular chunk of roof fall. "I first saw them when I was a boy, maybe as old as Dancing Leaf"—he pointed to Black Crow's oldest daughter—"and they were old then."

Three Toes continued to rub at the soot as Rattling Hooves cried out and whacked at a brown streak with her stick. "Got you!"

On the other side of the spiral, Three Toes uncovered pictures of two animals, obviously mountain sheep from the horns curling on their heads. Then he found a buffalo and an elk, both transfixed with darts. A series of grooves in the lower part of the wall he identified as scrubbings for platform preparation in the manufacture of chipped-stone tools, but above, hidden in the dancing shadow of the fire, he scraped the soot from one last figure.

"What's that?" Hungry Bull craned his neck to see.

"Wolf," Three Toes whispered, stepping back as the lines of the animal became clear. "Look! Like it's alive."

Little Dancer gasped, almost startling Hungry Bull. He managed to glimpse his son's face, seeing the color drain from his wind-nipped cheeks.

"Wolf was the Spirit Helper of the First Man when he came from under the world," Two Smokes reminded them from where he rubbed at his shivering arms. He nodded slowly. "We never cleaned the rock carvings when we were here."

Elk Charm's deadly stick smacked another skittering pack-rat as the fire burned into the nest. "That's two! Fresh meat tonight!"

"Hey." Three Toes grinned, stepping back to put his arm around Meadowlark and ruffle his children's heads. "This might not be such a bad place after all!"

Hungry Bull chuckled as Rattling Hooves whacked another packrat. The heat from the fires had begun to penetrate his half-frozen clothing. "No, it might not be bad at all."

Then he caught sight of Little Dancer, still pale, glazed eyes on the wolf that seemed to stare down at him from above.

Snaps Horn studied White Calf's shelter from a distance, seeing no one but the old woman. He waited for two days, making sure the others had left. Angrily, he looked up at the somber sky. White fluffy flakes fell wet and heavy. There'd be no trail now. He should have cut for sign earlier. He'd known the Short Buffalo People would be there.

The Short Buffalo boy should have come walking down one of the trails so he could drive a dart right through him. That'd teach him to fool with the woman Snaps Horn had chosen. Then no one would stand in his way if he took her for a wife.

Where would they have gone?

The old ewe trotted forward, stopping for a moment to look back over her shoulder.

"Slow up!" Rattling Hooves called, her voice barely raised in the chill air.

Little Dancer stopped where he was, trying to keep his footing on the steep slope.

Sunlight slanted from the winter sky, warming the southern face of the canyon. Behind the rocks, shadows of snow clung in the recesses. Bits of grass, winter-dry plants, and occasional patches of brush eked out a fragile existence on the crumbling slope of the mountain.

"Can't believe people hunt like this." Hungry Bull's words barely traveled to where Little Dancer waited, trying to catch his breath.

Ahead of them, perhaps four dart casts away, the little band of mountain sheep stopped in the old ewe's shadow, staring back at them.

"Now what?" Little Dancer asked.

"Forward," Rattling Hooves called in her throaty voice. "Just a bit at a time. We don't want them to spook and bolt. If they do, they'll miss the trap."

Little Dancer repeated the order, hearing it passed down the line of people threading their way along the slope.

Below him, the valley lay cloaked in snow. The willow-packed stream bottom lay in blue shadow, rounded mounds of snow marking the looping course of the ice-shrouded stream banks. Here and there a dark patch showed where the water ran too fast to freeze over. The winter-nude willows had been crisscrossed with deer and elk tracks. The slope opposite brooded in memories of summer. The perpetually shadowed spruce and fir slept mantled in deep snow.

Little Dancer looked up into the winter-blue vault of the sky, marveling at how the color seemed so much deeper in the short days. A faint glaze of clouds laced the heavens to the east. The nippy breeze played carelessly down the canyon. Curiously, he sniffed, seeing if he could detect any odor of the sheep. The air stung his nostrils.

Below him, Elk Charm picked her way carefully. As if she could feel his eyes on her, she looked up, smiling as she tossed her wealth of jet-black hair over a hide-wrapped shoulder.

A pleasant thrill rose peacefully in his breast. Finally he could smile, laugh, enjoy life as it should be lived. This bit of land had become theirs. Here they lived beyond the fear of Blood Bear, beyond the nightmare of Heavy Beaver.

He took another step, trying to dig his moccasin-clad foot into the side of the mountain. Gravel and dirt rattled and cascaded under his weight.

"Hey!" Hungry Bull griped in a muted voice.

Little Dancer chuckled from the pit of his stomach.

Ahead of him, the sheep began to move again, the old ewe leaping gracefully from rock to rock, the sun shining on her sleek winter coat. An old ram followed the rest, uneasy, hanging to the rear as if he didn't know quite what to do.

From where Little Dancer traced his way along the slope, he could barely see the low saddle. "Time for Elk Charm to work her way ahead and up," Rattling Hooves added.

From high above where Three Toes scrambled from one precarious perch to another came a robin's lilting call. Little Dancer shook his head at the incongruity of the birdsong until he realized he'd been tricked by Three Toes' talented mimicking.

Below, Elk Charm waved and began to move faster, walking along the more stable rocks. Black Crow and Meadowlark took up the pace, keeping the line more or less even. Hungry Bull kept his position.

The old ewe trotted ahead, kicking dirt and pebbles to bounce down the slope. The younger ewes and lambs followed, almost buckjumping across the loose scree. Reaching the secure footing on the other side, the lead ewe stopped, staring at the saddle as if she understood.

Little Dancer swallowed, thinking about the dwindling supplies of meat.

"Please, Mother," he pleaded.

She turned to stare over her buff shoulder. Across the distance, he could feel her eyes on him.

"*Please*, Mother," he whispered fervently. "We need your meat."

The drive line had come to a stop. The ewe shot a quick glance up toward the trap. She craned her neck, ears pricked behind her thin curved horns. One avenue of escape remained. She stared hard at the narrow gap where she could bolt and flank the drive line. The decision seemed to waver in her mind.

"Please, Mother," Little Dancer repeated under his breath. He tried to reach her, to explain the starvation that could befall a people without the gift of meat. Fists clenched, he cleared his mind, seeking to convey the need.

Time slipped. He didn't realize he'd fallen to his knees, arms lifted. *"Please, Mother."*

The feeling leached up from the sharp rock that bit into his knees. That instant of awareness stretched, the Oneness wrapping around him like fog around the scabby bark of the valley cottonwoods in morning.

"We're hungry, Mother. Lend us your life. Share your spirit with us." He didn't remember meeting her eyes across the distance. For the moment only the touching of their souls mattered. Only the pulsing of the ewe's heart, the rush of air in her lungs, the worry in her mind, filled his consciousness.

"Feed us, Mother."

Understanding, regret, acceptance, the emotions filled him, possessed him. He himself turned, walking on four nimble legs, starting up the slope. He watched a colorless world now flatly visible in shades of gray through the ewe's eyes. Through her ears, he heard the rest following, their scrambling feet grating on the loose gravels of the mountain, clacking on the rock. The odors of earth and frost and mold-rich leaves packed under the bitterbrush and squaw currant hung in his nose, mixed with the tang of winter-cured grass.

He relished the power of her legs as she bounded up the slope. He ran on her wondrous feet, surefooted with her padded hooves where a man would slip and tumble.

Then she passed between the two rocky outcrops, topping the crest of the ridge, running down between the stacked pitch-pine wing walls of the trap. Her muscles took the leap into the catch pen, while the others crowded behind.

Two Smokes' net rose behind and the other ewes and lambs began to bleat nervously. She waited, sharing the moment with him, uneasy, but accepting so long as he shared her mind. The bleating of the herd, the snorting of the jittery ram, stung every instinct.

The shouts of the hunters shot terror through the rest of the herd, adding to the panic of their bleating and dashing about. The net crowded them forward, handled by the crippled Two Smokes and the agile Rattling Hooves. They appeared oddly out of perspective, looking flat and awesome through the ewe's eyes. She barely flinched as the net lowered over her, a weight that couldn't be comprehended. The others stood trembling, trying to understand this thing, this binding of strings smelling of human and juniper bark.

He understood the clubs. And through him, so did she. The rising of the fire-cured juniper, the arcing descent, the hollow smash, shivered his being. The rich odor of blood carried on the breeze, its musk mixing with the scent of humans. One by one, the rest of the bighorns were clubbed. Inevitable death approached.

Little Dancer stared up at his father, huddling down as the club rose against a gray sky. He flinched as the whistling arc of wood descended.

Blackness.

Voices.

"He's waking up. Little Dancer? Can you hear me?"

The familiar feeling of hands—human hands—cradled him. Warmth rose from the body supporting him. He groaned, stirring, savoring the sensations of life, of the heart beating in his breast. A wonderful sensation of numbing chill saturated his legs and arms and led him to shiver.

Alive!

"What happened? Did you fall?" Elk Charm's concern brought him up from the layers of infinity to open his eyes to the bright light of a slanting sun. He blinked, finding himself on Elk Charm's lap. Hungry Bull crouched over him, holding his hands, half-frantic eyes searching his face anxiously. Around him, Three Toes, Black Crow, and Rattling Hooves bent over, expressions tense.

"You missed the hunt." Hungry Bull almost laughed with relief. "You fell down and—"

"I was there," he croaked, taking a deep breath. "The ewe and I . . . One. We were One. She was going to drop down, miss the trap. I pleaded."

The memories came rushing back, each step, each breath and heartbeat. The rising of the club, the inevitability of death. A violent shiver racked his body.

"We've got to warm him up," Rattling Hooves spoke from somewhere beyond.

Hands lifted him, people mumbled disjointedly as his body shifted beyond his control.

"Watch your step." The words muddled in his ears.

He floated off again, awed by the thought that he'd died with the ewe—and it hadn't been unpleasant. But what had happened afterward? A feathery feeling of drifting . . .

Warmth. A crackling of fire. Smoke tickled his nostrils. Bleary-eyed, he blinked at a fire set into a shallow pit. The odor of roasting meat filled his nostrils. A sudden hunger saturated him.

"And he keeps talking about the One?" Two Smokes could be heard to one side. "I saw the ewe stop. I thought for sure she'd bolt and we'd miss them. A feeling of Power prickled in the air. I knew it, the way a berdache knows. Then the ewe turned and walked right into the trap. She didn't even look scared, but her eyes . . . the way she stood . . . possessed."

"Shared," Little Dancer croaked. "Shared." And he stared into the crackling flames, drifting with the sparks.

* * *

"What do you think about Little Dancer and his visions?" Three Toes asked cautiously as they climbed. "You know, he's not like a child who . . . Child? I mean a man. He's killed his first buffalo and he and Elk Charm are obviously man and woman under their hides at night. But he's so young . . . and so old at the same time. You're his father, what do you make of it?"

Hungry Bull puffed a frosty breath from his laboring lungs as he looked up at the mat of snow-covered branches interlacing into a woven pattern above them. The boles of the fir trees had a washed-out grayish look against the snow and the crisscrossing of powder-mantled deadfall.

He shook his head, stopping to pack down a place to stand in the knee-deep snow so he wouldn't slip and tumble back down the steep trail. The pockmarks of elk tracks wound around the uprooted base of a blown-down tree and disappeared into timber. How could elk run up stuff like this? Magical!

"I worry about him." What more could be said?

"And Elk Charm?"

Hungry Bull shrugged, resettling the pack on his back. "He's a man, old friend. He's killed his meat and taken a woman. He's proven he can feed her. He's taken the responsibilities of a man—and he acts like it. He's strong and smart and has to make his own way now."

Three Toes sniffed at the cold, looking back down the tortuous trail they'd followed up the mountain side. From up where he stood, the slope looked worse than it had been. Up was always less scary than down. Long braided-hide ropes curled on their backs. "You feel cramped in here, like you can't see. Like some monster might reach out of all these trees and eat you or something."

Hungry Bull chuckled. "My odd boy—the one you worry so much about—would Dream you back."

"You think that's what he did?" Three Toes shook his head. "I don't know, maybe he did. White Calf always said he had Power. And Two Smokes, well, I always thought he was a . . . different. But, you know, these Anit'ah, they think berdache have some sort of Power, like Traders—"

"Not like Traders—they're berdache."

"Okay, berdache Power. I can start to believe that." Three Toes frowned, sucking loudly at his teeth before uttering the throaty rasp of a stellar's jay. The call echoed through the somber trees. A chickadee peeped in return.

Hungry Bull squinted up at the tiny patch of blue sky he could see straight overhead. "Yeah, I think Little Dancer has Power. I hear him at night while he's asleep. Dreams come on him. Not like normal people dream, but Power Dreams, and a lot of the time he wakes up . . . but he doesn't, you know? You can talk to him and he'll talk back, but he's not there, not *with* you in the shelter."

"I saw. Last night. You called to him and he answered that it was the fire. I looked, and the fire looked just fine. He had his eyes open, Hungry Bull. I could see that—but it was like he wasn't inside."

"You were awake when I asked him about it this morning? He just blinked at me, baffled."

"Yeah. That's enough to make my hair stand on end," Three Toes grumbled. "Makes Fun is getting a little spooked about it. Black Crow's told her to keep quiet, that it's a phase and Little Dancer will grow out of it."

"Come on, the snow's freezing my feet, standing still like this." And he wanted desperately to avoid the subject that had started to wear on all of them.

He took another step, following in the path of the elk that had climbed before them. The elk knew the best way to get to the top of the mountain. But then, where an elk thought the trail was easy and where a man did demonstrated two different realities.

"So we're going to snare an elk just like a rabbit?" Three Toes puffed and struggled up after Hungry Bull, continuing his peeping conversation with the chickadees. "Sounds real crazy."

"Why?" Hungry Bull wondered. "You heard what Rattling Hooves said. All we—"

"I didn't get all of it. I'm still trying to make sense out of that slurred pronunciation they talk in."

"Does sound slurred, doesn't it?" Hungry Bull reached up with a mitten to scratch back of his ear. "But then they say we cluck like sage grouse when we talk."

"Sage grouse?" Three Toes exploded with a snort. "That'll be the day! We don't sound anything like sage grouse when we talk."

"They think so."

"And what about you? You and Rattling Hooves seem pretty blissful under the robes. You and she are going to stay together? What about this One Cast? Is he going to be trouble for you?"

Hungry Bull pulled himself over a deadfall where the elk had already knocked the snow off, dragging their bellies across. He reached back and offered Three Toes a hand.

"She says it won't be trouble. She says that among the Red Hand a woman can leave a man . . . just like that. I guess, though, that it's considered polite to do something for the old husband. Take him a couple fine robes, maybe some meat.

"But One Cast married her more or less because she needed a husband. At least that's what she tells me. One Cast likes his first wife best, a woman called Wet Rain. Rattling Hooves sure liked them both. Said they helped deceive Blood Bear when he tried to take Elk Charm. I guess that's reason enough to like them."

"Well, I can see that. Anyone who doesn't like Blood Bear is all right in my view." Three Toes paused to take a deep breath before adding, "But then I don't seem to be doing any too good with Dreamers or leaders these days."

"Don't worry about it. You're safe now. We can all start over, learn new things, and stay out of Heavy Beaver's way."

"And Blood Bear?"

"I don't think he'll bother us. Not with White Calf speaking for us."

"Um, I don't want to rain on your buffalo hunt, but she's not as young as I'd like her to be."

"Thinking about another wife?"

"Oh, stop. White Calf? A wife? I could think of bunches of better ways to commit suicide. Like sneaking up behind a mad buffalo and slapping its scrotum with a prickly-pear cactus. But what if she decides to take her soul to the Starweb sometime soon? What do we do then? Our Spirit Woman protection's gone and died on us."

"That's why we go visit the Red Hand in spring. We go

as relatives to Rattling Hooves and Elk Charm and Two Smokes. We go and visit and trade and come back here. Rattling Hooves says that come spring, we'll have shooting star, balsam root, onions, sego lily, biscuit root, and all kinds of things growing up here. Then in late summer and fall there's serviceberry and currants and pine nuts and ruff-necked grouse and all kinds of good stuff. We might have to move a little to find the slopes with the best harvest—I guess that changes from year to year—but it won't be bad."

"You like all that stuff? You like not eating buffalo?"

Hungry Bull slapped his belly. "Put it like this. I've grown used to looking down and seeing my navel—maybe not so round as Black Crow's, but still, I haven't been hungry for a long long time. Not only that, but stuff like sego lily is sweet, wonderful. And baked biscuit root is like nothing else in the world. I could eat that—like you could buffalo backstrap—for the rest of my life."

"Doesn't seem right, all that digging in the ground."

Hungry Bull chuckled to himself. "Not more than a couple of weeks ago, I told my son the same thing."

"So what happened?"

"Rattling Hooves came into my life. For the first time since I saw White Calf up on the ridge that day, the sun shone. Now, well, look around you. It's pretty up here. The wind isn't as bad as down in the plains. There's color up here in the rocks and soil and trees and the flowers. And we can still trap. The sheep trap worked fine. We're after elk. What's better for hunters than to hunt, eh? And no Heavy Beaver is Dreaming trouble for us here."

"But it's so different from the old ways."

"Anything new is different. So learn and enjoy it."

"Like Rattling Hooves teaching you how to trap sheep? Blood and dung, if Heavy Beaver could hear that! A hunter learning to hunt from a woman?" He slapped his leg, laughing.

Hungry Bull lifted a shoulder in a shrug. "I don't care. I'm happy. Let me tell you, I thought I'd never live again, that my soul would rise to the Starweb like the black smoke from burned fat. Now Rattling Hooves has come, and she's warm, thoughtful, and she cares about me. I care about her.

The hole in my heart that opened when Sage Root was murdered, well, it isn't gone completely, but there's a part of me that's full where I didn't know it was empty. I feel whole now.''

Hungry Bull undid his pack, slinging it over a chest-high log the elk had jumped. "Give me a leg up here."

With Three Toes' help, he scrambled over, reaching back to pull his friend up. "Besides, your children like it here. I watched Two Moons, Laughs A Lot, and Grasshopper up with Black Crow's get. They were all rolling rocks down the hill, laughing and shrieking to wake the ghosts."

"They like it. We lived so far east with Seven Suns' band they didn't get many chances to roll rocks. Young ones should get that chance."

"And Meadowlark and Makes Fun will like it better, too. Work's not so hard up here. They won't have to go so far for firewood in winter. Water's almost everywhere. Food's easier to find. You don't have to pack as much on your back."

They cleared the trees, walking out into one of the lower meadows. Underfoot the snow crunched. A raven rose with a rasping of wings on air, sliding out of sight.

"I'd say—there." Three Toes pointed to a narrow break in the trees that separated their meadow from one above it. Near the break the snow had been dimpled by elk beds and stitched with tracks. The place stunk of the rich musky odor of elk. Piles of scat and urine discolored the snow.

"They cross through there, I'll bet." Three Toes kicked urine-crusted snow loose and sniffed, grinning like a fool as he exhaled a frosty cloud.

"Think those trees are strong enough to hold an elk?"

"Think our rope is?" Three Toes countered.

"Guess we'll find out." Hungry Bull plodded his way across the clearing.

"So, how sensitive are elk to man smell?" Three Toes wondered. "Will they pass through there even though everything smells like people?"

"Rattling Hooves said we should piss on either side of the passage through the trees. She said elk sniff and leave their mark on top of a man's."

"You're joking!"

"No joke. She told me that when she was married to Elk Charm's father, he used to backtrack and find elk had followed him for half a day."

"Hunted and hunter, huh? Like silver bears." Three Toes stared over his shoulder at the somber line of trees.

Hungry Bull stepped into the first elk bed—and almost fell. The animal's warm body had frozen the snow and coated the bed with a glaze of ice. "Frozen solid. They've been gone a while." He picked up a pellet from the pile, squeezing it between thumb and forefinger.

The passage through the trees looked excellent. The trail had been packed down by elk feet.

Hungry Bull boosted Three Toes as high up the tree as he could to tie off the end of the snare. Together they hung the loop just so, at the right angle to catch an elk's head.

Finished with their handiwork, Three Toes slapped the snow from his mittens and chewed at his lip. "So that's an elk snare? And I did it all on my own?"

"You trapped sheep, too. And knocked pine nuts out of trees."

"And liked them," Three Toes agreed. "Yes, I suppose I could get to like this life. But it's a little lonely. I miss hearing the old tales." He frowned. "Maybe we should have brought Little Dancer. He could have made a sign or something that draws elk better than urine."

Hungry Bull shrugged. He started to turn and froze, reaching to pat his friend on the shoulder. Three Toes turned and stopped short.

The wolf stood in the shadows of the trees, eyes burning curiously yellow, as if lit from a fire inside.

"Big, isn't he?"

"Yeah," Three Toes breathed.

For long moments they watched; then, as if by magic, the wolf disappeared.

Three Toes blinked and rubbed his eyes. "I didn't even see him move."

"Me either." A shiver went up Hungry Bull's back. "Did you notice the . . . Oh, never mind. Must be the light."

"You mean the way he looked just like the wolf drawn on the rock in the shelter?"

Hungry Bull nodded, staring at the place where the wolf had stood. "Just like the wolf in the shelter. Just like that . . ."

"The buffalo are worried!" the Wolf Bundle cried. "You can feel it. Confusion, frustration, starvation, they're half mad. One by one, they die. A species facing oblivion spreads terror through the Spiral. They know their time hasn't come. But what can they do? The soul of the land cries out. Feel death? Feel it drawing close, choking the warmth from the earth? Is this our future? Feel the fawn antelope in their need? Thirst. The land cries. What can we do? I'm tortured . . . dying with the land. Thirst, heat, what can we offer them?"

Wolf Dreamer's weary voice settled in an evening frost. "Hope."

Chapter 17 ✋

"You look worried, girl."

Elk Charm met her mother's eyes before gazing back down the valley. The slopes now had a faint green tinge that had begun to challenge last year's brown. Sagebrush gleamed bluish green against the tan of the sandstone. Overhead, the crystal sky stretched into a blue infinity that threatened spring.

"I was thinking of something Two Smokes told me . . . about Dreamers."

Rattling Hooves sighed and settled herself in the warm sun next to her daughter. "I've caught you looking into nothingness more than once. You sneak those faraway looks whenever you think no one is watching. Want to tell me about it?"

"I always thought it would be Snaps Horn. Then I met Little Dancer. I love him with a feeling like a fire's inside me. I never knew I could love a man this way. He's so . . ."

well, he's gentle, always thinking of me, and he holds me like I'm the most precious thing in his world.''

"I've seen."

"But he frightens me. There's part of him I can't share. Something that's beyond me.''

"And Two Smokes? You said he told you something about Little Dancer?''

Elk Charm shook her head, lip clamped in her lower teeth. "He told me once about how Power uses people . . . like humans use tools for a single purpose, and then discard them. He talked about a dart as an example, how it was so carefully crafted and finally cast at an animal. You know what happens to darts. Sometimes they miss and land in the rocks. When that happens, the point shatters, the shaft cracks. All that work for nothing. Sometimes they get lost in the snow or thick grass, forgotten. Left behind to rot away.'' The image lived inside her, haunting, painful.

"And you think the Power's that strong in Little Dancer?''

She filled her lungs, enjoying the sensation of air rushing through her throat, holding it to savor the full feeling. "Yes, Mother. I think he's more Powerful than he knows. The day at the mountain sheep trap was only a hint. I've watched trappings before. You know as well as I that they were about to bolt the wrong way. He Dreamed them in.

"Since that day, I've watched Two Smokes. He sits in the back of the shelter, not saying much, but his eyes are always on Little Dancer. Not only that, but when Little Dancer has Dreams late at night, he'll wake up, and stare at the spiral on the back wall of the shelter—or at the wolf. And when he has those Dreams, I wake up. So does Two Smokes, even though he sleeps across the shelter. I don't think Little Dancer notices, but Two Smokes is watching him, staring through slitted eyes.

"I asked him about that. He smiled funny—as if his heart were tearing—and told me that a berdache can feel Power, that they live in the halfway place between the worlds.'' Elk Charm lifted her shoulder. "And he won't tell me more. He just places his hand on my shoulder, like a reassuring brother, and walks off.''

Rattling Hooves put her arm around her daughter's shoulders. "Yes, I suppose Little Dancer does have Power. But as far as I'm concerned, he can take care of himself. It's my daughter I'm worried about. What do you think? Is he worth the trouble? Will you be all right?"

Elk Charm looked up into those warm eyes. "I . . . I think so. He's going to be a great man, Mother. I can feel it. Maybe as great as First Man was when he brought the People up from the First World to this one."

"But the legends tell us that First Man avoided women." Rattling Hooves lifted an eyebrow as a reminder.

Elk Charm settled her vision on the distance where the ridges rose against the skyline one after another until dun earth and tan rock met cerulean sky. "And if he's called, I guess I've had my warning." She cocked her head. "I can prepare for that day. And when it happens, I'll have had what time with him that I've had, won't I? I mean, if you could have known what would happen to Father—you'd only have so much time—what would you have done? Turned away from his robes?"

Rattling Hooves studied her pensively. "I didn't know that we'd begun raising adults at so young an age. When I was your age, just out of the menstrual lodge, I was interested in men, trying them all, learning what coupling was about. My concern was to make as many of my friends as jealous as I could. I tried to marry the most handsome man available. And here you are, worrying about only one and what he'll do to your life. Most girls your age are too wrapped up in themselves to think that far ahead."

Rattling Hooves paused, a frown lining her features. "Or is it that you've only had one man? Maybe it's a lack of experience? Hmm? Could that be it? You've thrown all of yourself into Little Dancer when he's the only man around who can—"

"No." She shook her head stubbornly. "I've thought about that. I've thought about all the things Tanager and Cricket and I promised ourselves we'd do. Sometimes, I lie awake at night and watch the firelight on the rock overhead and try to think what man I'd rather have. I don't just mean in our band—but among all the Red Hand. Snaps Horn had always been the one I dreamed of. But compared to the fire of Little

Dancer, Snaps Horn is a mild ember. I still like him, and maybe if Little Dancer left I'd still go to him. But Little Dancer's different."

"They all are," her mother reminded wryly.

"I mean it. He's . . . well, so kind. He's been hurt. Tell me, when you look into his eyes, what do you see?"

Rattling Hooves shifted uncomfortably. She considered for a moment, the gentle lines of her face thoughtful. "Yes, I know what you mean. I see the same thing in his father's eyes. But I can trust Hungry Bull. He wouldn't hurt me. He's mature, a man who knows himself and where he'll be tomorrow, or next year. He has that sense of identification with others . . . that what was done to him can't be inflicted on anyone else. I've known men who'd do that, turn their pain on someone else. Blood Bear would. He'd make another pay for what was done to him by life."

"Little Dancer wouldn't do that. He wouldn't hurt me."

"Not knowingly." Rattling Hooves shifted, taking up Elk Charm's hands; her serene eyes probed her daughter's. "What I wonder is, what he'll do if the Power asks?"

Swallowing hard, Elk Charm lifted her shoulders, enjoying the warmth of her mother's hands. "I don't think he knows himself. I've asked, and he says he's not the one. He repeats that over and over."

"Like he's trying to convince himself?"

Elk Charm's heart tripped. "Blood and dung, I hope not!" Yet she knew she'd made up her mind. She'd savor every moment with him, keep each of his smiles as her own. And if the Power proved stronger than she? Well, that rocky and forbidding ridge would have to be scaled when the time came. Pray to the Wise One that she could do it.

"You know"—Rattling Hooves paused, trying to pick her words—"the others are beginning to worry. When Little Dancer Dreams at night, and makes the noises, it wakes the children. Makes Fun and Meadowlark are getting nervous."

"They're living in a new land, learning new things. We're all cramped up in that little shelter and the winter seems like it will never end."

"Sure, we're all tired of each other. But part of the constant tension is caused by Little Dancer." Rattling Hooves pulled her knee up. "I've done a little talking to Two Smokes myself. He's no fool; he can feel things coming to trouble."

Elk Charm's gut twisted.

"Ah, yes, you know, don't you, daughter? You can feel it, too."

"What . . . what did Two Smokes say?"

Rattling Hooves lifted her chin slightly, tightening her grip. "Listen to me, Elk Charm, and remember that I'd never hurt you. Do you know that? That you're my most precious—"

"Yes, I know."

"And you know that I'd only tell you what I honestly thought was the best for you. That you don't need to do anything you don't want to and I can only advise."

Elk Charm nodded, a misery spreading.

"Two Smokes thinks that Little Dancer needs to go see White Calf. Wait! Hear me out first. Two Smokes thinks White Calf can help Little Dancer find his way, now that the Power's changed between them. That if Little Dancer keeps fighting it within himself, he'll tear his soul in half. When that time comes, you'll have to let him go."

Elk Charm swallowed against the numbness.

"Will you think about it?"

She nodded, a cry stifled on her lips.

Blood Bear lay on his back tugging at one long braid with a callused hand. The other hand batted a willow switch against the scuffed hide of the Wolf Bundle. Face pinched, he scowled at the talisman of his people. What did it all mean? The lodge around him pressed down, stifling, boring. This winter, he'd chafed, waiting for spring and the long summer light.

The Wolf Bundle rested on its tripod holder, dominating the lodge just as it dominated the thoughts of the Red Hand. Blood Bear frowned. The Bundle had changed, it looked different, dingy, and, yes, the kid had been right . . . *cold*.

Since that day when he'd left White Calf's camp, he'd wondered about the boy's words, and about his attachment to the talisman. White Calf had known something, perceived something he couldn't quite grasp. And that made her prophecy frightening. The moment that foolish Short Buffalo youth had come close to the Wolf Bundle, an electric feeling had charged the air. Since he'd been sitting almost on a direct line between them, he'd felt it for the first time—a prickling sensation like the one a person felt just before lightning struck the ridge top a couple of dart casts away.

In addition to everything else, Rattling Hooves had been championed by the Short Buffalo hunter. What was his name? Hungry Bull? The man had dared him, *dared* him to combat over the woman! And she'd accepted it. That affront needed to be paid back. But then, his own heart had raced when Rattling Hooves had stood at the end of his dart and looked him in the eyes. She'd been magnificent, face proud, thick black hair wild in the wind. What a woman, unconquered, bursting with spirit to save her foolish little daughter from meeting womanhood on Blood Bear's hard penis.

So the daughter had been virgin tight? What did that mean against the spirit and pride in the mother's eyes? Any man could tame a wide-eyed young girl to his needs, but what about Rattling Hooves? He smiled at the Wolf Bundle. That challenge could prove worthy of his attention. To bend such a woman to his will would provide a great deal of satisfaction.

He scowled and slashed viciously at the Wolf Bundle, watching it jerk and dangle on its carry strings. The tripod rocked back and forth. The scarred stub of his little finger burned.

"And I had it all in hand. If Rattling Hooves hadn't acted when she did, I could have skewered the old woman and we'd have killed the Short Buffalo refugees. Then I could have taken Rattling Hooves *and* her daughter. That old witch White Calf would have been out of my hair and that foolish Hungry Bull would have drunk deeply of my dart."

But it had turned around so quickly. The hunter had blocked his cast and everything shifted, just like a stampede of frightened elk that veered at the last moment, dashing off to the side for no reason.

"Oh, be quiet, Blood Bear," the old woman's words echoed in his mind. *"You're almost finished. You've some time yet. You'll be able to delude yourself a while longer and enjoy your status. Power's not with you . . ."*

He remembered the prickling he'd felt as the youth approached the Wolf Bundle. Curious how the boy's eyes had glazed over, but then a lot of things had been curious that day. A "turning," the old woman had said.

A turning of what?

He continued to brood, shuffling about on his bedding, trying to get comfortable. "A turning of White Calf's power, for one." He grunted an assent to his own words. The old witch had been far too powerful among the Red Hand. There had to be a way to rid himself of her meddling.

Nor could he forget the Short Buffalo People who waited out on the plains like an upslope storm, ready to smash into the Buffalo Mountains and the strongholds of the Red Hand.

"Ho-yeh!" a voice called though the evening silence. "Have I found the camp of the Red Hand?"

Blood Bear sneered at the Wolf Bundle and grabbed his soft calfskin robe. He ducked out into the chill air and lifted his hand, shading his eyes against the fierce glare of the setting sun. The light burned yellow across the snowfields.

A man trudged across the white, back bent to a pack that sat low on his hips. Other People emerged from smoke-browned lodges to watch. The stranger bore the staff of a Trader, the thin wood bent in a hoop and dangling with bright feathers and rattles.

"Three Rattles!" Blood Bear called, jumping and whooping. "What brings you to the camp of the Red Hand so early in the year? The trails have barely begun to melt out."

The Trader puffed and sighed, walking onto the packed snow of the camp, where he picked his way cautiously over the dimpled ice, careful of tearing the webbing of his snowshoes.

"I don't trust the plains anymore. Too many funny doings down there. We heard last year that a Trader from the Squashed Rock People had been killed by Short Buffalo warriors. A Fire Buffalo Trader was beaten and had his pack stolen. He barely got away with his life. This new Dreamer they've got. He's an odd one. You don't know what he'll do or why."

Blood Bear turned, clapping his hands. "Green Horn! Have Tanager run some stew to my lodge. Throw some of that deer on the coals. Three Rattles must eat. He brings news! And have Cricket bring some more wood for my fire." To the Trader, he added, "Come to my lodge and warm up. The Red Hand welcome you. Our camp is yours."

People called to each other, scurrying about, chattering with excitement. Everyone wanted to hear the news.

Three Rattles grinned, though his cheeks looked stiff with cold. Frost had frozen on his braids where foggy breath touched. The collar of his fur-lined coat had gone hoary, obscuring the fine fox-fur lining of his hood.

Ramshorn and Never Sweat already stood anxiously at Blood Bear's lodge flap. One Cast and Wet Rain came walking across the camp, holding hands, talking with animation. Green Horn ducked out of her lodge, a steaming haunch sagging between her gnarled fists.

"Come, warm up." Blood Bear held the flap back and motioned Three Rattles to the place of honor next to the Wolf Bundle. Someone handed a steaming bowl of stew to the Trader, who drank deeply. Hot, roasted meat appeared on a carved wooden plate.

The rules of hospitality seen to, Blood Bear looked around at his packed lodge. All the elders sat crammed, shoulder to shoulder, taking up every bit of space. Expectant expressions filled their faces, keen eyes on Three Rattles as they waited for him to eat and drink and warm his hands by the fire.

"Tell us all," Blood Bear began with a sweeping gesture of his hand as Three Rattles placed the empty horn bowl on the ground before him and politely belched with gusto. "You said a Squashed Rock Trader was killed last year?"

The listeners gasped, some placing hands over their mouths to signify the horror of it.

Three Rattles nodded, taking his stone pipe from his pack. He carefully packed it with red willow bark and snagged a half-burned stick from the fire to light it. He puffed and passed the pipe to Blood Bear. From his lips it went around the lodge.

"I don't know the particulars. I heard the story among the Cut Hair People. Their leader, old Fat Dog, doesn't speak highly of the Short Buffalo People—even if his mother was one of their women.

"Anyway, lightning strike me dead if this isn't reported in the same manner as I heard it, but Fat Dog told me that Heavy Beaver says his spirits have Dreamed to him that all the old Power is evil. And that includes the special Power that Traders live under. He's told his raiders that they can take what they will from Traders without fear.

"Apparently the Squash Rock Trader—who I'd met and knew as Jay Bird—wouldn't let the Short Buffalo warriors take his pack. Instead, he used his staff to slap one of the young men across the face. That so angered the warriors that they darted him on the spot and left him there in the sun after taking his pack."

A low murmur of discontent spread among the elders, faces going grim.

Blood Bear stared at the fire through slitted eyes. "Doesn't the fool know that he'll cut off trade along the mountains? How does he expect to get Knife River flint from up north? Or that salty fish—like that stuff you gave me that time—from the south? How are people supposed to know what's going on? Will the Traders start going west of the mountains?"

Three Rattles shrugged. "I don't know. Honestly, it's a hard journey to travel west of the mountains. The land is all broken with sandstone walls and huge canyons and high mountains here and there. The rivers run deeper and are more dangerous to cross. Water is harder to find and I don't know all the people who live back there. I don't know if they would honor a Trader's staff . . . and they don't know the signs to communicate."

"Could they go through the mountains, maybe?" One Cast wondered, pointing southward. "When I was a young man, I went down the spine of the mountains. There are big open valleys that run part of the way, but the passes are high, the trails irregular where they run through the timber. Still, it's a way."

Three Rattles had listened, nodding as One Cast spoke.

"It's a way. You're right. And I don't know how to answer your question. For myself, I can say only that I wouldn't want to try the high peaks. I think I'll try a different way, maybe go west over the mountains and catch the trail that follows the Angry White Water River to the Silver River to the ocean where Father Sun dives into the sea. The trading is supposed to be good there. Seashells come from there, and smoked fish, and good obsidian.

"I'll miss the buffalo plains and a lot of old friends, but even now, it's not the same. The Cut Hair have been pushed south of the Sand River. The Squashed Rock are nervous about the Cut Hair fleeing south. Some say they've fought with each other over who got to pushing who out of their lands. My people, the White Crane, have been raided by the Short Buffalo till we've had to move our hunting territory far north of the Big River to avoid the Short Buffalo People. Up there, we've had to fight with the People of the Mask, who don't want us in their lands. The Fire Buffalo People, who live where the Big River runs south to the Father Water, have also been raided. They've vowed to retaliate next year when they've purified their young men and made a new Power for their darts.

"With all the raiding and war, I'm not sure I want to be walking along by myself with nothing but a staff and Trader Power. If Heavy Beaver dies suddenly, with his skin shriveling like the stories say will happen to people who molest a Trader, then maybe I'll walk the plains again. For the time being, nothing has happened to Heavy Beaver in spite of his warriors killing a Trader."

"Maybe you could go all the way around the Big River?" Blood Bear asked mildly. "Maybe you could follow it clear down to where it meets the Father Water and follow that down to the salt water?"

Three Rattles smiled wearily. "That, my friend, is a long, long walk. I don't know the people on the Father Water. I've heard stories about them, of course, since the Fire Buffalo People trade robes and dried meat for their old-man fish and turtles and woven grass mats, but I don't know the language or whether they honor the Trader's staff. No, I think I'll go west to the Silver River."

"But will we still have your trade?" Green Horn couldn't help but ask. She'd been rocking from side to side, jostling everyone around her. Her old legs couldn't take the cramp and had gone to sleep under her. Nevertheless, she couldn't force herself to get up and leave—not with the Trader there. First Man alone knew when they might get another.

Three Rattles laughed, wiggling to get out of his coat now that he'd warmed up. "I'll bring my trade to the Red Hand. It's a little out of the way, but I'll come by here. I can tell you now that I can trade for mountain-sheep-horn spoons, dried-root breads, pine-nut paste, and lots of other things. I'll need to see what comes of this trip."

"How will you go?" Never Sweat asked, rubbing at his crooked nose.

Three Rattles settled on his folded coat, extending his moccasins to the fire despite the cramped quarters. As the heat went to work on them, the water steamed off the beaver-fur outers of the tops. The hard-smoked buffalo hide of the soles looked completely soaked.

"Most likely I'll follow the mountain south to the basin. There I'll head west to the Warm Wind valley and up over to the headwaters of the Angry White Water and then west. I don't know where the trails go out there. Green Hammerstone, my cousin's brother's sister's son, has been going out there, but he won't be back until fall. Maybe I should wait another year and go with him, but I think the time is now."

Blood Bear cleared his throat. "What about this Heavy Beaver? You've met him. What do you think of him?"

Three Rattles frowned as he stared into the fire, choosing his words. "I think he's . . . well, touched by something. But I don't know what kind of Power it is. He's different. He doesn't act like any Dreamer I've ever known. He's not anything like White Calf, who lives with Power and knows its good and bad uses. He's . . . listen, don't think I'm crazy, but I think he made his Power up. Imagined it and it came true." Three Rattles looked up to gauge the impact of his words. "You know, like when you believe a lie for so long you begin to think it really happened—even when you know it didn't."

An uneasy shuffling filled the lodge. Outside of the mention of White Calf—that brought bile to Blood Bear's throat—the speculation on Heavy Beaver struck very close to home. Heavy Beaver was the one who had thrown the Wolf Bundle into the dark to land in the weeds. Perhaps . . .

"Surely someone would see through it," Green Horn snorted. "Someone would challenge him, use real Power to break him and his hold, if it were all a lie."

Three Rattles lifted his hands, palms up. "I don't know, Grandmother. I thought that a couple of years back after he started Cursing people who opposed him. I thought then that someone would stand up to him, make a liar out of him. No one did and everyone he Cursed died. Maybe he really has Power or maybe they willed themselves to death."

"But the Wise One Above would strike him down!" Ramshorn insisted, disbelief on his strained face. "Power doesn't like to be made a fool of any more than a hunter likes to have someone tell him he brings home winterkill for a trophy!"

"Maybe," Three Rattles agreed. "I don't pretend to know the ways of Power, but I can tell you Heavy Beaver has more control over the plains now than any man I've ever heard of. His warriors run from south of Sand River to north of Big River. When the hunting is poor, they raid the peoples who have what they need."

"They haven't been too keen to raid us," Never Sweat added, staring at a dart point he'd taken from his pouch. "They caught us once, and we learned. They won't do that again. We know the trails. They don't."

Three Rattles pursed his lips, frowning into the coals. Blood Bear placed another chunk of thick sagebrush on the red eye of the hearth.

"Maybe not yet," Three Rattles conceded, "but I wouldn't count on that for very long."

"How so?" One Cast asked, cocking his head attentively.

Three Rattles shifted to unlace his outer moccasin. Mostly dry now, the hair had started to singe. As he undid the laces, his sober voice held them. "I think Heavy Beaver wants to cover his backside. He's like a bull elk in rut. For the moment, he's managed to kick the five-point bulls off his flank. At the same time, he's heard another six-point whistling in the next valley and that thought's eating away at him. For years, the joke has been that only crazy kids and people who eat larkspur war on the Red Hand."

"That's right," Ramshorn growled, shaking a fist.

"But that's changed. Heavy Beaver surprised a Red Hand

camp.'' Three Rattles looked around. ''The White Crane split off from the Red Hand for a couple of reasons. There was a disagreement over the Wolf Bundle. We also had too many people hunting the same game, digging the same roots. The White Crane moiety went north to the Big River. In doing so, we pushed the Short Buffalo People south against the Cut Hair. They never forgave us. But then, over the years, we always beat any ambitious young man who came to take the land back. This time, it wasn't just an ambitious young man. It was Heavy Beaver—and he killed and wounded a lot of our warriors.''

''*We're* Red Hand,'' Blood Bear reminded—and wished he'd kept his mouth shut.

''You are.'' Three Rattles didn't seem to take offense. ''But the Red Hand have never faced a man like Heavy Beaver. He's driving his closest competitors away, cowing them, just like that bull elk I was talking about.'' Three Rattles pulled off his outer moccasin to expose another layer, also waterlogged. ''Once he's reasonably sure he won't need to worry about rivals nipping at his heels, I think he's going to come up here, and he won't leave until one bull or the other controls all the herds.''

Blood Bear tried to smile, but he could feel his lips quivering with the strain. Without thinking, he turned his eyes to the Wolf Bundle. Well, if it came to unfold as Three Rattles suggested, he could still inspire his warriors. The raiding would be long and drawn out, both sides sneaking through the trees, ambushing, moving. An interesting way to fight. He had little doubt he would triumph over Heavy Beaver. After all, he was Blood Bear, Keeper of the Wolf Bundle.

A tingling irritated the stump on his little finger.

Black Crow walked down off the steep slope, a heavy pack on his shoulders. Hungry Bull rose, leaving the white willow stems in the pile of shavings he'd made as he peeled and straightened them for dart shafts.

The sun added a bit of warmth to his cold body. On days like this, people stayed outside as much as possible, avoiding the constant crowding in the shelter.

Hungry Bull met Black Crow part way up the slippery trail.

"Good to see you back. Rattling Hooves has been worried sick."

"Rattling Hooves? What about my wife?"

"I don't think Makes Fun understands the hazards of the mountains like Rattling Hooves does. Have a good hunt? Pack looks full."

"Three porcupines—skinned, of course."

Hungry Bull took the heavy pack, swinging it over his shoulder.

"I just had to get out. Be by myself for a while." Black Crow winced as he straightened his back. He rubbed his rotund belly with a mittened hand.

"See anything?"

Black Crow shot him a quick glance. "Tracks."

"Tracks make thin stew. Fortunately you found porcupines standing in some. I suppose you had to kill them to see just how fresh the tracks were?"

"Man tracks."

Hungry Bull stopped short, turning. "Fresh?"

"Maybe a week old." Black Crow squinted up at the sun. Frosty breath curled around his face. "Someone's up there. I wonder how much an Anit'ah hunter would hesitate running a dart through one of us out alone like that."

"They know we're here, that we're not enemies."

Black Crow lifted a shoulder. "I cut short my hunt. I found a place where he'd crossed elk tracks. He looked at them, and continued on his way."

"Too old?"

"Maybe. They'd drifted the same amount as his. I'd say he found them fresh."

"Blood Bear?"

"Or someone else. But you and I think along the same lines. Whatever he's hunting, it isn't elk."

Around him, the trees burned, fire leaping orange and yellow, searing, crackling and roaring, as entire conifers exploded in waves of flame. Blinding tongues of light leapt for the night-black sky, illuminating the cloudlike masses of tumbling smoke in an eerie reddish tint that receded into charcoal smudges of ruby and maroon as they rolled higher and higher into the flame-streaked sky.

The air roared and rushed to feed the tremendous inferno. Entire trees cracked like thunder as the trunks split, steaming and whooshing flammable gasses into the wall of racing flame.

The heat of it beat down like a fist, crushing him into the parching soil, grinding him down flat as the world burned around him.

In the heart of the roaring incineration a figure moved, stalking the white ash like a shadow.

Heart pounding, Little Dancer watched as Wolf pulled up, pointed ears pricked.

"Why don't you burn? What are you?"

"I'm the Dreamer of the People." And the figure blurred as a wall of flame swept past, searing an afterimage onto the back of his eyes.

Shielding his gaze with an uplifted arm, Little Dancer squinted, expecting Wolf to have been charred to sizzling grease and blackened bone. Instead, a man stood there, tall, handsome, the gaudy light of the burning world reflecting on his smooth skin.

"Wolf? What . . . Who *are* you?"

"I'm you, Little Dancer . . . and not you. I'm the Dream and the reality. I've led you here . . . and followed you. I'm who you will be one day, and who you'll never be. I'm the Way, the Spirit of the People. I drank from the Wolf Heart. I Dance among the stars and beneath the rocks. I Sing with the winds of the Sun, and hear the sigh of the Moon. I am Wolf, the guardian of the People."

Fear rose within while the roar of the fire grew louder and softer with the vision's words. With a throat gone dry, Little Dancer tried to swallow. He turned to run. Flames whipped and popped as sparks twirled like mosquitoes in the lee of summer willows. Fire leapt, searing tortuous paths across the crackling landscape.

"We're One, little friend," the warm voice cooed. "You see, I'm within. I am everything you are . . . and all that you are not."

"Go away! Leave me alone! *I'm not the one!*"

"Go away? And leave you to burn?" The voice mocked him, taunting with reality as a spear of fire lanced Little Dancer's heart. He yipped, jumping back only to feel a searing on the nape of his neck.

"Join me. I'm your path through fire. I'm your path through Power. Live in me. Dance in the One, and you'll rise above the world that deludes you, but you must prepare. One day you must answer for yourself. What will you give for the Power? What will you give for justice? What will you give to Dance with Fire, and heal the burns? Are you strong enough?"

"I'm not the one!"

"I'll give you all the time I can, little friend. Then, when I can no longer wait, I'll have to test you. In the meantime, prepare yourself. You can't help who you are, or what you'll be. You can only prepare . . . and Dance the Spiral. You can only prepare . . . prepare . . ."

"I'm NOT the one! NOT THE ONE! NOT—"

Fire blasted up with the clapping explosion of lightning, beating him into the heat, burning him into the very skeleton of the tortured earth, twisting. . . .

"Little Dancer!" Elk Charm's cry pierced his horrified sleep like a frosty dart.

He gasped and jerked awake, sitting up in his sleeping robes. He gulped to fill his lungs with the crisp night air. Around him, the others sat up in their robes, staring with wary eyes. Makes Fun talked in cooing voices, soothing Mouse Runner, who'd awakened echoing Little Dancer's cries.

"You were dreaming again," Elk Charm told him, placing a cool hand on his sweaty shoulder. "You're here. We're all here. It's all right."

He shot a frightened look into her worried eyes and swallowed, feeling his throat burn, as if still in the Dream.

"Sleep now, son," Hungry Bull called from where he and Rattling Hooves sat up in their robes.

"You bet!" Black Crow called from the bed he shared with Makes Fun. "Any of those dream beasts come in here, Three Toes will dart 'em one right after another."

"Hey!" Three Toes cried. "You dart those dream monsters yourself. Me, I'm running faster than an antelope with an angry wasp on his tail!"

No one laughed despite the effort.

Elk Charm had gripped his hand in hers. He took a deep breath and nodded. "Just a dream, that's all. Everyone go to sleep." *I'm just being strange again.*

Rattling Hooves stared intently at her daughter, a look that communicated something private. Two Smokes watched, eyes like slits where he lay curled in the corner. To Little Dancer, he might have been a knowing predator. His manner smacked of a bobcat waiting over a rabbit hole.

Little Dancer lay back down, watching the rock overhead where it glowed dully red from the embers in the remains of the night fire. Like the reddish billows of blackness that rose from the burning forest in the Dream.

Elk Charm settled herself next to him, pressing her body reassuringly against his, snuggling close and hugging him tightly.

"I worry about you," she whispered. "Tomorrow, Little Dancer, let's go for a walk. We've . . . well, I think I know something that will stop the Dreams. Tomorrow . . . we'll talk about it."

"What?"

"Tomorrow," her strained voice promised. "Tonight, just hold me. Hold me like it was the last time."

He pulled her against him, reaching to run her long black braids through nervous fingers. "Shhh! Sleep now, I'll be fine."

She hugged him with all her strength until her arms shook. A warmth rose to fill him. Yes, let the Dreams come and do as they pleased. So long as he had her, he could stand them. Why had she sounded so lonely, so desperate and frightened?

The afterimage of the fire burned behind his eyelids. He stared straight overhead, memorizing each of the angles of rock, noting which had the thickest soot, listening to the night wind beyond the hangings that kept the shelter warm and moderately protected.

In the darkness, a wolf howled, the sound cutting like a quartzite blade in his heart.

He looked toward the back wall of the shelter above where the children slept and his soul chilled. There, the wolf effigy watched him with burning eyes.

"How much more of this must I stand? This . . . human treats me like a bit of dung. Each time my anger grows. I weaken, yet you tell me to remain helpless! Power leaks away like heat from a winter lodge and I can do nothing? I would break him, twist his bones like grass stems. I would sear his soul in his body! You've seen, felt, yet you do nothing but torment his little finger!"

"Patience," Wolf Dreamer soothed. *"The boy is walking into our net."*

"I haven't much patience left."

"We need the boy desperately. Humans live with time. They Dream the future as well as the past."

"My patience has limits. I see no progress with the boy. Heavy Beaver plans to send his warriors to the mountains with the spring thaw. What are you going to do?"

"I know my options. I have another gamble to make."

"Like the last one?"

"Wait. The Watcher follows the boy."

"As I wait, desperation grows. I must act . . . or die."

"Wait! Or you will destroy it all."

Chapter 18 ✋

Hip aching, White Calf hitched her way through the snow. A pack of firewood hung from a tumpline pressed into the parchment skin of her forehead. Her breath puffed in a white wreath with each laboring of her lungs. White hair hung in straggles from under her fox-hide hood.

She worked her way out of a thick stand of timber she'd hesitated to harvest at first. For one thing, it sat on a steep slope, which increased the risk of her falling in the dense, interlacing tangle of deadfall. At her age, alone, in winter, a broken leg meant death—but then so did freezing from lack of firewood.

She stopped, grimacing at the pain in her hips and the trembling of her exhausted legs.

"Getting too . . . too old . . . for this kind of thing." She swallowed, bending over to brace birdlike hands on thin knees, easing the strain on her back.

She hadn't realized how much simpler life had been with Little Dancer to carry wood and water. And what a joy it had been to talk to Two Smokes around the night fire. In the company of the berdache, she could sit by the hour and reminisce about Broken Bill and old Has No Sense and Eats Too Fast. All gone now; they lived only in her memory. Did that constitute the sum and total of existence? Only to live on for as long as someone remembered you? And what then? Did that fragile link between this world and the Starweb break? If only the ghosts could speak instead of just haunting the quiet, green-shaded places and the hidden crevasses under the snow. If only they'd give tongue to their musings instead of silently watching the ways of the world.

Her lungs made a wheezing sound as she tried to get her breath. A trembling had begun in her leg and the joint of her hip burned as if someone had dropped a small ember from a smoldering fire down inside. She hadn't realized how much she'd aged in the last five years since her final return from Heavy Beaver's camp.

She growled to herself and squinted up at the sky. Worse, she, White Calf, who had always chosen to reject the ways of people for the solitude of a Dreamer, missed the company of others. "Sour old excuse for a Dreamer you are, girl," she mumbled to herself.

Taking a resigned breath, she hitched her pack up and began breaking a careful trail down toward the path. Despite the newly crusted thickness of spring snow, the elk had used the route through the winter and beaten down a track. With that footing, travel wasn't as horrible as it could have been. Spring, despite its sunny days, made traveling far more difficult. The snow, loose and crumbly in winter, melted and froze while new water-rich spring snow covered the old ice. It never froze hard enough to support a person's weight. Sooner or later, her foot punched through the thin ice, leaving her wallowing and cursing as she fought to get back up. Nor did snowshoes help much, for each ridge had been blown free of snow, leaving gnarled brush, rocks, and sticks and other irregularities to puncture the webbing or break the willow hoops.

"I hate spring," she growled, feeling the cold bite of the wind. "In the dead of winter, the deep cold lies on the land and that's that. But spring? So what if the air's warmer? It's wetter . . . and blowing all the time. The wind goes right through a person. Then you wade around in the wet snow and everything gets soaked. Then darkness comes, and the temperature drops, and then what kind of shape are you in? I'll take a blizzard in the deep cold compared to this any day."

She jutted her jaw out in silent assent and considered the mud that always made such a mess of spring walking. She hissed at herself, and put all thought of it out of her mind. Why be depressed when she had a hard walk ahead of her?

On quaking legs, she rounded the last bend in the trail and stopped to take another breather, waiting for her lungs to recover and her heart to quit trying to batter through her breastbone. Only when she looked up did she see the faint trace of smoke rising from her shelter where it nestled under the gray brooding limestone cliff.

"Who . . ." Perplexed, she found some reserve in the depths of her antique body and forced her legs into a vigor they'd forgotten they'd ever had.

"Ho-yeh!" she called. "Greetings! Who's there?"

The surprise increased when Little Dancer parted the flap and stepped out, squinting in the brighter light. He smiled and hurried to help her, easily lifting her load with one hand and swinging it over his back. She narrowed an eye—a nasty retort on her lips. Strength always seemed to be wasted on the young—who were forever too foolish to know what they had.

"Thanks," she wheezed. "Whew. Let me catch my breath and I'll tell you hello."

He cocked his head, inspecting her. "I thought about tracking you down, but I figured you might be up on the mountain. You know, up where you've got the stone circle with the lines in it. I didn't want to disturb your Dreaming."

She huffed and puffed up the slope to the hangings, slipping in and waddling over to her hides. After the snow and bright sunlight the place looked like night. Despite the graying of her vision, she knew the way by heart. Grunting and creaking, she let herself down and sighed, staring absently at the crackling fire. "You could have tracked me. For a bit there, I wasn't sure I'd make it back."

He settled her bundle of wood onto a stack, which—to White Calf's eyes at least—looked of mythic proportion.

He gestured at the wood. "I noticed you had about run out, so I carried some in."

"You got a man name yet?"

He shook his head, lifting a shoulder shyly. "No. I've never . . . well, it just never gets done. And you know, it's not so important anymore."

She grinned at him. "If I didn't think it would kill me, I'd get up and hug you."

A flicker of worry ceased his face. "You're not feeling well?"

Her lungs spasmed, leaving her coughing. She finished the spell and waved off his concern. "No, it's not that, boy. It's just . . . well, age, you know? Seems like every day I'm faced with the fact that I won't live forever."

"You'll be around," he said simply.

"Think so?"

"Too mean to die."

She chuckled at that and ended up coughing again. He waited her out before noting, "You didn't used to cough so much."

"It only comes when I've pushed myself too far." She worked her toothless jaws and twitched her lips. "Seems like the wood gets farther and farther away. Pull that flap open, let some light in here. It's warm enough yet that we won't freeze and it's an excuse to change this old air for new.''

"You should move camps. When I was looking around, I noticed the timber across the valley has been picked pretty clean. The lower branches have all been stripped. The dead-fall has been pulled out. Only the big logs are left.''

She shrugged. "I like it here.''

"How's your food holding out?''

"They send you up here to ask me questions?''

He grinned at her, a sheepish curl to his lips. "Not really. They've been talking, of course. Two Smokes is worried sick about you.'' He paused, a wicked light in his eyes. "Maybe he's not so wrong.''

She growled at him, narrowing her eyes evilly. "So why did you *really* come? Just to make me miserable? Well, don't just sit there like a mushroom on a log, tell me. What's the news? Why are you here? Nobody to harass you?''

He threw another couple of branches on the fire as she undid her moccasins and propped them on the rocks next to the glowing coals. Drying moccasins had to be done just right. To begin with, they must be made of thoroughly smoked and excellently tanned leather, lest they shrink or harden, or crack. And if a person got the footgear too hot, the heat would drive out the oils and fats that helped water-proof them.

"I get harassed plenty.'' His grin faded. "People have just been wondering about how you were getting along, like I said. We've—''

"Everyone's all right? No one's sick or hurt? You didn't come for help to heal?''

"No, everyone's fine. But we'd started to worry about you. The idea came up more than once to send someone up to see how you were doing.'' A twinkle came to his eye as he added, "Maybe make sure you weren't going to freeze.''

"*Bah!* That'll be the day!''

Ignoring her outburst, he continued, "I just sort of volunteered.''

She perked up at that. "Volunteered? You? I thought you didn't like me.'' *And you're hiding something. No, there's more to this. What?*

He avoided her eyes. "It's not that I don't like you. It's just that you kept pushing me about Power. You always seemed to know I'd Dreamed. You always knew everything. You wanted me to be more than I wanted to be. That's all. I didn't hate you or anything."

Liar! The old keenness had returned. "Then why did you decide to come? The Dreams still bothering you?" *Ah, that's it! Look at him squirm like a packrat in a snake's hole!*

He nodded, rubbing his hands together, suddenly nervous. "Look, I'm not your Dreamer. I don't want to get all tangled up in that again."

"Well, quit worrying. You're not *my* Dreamer." She shifted the moccasins on the rock, watching the steam rise from the warm hides.

"Good."

"But it's the Dreams, isn't it? That's why you came all the way up here."

He stared silently into the fire, a faint puckering visible about his lips, lines forming in his brow.

Dropping her voice, she added gently, "I won't push you about it. I . . . well, I made a mistake. Handled the whole thing poorly. I learned that day Blood Bear came down here and tried to start a war. That's when it all came clear." She made a gesture as if to wave it all away. "So just talk. I'll help any way I can. I'll just listen if you want."

He hesitated, seemed to stumble, then said: "It's the Dreams. I'm making everyone but Two Smokes crazy. Hungry Bull says it's like being on a peak in a lightning storm, you don't know when to jump."

"Power does that."

"Anyway, the Dreams come and go . . . more so lately. I get one that comes back time after time. I'm alone in the middle of a forest fire. And a Spirit Wolf walks through the flames and turns into a man. When he talks to me, he talks in riddles I can't understand, about being everything and nothing at the same time. I get the shakes for days.

"Then I've had other things happen . . . like a living Dream. One time we'd gone to trap mountain sheep and I . . . lost myself in the sheep, I guess you'd say." He swallowed hard, changing the subject. "Two Smokes and Elk

Charm are worried. I guess everyone's worried. I see it in their eyes. They know I have Dreams—but they don't understand. Makes Fun and Meadowlark, they're nervous about their children. Don't know what I'll do to them. Elk Charm and Two Smokes thought I should come see you.''

She lifted an eyebrow. "Elk Charm?"

He began to fidget. "We're married.''

She sighed and rubbed her forehead where the tumpline had bitten so deeply. Her dry laughter surprised him. "Circles, boy.'' She shook her head. "Married, eh? Well, I wish you better luck with it than I had.''

"I'm happy. She knows I have trouble with the Dreams.''

"Good, it makes things easier to explain.'' She reached into a pouch and pulled out a stick of dried sego-lily bread and tossed it to him. "I hope Elk Charm understands what she's gotten herself into. Don't look at me like that. I know what I'm talking about. I inflicted myself on both Big Fox and Cut Feather. Well, thinking about it, I didn't know what I was doing when I married Big Fox. That was the first time. I was young—well, not so young as you—but young. Thought I could simply settle down and live like a real person. Thought I could deny the Dreams.''

"And it didn't work?'' He chewed the breadstick absently, jaws working under smooth skin. Unconsciously, his eyes kept straying to the spiral pecked in the back wall where the sunlight illuminated it.

"No. It never worked.'' She laughed at the idea. "There's something about the way a human is put together. We're no different than the rest of the animals, I suppose. I mean, take a beaver. It doesn't matter that he's got a dammed-up pool full of willow twigs all cut and stuck down there in the mud. He's still got to crawl out and chew down trees—even spruce trees if they're the only ones available. I guess you'd say that's the way the Wise One Above made him. With humans, well, we have the need to be with each other, and when men and women are together, the robes get parted and what makes men men and women women meets. I had all those urges and I thought coupling would overpower the Dreams.''

He looked miserable.

She smiled wistfully. "It works for a while. You'll be able

to lose yourself in Elk Charm for a time yet. It's all new and wonderful—and there's the coupling itself. Ah, yes, the coupling . . .'' She lost herself in the memories for a moment before sighing and returning to the subject. ''The problem is that it tears at you. The lure of the Dream pulls against the lure of the person you love. And what then? You can't do both.'' She waggled a finger at him. ''Don't lift your eyebrow like that. I mean it, you *can't* do both. Well, all right, don't take my word for it. You'll find out on your own anyway.''

''Maybe.''

She reached down and massaged her toes where they warmed by the fire. Her toenails were getting too long again. Have to trim them. ''I don't know why the Wise One Above does it this way. Seems a shame, but I suppose it's just another reflection of how the universe was made in the first place.''

''What are you talking about?''

''Circles. Hmm? Oh, I mean about the way every person learns things. Truths, if you will . . . laws about the way the world works. Then when people get old, they got all this stuff they've learned packed away in their brains and they can't show young men and women why it's the way they say. The young have to go out and find out everything the way the elders did. Damned inefficient—unless, of course, I'm missing something important.

''Old Six Teeth, the Spirit Man who taught me, he used to wonder if we all weren't the same person just living the same life in different ways.''

She wondered, *Is this the way of it? When I had the boy, I didn't have him. And now, when he's left and on his own, I get him? Is that the trick that's been played on me? The lesson I needed to learn? Perhaps that's the Spiral of teaching, that knowledge can't be forced—only withheld. But what does that mean?*

''That doesn't make any sense. How could we live the same life in different ways in different bodies?''

''Illusion.''

''What? Illusion? I don't . . . That's crazy.''

''So's the whole world.'' She resettled herself and raised a finger to point at him. ''Tell me, Little Dancer, what's real?

The world? This one?'' She gestured around at the shelter and thumped her knuckles on the rock next to her. "Or . . . are the Dreams real?"

"This is real." He crossed his arms, kicking out his feet. As if to emphasize his point, he thumped his heel on the packed dirt.

"How do you know?"

"Because if I pick up one of those coals and rub it against the bottom of your foot, you'll scream."

She clapped her hands, laughing. "Will I? Or will you just *think* it's me screaming? Hmm? Maybe everything around you is your Dream of what the world is really like?"

"Then if I believe otherwise, you won't?"

"What if that depends on how hard you believe it? Can you be sure you really know that burning me makes me scream? Can you be sure some little part of your mind doesn't say, burn her and she'll scream? 'Cause if you burn yourself, you'll scream. Maybe it's shared reality, hmm? You think I feel pain the same way you do—so I do."

"But don't you?"

"That's not what's at issue here." She continued to jab a hard finger at him. "We're talking about how you know what you think you know."

"But I can *feel* you, touch you, hear you . . . and this late in the winter, smell you, too!"

"You think so. But tell me, am I always this way? What happens when you can't see, feel, and smell me? Maybe I don't exist when you walk out of that flap, hmm? Maybe Two Smokes and Elk Charm and Hungry Bull don't exist until you get back and find them where you expect they'll be. Maybe we're all part of *your* imagination of what's real."

"They exist!" he cried. "I know they do. When I get back, Three Toes will have made new dart points. Father will have snared some more elk. It'll all be there when I get back."

"Sure it will, but you can't prove that it's there right now. Do you see?"

He shook his head, bewildered. "No. It's obvious that they're there. They have to be! Otherwise . . . otherwise . . ."

"Exactly, otherwise. You see, you have no way of proving

to yourself that your father really exists. You could have made up this entire world. The only person who *knows* this world is real is you. And you can't prove to me that it exists the way you think it does.''

He gaped. ''But suppose I pick up my dart and drive it through you. You'll feel it . . . die from it.''

''Will I?'' She leaned back and crossed her arms. ''Or am I only a part of your Dream? Maybe you only imagine that I'll feel it, that I'll die. You see, *you* can't prove to *me* that I really exist!''

He shook his head, confused.

''Ah, Little Dancer. Old Six Teeth told me once long ago that life is the Great Mystery, that only within ourselves can we know what we think is real. I can't prove to you that you're real. I can't prove that this fire is real—that it isn't just a tool of the Dream. Sure, it will burn me if I let it, but is the pain real? Or is it imagined? Illusion?''

''It's real.''

She pursed brown lips over toothless gums. ''I wonder. Six Teeth told me he'd seen a Dreamer Dance with fire once. The old legends, the ones you youngsters don't hear anymore, say the old Dreamers learned from First Man—and they Danced with fire.''

He went pale before quickly adding, ''That could mean a lot of things. Maybe they waved it around on sticks and—''

''No,'' she insisted. ''Memory is a tricky thing—like a Dream, it changes. Memory itself is illusion. But I remember Six Teeth so clearly, remember the look in his eyes, like crystal beads of water lit by spring sunshine. He'd seen it. He said the Dreamer Danced with the coals in his hands, Danced barefoot in the Fire, and didn't get burned. According to Six Teeth, the way it was done was to retreat to the One, to change the Dream so it was real and this world illusion.''

''I'd trust in a sharp dart, myself,'' he added. ''I mean, think about it. I do things to myself all the time, cut myself flint knapping when I don't know it and I see the blood afterward and wonder when I did it. If I made the world up, like you suggest, I wouldn't imagine myself getting hurt. That doesn't make sense."

"Unless the rock Dreams it's hurting you."

"The rock . . ."

Through slitted eyelids, she watched him. "And you don't think the world around you Dreams? How do you know you're not the illusion of a rock? Or a bat? Or maybe a tree? What if a mouse is curled in its burrow somewhere, Dreaming your thoughts and experiences for you at this very moment? Can you prove to me beyond any doubt that you aren't part of someone's . . . something's Dream?"

He jumped to his feet, twirling around, arms out. When he stopped, he looked at her. "There, see, I just decided to do that. *I* decided to get up and spin around. Me." He pointed to his head. "In here, inside. *I* thought to do that."

She laced her fingers, cocking her head. "Did you? Or did whatever Dreams you plant the idea? Am I talking to Little Dancer? Or to the Dreamer through the illusion of Little Dancer?"

Frustration reddened his face. "I'm *me*! This is crazy! How can I prove to you that I'm me? Anything I think up, you'll say it's Dreamed. That I only think it, or someone else only thinks it. I—"

"Exactly my point!" she cried, and clapped her hands.

He looked crestfallen. "Then how can you believe in anything? Why even talk to another person? Ignore me. I'm not real."

She winked at him. "Because for whatever reason we're here, alive and living, there's a purpose. So what if we're Dreams? For the time being, act it out. Besides, accepting the illusion works, for the most part."

"I think it's crazy." But he didn't look any too sure of himself as he said it. A frown had engraved itself into his forehead.

"Maybe," she whispered, dropping her chin on her fingers. For the moment, she lost herself in the images of Six Teeth and his wonder that man could Dance with fire. But how? She blinked and looked up, seeing the amused disbelief in Little Dancer's eyes.

"Thinking about not being real?" he asked.

"No, I was thinking about what it would take to Dance with Fire."

"Skin made of water. Even if you don't exist, that's impossible," Little Dancer replied.

"More things are never tried because they're impossible than are tried because people believe in them." She reached for her stick to stir the fire. "And what kind of world would we have if people believed in the impossible? Think of what we could do. Now, there's a Dream for you."

She pointed with her walking stick. "That line there means the worst of the cold is over. When the sun rises there, it's halfway to the summer solstice."

Little Dancer moved around the outside of the circle, seeing how the rocks aligned. Only the gray tops of the stones stuck out of the windblown snow that had mounded and begun to melt as Father Sun picked a more northerly path through the sky.

Where they stood on the ridge top, the cruel fingers of the wind shot through hide and flesh like obsidian-tipped darts, chilling the very soul. Still, this high ridge had an unrestricted view of the irregular horizon.

"But how did you figure this out?" he called against the gale.

"Time, boy." She cackled like a sage hen over a green sprout. "By watching the sky, the path of Father Sun, and how the Starweb has been woven over the earth. It's all part of the Circles. You see, when you come stand here and look down this line, you'll find that on the day the sun comes up over that rock, it's the height of summer. Days get shorter until just after the beginning of the deep cold. Then, on the shortest day, the sun comes up over that rock down there."

He walked around the stone circle, sighting down each of the transecting spokes. "So you always know when the seasons break? I never knew it was that easy."

"Bah!" She waved it away while the wind flapped the skirts of her dress. "Most of knowing how the world works can be figured out by just watching it. For instance, which way is really north? Point."

He did, picking the mountain he'd always thought lay north.

She hitched around the circle, picking a line of rocks. "There. Come stand here and look and you'll see straight north."

"And how do you know that?"

"Simplest thing in the world. I sat up here and marked where the stars appeared on the horizon. Then I marked where they set. A person just sits there in the same place all night long marking the star paths, the place in the middle is north. That's how you prove the north star is really the north star. Must be pretty Powerful not to move in the night like the others."

"That or it's dead."

"Maybe, but I doubt it. It twinkles like all the others. It just doesn't move." She tapped her walking stick against the rocks to make a clicking sound. "Yes, all it takes is watching long enough and you can figure out how things work. Of course, I still haven't figured out what the sun burns. Can't be wood, there's no smoke up there. And the light's too bright. You ever noticed? Not like firelight, it doesn't have that yellow cast to it. And then there's the moon. Whatever it burns, it doesn't put out heat—and no smoke there, either."

"But I remember you saying everything has a spirit of its own."

She nodded. "It does. Spirit Power lies in everything, it's just a matter of opening parts of your soul to feel it. Animals, of course, have souls, but so do trees and mountains, and streams and the clouds in the sky. It's all pulsing and throbbing around us all the time. It's just that humans are always throwing mud in the waters of their lives to muck it up. They're not happy unless they're floating along in dirty water so they can't see where they're going or what the channel looks like."

He laughed, shivering despite his warm sheep-hide cloak.

She saw and hugged herself. "Come on, let's get off this hill. I'm about frozen to the bone."

"No, you're not cold. It's all illusion!" he teased, helping her down off the steep trail. He had to grip her hand to keep her steady on the treacherous parts. Rocks rolled underfoot and ice had packed the shadows. "How long did it take you to make the wheel up there?"

"Couple of years. Sometimes it's cloudy in summer and you need to wait another year to get the rocks placed just right. The hardest part is the winter. Lots of clouds then. And it takes a certain amount of dedication—or idiocy—to sit up there in the dark waiting for morning while the wind blows snow up your skirt and your skin turns blue. Ice freezes in your hair and you get to shivering so bad you're not certain if the sighting you took on the top of the rising sun was correct or not because your teeth were clattering so hard as to jar your eyeballs in the sockets. It reminds you this world might be illusion—but it's a cursed powerful one!"

"What gave you the idea for the star wheel? Did you Dream it? Just think it up one day?"

She shook her head and wobbled out onto the flats at the bottom of the trail. Snow crunched under her moccasins. "Dung and flies, no. I saw one up on a butte overlooking Big River one time when I went up there with Cut Feather to see some of his relations among the White Crane People." She paused, seeing it again in her mind. "I remember going up there one night because the White Crane thought it was a Power place. I lay down to sleep between the spokes and had a wonderful Dream. I woke up just at dawn. I got up and was rolling up my bedding as the sun was coming up. I noticed a spoke pointed right into the red eye of the sun. That set me to thinking, so I watched that star wheel for a while. The whole time we were there I watched where the sun came up and set. Watched it move around the wheel.

"No, I didn't make it up. I don't think there's much to make up in the world. That's the beauty of the Spiral, you see. Everything comes around and happens all over again. Like life. A baby is born, learns to walk, learns to talk and play, and gets to be a young person. Then the young person learns to be an adult. A penis finds a vagina and another baby is born and learns to walk and talk and do everything over again. Circles within Circles, but all connected: the Spiral."

He paused to take a swipe at a snow-heavy branch. "And where do you think Heavy Beaver fits into all that?"

White Calf ran her tongue along the insides of her cheeks, a determined look on her face as she walked. "The problem with Heavy Beaver is that he's found Power without knowing how he did it."

"But you've told me for years that he's a liar, that his Power is all made up."

"It is. You see, he does make it up. But think about it for a bit. I know you hate the idea that the world is illusion, but consider this because it's the secret of his strength. Heavy Beaver's Power is in the heads of others."

Little Dancer stopped, turning on his heel. "Huh?"

She gave him a knowing squint, a trace of satisfaction in the set of her lips. "That's right. His Power is in the heads of other people. They believe for him. If you will, they Dream the reality of his Power—and it's all illusion."

"Illusion?"

"As compared to the One."

"But what if Oneness is illusion, too?"

"Then it's the ultimate illusion. But it works. Since you've been here, you've told me about the bighorn trap. You've told me how you Dreamed the antelope to come to your mother's trap and feed the People. You've told me about the Dreams, but what *I've* never told you is that your Dreaming with the One was so powerful that time that I shared it."

He stared at her. "You . . ."

She waved it away. "Oh, yes, I felt you and your hunger. So did the antelope . . . and the mountain sheep. That's why if the One is illusion, it's the most powerful. Think about it and remember when we had our argument that first day about me proving you really existed. I knew you were real by having shared that Dream. And that's how you know antelope and mountain sheep exist. You've been One with them."

A chill realization, colder than the icy wind tearing over the rocky crags, ate into his very soul. For long moments, he stood, locked in his thoughts as the pieces began to tumble into place. He nodded absently, raising his gaze from the crusted, ice-flaked snow to ask her more, but she'd left. He stopped to kick at a sagebrush, exulting, before racing after her disappearing back.

* * *

Lost in thought, Elk Charm handed Two Smokes a horn bowl of steaming mountain-sheep stew. She walked over to sit cross-legged on the fill before the shelter, eyes unconsciously straying to the trail that led down from the high ridge.

"Still waiting for him?"

"Yes." And her heart tore.

"He'll be back," Two Smokes told her, sipping the hot stew.

"He'll be back," Rattling Hooves echoed from where she sat weaving grasses together for a collecting basket.

Elk Charm didn't need to turn to know the worry in her mother's face. Although she'd been a child at the time, that assurance had filled many a night in her father's lodge during the long spring of his absence. Not until Ramshorn found his body melting out of the snow slide the next spring had the phrase been dropped.

She bit her lip as she did so often these days, anxious gaze tracing every crook and turn of the trail as it made its way up the slope, over the outcrops, and around the patches of rabbitbrush and sage.

"He had to go," she reminded herself, trying not to think of the things that could have happened. A broken leg in the black timber would have meant a terrible death. A careless step on an unstable slope could trigger an avalanche. A misstep on an icy trail and a fall could . . . *No, don't think it.*

"Yes," Two Smokes' voice soothed. "He had to go. Someone had to check on White Calf. I think, too, the Dreams were . . . Well, he needed to talk to White Calf. Maybe, after all the fights they had over the years, this was good. Maybe they needed this time to finally talk."

She couldn't deny it. How many nights had he tossed and turned, waking to stare at the wolf face that had been so laboriously pecked into the rock in the back of the shelter? Even sitting in the sun as she was, she could feel the wolf effigy staring at the back of her head. Sometimes, when she'd been awakened by Little Dancer's troubled sleep, she'd look up, and could swear the eyes glowed yellow in the night.

And the tension had ebbed in the shelter. People no longer snapped at each other, looking furtively at Little Dancer.

Laughter had returned, the Short Buffalo People learning Anit'ah, while the Red Hand learned their language in return. Stories had been told in both languages—a healing. And Little Dancer's leaving had triggered it all.

The memory of that last day stung with the burning of cactus in a finger. "You've got to go. You've got to see White Calf."

"I don't like her. She'll just push me."

"Please," she pleaded. "Otherwise, the Dreams will tear us apart. Two Smokes knows. Go, ask him. I love you, Little Dancer. If not for yourself or the others, do this for me. Please."

And he'd gone, knowing all the while that he'd wanted to, and refusing to admit it to himself.

"But so long?" The question she dared not allow herself slipped out.

Her mother's feet grated on the pebbles and a warm hand settled on her shoulder. "It hasn't been so long, daughter."

"Almost three moons."

"The weather's been bad, perhaps White Calf needed him. She might have been hurt. You never know."

Elk Charm nodded slowly, a grisly memory of her father's curiously swollen body rising from the depths of her memory. At first, she hadn't believed that hideously deformed face had been his, with the lips all pulled back to expose the teeth, the jaw cocked at an angle under empty orbits where his soft brown eyes had once been. But she had recognized his clothing.

Could that same ghost-mask face now belong to Little Dancer?

Little Dancer stepped out, blinking in the gray morning light.

White Calf parted the hanging skins behind him, pushing on the small of her back as she straightened. "Looks like good weather for traveling. Watch the talus slope when you go over the divide. This time of year, it'll be tricky footing. No telling what's frozen and what's loose. Stuff shifts, too."

"I'll watch myself."

White Calf worked her toothless gums, looking up at him

with sparkling eyes. "And give my best to Elk Charm. I don't know what you'll tell her. I suppose that you're just fooling around with a woman old enough to be your grandmother."

"*Great*-grandmother," Little Dancer corrected. "And you are."

"You get all the questions answered?"

"I think so. All but that one Dream."

"The one with Wolf in the burning forest?"

He nodded, looking away, down the trail.

She smacked her lips. "Yes, well, enjoy Elk Charm while you have time."

He tilted his head, staring down at her. "The Wolf-Man said I'd have time. And besides"—he smiled wryly—"Power can't make me into something I don't want to be. No, that I *refuse* to be."

"Care to bet?" she asked dryly.

He nodded soberly. "I promised my mother. Every time you talk about Power, I hear her words echoing in my mind."

"Your mother was Clear Water."

"My mother was Sage Root—and besides, look what listening to Power did for Clear Water."

White Calf grinned at him, exposing empty pink gums. "The problem with Power, boy, is that we mortals can only see a tiny piece of the Spiral."

He clapped her on the back with an affectionate pat. "And I don't even want to see that much."

"Go see your woman. Her bed's been empty for a long time. If she's as passionate as I was at that age, she'll be dragging you between the robes before you've set your pack down."

He shook his head and hugged her good-bye one last time. "Thank you for the talk . . . and the lessons."

"Thank you for the firewood. Come back when you feel like it. Send Hungry Bull and the rest, too. I like the company."

He waved as he set off down the trail.

As he warmed his sleep-stiff muscles, he struggled to make sense of the ideas spinning in his mind. A framework lay there, starting to sort itself out, a means for understanding the Dreams, the way of Power—and, he hoped, the trick to avoiding its snares.

Ahead, the trail wound around through the timber before dividing one way, heading down toward the Clear River, the other climbing up through the trees to the ridge top and following the elk route to the south. He took the high path, following the way of the elk—fitting, the way that led to Elk Charm.

At least now, after months of talking, of listening to an old Dreamer's words and thoughts, he could keep the Dreams in perspective. Besides, he had a week's worth of travel ahead. In that time, he could work it all out, rehash the arguments with White Calf, figure out how to combat the Dreams and keep himself happy while living with his wife. It would all work.

She says a person can't do both. Very well, Mother, I hear your warning. Your son will never do what Heavy Beaver did to others. No one will feel like that. I choose my wife. The Dreams, Wolf, and the ghost of the First Man can make their own way.

For the first time since Sage Root's death and the defiling of the Wolf Bundle, he felt satisfied with himself and who he was.

Charging along the path, he laughed aloud, enjoying the fire of sunrise among the clouds.

A movement in the trees caught his attention; as he looked eagerly, hoping to see an elk, a patch of black slipped through an opening in the trees.

Deer?

Then the animal darted across a meadowed pocket in the trees. The huge black wolf stopped, a foot lifted as he stared at Little Dancer with large burning yellow eyes: the Watcher!

His feet lost their lightness as a tightness restricted the bottom of his throat, making it difficult to swallow.

"Go back!" He waved his darts at the animal. "Go back and tell First Man I'm not his Dreamer! You and he . . . well, you can't make me if I don't want to! You hear?"

Wolf didn't move.

"I'm Little Dancer . . . and I belong to no one but myself!"

Wolf lowered his head, nose coursing over the crusted snow, as if casting for scent, wary eyes on Little Dancer.

"Go!" He pointed toward the timber with the darts.

Wolf turned, head low, tail down, and trotted silently into the trees.

Little Dancer grinned, knocking his dart shafts rhythmically together as he hummed a song. The lightness had returned to his feet and again he practically danced his way down the trail. Images of Elk Charm, along with the vanquishing of the wolf, competed for attention in his mind.

Only then did he notice the few strands of cloud overhead had dulled, losing the enflamed look of the sunrise. Now they seemed to darken. As he topped out on the ridge, he studied the western horizon, slightly unnerved by the bank of black clouds rolling down.

Snaps Horn eased out onto the trail, bracing his feet. The dart—so carefully crafted—rested in the hook of his atlatl. He measured the distance, centering his aim in the middle of Little Dancer's broad back. The oblivious youth walked with eyes only to the front. From this distance, Snaps Horn couldn't miss.

"For Elk Charm," he whispered under his breath. A tingle of victory shot hot through his heart. A grim smile played on his lips.

Arm extended, his powerful muscles rippled—and he almost fell over backward as the atlatl was seized from behind.

A cry stifled in his throat as he caught himself and whirled to face his assailant.

Tanager!

She placed a finger to her lips, gesturing him back. Then she skipped lightly into the thick mat of timber.

He followed, burning rage building. Once in the cover of the firs, he gritted, "I don't *believe* you! What kind of crazy idiocy—"

"Shhh!" She shot him a reproving look, craning to stare down the trail.

He sat, practically trembling with anger. "This time you've gone too far! This time—"

"Fool!" she hissed. "Come on, we've got to talk."

She led him farther from the trail, winding around through the timber. She slipped lightly over a deadfall he had to clamber over.

Finally satisfied, she stopped and wheeled, hands on trim waist. "Sit down!"

"Don't you go—"

"*Sit!*" She thrust a straight finger down.

Despite himself he settled to the cushion of the duff and she dropped to face him.

"I just saved you from the worst mistake of your life."

"Worst mistake! I almost—"

"Ruined yourself!" Tanager shook her head, eyes flashing. "What did you think? That you'd kill him and Elk Charm would come running into your arms? You've got less sense than a bull elk in rut!"

Snaps Horn glared at her.

"Listen," she explained, hands wide. "Elk Charm loves him. Yes . . . *loves* him."

"How do you know?"

"Because I've watched her. You were looking too high. They're way down on the south end. In a shelter in one of the canyons."

"I knew he'd come back to White Calf's."

"And then what? You'd kill him? Elk Charm would hate you for the rest of your life! She loves him. And if you killed the man she loved, then what? You think she'd ever look at you?"

"How would she know who killed him?"

"How would she know?" Tanager laughed, a slim hand to her mouth. "Who else has spent the winter out roaming around the timber like a fool? You're the only one, foolish calf! That's how she'd know. And every camp of the Red Hand is talking about it, speculating."

Through the mist of his anger and confusion, it made sense.

"Yes, you finally understand." She grinned at him. "Listen, we've been friends for a long time. I couldn't see you ruin two lives because your penis has overloaded your brain."

"How do you know so much, girl!"

An impish look crossed her face. "Because I might be strange. But I watch. I watch everything—animals, people. I know what makes people act the way they do because I've always lived apart. While most people are all wound up in their problems, I'm watching, learning why they do what they do. Like animals.''

He tried to figure out what to do next. The dominant urge was to stomp away. Then she grinned at him again and destroyed his line of thought.

''And I haven't been a 'girl' for three months now.''

''But . . .''

''No, I haven't been to the menstrual lodge either. I'm Tanager. When the signs first came, I left for the timber. When I'm ready, I'll go let them fawn over me and paint me up. But I'm not ready yet.''

He shook his head, baffled. ''But that's the most important thing that happens to a woman. It's special!''

''And I'm Tanager. I'm special in my own way.''

''You don't want to worry about avoiding Blood Bear?''

''Blood Bear?'' She giggled to herself. ''He'll have a merry chase catching me. No, I'll vanish when the ceremony is over. And I think most people will expect it. Even Mother's given up on me.''

Snaps Horn rubbed his face with a cold hand. ''So I'm supposed to let Elk Charm go?''

''Of course. You weren't meant for her anyway. You're too different. She wants more than you could give her. And that's not a slap in your face. She daydreams too much. You need a woman more practical.''

''Oh? Who?''

''Cricket. She's dying of love for you. She's been pacing around the camp staring down the trails practically dying inside. She's always loved you. And you've always been out of her reach.''

''Cricket?''

''Yes, Cricket. And here you are out trying to ruin your life and Elk Charm's and Cricket's! If you killed Elk Charm's lover, Cricket would have been miserable.''

''But she's just a girl!''

''That's because you've only had eyes for Elk Charm's body. You've blinded yourself.''

"What about you? Maybe you're jealous because I want Elk Charm?"

Tanager gave him a level look. "I'm not sure I want to couple with you. For one thing, the elders would whisper about incest. We're too closely related, second cousins. And besides, you couldn't stand me. It's fun to play tricks on each other, but you'd want a wife that was always home with you. You know me. You know what I like to do. Can you see me as a wife?"

He shook his head.

She looked up at the threatening clouds that dropped low. "Listen, we're not going anywhere. I know a place close to here. This storm's going to be bad. Let's go build a fire. I've got some jerked meat in my pack. Enough to hold us. We'll have plenty of time to talk."

She shot to her feet, leading him out of the timber.

Was she right? Would it have been a mistake to kill the Short Buffalo youth? Would Elk Charm have hated him?

Worse, had he been *that* much of a fool?

"Hope that man of Elk Charm's has enough sense to head for cover," Tanager muttered as she stepped out of the trees.

Snow. Weaving patterns like wraiths of wind, it fell in sheets. Flakes half the size of a woman's hand came tumbling out of the opaque gray of the sky, whirling, piling up on the land, mounding into humps over the tall sagebrush, and capping the rocks like curious giant mushrooms until the caps themselves disappeared—melding with the increasing depth. Where Hungry Bull's group huddled in the shelter, they could hear the patter of flakes on the hide hangings.

"Lot of snow," Three Toes offered, expounding on the obvious. "And it's come so late." He whistled like a meadowlark, as if that plaintive trilling would somehow bring an end to the monotony of waiting out the storm.

"I hate to be the one to remind you, but the wood situation is getting a little worrisome." Black Crow scratched behind his ear and walked over to pull the hides apart, allowing only a sliver of gray light into the shelter. He craned his neck as he inspected the falling flakes and let the hangings close.

"I'm not up to it," Hungry Bull groaned.

"Lazy!" Rattling Hooves chided from the side. "Makes Fun? Meadowlark? Do we go stumble around and get wet and cold while these tough men shiver and shake?"

"Men do have that frail streak in their constitutions," Makes Fun agreed, a devilish glint in her eye as she studied her husband.

"And we went for it last time." Meadowlark pursed her lips over her sewing while the children argued about something in the back of the shelter. For the moment, they'd snarled themselves in a loud game that involved crawling through the bedding while holding on to each other's legs to create what they called a monster worm.

Meadowlark shook her head. "If that's the only time I have to cover for my lazy man, I suppose it'll be as much a miracle as a white buffalo riding me to the Starweb for a visit." She set her awl and sinew aside, reaching for her sheep-hide coat.

"All right!" Three Toes exploded, leaping to his feet. "We'll go find wood! Maybe that big blown-down fir across the canyon. It's in the middle of the trail anyway."

"Great idea!" Hungry Bull crossed his arms over his chest. "You go hack it in half and give us a call when you're ready to move it."

"How about something a little less ambitious, like a couple of loads of small stuff?" Black Crow suggested, pointing a finger at Three Toes and lifting an eyebrow.

"I'll bet Heavy Beaver doesn't gather any firewood in the middle of snowstorms."

Meadowlark's musical voice chimed, "You can always go live with him. I'd never try and keep you from something like that."

Three Toes finished pulling on his outer moccasins and grinned at Hungry Bull, hooking a thumb back at his wife. "Is that gratitude? After all the years I looked out for that woman, kept her from—"

"Yes?" Meadowlark leaned forward, lips parted, waiting. "You did what?"

Three Toes hopped lightly to his feet, whirling a sheep hide around his shoulders and pulling a fox hood over his head. "Nothing! You two hunters coming on the chase? Or are you demented enough to sit around here with this bunch of sage hens?''

"Ah, the sacrifices we make in the name of family tranquillity!" Hungry Bull slapped Black Crow on the shoulder and ducked out into the storm.

Two Smokes chuckled from his place in the back where he stitched his incomparably tanned leather into a new pair of moccasins. No one, not even the best, could compete with Two Smokes' work.

Rattling Hooves kicked at a high-piled bundle of bedding. "Hey! Girl of mine. Wake up!"

The furs rose and shifted, Elk Charm's sleepy face poking out from under the mass. "Huh?"

"We just sent the men out for wood. Since they're bringing a bunch back, we might want to take some of that biscuit root we dug the day this storm started and turn it into something roastable. You know, make a deep pit fire and cook it good.''

Elk Charm yawned, rubbing at her eyes. "Still snowing?"

"Like you haven't seen for all your years."

"Little Dancer didn't come back?"

"Now," her mother replied gently, "you wouldn't want him traveling in weather like this. Think about the footing, how you can't judge the surface. Walking in this, a chance misstep could leave him . . . And there's ice and thinly crusted snow that would . . . Well, you'd want him safe, that's all, daughter." Rattling Hooves lowered her eyes, looking away as she fumbled with the hem of her skirt.

"He'll be staying with White Calf through this," Makes Fun decided firmly. "She wouldn't send him out into a mess like this. White Calf's just that way. She knows. A woman doesn't get that old without knowing a few things at least."

"She has a way with weather," Two Smokes agreed. He laid aside his moccasins and picked through his collection of grasses as if he'd just had a thought. He lifted one after another to inspect them against the weak light. The puzzled look didn't leave his weather-beaten face.

Elk Charm pulled her mussed hair back, fishing a long-toothed comb crafted from a deer scapula from her pack. Picking at the snarls, she worked her hair into long shining lengths before braiding it. Rolling and stowing the bedding, she stepped out into the weather, following the trail down into the willows to relieve herself.

Watching her go, Rattling Hooves pressed at her forehead with a knotted fist. "By First Man, I hope he comes back. She's too young to go through what I did." Her face lined. "I had her . . . and Wet Rain. But she's so young."

Meadowlark placed a warm hand on her shoulder. "What will be, will be." She shook her head. "I don't know. After what Little Dancer's been through, well, I don't think the spirits would abandon him now."

"Chokecherry always said he was going to do great things," Makes Fun reminded. "I'll put my trust in Chokecherry."

"I've known him the longest." Two Smokes sighed. "Myself, I don't think Power will abandon him. I don't know what it will make of my Little Dancer, but I don't think he's come this far just to be left beside the trail." He smiled and winked at Rattling Hooves. "But then, you know about berdache. We feel things."

The children giggled and squealed where they rolled and wrestled in the robes. "Hey, you little ferrets, settle down. People live here, not a pack of otters." Makes Fun slapped at the pile with a grass flail.

"Power?" Rattling Hooves shook her head. "Why does the very thought of it still make me nervous?"

"Because you've been around us too long . . ." Meadowlark said in half jest, "and we were around Heavy Beaver too long before that!"

"Wait and see." Two Smokes replaced his grass in the leather holder. "When people deal with the long terms of Power, all they can do is wait. Power picks its own time and place. It does what it does when it thinks the time is right."

"That's reassuring," Rattling Hooves grunted dryly. "She's *my* daughter."

Two Smokes said no more, dropping his eyes and lacing his fingers across his sagging belly as he thought about his grasses.

The flaps parted and Elk Charm stepped through, head already matted with snow. Without a word she went to the parfleche that stored the freshly dug roots. She had to step over squirming children to reach for the grinding stone. She scrubbed the dirt from the root skins one by one with a handful of stiff grass. Then she used the mano to smash the thick roots before milling them. The mano sounded hollowly in the room, rasping, knocking, and rasping again.

As she worked, the muscles in Elk Charm's forearms leapt and tensed under her smooth skin, a reflection of the turmoil in her mind. She attacked the woody roots, grinding the fibers against the stone as if, by the very action, she could exact some measure of vengeance on the world that frustrated her so.

Only Two Smokes saw the tear that slipped down her cheek.

Little Dancer shivered in the hollow left by a deadfall. Overhead, its twisted roots thrust gray skeleton fingers up into the stormy sky. Clutched in its grip, rocks, dirt, and a mass of debris created a slight shelter from the ceaseless dance of falling snow.

He blinked, tucking his arms tighter about his middle. A pain ate at the side of his head. Stupid, foolish . . . of all the idiot stunts he'd ever pulled, he knew better than to travel in a storm like this. His first action should have been to turn around and race back to White Calf's. His second should have been to make a shelter, stock wood, and wait it out.

But he hadn't. Images of Elk Charm's face had led him on. Thoughts of her body hot against his had spurred him into the storm, leading him to follow a path he'd traveled only twice before. For a while, he'd fooled himself into thinking this might be just another spring storm—wet, wild, and quick to dump its load of snow and hurry on across the plains to the east. Instead, this one had clung over the mountains like a patient bobcat over a cornered rabbit.

At that thought, he shivered even harder.

Then he'd climbed to the ridge top, figuring to find better footing where the wind had blown the snow away. The cornice had fooled him. He'd stepped where nothing but snow supported his weight. He remembered the lurch in his stomach, the flailing of arms, and falling. . . .

How long had he lain unconscious in the snow? He'd been

lucky to come to at all. He'd blinked, feeling the frostbite eating into his fingers and face. A glazing pain hammered at his brain, a stiffly clotted cut burned and stung on his cheek where the blood had leaked into the snow and frozen.

His darts were gone, as was his pack. Now, only hope remained for him. Hope that a miracle would occur, that the storm would break, that a blistering chinook would replace the heat of life that had evaporated from his icy flesh.

He groaned as he looked out from under the roots, staring up at the forbidding sky. The endless fall of giant flakes continued to spin out of the murky clouds. Endless, dancing with the air, the fluffy white tufts of snow whirled down to pat with a soft whisper to the ground.

"Got to . . . to move. Make heat."

He gritted his teeth to keep from crying out, and staggered to his feet. A nagging ache reminded him that he'd fallen hard on that leg. It didn't seem broken, but his thigh had swollen to stretch his hunting pants. He almost collapsed as he realized the feeling had gone from his feet.

Uncontrollable shivering possessed him as he stumbled along, arms clutched to his chest. He had to generate heat through movement, no matter that his leg shot agony through him with each step. How long ago had it been since he'd eaten anything besides snow? How long until his body exhausted itself and could no longer produce heat?

Blinking stupidly, he crashed through the snow-sodden branches of a fir and cried out at the icy dusting he got as the snow load emptied on him. Batting at himself with hands like clubs, he staggered on, weaving on his feet.

The world pitched and slapped him facefirst into the snow. On trembling limbs, he got to hands and knees, cold clamping his soul like a bear's jaws on elk bone.

His vision shimmered as if he looked through a veil of silver tears.

Where am I? Where am I going? Why am I out here? Where's home? I'm . . . lost . . . lost . . . Elk Charm? A sobbing cry stuck in his throat as fingers of ice water melted from the snow packed in his hood and trickled down his back.

Dumbly, he fought his way to his feet, kicked his way forward for another three paces, and pitched on his face again.

Even the heartbeat seemed sluggish in his chest as he forced himself to keep going despite the pain and weariness.

A warm feeling began to replace the numbness in his feet and hands—delightful warmth—and he'd become so tired. If only he could lie down for a moment . . . sleep . . . for just a moment. . . .

Firelight cast red-orange shadows on the irregular rock of the shelter.

Elk Charm gasped, bolting upright in her bed.

"What is it?" Two Smokes asked from where he sat tending the fire over the pit full of sweet-smelling biscuit root.

Elk Charm struggled to get her breath, a panic on her pretty face. "I . . ." She buried her head in her hands.

Two Smokes stood, carefully maneuvering on his maimed leg so as not to disturb the sleepers. He settled himself on her bed, placing an arm about her shoulders as she sobbed softly to herself.

"Shhh. Here. Come on, now. This is old Two Smokes. Tell me what's wrong. A dream?"

She sniffed and wiped at the tears flooding her eyes, nodding her head. She refused to look at him, suffering on her own.

"Hush, now. You're safe. you're here, and warm, and surrounded by people who love you. What was it? What was this terrible dream?"

She looked up, desperate eyes meeting his for the first time. "L-Little Dancer," she moaned. "He's . . . Oh, no . . . he's dead." And she burst into tears again.

Two Smokes started to say something, hugging her close, patting her—but his eyes caught the wolf effigy where it had been pecked into the sooty rock.

Power had been at work this night. He could practically taste it in the air. And he'd felt the lurch, the same sort of wrenching as the night the Wolf Bundle had been desecrated.

His heart skipped, for he could have sworn the wolf's eyes gleamed for that brief instance, and it looked like triumph.

* * *

"So close," the Wolf Bundle whispered. *"We hang by a thread. Must you play so perilously with the passions of youth?"*

"The girl, Tanager, acted on her own. The storm took all of my ability. Let's hope it's enough. I had to throw the Spiral out of balance to effect this." Wolf Dreamer sounded weary. *"Perhaps I bought us time. Perhaps I can reach Little Dancer. The Watcher is ready."*

"Or you may have just condemned us."

"It's up to free will now. Heavy Beaver's . . . and the boy's."

Chapter 19 ✋

Heavy Beaver glared at the snow blowing out of the sky around his camp. Icy wind roared down from the Buffalo Mountains, moaning around the cap rock on the hogbacks, twisting across the flats before lining out to blow wraiths of snow across the sage flats, piling little diamond-shaped drifts to taper away behind the craggy sagebrush.

He wet his lips, tasting the flakes, feeling the crystals battering against his skin. Eyes slitted to the gale, he stared into the storm, wondering. Never since he'd first heard the stories had such a storm as this come so late to the plains. Never had he seen the buckwheat, the phlox and aster, frozen on their stalks.

He contemplated the fate of the warriors he'd sent to scout the trail up Clear River, past the Red Wall and into the Anit'ah country. The snow should have been melting by now, the trails opening. Anit'ah camps, lean from winter, should have been easy pickings for his young men.

Not all of his youths had gone to scout Anit'ah. Many had gone for spring buffalo, hoping to pick up fresh meat from the nursery herds, and perhaps waylay antelope at the same time. This was the time when does left the big herds, wandering out by themselves to look for fawning grounds in the thick sage where coyotes wouldn't find the newborn twins.

And how did those young men fare? So far, a handful had come stumbling in, feet frozen, faces frostbitten and burned. Not good. The flesh had gone black on the ones he'd treated. The ability to feel ice in a living human limb appalled him. And the ones who hadn't returned? What of them? They'd left camp dressed lightly for the hunt, not wearing much in the way of clothing. After all, a hunter didn't take a pack dog with him. What kind of foolishness would that be?

The wind battered at him, seeking to push him back, whipping his clothing about his legs and tugging at the fox lining of his hood.

Impassive, he stood before the storm, slitted eyes seeking the Buffalo Mountains, and the people who resisted him. Sometime soon, he'd move into those hills with their lush viridian meadows. He'd have to. The drought had been stealing back on them, the rains ever more scarce. Buffalo had become almost as few and far between as the year he'd cursed Sage Root and broken the power of the elders among the People. This time, he'd need those Anit'ah hunting grounds. If he couldn't find new lands for his people to hunt, if he couldn't raid enough spoils from the Cut Hair and White Crane and Fire Buffalo, then they might begin to question the vision he'd imparted to them.

"Dreamers can be killed," he whispered into the wind. "But only Dreamers with no imagination need worry."

Filling his lungs with the icy air, he frowned into the storm. Where were his young men? Had they all reached safety? Or did they lie dead and frozen even now, sightless eyes blown full of snow, stiff fingers rising above the drifts, clawing at the driving wind?

Illusion. Life, the world, everything was created of illusion. He Dreamed . . .

. . . Sinking into the warmth, like a feather on air, he drifted, slipping back and forth as he settled into the haze.

"Your soul could be mine now. You're on the verge of

parting with your body, of turning ghost or rising to the Star-web. What is your wish, Little Dancer?

"Would you see your wife again? Would you conceive your children? Would you leave your people to the false Dreamer's ways? Will you leave the Wolf Bundle to die? Why will you do this thing? Why will you ignore the cries of the Spiral? Of the Circles? Of your people?"

In the haze, Little Dancer floated, enjoying a feeling of relief, aware that his suffering lay somewhere behind him—up beyond the haze of warmth that soothed his tired soul. "But it's so nice here. So . . . nice . . ."

"What you feel is the world of death. Your soul balances on the edge."

A gentle surface, which appeared to be a giant human hand, stopped his descent, cradling him while the hazy warmth stirred around him like clouds over the peaks.

"What happened? Where am I?"

From out of the billowing warmth, the features of a man formed. His face gleamed radiantly, lit from within. Sparkling black eyes stared out from either side of a straight nose.

Little Dancer's breath stilled in his throat; never had he seen so beautiful a man. Never had he been so captivated by the Power and empathy in a man's eyes.

"Who are you?"

The man laughed, the sound of it rippling the haze, turning it this way and that like he'd seen schools of minnows in the Moon River. The very air seemed to live with his laughter and Little Dancer's soul leapt while his nerves tingled.

"I am the Wolf Dreamer, the one you call First Man. I chose, once—as you must do now. Only perhaps in those days, the choices were a little less difficult."

"Why am I here?"

"You're dying, Little Dancer. Your body is freezing and your soul is drifting free."

The warm haze around him shifted for a moment, changing from featureless to wind-whipped snowflakes. Slightly below him, he could recognize the mounded lump of his body, snow-packed and already becoming one with the drift that formed about it.

"So you see, this choice is yours. Live, and you will have

a short time with your Elk Charm.'' The scene shifted, and Little Dancer stared down into the familiar depths of Hungry Bull's shelter, seeing Elk Charm in fitful sleep. To one side, Two Smokes stared up, as if he could see him. Through the vision, Little Dancer could feel the soul of the berdache as it savored the Power.

His eyes went back to Elk Charm and the love cried out from within. He tried to imprint the memory of her delicate face, of the lines of soft cheek and firm jaw. The wealth of her long hair spilled over the hides, framing her intense beauty.

He ached.

"I'll give you what time I can. The Spiral is coming full. I've kept Heavy Beaver from moving. I can keep your people safe for a while longer, give you more time. You're so young, but then, Clear Water resisted for a long time, too. She couldn't stomach the thought of Blood Bear touching her.''

"Blood Bear? My father?"

"You needed his strength, his indomitable courage—mindless and thoughtless though it might be. Oh, I've put a lot of thought into you and your life. You've been given everything I can give you—except the will to do what needs to be done.''

"The will?"

"Exactly that. The Wise One Above—the Creator—made the universe so. As it turns, the cycles of stars and worlds and insects and even grains of sand make their own way. The Creator allowed for free will, for things to choose. What you wish to observe is what will be. You make up your world around you. Suppose I told you that what looked like solid rock was mostly empty space?''

"That the world is illusion?"

"White Calf told you the truth—only she doesn't comprehend the depths of her understanding yet. The patterns that are generated are fascinating, spinning, changing always. The very essence of the universe is like a brewing storm. It's so difficult to keep from watching, wondering. . . .''

"Then why don't you?"

The Wolf Dreamer smiled, a hollow pain filling his eyes, the power of which left Little Dancer in tears.

"I'm not perfect, little friend—as nothing in creation is.

I, too, have my faults. I . . . I have too much love in my spirit. In its way, too much love is as terrible as too much hate. Each hurts. You must understand that if everything existed in harmony, nothing would change and the universe would become stagnant—and die.

"But now you must choose. Will you choose to live? Or will you die? If you live, I'll keep you until the very last. I'll let you have as much pleasure as I can. At the same time, my people—all of them—need you. Heavy Beaver has changed the Spiral."

Wolf Dreamer's gentle smile turned wistful. *"Curious how powerful a single idea can be . . . how it can change the minds of so many until the very fabric of the universe ripples. You, however, can change it back. You can meet Heavy Beaver, and prove him false. Doing so may put the Spiral back the way it was. The last time, we lost the mammoth, and camel, and horse, and sloth. This time, I wouldn't lose the buffalo, and antelope, and I wouldn't have the People go the way others are."*

"And if I choose to die?"

"That is your will. I can't lie to you, my friend. The way of death will be much easier, more pleasant to float off to the Starweb with Sage Root, Heron, Clear Water, Dancing Fox, and so many others. There, they Sing and Dance and hunt with other souls as they watch the universe in all its wonder."

Another voice whispered through the mist, *"And I will die with you."*

"Who was that?"

"The Wolf Bundle. Your fates are tied. Already its Power is ebbing. If you decide to live, you'll have to take the Wolf Bundle from Blood Bear. To do that, you'll probably have to kill him. Are you stronger than your father? Do you have his strength?"

Little Dancer stared into the kind eyes of Wolf Dreamer. "I don't know." He couldn't lie . . . not to himself, not to Wolf Dreamer—and not in this place.

"If you decide to live, you'll find out. That's another thing: I can't assure you of victory. Remember free will? Like rock

is the foundation of earth, so is will the foundation of the universe.''

His mind had begun to work again, honed by the arguments he'd had with White Calf. ''And if I chose to live, what will it cost me?''

Wolf Dreamer's eyes shimmered, tearing, so painful it hurt to look at him. *''Everything you hold dear. Once you start on the trail of a true Dreamer, you can't go back. White Calf told you the truth. You can't be both.''*

''And if I die? What then? What happens to Elk Charm, and my father? You've already told me the Wolf Bundle will die—and the buffalo, too. What about the people I love?''

Wolf Dreamer's expression mirrored the concern within. *''A spirit can see only so much of the future—and not all will come to pass as we foresee. But I foresee them fleeing, finding a place to be safe on the shores of the western ocean.''*

Little Dancer hovered on Wolf Dreamer's hand, looking into those kind eyes. Memories slipped and slid through his mind. His mother's words echoed hollowly, dominating his thoughts. Heavy Beaver's arrogant smile lingered, and he relived the moment the shaman walked forward, club raised to dash his brains out. White Calf's angry face formed for a moment, before it faded into Elk Charm's anxious features. The Spiral on the rock shelter wall before him seemed to pulse with life. The Wolf Bundle fell with a sickening thump from the night sky and the world reeled. In the silence that followed, he could hear the echo of Heavy Beaver's pot drum, singing Sage Root's death. Death . . . She sat propped in the sun-bleached crook of a weather-stripped cottonwood. Flies walked on her face, rising to hover over her slit wrists and suck greedily of her blood. His mother's dead eyes burned with Power, searing his very soul.

''I'll live.'' The words caught in his throat. ''Just give me as much time as you can.''

''It will hurt worse when it's time.''

''I know.''

Wolf Dreamer nodded. *''I'll come for you. You'll know, of course. But I'll meet you . . . like this . . . and we'll talk. I have some things to teach you.''* A pause. *''Why did you choose the way you did?''*

He looked into Wolf Dreamer's eyes. "Maybe . . . maybe like you . . . I love too much."

"Wolf will save you. He'll take you to his den and warm your body. He'll go with you, guard you, keep you and your family safe for as long as I can allow. He's my promise to you."

Haze drifted down, spinning the Wolf Dreamer away. As if Little Dancer had jumped into a pool, his body rose, twisting slightly as it rocked. Around him, the comforting warmth began to ebb, replaced with chill that leached into his very bones. Pain and fear began to pound with each muffled beat of his heart. A throbbing agony fired the side of his numb head.

He whimpered at the pain of his body pressed onto the angular rocks. Crying out, he tried to move. Snow restricted his progress. Pain. Numb-tingling cold—his flesh shrieked of it. Broken and battered as he was, the memory of the warm drifting haze of death seeped away into miserable reality. He lay dying as light fled and darkness dropped on the land.

He raised his head, blinking at the ice crusting his lashes. The shivering had gone, a sign that the last of his heat had vanished. Death lay so close.

The black form detached, slinking close, circling uneasily.

"Wolf!" The sound of his cracked voice frightened him.

The big black animal sniffed at his face, whiskers barely felt as they brushed his numb skin.

Little Dancer summoned some hidden reserve and lurched, getting hands and knees under him. His entire body hurt, stinging, aching as he got to all fours.

He almost fell, reaching out, bracing himself on the wolf, half expecting the animal to whirl and snap at him. On legs that refused to function, he crawled. Using an angled deadfall, he managed to get to his feet.

One step after another, he moved doggedly forward, keeping the huge black animal in sight. Around him, the timber grayed to blackness, as if seen through a hole in the night. He staggered and stumbled on. He walked in a daze, images of the Wolf Dreamer hanging in his dull mind.

"Won't die," he whispered through unfeeling lips. "Won't . . ."

He fell hard, the impact jarring his tortured body. Cold,

so terribly cold. The hurt seemed to cause a ringing in his ears. Spent, he struggled to stand, struggled to . . .

Consciousness faded.

Elk Charm sat on the uncomfortable hardness of a worn boulder where it stuck out of the hillside. She could see the length of the valley where it ran southeast out of the Buffalo Mountains and down to the distant hogbacks. An abrupt ridge hid the far horizon she'd memorized that evening she'd sat next to Little Dancer—and finally coupled with him. Until the day she died, she'd remember the look in his eyes as he stared out over the plains. A premonition of trouble; pain at what he'd left behind; confusion; it had all come together in the set of his face. What a cruel legacy.

Now the final shadows of the terrible snow melted out of the stands of timber on the north slopes. Below, in the valley, the creek ran full with runoff, white water dashing and crashing around the oxbows of the broad valley. The willows had gone viridian in the warm sun. About her, grasses shot lush spikes of leaves up through the brown clump of last year's growth. Life had come again to the mountains—and found only a barren grayness in her heart.

The delicate yellow heads of sagebrush buttercup and purple shooting star added no color to the drabness of her thoughts. Not even the calls of the rosy finches and the flocks of juncos could dent the lingering edges of her grief. Little Dancer's memory suffused her life. His words ghosted through her ears. She saw his face, the way his smile went from serious to irreverent. Her body tingled with the lines of his caress. Her loins ached for him, knowing his light had flickered and gone dim in the world.

Worse, she dared not think of him, how his body must look as it melted out of the snow. She'd seen her father, she knew.

"There you are."

She'd missed his approach.

"Mind if I sit down?"

She shrugged, looking up listlessly.

Two Smokes grunted as he lowered himself, making room for his game leg. He pulled his good knee up, hugging it in the loop of his arms. "Spring has finally made it. I'd come to think we'd spend the rest of our lives staring at each other. Have you noticed how everyone has disappeared over the last couple of days? That comes of living with each other for too long in the same shelter."

She said nothing.

"I think what we'll do is when everyone gets back, we'll move over to the west side. I know some wonderful places over there that have a spectacular view. You can see right across the basin, for maybe . . . I don't know, four days' hard walk, to the mountains on the other side. Good grass up there. Lots of sego lily and balsam root for the digging. Yampa's pretty thick, too. We could find one of those valleys cut down through the cap rock. Lots of shelters there so people don't have to crowd together. Another winter with those children and I think I'd rather slit my wrists with dull quartzite."

She swallowed at the lump in her throat, wishing she could talk back—finding no words in the desert of her thoughts.

"There's a good deal of wood, too. Won't be so long a hike to pack it back as we had this year. I know of a couple of excellent sheep traps. Used to be buffalo down in the basin, but that's a lot of packing to get the meat back up to the shelters."

She traced the path of a red-tailed hawk as it danced on the air currents. Before long, the ground squirrels would be out, wary of the hawk's sweeping flight. For now, the hawk waited, seeking instead any red squirrel or unwary cottontail.

"You know," Two Smokes added kindly, "I'd like to know what you feel. I can't bring him back; berdache don't have that kind of Power, but maybe we could talk. It might make his spirit rest easier."

Her insides wilted and she could feel her chin quivering. Blessed Wise One, did it *have* to hurt so badly?

"All my life, I cared for him." Two Smokes shook his head, the gray in his braids glinting silver in the sun. "I can't figure. It used to be that I could feel the link between the Wolf Bundle and Little Dancer. That Power feeling, you know?"

She reached for his hand, feeling the warmth of his skin under her fingers.

"It's my fault," Two Smokes added. "I failed both the Wolf Bundle and Little Dancer. I should have stood that night . . . and run a dart clear through Heavy Beaver. They might have killed me for it, but I could have washed the insult in Heavy Beaver's blood first. Sage Root would have seen that the boy got the Wolf Bundle. Maybe I could have saved us from all of this."

"It's not your fault," she managed. "Two Smokes, you did the best you could. No one can know the future. People just have to do the best they can."

"Perhaps. Maybe we can't know the future, but the past is forever. How are you feeling? What's in your heart?"

She looked up at him, seeing the lines that had eaten so deeply into his face. A perpetual squint, like that of a man in pain, etched his eyes. These signs, and his graying hair, showed that Two Smokes had passed the threshold to old age. But was he that old? No, Rattling Hooves had been born even a year or two before Two Smokes. Had life treated him so poorly? Her wounded heart beat with sympathy for the old berdache.

She reached up to hug him, burying her head in his chest to let tears relieve the hurt for both of them. For a long time, he held her, let her hot tears wet the front of his quill-decorated shirt.

"We're a pair, aren't we?" he murmured, stroking her hair.

"It's just like what happened to my father," she mumbled, and straightened to stare off into the distance, watching the hawk turning slowly with the winds. "I know how my mother felt now. Did we do something wrong? Did we offend some spirit somewhere? What? All I did was love him."

Two Smokes took a breath and hugged her. "It wasn't you. He'd been picked for something by Spirit Power. Remember? I told you that day above White Calf's camp. I didn't know that it would happen this way."

"The others still say he's coming back."

Two Smokes slapped at a fly that had begun to buzz around them. "I'd like to believe that. Only I trust your dream. I thought I . . . well, I thought I felt him go. A berdache can do that sometimes, feel a person's soul like that.''

"I guess I'll always have the memories. Dung and flies, I knew I'd have to share him with the Dreams. I could have stood that. At least I'd have him part of the time. But dead is . . . forever.''

"Come on. Let me take you back to the shelter. I made some biscuit-root bread this morning. It should be about baked. I'll bet it's steaming and hot and so sweet your teeth will ache to bite into it.''

She hesitated for a moment while he stood. "I don't know. Maybe I'll just—''

"Girl, you haven't eaten for days. Come on. If Two Smokes has lived through all the terrible times he has, then he's learned something from it. Food first. Keep your strength.''

She let him pull her up. With her helping him over the rough spots, they worked their way along the slope. In places, the mud remained slick and treacherous.

As they topped a rise, the camp lay visible. The hangings looked worn and tattered after the winter. The yellowed sandstone of the outcrop looked dingy as did the trampled trails through the willows and along the slopes.

I'll never be able to come back here, she thought, hearing Two Smokes grunt as his bad leg took a jolt.

"Look! Someone's coming.'' Two Smokes paused, lifting a finger to point.

She squinted up the hill, seeing a person walking with a big black dog. "Looks like he's had a tough trip. Almost staggering as he walks as if . . .''

And she was running, pounding up the hill, barely aware of the throb in her lungs as she ran out of breath.

She slowed to a stop, lungs exhausted, legs trembling as she looked at him. He smiled weakly. A terrible cut on his cheek had scabbed over. His clothing hung in tatters, muddy and dirty.

The huge black dog had become a wolf, staring at her with wary yellow eyes.

"I'm back,'' he said in a raspy voice.

And she threw herself into his arms.

BOOK THREE

The Challenge
of the Man

"Where are you?" Wolf Dreamer called from the shimmering wealth of the Spirals.

"Death . . . all is dying," keened the Wolf Bundle.

"The time has come."

"Hear their pleas? Hear the last calls of suffering?"

"Wolf Bundle, the time has come."

"Perhaps . . . too late . . ."

Chapter 20 ◉

The hot wind blew down from the northwest, sucking the last remaining moisture from a land that had had no winter. The faint dusting of snow that had fallen at the height of the deep cold had vanished like the memory of a wistful smile from an old man's lips.

A man could count the number of rainstorms that had passed this year on one hand—and those had been cloud-bursts that scored the earth and filled the drainages with muddy water, only to vanish into the hot air.

Where buffalo had once grazed, whirlwinds—said by some to be the unhappy ghosts of the dead—lifted yellow-white dust plumes to the skies and exhausted themselves.

Among the buffalo, the old and weak collapsed on the long trek between water holes. The cows remained gaunt. Fetuses aborted from the stress, their fragile carcasses marking the back trail of dusty imprints left by cracked hooves on the sunbaked clay. Behind the dwindling herds, buzzards and ravens followed, waiting their turn. The gorging wolves left red, chewed remains for the coyotes. After the coyotes slunk off with full bellies, the birds got their chance, and when they left, only the rodents could make use of the bleached bone. Not even enough remained for the shining bottle flies to blow.

Through it all, only the wind seemed eternal, blowing, grating on the souls of human and beasts as it lifted silts and sands, driving the grit with a force to fill every crack and crevice. The hollows behind hills puffed underfoot, while the windward side consisted of deflated rock denuded of grass, dotted here and there by a sandblasted skeleton of sagebrush. When rain fell on the exposed rock, it could only run away to the sheer-walled drainages, carrying more of the dying soil with it on the long march to the sea. The rivers ran so turbid even the wiry antelope hesitated to drink.

On the plains, buffeted by the wind, continually grimy from the blowing silt, the People cast tired gazes to the heavens, following the cycles of day from bloodred sunrise to flaming sunset. Weary eyes forever searched the western horizon for storm clouds that never came. When the People ate, blown sand grated in their teeth. When the young men returned from the hunt—usually with empty hands—the faces of the People turned to their Spirit Dreamer.

Heavy Beaver stepped out behind where his camp lay sheltered in the lee of a sage-studded bluff. He'd chosen this place just up from the brown waters of the Moon River. As he stood, arms crossed, the sun lowered in the west. This day, the gaping red eye of light—a macabre wound—bled through the dust-heavy air. It settled on a specific rocky tor high in the Buffalo Mountains. Even from where he looked to the west, Heavy Beaver could see the retreating snow line on the high peaks. As usual—no matter what the drought in the plains—the mountains had snow. Where snow melted, the plants grew green and the buffalo grew fat.

"This year," he promised. "This year we come, Anit'ah. With all our young men, we're taking your mountains. I'm the new way. You can't stand before my mother's vision. I'm the new Dreamer for all men. I'm the cleanser of pollution."

The time had come; he had no choice. If he and his frustrated warriors didn't take the Anit'ah lands, the People would starve. When a people starved, they came looking for the Spirit Dreamer who'd led them falsely. Already, too many whispered behind their hands that Heavy Beaver's Power had begun to slip, to fade into memory like the rain that never fell.

If he couldn't keep Two Stones, and Seven Suns, and Elk Whistle crushed under the weight of his power, then one day soon, a dart would transfix Heavy Beaver's guts and a different man would take his place . . . and his barren women.

And if that man begot a son from Heavy Beaver's wives, that would be an even more damning indictment.

"Prepare yourselves, Anit'ah. This year we're coming. We

have nothing left to lose.'' *And Mother, even possession by the evil ghosts would be better than failure.*

Elk Charm's calves ached, a stitch burned in the joint of her hip, and every muscle in her lower back and pelvis screamed for relief. But she could not remember being happier.

Not every day turned out like this one. Elk Charm followed the trail that skirted the cap rock where it hung out over the canyon. Behind her, to the east, the tall peaks rose, snow-packed and glaring white against the crystal-blue dome of the sky. Spring had come again—another cycle finished, a new one started.

Ignoring the ache in her back and the strain in her legs, she grinned at the whole world. Outside of the exertion, her biggest worry was that the bottom would split out of the pack she carried. This was, indeed, a special day. She had gone to dig roots where the snowbanks fed the verdant green slopes and the prize biscuit root that grew there. No more than an hour's worth of driving her hard chokecherry digging stick into the ground had netted an entire packful of roots and greens. She'd stopped to pick some newly sprouted yarrow for seasoning and heard the doe.

Purely by luck, the deer had stepped out from where she'd been bedded in the juniper, ears pricked, curious at the disturbance to her morning nap.

Without a second thought, Elk Charm's arm went back and she drove a finely fletched dart through the deer's chest. The doe jumped, wheeled, and made no more than fifty paces before her knees went weak and buckled. Reeling on her feet, she'd fallen, struggled to get up, and fallen again.

Wary, Elk Charm had frozen in place, waiting. Only a fool rushed up to a wounded animal. To do so might lend the prey that final rush of fear and send the quarry on a wild run. Accidents happened that way. Hunters lost their fatally wounded game. On such an occasion, a wounded animal's spirit might stalk the hunter, watching, scaring away other game and causing bad luck.

Elk Charm had stood still as lightning-riven deadfall, waiting, watching the doe bleed out, her sides working harder and harder as the blood emptied from her pierced lungs.

Finally the head had dropped and the doe rested her chin on the buff-colored rocky soil. She'd sighed a couple of times, the sound rattling and loud as blood leaked from her nostrils to soak the arid stone and dirt. Only when Elk Charm could see no movement did she creep closer. By the time she reached the doe, the animal's spirit had passed from the body.

Reverently, Elk Charm had said the prayers, Singing the spirit to the heavens above. She asked fervently that the deer's soul might run with the wind, and Dance with the stars. Gratefully, she thanked the doe for the gift of life and what it meant to her family. Then she straightened and lifted a hoof, rolling the animal over.

Not even Hungry Bull could have made a better shot than that! She'd pulled her butchering kit from the pouch hanging at her waist and quickly slit the gleaming white belly hide open. With her quartzite chopper she split the ribs from the sternum. She'd emptied the heart of clotted blood and cut it from the tough sack that surrounded it. The windpipe came out next. The liver, kidneys, and fetus had gone into her pack as delicacies for tonight's feast. Then she'd halved the carcass, unloading part of the roots so she could carry the organs and hindquarters back. The rest she propped in the juniper branches to cool.

Only after she'd finished butchering did she drain the paunch and intestines. Turning the paunch inside out, she coiled the intestines and laid them inside where they'd stay moist and flies couldn't get to them. She'd return with Little Dancer before dark and retrieve the rest of her roots and the extra meat and organs.

Remembering the events of the day, she walked in a glow, and grinned, and chanted a song under her breath in an attempt to ignore the pain her load caused her. That didn't stop her from worrying about the strain on the pack. She'd sewn the straps herself, using the finest sinew, and most of the leather had been doubled. Still, what she carried had to be almost half her weight. Not even the best packs could take that for long.

Besides, she *had* to get back. The milk in her breasts had

begun to ache in addition to her muscles and bones. Already she could feel the wetness and smell the musk of leaking milk.

"Ho-yeh!" The cry came from behind her.

She slowed and turned, lifting a hand to shade her eyes. A man trotted briskly down the trail.

"Ho-yeh!" she called back, trying to place the figure. "Catch up! This is heavy!" And she started down the rocky path again, using her digging stick to help with balance.

She heard him closing, heavy feet crunching on the friable sandstone pebbles that littered the cap rock.

"Who is it?" she called.

"I am Ramshorn, warrior of the Red Hand, and I'm betting the front side of that big pack is Elk Charm, also of the Red Hand and my cousin on top of it all."

Elk Charm bit her lip, knowing full well what he wanted. She'd hoped Blood Bear wouldn't be foolish enough to send someone down. She'd hoped it had all gone away, blown like the dust on the west wind to some other place far away.

"Ho-yeh, Ramshorn. Welcome to the camp of Hungry Bull. You've timed it well, I've got fresh deer in the pack and roots, too—albeit a little blood-soaked by luck."

He laughed. "I stopped to look. You'd scuffed up the tracks, but it looked like a neat one-shot kill. How far did you throw from?"

"Maybe twenty paces." She grinned despite his presence; pride over something like that didn't come every day. "When I opened her up, the dart had cut through the lungs."

"Well, if you do that sort of thing all the time, why don't you leave this Little Dancer of yours and come be my number-one wife? The others can step aside for a hunter like that."

"And you'd never sleep," she shot back. "All those wives you displaced to bring me in would slit your throat some night—and mine, too, no doubt. If they didn't, someone else would, *cousin*, because marrying you would be incest."

He laughed with her and offered, "I could carry something. Maybe those back legs? I see the hocks sticking out the top."

"Not worth it," she puffed. "We're almost there."

The trail forked. The less-traveled route to the right continued to follow along the cap rock. The other split left and dropped down through a crack in the thick sandstone. Elk Charm slowed, placing each foot just so from long practice.

"Heard you had another baby. A boy this time?"

She frowned as the pack scraped the rock on both sides of the narrow way. *Please, don't let those straps fray!* "No, to Hungry Bull's dismay, Little Dancer got another daughter."

"Hmm. I'll bet you heard about that."

She picked her way along the top of the slope where the colluvium fanned under the tawny sandstone. Rabbitbrush, bitterbrush, serviceberry, and sage rasped against her moccasins and skirt, scratching loudly on the pack. A warmth rose within her. "No, not Little Dancer. To him, any child is a blessing, a special gift he accepts with thanks . . . the way most people should consider every sunrise and sunset. For you never know when you'll see the last one."

He grunted.

The thought of the future settled around her heart like a frosty spiderweb on a winter-blue day. Yes, she knew why he'd come. The nagging worry had begun to eat away at the glow of both a perfect kill and the full pack.

"This is your shelter?" He stepped around the brush and pointed.

"Next one down. That shelter belongs to Three Toes and Meadowlark." As she spoke, Grasshopper came charging up the slope.

"What did you get? Who's come?" Grasshopper demanded, popping from foot to foot, eyes wide as he studied Ramshorn.

"This is the Red Hand warrior, Ramshorn. He's come to see Hungry Bull and the rest of the men."

"To get them to go off to war against the Short Buffalo People?" His jumping increased. "Didn't Blood Bear send someone last year and Hungry Bull and my father told him they couldn't fight against their relatives and—"

"Yes, yes, but this is a new year." She poked at him playfully with her walking stick. "So go tell your father and the rest that Ramshorn has come. Go on. At least we'll feast him until his belly pops and send him on his way happy and full of good memories."

Grasshopper grinned, whooping and jumping as he bolted back down the trail. Before her shelter she could see the big black wolf. As always, a shiver shot up her spine.

"I could help you with the pack," Ramshorn offered again, carefully avoiding the issue Grasshopper had broken open like an overripe gourd.

"Path's better here. We're almost home." *And better to be no more in your debt than possible.*

As they neared the shelter she inhabited with Little Dancer, the angry squall of a baby could be heard. "That sound grating on your ears is the young one. Little Dancer might be the best father among the all the people in the world, but for some reason his dugs just don't keep the little ones happy."

Ramshorn smiled politely and gave her his hand as she climbed up the fill before the shelter. The big black wolf slunk off the other side of the midden and paused downwind, testing the air guardedly. She groaned as she lowered the pack and ducked out of the tumpline. "Hey, lazy man of mine! Come see what your wife got while you were fooling around with the infants!"

Ramshorn looked around, sniffing the air. "I figured it would be a little more like a . . . well, you know how a camp gets after it's been lived in. And you've stayed her for how long?"

She grinned at him, hearing Little Dancer pulling the flap back, yawning. How could he sleep through the baby? "We have a lot of children around here. They need something to do, so they clean up the winter scat and throw them in the drainage where the rains take them away."

"Deer hocks?" Little Dancer asked, blinking himself awake. He nodded to Ramshorn. "Blood Bear wants warriors again?"

"The Short Buffalo People have already sent scouts up the trails. More than ever before. We've caught some, others get through. They're learning, though. We had three women killed and a couple of children. Snaps Horn and some others caught them at a steep place and rolled rocks down from above. The ones that lived were darted and cut up. Their pieces hang from thongs over the old trail up the Clear River."

Little Dancer nodded, flinching slightly, which accented the scar in his cheek. "Seat yourself. It's nicer outside than in. Are you thirsty?"

"Water would be wonderful. It's a long walk since the last spring."

"Up by Monster Rock?"

"Is that what was pecked there?"

Little Dancer nodded, reaching for a buffalo-gut bag that hung inside the door flap. "I think it originally showed men throwing darts at the monster, but you can only see that when the light's right. I guess it proves that not even the rocks last forever."

Ramshorn took the water, drinking greedily.

"How's White Calf?"

"Immortal." Ramshorn wiped the water from his lips, handing the bag back. "I imagine she's no different than when you saw her this last winter. The skinnier she gets, the feebler she gets, the keener her old mind is. Blood Bear stopped there with a war party and she poked and prodded at him until he left in disgust muttering that he should have killed her long ago. She just cackles and feeds it to him. The Red Hand love it and most of the warriors can't wait to make it home and tell the stories."

"I don't trust Blood Bear when it comes to his dealings with White Calf. I don't suppose with all these Short Buffalo warriors roaming everywhere that she'd move?"

"I doubt it, she says they won't bother her. That she'll show them the real meaning of a Curse if one tries anything."

"It would be best for everyone if the Short Buffalo left well enough alone and went back to their plains."

"Perhaps." Ramshorn settled himself comfortably as Elk Charm ducked inside. After she rescued the infant from its cradle board, she slipped her shoulder out of the dress and emerged with the infant attached greedily to her right breast.

She eased herself down, sighing as her weary back relaxed and the ache went out of her hips. "We'll have to go back for the rest of the roots and the front half of the deer. I put brush over the head so maybe the ravens and magpies won't get the eyes. That's your father's favorite part."

Little Dancer shot her a radiant smile. "A good kill?"

"One shot." She beamed. "First thing, I Sang for her spirit."

"Well, let's get Ramshorn comfortable and make him at home. Then if you'll show the way, I'll carry the second load."

"Meadowlark might even look after this one." She indicated the infant. "Your other daughter didn't get eaten by a bear when I was gone?"

"She's off at Black Crow's making Cradle Girl miserable." He frowned. "I wonder if that isn't her mother coming out in her."

She plucked up her digging stick and poked him until he cried in surrender and scrambled away on all fours.

Ramshorn laughed heartily. "It's good to see people having fun again." He took a deep breath and pulled one muscular leg up to his chest. "The Red Hand worry so much, I think we've forgotten how to laugh."

Elk Charm cocked her head. "We don't hear much here on the west side of the mountain. Is it really that bad?"

Ramshorn dropped his eyes. "One of the women killed in that raid I told you about . . . well, her name was Wet Rain."

Elk Charm's stomach lurched as if she were falling.

"So, what are you going to tell him?" Elk Charm demanded.

Little Dancer pursed his lips and took a quick look at the sky, gauging the time left until dark. "What I always tell them. It's their war. Until Heavy Beaver comes here, I don't have to face him. And if I get a warning, I'll take us away first."

"You're worried about the Dream, aren't you?"

He nodded slowly, like he always did, eyes straying to the huge charcoal-colored wolf that padded quietly beside them, tongue lolling, yellow eyes always alert. The Dream had lingered, almost like a dizzy haze. Consciousness had returned to him that bitter winter day in the wolf's den, and with it the memory of the choice he'd made while his soul rested in Wolf Dreamer's hand. He'd chosen life—and pain—over the soft wonder of death.

True to the First Man's words, the wolf guardian had saved him from freezing and dragged him to its lair. There the animal had curled around him, the warmth of life leaching into him like spring rain through uncured moccasins.

Nor had the animal abandoned him on the miserable trip to Two Smokes' shelter. He'd hobbled along on his bruised and swollen leg, living off rose hips as they melted out of the drifts, sharing part of wolf's catch, finally plucking the tops of biscuit root and shooting star as they peeked through the snow. As he'd come closer to camp, he'd fashioned a crude digging stick from branches snapped off a dead juniper and dug biscuit root, consuming the rich sweet pulp raw.

The Dreams hadn't plagued him again until it got on toward winter. Then, when the Dreams invaded his sleep, wolf became restless, giving notice that time had come to make the trek to White Calf's for the deep cold. And each year, he'd gone, spending the frigid nights in deep discussions with the old woman, hearing the stories, talking about the ways of the world, how Monster Bone Springs had almost washed away.

The world was changing—and he lived day by day, hoping each wouldn't reach out and snatch him away.

"I made my choice that day on the mountain," he said. "Wolf Dreamer said he'd give me as much time as he could. That same spring blizzard froze half of Heavy Beaver's war-hungry young men. That loss bought us the time we've had so far."

He turned, searching her eyes, reveling in the love he saw reflected there. "Listen, I made the promise. In the end, it's up to me. I know it, Wolf Dreamer knows it, and you know it. We live one day at a time, remember?"

She forced herself to smile, jerking her chin in a nod. She stepped close to hug him tightly, the power in her arms practically driving the breath from his lungs. "I love you, Dancer. Don't leave me."

The greatest pain in his life came from the fact he could never tell her, *"I won't."*

Tanager ran, lungs heaving as she fled through the trees. The enemy had come out of nowhere. One minute she lay on her stomach, chin propped on her elbows as she watched Cricket nursing her new baby. The next, Short Buffalo warriors had charged out of the timber, screaming, casting darts here and there as the camp erupted into bedlam. She'd jumped up, grabbing her atlatl, trying to nock a dart as Cricket screamed.

A tall man had grabbed her friend by the hair from behind, bending Cricket's neck back. Tanager's reaction had been instinctive. She'd clubbed the man with her atlatl, smashing his face. As he staggered back, she'd driven a dart into his belly. She'd taken Cricket's hand and run in panic, the warrior's shrieks in her ears.

Now, so far from camp, Tanager ducked to the side, diving under a tall fir. Cricket, gasping and moaning—Snaps Horn's tiny son in her arms staggered after.

Seeking to still the burning in her lungs, Tanager crept to look back the way they'd come. Nothing moved.

Cricket had sunk gratefully to her knees, her infant wailing softly. Eyes closed in misery, she gasped for breath, trickles of sweat running down her flushed face. "What . . . now?"

Tanager's starved lungs struggled for air. "I don't know. Can't go back."

"But . . . where?"

"I know. Elk Charm's . . . camp. You know . . . the way?" Tanager managed between pants.

"Down on the . . . west side. Where the . . . big canyon . . . cuts down to . . . the basin?"

"Yes. Go there. Take any others . . . you find along . . . the way . . . and go there."

"What about you?"

Tanager grinned, feeling the uncertainty in her gut. Her breath was coming back. "Look, you're the one with a child. You've got Snaps Horn for a husband. Me, I'm still free. For all the good it's done, a man's seed might be cast on bare rock as well as inside me."

"Tanager, please. Don't do that to yourself. You're the most beautiful woman in the Red Hand. You can have any man you want for a—"

"Shhh! What's the matter with you? The camp's just been raided and you want to talk about me? Go! Quickly! Make your way to the high trail and cross to the valley west of here. From there all you need to do is follow the streams down."

"What about you?"

Tanager winked at her friend. "I'm sneaking back. Someone has to find out what's happened. My hunting weapons are back there. Besides, Snaps Horn is out with the rest of the men. They need to know where you're going. I'll have to tell people to run to Rattling Hooves and Elk Charm. How else will they know? How will Snaps Horn know?"

Having no other choice, Cricket nodded. "All right. I'll take the baby to Elk Charm's. But . . ." She reached out, placing a hand on Tanager's arm.

"But what?"

"Be careful."

"You know me. Not even smoke moves as quietly as Tanager in the timber."

Cricket shook her head. "I know you're a good hunter. I know you'd rather be out roaming around than in a tent. But Tanager be careful. I just have a terrible feeling, that's all."

Tanager grinned at her. "Remember, don't stop until you get to Elk Charm's. She'll take care of you."

And she forced herself to her feet, feeling a tingle of excitement as she started back toward the camp, wondering who might have been killed and who might have survived.

Why did she always have to be different? No wonder none of the men she'd coupled with could plant a child in her. She moved around too much for the seed to catch.

She glanced down at the whipcord thinness of her body. Not an ounce of fat padded her firmly muscled flesh. No, she might not have a man's strength, but she had that special balance and speed that gave her a slight advantage. No man among the Red Hand could cast a dart as accurately as she. She had the eye for it, and the talent for the hunt seemed to be inbred—a Power all her own.

Suddenly they were around her again. She couldn't believe they had come so far so fast. She might have been moving like the smoke she bragged about; nevertheless four men leapt out of the trees. She spun like a deer and hesitated for a moment since the only avenue of escape led back to Cricket.

She easily ducked an arm and bolted to the side—too late. Thick arms grabbed her around the middle in a grip that crushed her to the ground.

She struggled, almost breaking free before another grabbed her arm. She twisted, looking up into an unfamiliar enemy face. The man grinned at her, a burning light in his eyes.

Makes Fun bent over her grinding stone, enjoying the feel of the mano clutched in her hand. The muscles of her forearms tensed and rippled with each stroke. The *grate-clack*, *grate-clack* of mano and metate sounded a hollow cadence through the shelter as she milled the last of last year's pine nuts into a fine paste. When she found a nut that had dried, she'd use the pecked edge of the mano to smack it flat for grinding.

With deft hands, she scooped up the mush and placed it in a grass basket, reaching for the final handful of unprocessed nuts. With a staccato of raps, she used the mano butt to mash them down before beginning the rhythmic grinding again.

"Hard to believe how much things have changed," Black Crow offered, scratching at his protruding belly. He squinted at the pile of carefully cut rawhide strips separated into three coils before him. Each contributed to the long section of rope he braided for a new elk snare.

Makes Fun nodded, a pinched look to her brow as she concentrated on the grinding. "If I would have had to guess, I'd never have thought the Anit'ah would come seeking *you* to fight against the People—and never twice in a row."

"Things have changed." He hesitated, head tilted back, accenting the prominent spike of his Adam's apple. He scanned the afternoon sky as he thought. "You know, it was always Little Dancer at the center of it—kind of like the trouble in a dog pack can be narrowed down to one puppy. Next time, maybe I'll pick my friends better."

She laughed sarcastically. "Oh?"

He shot her a curious glance. "You like what's happened to us? All this running, living in holes in the rock like packrats? And there are only buffalo to kill every once in a while up here."

"Fool," she told him softly, a warm light in her eyes.

"Look around you. This place is beautiful. Unlike the plains where spring is green and the rest of the year is brown, there are colors here, and the land changes with each moment as the sun moves.

"I've never been as warm in a hide shelter as I am in the rocks. Maybe brother packrat is smarter than you think, huh? And when was the last time we were hungry?"

"But we eat seeds and roots and things like that!"

"Uh-huh, and elk and mountain sheep and deer and jack-rabbit and bear and . . . yes, even a buffalo on occasion. You remember, Black Crow. You think real hard and you remember just *how much* buffalo we ate those last years with the People." She waggled her mano at him.

He lifted a sheepish shoulder. "Well, maybe we were a little hungry."

"And besides, what if we had stayed, and Heavy Beaver hadn't Cursed us all dead? What then? You'd be the one going up into the mountains to fight the deadly Anit'ah. Think of that. Now, here we are on the other side of the mountains. And we're safe for a while." She paused, a pensive look in her eyes as she stared off to the west where the sun sank slowly. The canyon hid the view, but she knew what lay there.

"And besides, husband, if things change again, we'll cross the basin out there. Maybe find a place to live in that next bunch of mountains."

"And if there's a war there?"

"We'll keep moving until we find a place where there isn't war. What do we need? Someplace out of the rain and snow? Animals and plants to eat and make clothing out of? Can you think of anything else?"

"People to talk to."

She winked at him. "You're tired of Hungry Bull and Three Toes and Meadowlark and—"

"No, I mean *people* to talk to." He scowled at his braiding where it lay in his hands. "I miss the old stories, seeing different faces, hearing the jokes from someone new. I miss the coming of the Traders, and hearing what they've seen. We're cut off here. That's all."

She nodded, callused hands going still as she thought back to those other days. "Yes, I miss that, too." For a moment they sat in silence, until Makes Fun shook her head violently. "But no matter, I wouldn't trade anything for Sage Root's fate."

She reached over and placed a white-powdered hand on his knee. "You know, husband, sometimes the world just changes. Maybe we could have done something about it if we'd known how far Heavy Beaver would take things. But we didn't, and even when I finally started to wonder, and Chokecherry tried to tell me, I still didn't believe it. But that's past, the buffalo's out of the trap."

"Out of the trap and running!" He laid a hand tenderly over hers. "And we have strong healthy children who don't scream for war. So the world changed? We got the best of it, didn't we?"

"And that only leaves the Anit'ah."

He nodded, gazing toward where Ramshorn sat in the sun with Rattling Hooves, talking. "We can't go fight the People. No matter what Heavy Beaver's made them do. They're our relatives."

"And one of the these days when Blood Bear comes to make us?"

"We'll leave, wife. We'll leave and go see those mountains over there across the basin."

Ramshorn had timed his visit perfectly; for the first time that year the warm air off the basin rose with the night, sending pleasant dry breezes up the canyons. The gentle scent of sage, juniper, and limber pine mixed with the perfume of blooming phlox, buttercup, and yellow bell.

For the feast, a large crackling fire had been laid before Hungry Bull's ample shelter. The dance of the flames reflected in yellow-bronze tones off the high arch of the overhanging sandstone and cast darting shadows over the juniper that crowded the rimrock, seeming to weave eerie forms against the background. Shadow patterns jumped in accordance to the rising and falling of speech, animated by laughter.

Over it all, the night sky stretched endlessly. The Starweb sparkled in brilliant radiance as each point of light glimmered and danced in the velvet night.

The people of Hungry Bull's band sat around, talking and joking, knowing the night would bring good and bad. Ramshorn came with news—and Rattling Hooves had already cut her hair short in mourning. Elk Charm had not only cut her hair, but wore her worst clothing. She wouldn't change until at least a moon had passed. Among the Red Hand, the death of a mother—even by marriage—did not occur without sorrow.

Then, when everyone had eaten, they would talk of Blood Bear's request for warriors.

Little Dancer had found himself a place to sit in the rear, where he could see and hear and avoid involvement in the talks as much as possible. For the moment, he simply enjoyed the night, watching the firelight play on Elk Charm's beautiful face. Already, he missed her long luxurious hair. How would it be to make love to her in the evening and not have that soft wealth spilling around him? How would it be, not to be able to reach over in the night, as he so often did, and run the silky strands through his fingers?

His infant daughter had dropped off to sleep in Elk Charm's arms. Her mouth—toothless and pink—hung partly open in her fat face while tiny fists clutched nothingness. She'd pinched her eyes shut, giving herself a strained look. Only infants worked that hard at sleeping.

He looked over to see his oldest daughter—finger in mouth, dirt and soot smudged around her face—watching wide-eyed as Grasshopper attempted to flake a stone tool. Dancing Leaf, Black Crow's number-two daughter, rested on her knees, offering sarcastic advice—to Grasshopper's infinite disgust. The clacking of his futile stonework lent background to the rising and falling talk of the adults.

Meadowlark and Makes Fun hovered about the fire and poked anxiously with their digging sticks where the deer fawn roasted under layers of dirt covered by a bed of glowing coals. The meat had been wrapped in balsam leaves and packed with biscuit root and yarrow leaves for flavoring. So sealed, it simmered in its own juices. Unborn fawn cooked over an open fire fit anyone's description of delicacy—but roasted like this? Little Dancer's mouth watered at the thought.

Meadowlark shot wary glances toward Three Toes, who

listened with interest to whatever Ramshorn said. The hunter still had to concentrate to keep track of the Anit'ah tongue, but he'd learned over the years. Black Crow simply nodded, smoking willow bark in his straight clay pipe. Rattling Hooves monitored the roasting pit full of pine-nut patties Makes Fun had produced that afternoon. Already the sweet odor had begun to seep from the insulating layer of earth to tantalize the air.

Two Smokes, looking like the elder he'd become, sat propped comfortably, maimed leg stuck out. He used a small rock to press a bone awl through an elk hide he'd tanned and cut to size. As he punched the hole, he'd double-stitch the seam of the jacket he worked. His attention did not wander; no single word uttered by Ramshorn missed his keen ears. Only a careful observer would notice the flash of his eyes as Ramshorn told of this or that occurrence. The weathered expression of Two Smokes' face seemed to tighten at each mention of Blood Bear.

Beyond the ring of the fire, Little Dancer could occasionally make out wolf's shadow as he slipped through the sagebrush, perpetually alert. That link—now so familiar—never seemed to weaken. They both waited, always knowing it must happen some day. Wolf tolerated the People, and they watched him skeptically, understanding instinctively that this wasn't simply a displaced animal, but something more. In the passing years, that knowledge had set Little Dancer apart. Even Hungry Bull treated him with respect and no little awkwardness.

The people didn't know quite what to make of his yearly winter visits to White Calf's. They simply accepted. Spirit Power was good to have around—and unnerving at the same time.

Little Dancer had built his own Power wheel out of stones on the windblown flat above the canyon. There they'd find him every so often as the sun came up, checking the alignment of his lines of rocks where they transected the circle. They looked at him with awe when he calmly told them that a certain day was the longest of the year, or that winter would only last a moon more before the final melt started.

When someone got hurt, they came to him, expecting him

to mend broken legs, heal cuts and burns and toothaches. Last fall, an old man known as Flat-Nosed Badger had come all the way from the Red Hand camps for advice on a lump that had formed under his armpit. Remembering something White Calf had told him, he gave the man a hideful of ephedra and sent him back with instructions to boil it into a strong tea. When visiting White Calf, he'd been told the man had died, but that the ephedra had helped ease the pain.

Now he waited, watching Hungry Bull, the leader of the small band, pacing back and forth, helping with the cooking, adding wood to the fire, sharing a joke with Ramshorn. Then Hungry Bull teased Grasshopper over his crude turtle-backed scraper, chiding him over the cuts he'd made in his fingers.

"You look happy, husband." Elk Charm reached up to lace her slim fingers in his.

"It's a good night." He filled his lungs, enjoying the smells of plants and food and the familiar pungency of sage smoke. "This is the sort of occasion a person should savor and memorize so that he can have each detail to enjoy for the rest of his life."

She squeezed his hand, a signal that she sensed his hidden desperation. Unconsciously, his attention went to the dark, searching for the ghost shadow of wolf, seeing nothing but the uplifted spikes of the sage protruding from the clusters of white-green leaves. Nevertheless, he could feel the animal, waiting, guarding.

Yes, you're there. Wolf Dreamer didn't need to send you. I made my decision that time in the snow. I understand what's coming—but I don't have to like it.

At that moment, he caught sight of wolf. He could only make out the head, but both eyes burned in the darkness, catching and reflecting the light of the fire, looking identical to the old rock carving in Two Smokes' shelter on the south side of the mountain.

Now, when he thought of things like that, the path of the Spiral could be followed so clearly. Many a night he'd lain awake, thinking back on who he'd been forced to become and where his path would eventually lead. He felt frustrated, impotent; but then, what good had resistance ever done him? Almost with anguish, he remembered his excitement that day

Chokecherry had tried to tell his mother about Spirit Power—and the whole time, he'd been no more than a feather in the spirit wind. Meanwhile, he drifted on the gusts and eddies, his friends around him, like unfettered birds, darting and dashing where they would, without restraint.

And therein lay the irony. He studied Hungry Bull—the man who'd always disliked involvement with Spirit Power, the man who'd been cast loose from his people and had reluctantly agreed to lead this unusual band of refugees. Hungry Bull, who seemed so much adrift in life, could fly where he wanted, unaware of his freedom to choose.

No one cared that Little Dancer—whose Power people had begun to revere—remained a captive of the Spirit Wind, waiting for the Power to blow him where it would.

Things can change. Wolf Dreamer worries about free will. Perhaps someone will kill Heavy Beaver. Perhaps some An-it'ah will drive a dart through him, or some illness will take him. I may not have to give this up. I may escape!

Hope, like a sliver of fire-treated chert, rose hot and sharp within his breast. Fervently, he clutched Elk Charm's hand—praying with all his soul that some hole would appear in the net of fate to allow him to wriggle free.

"Hey." She tugged at him. "You're about to break every bone in my hand! You're squeezing so hard the blood will pop out the ends of my fingers!"

"Sorry, I was . . . just . . . ." He let her tug her hand away, watching her rub it as she stared soberly up at him, a sly smile on her lips.

"Got lost in your head again?"

He nodded—the familiar longing pumping with his blood. How could he let this go? How could he turn his back and walk away from this woman and his children? The very thought of it wrenched his heart.

Hungry Bull's cry drew his attention. "I call this food done!" He looked up at the night sky, raising his hands over his head. "Hear me, spirits! We call on you to lift the deer mother to your safe heaven in the Starweb. Lift her unborn fawn and place him in an honored spot. From them, we receive life. So, too, will we one day die in our physical forms and go back to the Earth Mother. And from us, the worms will feed and brother coyote will eat. Our flesh will nourish the plants that nourish the deer. We are the Spiral of life. What we take, one day will we give back. Perhaps on that day, mother deer and her fawn will pray our way to the Star-web.''

Little Dancer added his voice to the prayer, Singing the doe and her fawn to the stars, thanking the plants for their bounty, feeling the harmony of the Spiral of life.

And that's why you'll turn your back on those you love. Because you know your place, your responsibility. You are the lever that will move the Spiral back into place.

''But can't someone else do it?'' he asked under his breath.

Chapter 21 ◉

The taste of warm blood in Tanager's mouth gave her strength. Blood, the life that pumped strength through a person's veins. Her blood, her life, feeding her with her own strength . . . a Circle within.

She bit her lip hard again, the pain acting as means of stifling the scream born in the bottom of her throat. Anything to keep from screaming, from admitting the pain or the reality of what continued to happen to her. Each time she bit down on the inside of her mouth, more blood seeped from her ravaged lip, feeding her strength, keeping her going.

She'd closed her eyes long ago, refusing to see what she couldn't help feel. Eyes could be closed—one small comfort in her situation. Ears, however, continued to hear. Her body continued to feel, and the pain lingered, dull, aching. No longer did the men's entry and movement make a tearing hurt. For the moment, the fluids had eased the discomfort to a burning chafe. Where they'd bitten her, the sting lasted, irritated by their salt-sweaty skin rubbing the wounds.

She felt the one on top of her stiffen, groaning, his organ

pulsing inside. She swallowed hard, enjoying the taste of the blood in her mouth, taking strength from her life.

He lay limp on her while they chattered among themselves in their guttural tongue.

How long would this continue? Hadn't they exhausted themselves? She kept her eyes pressed closed, bloody lip pinched in her teeth. She felt him rise, cool air drifting over her sweat-dampened chest and belly.

Was he the last? Was he the—

Another body dropped on hers, almost driving the air from her lungs with its weight. They'd ceased holding her legs and arms long ago, figuring her resistance had broken. She bit her lip as he thrust.

She'd lost count, but there hadn't been that many, only seven in the party that had captured her. Only seven, but they'd been young, eager, with that keen look in their eyes. This way they could hurt back, do to her what they couldn't do to the Red Hand.

She bit her lip again as he hurt her, stifling the scream, feeding herself on the taste of her blood, battling the pain they caused by drowning it in pain *she* controlled.

I'll live. I swear, I'll live and repay them all. She swallowed again, subsisting on the strength she drew from herself.

Finally, he lay spent on top of her. He didn't rise. She waited, suffering to breathe under his weight. Through slitted eyes, she saw they had seated themselves, talking in a desultory way. A fatigue had crept into their faces, dulling the eyes, sagging muscular shoulders. Each clutched his weapons, the camp dark lest a fire bring the Red Hand down upon them.

She lay quiet, unable to move, feeling the warrior on her relaxing, drifting off to sleep. Did he lie like this on his woman at home? Was that his weakness? She opened her eyes in the darkness, carefully searching for anything to use.

Someone called. She clamped her eyes shut again, hearing feet in the grass, feeling the man on top of her start as he was nudged by his leader.

The man raised himself, and the toe nudged her. She looked up, seeing him gesture, pointing toward a blanket.

The chill of the evening iced the man-sweat on her skin. She fought the groan as she sat up, knowing how she'd hurt the next morning.

The leader spoke in gravel tones, gesturing toward his bedding. She waited.

In response, he kicked her hard and she couldn't stop the pain cry. Numbly, she crawled to his blanket and pulled herself into a ball, hugging her knees to her wounded breasts, aware of the burning inside. Her captor stood tall, well muscled and poised, the braids of his black hair hanging down over his shoulders.

From a pack he took a thong, gesturing that she extend her legs. She did, and waited.

Satisfied, he laid his darts to the side and bent down to tie her.

In that moment, she moved, powered by the strength she'd garnered from her blood. She snatched his darts, kicking out, whirling, using all of her anger to drive the sharp point into his flesh and up.

He shrieked, backing away, grabbing futilely at the feathered shaft that stuck out from his lower ribs.

She stood, nocking a dart in his atlatl, knowing the balance would be different. She held a man's weapon, awkward for a woman's muscles. Nevertheless, she drove a dart into the next man on his feet and, turning, bolted for the trees and the safe haven of the darkness.

They shouted in the night behind her. She gripped the darts, pounding through the trees, head down as the branches tore at her, lashing her bare skin. She used the branches as scourges to keep her fear charged, to spur her flight into the night.

Her feet ached from the bruising of rocks. She stubbed unprotected toes on sticks, stone, and deadfall. Still she ran, lungs heaving, body burning. Nothing remained now but pain and escape.

The first blind panic drained as she staggered on. They couldn't track her until morning. She slowed, taking note of her surroundings, trotting into a clearing to study the pattern of the Starweb. Finding her bearings, she pushed onward, climbing a ridge to stare across the jumbled landscape. She picked out Cloud Peak, realizing where she was. Not *that* far from Blood Bear's camp—if he still remained there during the raids. White Calf's would be closer. She turned, locating the valley of the Clear River and changing her direction, staying to the rocks and pine duff where it lay thick under the trees. Her bare feet wouldn't make a track—so long as they didn't bleed too much.

In her hands, two darts remained.

"You know, if we can't stop the Short Buffalo People, you're not safe either." Ramshorn met their gazes one by one with his own. "I've heard the stories. You're all fleeing from this Spirit Man, this Heavy Beaver and his new way. Just because your relatives are among his warriors doesn't mean they won't skewer you. I may not be much of a judge on why humans act like they do, but I'd bet they'd love the chance to kill people who had the nerve to leave."

Three Toes pursed his lips, a deep frown lining his face as he stared down at his feet.

Black Crow caught the look in Makes Fun's hard eyes and cleared his throat. "Ramshorn, everything you say is true. We don't deny it." He spread his arms. "But I ask you, as a host to a guest. Place yourself in my shelter for a moment. Look out at the world through my eyes. We came here at the bidding of White Calf. She told us that if we could go no other place, to come to her. We did that, and Blood Bear came with warriors—yourself among them—to kill us."

"And I, for one, have apologized for that. You must remember the times."

"We do." Black Crow tugged at his braid, composing his next words. "But many things have happened since then. Rattling Hooves and Elk Charm have come to live among us. We've adopted many of the ways of the Red Hand, but we've become a different thing—a new People, not Anit'ah, not Short Buffalo. We are us, even if there aren't very many of us."

"And what will you do when Heavy Beaver comes?" Ramshorn crossed his arms over his chest.

Hungry Bull pointed to the west. "We'll go there, to those

mountains. Or if not, we'll find a place where the people don't war and we can live by ourselves."

"The Fish Eaters live over there." Ramshorn's lips twitched. "Would you want to be a Fish Eater?"

"Once I would have died rather than eat roots and leaves." Hungry Bull's wry smile beguiled. "Food is food, my friend. So long as it keeps blood and bone strong, the soul can take care of itself."

"I agree with Hungry Bull," Meadowlark added. "I don't understand the changes that are occurring. The fact that my children are threatened by this is enough for me. I know Heavy Beaver. I grew up with him. Maybe I could have done something to stop him. Maybe it would have gotten me Cursed, too. I don't know. All I know is that I can't keep my family fed and clothed if my foolish husband runs off and gets killed in your war like his heart wants him to do."

Three Toes sighed and lifted his hands. "Yes, yes, I want to. What can I say? I wish I could drive a dart right through Heavy Beaver. Look what he's done to us! You find trouble everywhere these days—and it's Heavy Beaver at the bottom of it!" He looked around. "I don't like the idea of fighting alongside the Red Hand. They killed my father."

"And your father killed more than one Red Hand," Rattling Hooves reminded, her mind obviously on Wet Rain.

"That's precisely the point," Makes Fun agreed. "And at the same time, Rattling Hooves, here we are. What do we call ourselves? We're something new, a new People made of two old ones. Your relatives killed mine, and mine yours, and now we're living happily, sharing jokes and work and food. You care for my children when I go out hunting with Black Crow, and I open my camp to you as if you were my sister." She shook her head, making the gesture for "no more" with her hands. "No, I think if we get involved, it will only lead to trouble, to bad feelings and hurt and anger among ourselves."

Elk Charm cleared her throat, asking, "Ramshorn, if we don't want to get involved in this, what will Blood Bear do? Will he come here, angry, and try and kill us? I don't know Heavy Beaver, but Blood Bear isn't reasonable either. You never know what he'll do from day to day. Please, you're my cousin. Once you were my father's best friend. Tell me from your heart.''

Ramshorn reached up to rub his eyes. "I don't think Blood Bear will come here. At least not until the Red Hand have driven the Short Buffalo People out of the mountains for good. And if we lose? I don't think Blood Bear will be among the people fleeing the mountains. I think he'll die before then.''

Rattling Hooves nodded to herself. "Then I say we stay out of the insanity.'' She looked at Makes Fun. "I'm sorry I spoke in the tone I did.''

Makes Fun winked at her. "Grief does that. Tomorrow, when you have a chance, would you come cut my hair? I'll share your grief with you.''

Rattling Hooves, ever invincible, nodded slowly, lower lip trembling as she averted her eyes.

"Little Dancer?'' Hungry Bull asked. "Do you have anything to add?''

He shook his head. "I accept what the rest of you do.''

"We can't go.'' Hungry Bull summed up the reactions of his band. "We can't take the chance of killing our relatives. We can't take the chance of splintering the new family we've become here. If Blood Bear is angered and would retaliate against us, I'd ask you, Ramshorn, as a brave and honorable warrior, to send us word, and we'll leave here, go someplace else, maybe the valley of the Warm Winds.''

"I'll make sure you hear.'' Ramshorn smiled wistfully. "And if the Short Buffalo People drive us out, if I live, and if I'm welcome, maybe I'd bring my wives and live with you?''

"You'd have a place with us. You could bring your family now, if you'd like. Our hearts and homes are open to you. Let's hope it doesn't come to that.''

Blood Bear stared up into the night sky. This night, like so many others lately, he couldn't sleep. Instead, he paced around the dark cold camps of his warriors, stalking the shadows, staring at the darkness, wondering what would come next.

The Short Buffalo People had entered the Buffalo Mountain trails in a flood this year. What Heavy Beaver had intended years ago, only now could he do. The strange blizzard that had roared down on the plains five years past had wreaked havoc with the Short Buffalo People. Many had frozen—and in the interim, the White Crane and Cut Hair had struck back, seeking to break the power of the weakened Short Buffalo.

What Heavy Beaver had so laboriously created had tottered—his alliance of bands almost breaking under the strain. Nevertheless, he'd prevailed and pushed his plains enemies back. Now, once again, he could turn his attention to the defiant Red Hand of the mountains and seek to separate them from their rich hunting grounds.

There are so many enemies! Blood Bear let his vision roam the Starweb while he thought. Around him, the night lay cool on the land, the air rich with the smell of firs and pines. Insects clicked and whirred in the silence. The land lived, pulsing for him, sharing itself in this hour of worry.

All the years of wandering had given him a skill almost unequaled by his peers. He could drift like eagle's shadow through the trees. He could steal into their camps at night and kill them one by one, but he couldn't be everywhere with his warriors. What he and his Red Hand could do with cunning and bravery, the Short Buffalo could do with numbers. Where had they all come from?

Something had happened to the Red Hand, some essential spark had gone from their eyes and hearts. He scowled up at the heavens. What? No matter how he exhorted, it seemed that the inner core of resistance that had once been theirs had fled. He could berate, pray, dance, and sing. He could return, blood-soaked and victorious, but his warriors seemed faded and tired despite their triumphs. No matter what tack he tried—from hanging body pieces of the enemy in trails, to offering their hearts to the fire—nothing seemed to touch that flagging spirit. Why? What logic could he use? What spur could goad them to carry the fight to the Short Buffalo People instead of waiting for it come to them?

"We'll be destroyed," he whispered, staring up at the stars. "Like smoke on the wind, we'll be blown away. Only the rocks will remember the name of the Red Hand."

And that thought enraged him. While he fumed, he

dropped his eyes from the heavens and looked around his camp. His war party consisted of six men and two women, all awaiting the next advance of the enemy up the Clear River trail. Heavy Beaver had to try to force this way. It made sense considering that a large party of warriors had tried to scale the twisting steep trail on the north side. Only a fool wouldn't try a second offensive up the back.

Rage left a bitter taste in his mouth.

While he brooded, the pale form of the Wolf Bundle caught his eye where it rested on its tripod in the center of the clearing. The leather had cracked and peeled, the curious lines drawn so carefully into the hide had faded where they hadn't been abraded away. Shabby, he thought, just like the hopes of the Red Hand.

Viciously, he slashed at it with the back of his hand, knocking it rolling into the grass.

The action had been foolish, he realized, staring owlishly around in the darkness, thankful that the rest of his band remained locked in sleep. He picked it up, replacing it just so on the tripod, checking again to assure himself that no one had seen.

He massaged the sudden ache in the stub of his little finger. Foolish symbol of a dying people—no wonder they couldn't win a war—not with a silly thing like the Wolf Bundle. Now, if they had something powerful, like a grizzly skull, or . . .

He winced, startled by the sudden pain in his little finger. Of all the stupid things he'd ever done, cutting the tip of his finger off had been madness! All it ever did was ache and burn. He swore, it would be the death of him yet.

"Help me! The time has come, Fire Dancer. Help me! HELP ME!" The voice thundered in his skull, shattering the dream into jagged fragments, blasting through his mind like a clap of thunder burst upon unwary ears.

Little Dancer shouted in fear and struggled out of the bedding. His stomach lurched. He vomited violently, trying to suck a breath over the foulness in his mouth and nose. Again his stomach heaved in accompaniment to the convulsions.

He tried to brace himself against the reeling sensation, the feeling that the world had come apart. Dizzy, he propped himself with one hand; the other clutched his throat.

"What is it?" Elk Charm's voice penetrated the ringing in his ears.

He finally got a breath into his burning lungs, almost choking on the smell of his vomit. He coughed, his whole body jerking in response.

Some dislocated part of his mind identified the sound of Elk Charm shuffling as she teased an ember to life with shredded bark tinder. The first flickerings of firelight shot pain through suddenly sensitive eyes.

"Little Dancer?"

He could have cried at the concern in her voice.

Her arm went around his shoulders, hugging, warm and reassuring against the trembling that possessed him. "Cold," he whispered, "so cold." The weight of her arm on his shoulders almost collapsed him into the mess his tortured gut had spewed out on the floor. Not since the day he'd almost frozen had he experienced such a chill, as if the winds of winter blew through his soul.

"You're burning up," Elk Charm told him seriously. "Fever. Little Dancer, are you . . ."

"No, not fever," he managed through chattering teeth. "Power. The Wolf Bundle." He shook his head, trying to fight the shiver that wound through him like a tangled vine. "Last time I felt like this . . . the Wolf Bundle . . ."

"Hush. Don't talk like that."

"It's calling. I heard it, the words burn in my mind. '*Help me,*' it said."

Her lower lip had started to tremble. A glittering filled her eyes like the coming of tears. "No," she whispered miserably. "*No.*"

He managed to swallow, almost heaving again from the taste of his emptied stomach.

"Come on, come back to bed. You need to be under the hides. You'll catch a chill out here. . . . The Wise One knows what. Here, get under the cover. We'll talk about it in the morning."

He let her push him back into the bedding; any strength to resist vanished in his trembling. "Power Bundles can die, you know. They can be killed, just like a man. Dead . . . cold . . .''

"Hush. Sleep now."

He blinked, aware that vision had gone fluid like the time he'd opened his eyes underwater and looked up at the shimmering world above.

Elk Charm scampered busily about, scraping up his mess, carrying it out into the night to throw it away. Only when she'd returned and crawled in next to him and hugged her night-chilled flesh against his did he try to relax. She spooned herself against him, the firm feel of her flesh reassuring.

Little Dancer tried to still his racing heart, looking up at the hangings, startled to see a sliver of the Starweb where the hides had been pushed aside. The silhouette couldn't be mistaken. Wolf stared at him.

Even through the darkness, he could feel those yellow eyes burning into his.

"The Wolf Bundle," he whispered, staring miserably into the night. *"It called me."*

White Calf cried out and jerked awake. She tried to catch her breath, gulping at the cool night air. Her heart raced, the feeling in her tingling limbs the same as if she'd run a hard day's race. A queasiness churned in her stomach. Her head ached as if split with a stone ax.

What had it been? A Dream? She felt as if she'd been hit in the stomach—and the tingle wouldn't leave. Cold sweat broke out on her ancient skin.

Shivering, she sat up and pulled her robe around her. Grunting with the effort, she hunched over the fire pit, stirring the ashes for a hot coal. When she found one, she placed tinder over it and blew until she had a finger of flame. This she fed until the blaze crackled. Extending her fingers, she sought the warmth, only to find it wouldn't ease the chill from her flesh. That cold came from inside her.

She looked up at the Spiral on the wall. "So, the time's come full around? Is that it?"

From her pack, she took sage, and wet it, throwing it in among the coals. She stood, letting her robe slip from her ancient shoulders. Naked, she stepped into the steamy smoke that billowed from the fire, letting it wash over her, purifying, cleansing her very soul. Sage, the lifegiver, seeped into her very pores.

In the dim light, she looked down at her body, at the flat breasts that hung like flaps. Her belly sagged, the skin loose and wrinkled on her legs and arms. Hollows, like sockets, had formed where gaunt bones stuck out of her shoulders. Her hair gleamed white where the short braids hung down to her shoulders. What had once been the black glistening mat around her pubis now consisted of scanty wisps of white that she could barely see over the sag of her abdomen.

"You're finally old, Green Willow." She chuckled, remembering her first menstruation and how proud she'd been to become a woman. Another year had passed before she could attract Big Fox to bed her. Such things were difficult when a woman had a reputation for being odd, for talking to spirits; besides which, men had peculiar ideas about their manhood, and what sex with a witch might do to their holy penises.

She'd made it all the more difficult for them since she'd had an uncommon beauty. In that year, until Big Fox had taken her, the men had warred with themselves: lust for her full young flesh battling with their fear of her Dreams and the Spirit Power she seemed so easy with. In the end, Big Fox, full of pride and virility that not even fear of Power could daunt, had bedded her. Even before the others could convince themselves to try her, she'd conceived.

"Big Fox." She said it wistfully, remembering his rippling muscles, the way he smiled and joked. Ah, if ever there had been a man built for a young woman's passion, it had been him. No matter that he'd attracted every eye, he'd been an exceptional man—and worth every minute she'd spent with him.

Then Power had come and driven itself into her with more power and vigor than even Big Fox. The same way he'd possessed her body and made it his, so had Power possessed her soul—and the soul couldn't be denied like the body.

So she'd left, following the trail that led at last to this shelter, learning the ways of Power from Six Teeth until the old man had died and she'd carted him up the slope, sticking his body in a crack in the rock, walling it up to keep the predators out.

Her beauty hadn't faded, for when she first discovered Cut Feather spying on her, she found that he'd lost himself in wonder over the secrets of her body. What she couldn't share with Big Fox—all the speculations on Spirit Power and Dreams—she could discuss with Cut Feather. So they'd bedded, and again she'd conceived. Only unlike Big Fox, Cut Feather had understood when at last she'd had to leave. He'd felt the Power of the Dream, and knew the dilution that came with coupling.

"Cut Feather," she whispered fondly. "You were a balm to my soul." She stooped and dropped more wet sage into the fire, inhaling deeply of the steamy scent and exhaling to clean her lungs.

"So it's nearly come full circle. Look at yourself, White Calf. See what you've become at the end of your long life." She meditated, trying to put it all into perspective. Just what purpose could an old Dreamer find in life? Of the children she'd borne, of the Dreams Dreamed, of the lessons taught, what made her life worthwhile? The sensations? The thoughts? The actions?

Finally she raised her hands to the Spiral, straddling the fire, feeling the heat burn painfully into her thighs. Like a memory, a sexual fire stirred once again, stimulated by the pulsing heat and the purifying sage.

Losing herself in the pleasure of it, she stared at the Spiral and closed her eyes, seeing it in her mind, Circles upon Circles, one leading to another, never touching. Life, wondrous life.

The sound of the hangings parting didn't startle her. Instead, she took another deep breath of the sage and exhaled. She swallowed and opened her eyes, losing herself in the Spiral again. Then she turned.

The girl stared at her, wide-eyed, a terrified look in her eyes. She, too, stood naked, an atlatl in her hand, a dart nocked and ready to cast. Her body had been used hard, bloody in spots, bruised in others. She stood on trembling, scratched legs, abused breasts heaving as she fought for breath. Gooseflesh accented the shivers that ran through her.

The lines of her belly looked firm with muscle. Her hips hadn't borne the burden of swelling with a child.

Yet her face absorbed all of White Calf's attention. Black flashing eyes—those of an angry she-cougar—met hers. Behind the terrified fear lay the Power look of rage and commitment. Her delicate cheeks accented the straight line of her nose. A high forehead rose over a graceful brow. Her jawline matched the firm chin, although her lower lip had swollen out of proportion.

"Come in, child." White Calf stepped away from the fire, reaching to drop another couple of pieces of firewood on the coals. "Come here, come and warm yourself. You look about all in."

The young woman took a timid step forward, eyes darting about suspiciously. "What are you doing up . . . awake at this time of night?"

White Calf chuckled dryly, taking note of the abused flesh, of the streaks down the insides of her legs. "Maybe more than you know is afoot tonight. Maybe I was waiting for you." *Yes, The Spiral has turned. The end is near.*

The young woman tensed, half crouched as if to spring. The wary, haunted look had returned.

"Oh, come on. You're in no danger. Power's loose on the night." She gestured at the Spiral. "This night is the end of a lot of things—and the beginning of many more. It's a night of change . . . where Power is shifting. Come. You're not in any shape to run anyway, so you might as well relax and take refuge for the night."

She reached out, taking the young woman's icy hand. The blood that stained it had come from another. So, she'd killed in retaliation? The darts she carried belonged to a hunter of the People—and she obviously belonged to the Red Hand. The way of the rape became clear.

"Come, stand over the fire. That's it. Just as you saw me."

"You're White Calf—the witch?"

"And who calls me a witch? Ah, Blood Bear, of course. Poor fool."

"Why should I stand over your fire?"

"Because this is a turning of the Spiral." She pointed to the rock. "And because this might be a turning of the People.'' White Calf gestured at her own sagging flesh. "Just before you arrived, I stood in the heat, bathed by the steam of the sage, and wondered about life, about all that I'd been and done.''

She took the reluctant woman and led her, placing her just so over the fire pit, casting wet sage into the flames, the cloud of steam rising in a billowing column.

"I'd stared at the Spiral, thinking of all that it symbolizes about life coming full circle, and how one thing leads to another, attached yet separate.'' She chewed her lip, seeing the young woman close her eyes as the warm steam bathed her.

"You see, where you stand now, so once did I stand. As you have the blood of another who wronged you on your hand, so did I. Perhaps it's the way of the Spiral, hmm? I mean that we can't understand the bounty of life until its frailty and suffering is proved to us.''

The young woman had opened her eyes, staring at the Spiral. "I'm not a witch.'' And it came to her: beginning and end.

"Neither am I,'' White Calf added with a sigh. Yes, that's what had caused her to awaken. Transition. "No, you're now the mother of the People, although you don't understand that yet. It's curious, I came here with Six Teeth, to stand and cleanse myself like that. Only I came bearing a chokecherry digging stick.''

"And what did you do with your digging stick, old woman?''

White Calf chuckled. "It's over there, against the wall. From that moment on, it became a walking stick.''

"War darts won't become a walking stick—even if I were gullible enough to believe you.''

"No, I suppose not. But Power chooses for its needs. When Power called me, it wanted the Dream. With you, well, the darts speak for themselves.'' White Calf stared up into hot eyes, meeting them, feeling her Power mingling with that of this indomitable woman. "A Dreamer is coming, Tanager.''

"How do you know my name?''

"I know a lot of things. Listen to me. A Dreamer is coming. He's coming to make peace between the People and the

Red Hand. I can't see it all; I don't have the Power I wish I did. I never did have, you see. Oh, never mind, I'm talking about myself again. But the Red Hand are yours. I can't tell you what to do with them, but they'll listen to you. You, in turn, must listen to the Dreamer.''

"I'm not sure for the moment that I want to listen to any man. Not after—''

"He's not just any man.'' White Calf worked her old hands over the woman's chilled skin, avoiding the abrasions, seeking to restore circulation and warmth. "You wouldn't have made it this far without drawing on something deep inside yourself, some strength that runs in your very blood.''

White Calf caught the gleam in the woman's eyes, the slight quiver of her lips. "Perhaps.''

"Perhaps, nothing. This is an age for strength. That doesn't mean it's an age for stupidity—despite what Blood Bear would have anyone believe.''

"He's a great warrior.''

"He's a fool!''

"Oh? I've seen him kill. I've seen the bodies of the dead that he's—''

"He's driven the Wolf Bundle to abandon the Red Hand! Why do you think we're falling apart? Why do you think the trouble has come upon us? Why do you think you were raped out there? Why do the People prowl the lands of the Red Hand? Why are the Spirals changing?''

Hot black eyes flashed. "What are you talking about? The Wolf Bundle goes everywhere Blood Bear goes.''

"And how does it look, hmm? Tell me, Tanager. What kind of look is in Blood Bear's eyes these days? One of a man at ease with himself? Or a man driven to a desperation he doesn't understand?''

She frowned, wincing as it stung some hurt. "He spends most of his time rubbing his little finger and looking worried. But that's because the Short Buffalo People are—''

"It's because he's about to die.''

Tanager turned to glare. "The warrior hasn't been born who can drive a dart into Blood Bear!''

"The warrior's been born,'' White Calf admitted wearily. "That warrior just doesn't know it yet.''

"What are you talking about?"

"Just stand there. Let me warm some water and wash these cuts. These bite marks on your breasts worry me the most. If they get full of pus, you'll really regret it."

Tanager watched her warily, some of the trembling gone from her limbs. The gooseflesh had eased to reveal reddened, scratched skin.

White Calf winced at the pain the girl must be feeling as she cleaned the wounds; but Tanager showed no change of expression on her stoic face, despite what had to be agony.

"Like I said, you've got an inner strength." She frowned. "Perhaps that's what I never had. Ah, well, this is an age for heroes."

"I still don't understand."

White Calf found a robe and handed it to Tanager, who'd begun to fidget and finally stepped back from the fire, a faint sheen of sweat on her muscular legs and belly.

White Calf waved the words away. "You don't need to. Not yet. The thing you have to remember is that you've got to trust the Dreamer. You've got to be the strength of the Red Hand. Do you understand?"

"Trust the Dreamer?" A wry smile began to bend her lips until she flinched from the pain.

"Trust the Dreamer," White Calf agreed fervently. She cocked her head. "Tell me, Tanager, are you strong enough? Can you—"

The keen tip of Tanager's dart dimpled White Calf's throat. She looked down the shaft into the deadly eyes of the young woman. "I killed two of the crawling maggots that raped me, old woman. Don't tell me of strength. Where I should have been a broken wreck, I killed and got away—and so help me, by the Wolf Bundle, I'll make them regret it!"

White Calf ignored the prickle of the razor-edged stone. "That's passion, the need for revenge. Anyone can whip themselves to rage and attempt the impossible. I asked you about strength. Can *you* do what you *have* to? Can you rise above yourself? Can you carry the weight and responsibility of the Red Hand on your shoulders? Can you lead them, no matter what it costs you?"

"I killed, didn't I?"

"Any damn fool can kill. Can you give all of yourself for your Red Hand? Can you force yourself to look beyond your rage? That's what I'm asking. I'm looking for strength—not another weak fool like Blood Bear."

"You call *him* a weak fool?"

White Calf nodded, feeling a trickle of blood down her neck. "He's no better than Heavy Beaver—just less capable. He, too, spurns the Power."

The dart tip withdrew. Tanager shook her head. "I'm surprised. Had it been me on the point of the dart, I'd have thought my life over. Don't you fear, White Calf?"

She dabbed at the blood. "I fear. But not death. I've been waiting for it. I have a lot of questions I want answered. But that's not the issue."

"My strength is?" She lifted an eyebrow. "Right now, I could kill the world to pay it back for—"

"*That's* what worries me." White Calf filled her lungs. "I want to know if you're strong enough to use your wits over your anger. Can you do that?"

"Wits? Anger? What are you talking about?"

"If you can't figure it out, then Wise One Above help us, you'll probably kill the Red Hand."

Tanager simply stared, the hot burning of fury pulsing behind her eyes.

"Forget it. There's the stew bowl. You're about to fall over from fatigue. Eat and sleep, and if we have time, we'll discuss it in the morning."

Little Dancer took another handhold on the hot rock and pulled himself up, panting as he fought for breath. Below him, a sheer cliff dropped away to tumbled and broken rock. Wolf sat below, watching, tail wrapped around his front feet.

From where he'd climbed, the view could literally steal a person's breath. Even eagle didn't have a better perspective of the world. To either side, the sandstone cliffs dropped away from the pinnacle Little Dancer scaled. The land had been thrust up here, and he could see out across the entire basin to the blue-green mountains to the west. There, the peaks rose gray and jagged to rake the blue eminence of the sky. The flanks of the Buffalo Mountains stretched in buckled and dissected shoulders, each stippled with pine and juniper. Higher, dense mats of fir and lodgepole blanketed the slopes until the rounded peaks protruded like eroded and cracked skulls from tattered scalps.

Against this vista, Little Dancer pitted himself, trying to sweat out the misgivings and queer fingers of fear that gripped and slipped along his very heart. The danger of a fall, the chance of a misstep, only heightened the challenge—and the gnawing question that ate away inside him.

He couldn't go. He could feel the call, feel the pull of the Wolf Bundle—but Elk Charm pulled him more. He couldn't look into the eyes of his children and walk away to follow the call.

"I promised," he rasped through clenched teeth. "I made my decision!" Under his sweaty cheek, the gritty sandstone bit into his flesh.

He reached for another handhold. "Wolf Dreamer!" he screamed. "Where are you?"

Despite his bleeding hands, he braced himself and pushed up, torn fingers reaching frantically for another hold. He found a slight fissure in the rock and pulled himself higher. His muscles quivered and ached under the strain.

"Wolf Dreamer?"

He got his foot propped on an angular projection and forced himself up. With a final burst of effort, he flopped over the top of the rock, gasping, sweat tickling as it dribbled down his fevered cheeks and traced irregular paths under his scalp.

Flat on his back, he stared up at the sky. The endless blue seemed to beckon, to call him into an eternity he couldn't reach no matter how high he climbed. There, up beyond the vastness of sky, lay the land of spirits.

"Wolf Dreamer?"

He closed his eyes, the faces of his wife and children spinning out of his memory. "I can't go, Wolf Dreamer. I can't leave them. I love them too much. I like being who I am. Not who you'd make me. I'm not a hero . . . not like you. I'm only a man, a husband and father. Take someone else, someone stronger to fight your war for you."

Tears trickled down, mingling with the sweat on his cheeks. "Please, Wolf Dreamer. Find a hero to do your work. I can't save the Wolf Bundle. I can't destroy Heavy Beaver. I love too much. I can't fight.''

Only the hot whisper of the wind sounded around him. Somewhere below, a raven cawed—bringing a chill memory of Heavy Beaver's curse. A vague flash of Sage Root, wrists gaping, flies buzzing, passed like a snow flurry through his mind.

''*Not* me!''

He rolled over and pushed himself to his feet. He stood on a rocky flat no more than four paces east, west, north, or south. Small tufts of bitterbrush and saltbush clung desperately to cracks in the rock. Washed by rains, scoured by the wind, nothing but a scatter of head-sized rocks remained.

He froze, heart thudding dully in his breast. The work looked ancient, weathered away in places, clear in others. Dirt had drifted to fill part of the grooves, scrubby grass having taken root. He choked a hard swallow down his throat. The entire top of the rock had been laboriously pecked into a large Spiral. He shook his head, trying to back off the huge carving, realizing he had nowhere to go. Numb, he looked up at the sky, at the glaring sun.

He faced the east, raising his hands.

''Wolf Dreamer? Come speak to me!''

The sun burned down on him, baking his body. A pleading in his soul, he stepped forward, grasping fingers trying to pull the sky down. Scaly brush crackled underfoot, scratching his ankles.

''*Wolf Dreamer?*''

The sting seemed to come from the trampled brush at first, then the burning reached past his desperation. He looked down, seeing the triangular head where it stuck to his leg, injecting the venom of its wrath. Black slits of pupils stared malevolently up at him, the scaled diamond patterns catching the sun in a gray-buff sheen.

He cried, kicking out, snapping the reptile loose to coil in the corner of the rocks, the tail that he'd crushed buzzing furiously.

''No,'' he croaked, bending down, staring in horror at the punctures in his dark skin. ''No!''

He fell, hard stone beating against his flesh as he grabbed

his ankle. A searing dizziness gripped him, his stomach convulsing as he fought the urge to vomit.

"*No!*"

Through fear, he felt the world lurch. He blinked with glassy eyes, feeling the poison working within him, burning along his veins. Frantically, he looked around, seeing nothing with which to puncture the wounds—perhaps to bleed some of the poison out, for he couldn't bend to suck it.

The clicking sound came from his chattering teeth. He rubbed tears from his eyes. He could feel the grooves that had been pecked into the rock. He blinked, seeing he'd fallen in the center of the Spiral. Beginning and end—birth and death.

He waited as the sun angled across the sky. Sick, nauseated, he felt death eating its way up his throbbing, swelling leg. The sun slanted to the west.

The words spun out of the clear air. Little Dancer stared up into the weaving glazing of sky, hearing the old woman as clearly as if she stood above him.

Monster Creatures on bellies crawl.
Bite a man's foot. Watch him fall.
Legless, armless, hair of scale.
Shakes a rattle on his tail.
Teeth of poison, hollow flail,
Makes blood black and frail.

"Who . . . Who are you?"

The Sky? Aye, always the sky.
Blazing hot, and white the land,
Scorched as by burning brand.
Dream the big beasts to the stars, away.
Their corpses bleach on dusty clay.
Change the land the People tread.
Find a new way . . . or we'll all be dead.
Learn the grass, learn the root, the berry.
Time is short, life not merry.
Pound and grind, grind and pound,
While the hot wind blows around.

"What do you want?"

The dry wind gusted in answer. Blinking frantically, Little Dancer reached up, ever up, toward the blue inevitability of the sky.

Not for years had Heavy Beaver seen a summer coming this hot and dry. Not since the deep cold had any snow fallen, and then but a wisp that had dried the next day. Only the Buffalo Mountains, from all reports, had received anything like adequate moisture. As if they understood, the buffalo had taken the trails up to the high meadows, filling the land of the Anit'ah with their wealth. Other herds had dispersed here and there, scattering until only lone animals could be found in the uplands. Along the rivers, where the flow fed the riparian grasses, his hunters had ambushed and killed many of the animals, knowing that they must return to the only water available.

With his main camp, Heavy Beaver walked, following the trail left by his warriors. The trail wound round about, tied by necessity to the availability of water. They walked over a scarred land—rivulets had eaten into the denuded soil, only to fill with blowing dust and sand. Even the dogs looked miserable, panting and laboring under their loads as the pads of their tough feet bruised on the deflated pebbles and cut on angular rock.

Heavy Beaver did not lead the only band of the People. Two Stones came from further east, and Seven Suns' runners reported that he traveled south from the mouth of Mud River where it met the Buffalo tributary of Big River. From the south, Elk Whistle's tattered band picked their slow way up from Sand River, reporting that the blowing sand now blanketed the very sky, leaving the gritty air black. They had already taken to eating their dogs.

Heavy Beaver squinted at the rising parapets of the Buffalo Mountains. Here his warriors would win him a victory—or he would face a challenge more terrible than any they faced warring with the Anit'ah.

"The Anit'ah eat roots and seeds," Red Chert had told him. "Perhaps that's a way to keep hunger away?"

He'd slapped her, glaring down at her where she had fallen,

a hand pressed to her mouth. "We're men, not diggers in the dirt like Anit'ah. Buffalo Above and the Wise One placed buffalo here for men to eat. Meat is the food of strength, of Power. Roots will weaken my warriors." He'd looked to the rising swell of the Buffalo Mountains with their gleaming cap of snow. "No, we'll go where Buffalo Above leads us. This year, yes, this year we take the mountains."

But he'd heard others when they thought him far away. *"The Anit'ah eat roots—and I don't see their blood going weak!"*

"I'll take your mountains," Heavy Beaver promised. "On my mother's soul, I swear it. By the very blood in my veins, I'll not have silly women out gathering roots, gaining power in the lodges through the food they obtain. No! No man will be held hostage by that. They won't turn the cleansing of the People back in that manner. I'll have every last one of us dead by an Anit'ah war dart first!"

He clenched a fist and shook it at the mountain wall.

"Wolf Bundle? Reach . . . reach for him now! Fill him with your need. Act. Act now!"

Chapter 22 ◎

White Calf awoke with the feeling of premonition. Power had disturbed her sleep, playing with the little corners of her Dream mind. The last of the Dreams, however, had played as powerfully as life itself. The images lingered, sharply edged, so real she could practically reach out and touch them were she to extend her withered arm.

So her time had come at last. She opened her eyes, focusing on the comfortable interior of her shelter. In the peace of the morning, she let her vision trace the familiar belongings that hung from the pegs and rested in the niches. The ancient

Spiral pecked into the back wall seemed to dominate the room this morning. As the morning sun peeked over the distant mountains, a single sliver of sunlight pierced the hangings and lanced the Spiral with a brilliant shaft of light.

White Calf pulled her hair back, working her mouth to rid it of the stale night taste. Her bones crackled and groaned as she got up from her bedding, walking over to stir the sagebrush ash in the fire. She dropped tinder on red-eyed coals. Blowing gently, she coaxed a fire and began heating boiling stones.

Tanager lay covered with hides, a slender arm projecting from under the covers. Her slim hand lay limp, fingers in a curl. Here and there wisps of shining black hair poked out from under the protection of the bedding.

White Calf sucked thin lips in over her gums. A longing went out to the girl. Curious how Power worked. Tanager, the wild girl of the forest and hunt, had been drawn up, lifted into the Spiral.

Building a roaring fire, White Calf waited for the stones to heat while she used a sharp chert flake to shave dried meat into the boiling pouch. After the water floated thick with chips of meat, she added biscuit root, balsam, and the last of her carefully preserved onions. What little ephedra she had left, she threw in. Tanager would need it.

After that, she stepped over Tanager and inspected the stack of things propped against the back wall. She took her atlatl and the bundle of darts she'd so carefully crafted. One by one, she inspected them, checking for cracks in the wood, making sure the fletching hadn't been ruined by the rodents. The bindings remained tight where the deadly stone points fastened to the shafts. Good work, some of the best she'd ever done. The points had been crafted by Three Toes, who—with the knack of the plains people—created the most wonderful points she'd ever seen. Now the stone rippled in the morning light. She ran a caressing finger over the darts, blessing them, lifting them to her lips to blow a bit of her soul into them. The missiles—along with her atlatl—she placed next to the two darts belonging to Tanager.

She turned back to the fire, using her hearth sticks to pluck the cobbles from the coals and drop them into the boiling pouch. At the hiss and sizzle of the water, Tanager jerked and sat up, staring wild-eyed around the shelter.

"We'll eat in a bit. There's not much time this morning—but maybe enough."

"You keep saying that." Tanager combed her thick tangles of hair back with long thin fingers.

"I thought as much last night. This morning, I know. Dreams were loose on the land."

Tanager nodded, closing her eyes and shaking her head, as if to rid it of her own apparitions.

White Calf nodded to herself, well imagining the nightmares Tanager had relived. She took one of her beautifully carved horn spoons and dipped it in the steaming stew.

"Here, girl, eat. Eat all you can. You're going to have a hard day."

Tanager winced as she stood, color draining from her face.

"Here, take this with you. Chew it as you need." She handed the young woman a small pouch. "It's an extract I make out of willow bark. You peel it, and boil it, and when you boil the water away, scrape up the residue. It works on pain for some reason. Willow has lots of wonderful properties."

Tanager took a stiff step, trying to keep her expression neutral. She lowered herself carefully and took up the bowl, sipping cautiously at the steaming liquid. She glanced up. "You talk like you know something's going to happen today."

White Calf smiled absently, eyes locked on eternity. "I Dreamed . . . Dreamed like never before. I don't understand it all, not yet. But I heard the Wolf Bundle. It whispered in my Dreams."

Tanager studied her from the corner of a suspicious eye.

"Ah, skepticism. Is that what Blood Bear has taught you all? No wonder the heart's gone out of the Red Hand. Indeed, the Wolf Bundle whispered in my sleep. And I Dreamed of the First Man, saw him, shining and wonderful, smiling and reaching down to me after the Wolf Bundle had given me its message."

Tanager drained the horn and looked across. "And what

message was this? What does the Wolf Bundle want you to do?"

White Calf smiled, propping her chin on gnarled fists. "Not me, girl. It's you the Wolf Bundle wanted to talk to. It said, tell Tanager to help the Dreamer."

She shook her head, standing up, wincing at the pain. "You keep saying that. Are there any clothes for me here?"

White Calf sighed, grunting as she got to her feet. "Before you dress, let me clean those wounds again. Yes, I keep saying that. It's true. The Dreams have been driving me half-mad for days. I just didn't know who you were."

She turned, a fire in her flashing black eyes. "Why me? What is all this nonsense?"

White Calf found her medicines and looked up at the tall young woman. "Because, girl, if you choose to help the Dreamer, you'll become the leader of the Red Hand."

"Leader of the Red Hand?"

"And a way to restore the Spiral. Balance, you see. What the universe always tries to maintain—and never can. But you have to take that chance. Right now, you don't care for anything but your anger. In the Dream, the Wolf Bundle showed me how it would be. If . . . and I say *if*, you choose to support the Dreamer, you'll destroy the Short Buffalo invaders. If you don't, well, who knows? Maybe Fire Dancer and Two Smokes can pull something out in the end."

"Two Smokes? The berdache?"

White Calf nodded as she began working on Tanager's wounds. "I told you Power was mixed up in all this."

"And these weapons lying beside mine?"

"You'll need them in a short time. That's why I'd suggest you take that willow-bark extract. It'll make your pains—"

"What do you mean, *I'll* need them?"

White Calf tended the last of the bites and abrasions before producing a sheep-hide dress, an example of Two Smokes' talent in tanning and sewing. Even Tanager hesitated, taking a moment to run her fingers over the finely tanned leather. A radiant glow suffused her eyes as she slipped it over her head. The incredibly soft leather wouldn't aggravate her abused flesh.

"Don't know about your feet, but my moccasins look about your size. If not, you can make do with winter outers."

"You said I'll need the weapons?" Tanager looked up as she pulled footgear over her battered feet.

"You will. The Short Buffalo People who captured you are on the way."

"What?" Tanager's icy composure crumbled.

White Calf grinned wickedly. "Of course. I Dreamed them, you see. It's a deal with the Wolf Bundle. I've brought them to you. But one has to escape . . . to take the story back."

"*What?*"

White Calf sighed heavily. "How else will you believe what I say, that the Wolf Bundle needs you . . . the Dreamer needs you."

"But here?" Tanager's panic spread.

White Calf glared at her. "You would be leader of the Red Hand? Hah! Then you'd better start to prove it, girl. You've got four men to kill."

"There's five!"

"One has to live."

"One?"

White Calf dropped her eyes. "Let's say that's my price."

Straight Wood followed behind, watching while Left Hand worked out the trail. Just luck, that's all it had been. After they had lost the Anit'ah woman completely, a single track in the dust had pointed the way. By then the woman had to have believed she'd lost them. The tracks had to be hers. How many women would be walking around barefoot? And from the scuffs, she'd been near exhaustion and limping slightly.

Left Hand continued at a trot now, pointing here and there at a faint mark along the way. They worked up from the Clear Water River, following a well-used trail. Ahead, a grayish-white limestone cliff rose up to a high peak above the dark green tangle of trees.

"Look!" Firm Dart pointed. "Someone's gathered firewood in here."

Straight Wood could see the places where the branches had

been broken off. So they might have an Anit'ah camp here? He let himself fall slightly behind. Five of them? To attack a Red Hand camp?

"I don't know if this is such a good idea. With only five of us, what happens if we run into—"

"She killed Two Blue Moons and Tiny Ant," Left Hand insisted, trying to keep his voice down.

Firm Dart raised his hand for silence. "She killed our people—one of our greatest warriors. Most of their camps are small, with few men—and those old. I say we hit them hard, In the confusion, we kill the woman, and who knows, maybe we rout them all. The heart is gone out of the Anit'ah anyway."

Left Hand nodded curtly, taking to the trail again.

Straight Wood gritted his teeth, again taking the last position. Left Hand pulled up before the trees thinned to a large meadow. From where he stood, Straight Wood could see tan hides covering what looked like an overhang in the cliff. No other sign of a camp, no barking of dogs, no calls could be heard on the still air. The old woman sat in the sun, legs folded under her, face lifted to the morning.

"One old woman." Left Hand waved them forward.

Straight Wood felt that tug at his heart, the feeling of premonition. Why? Hadn't Heavy Beaver Sung over him and made him powerful? Reassured at the thought, Straight Wood followed.

The old woman could have been oblivious. Straight Wood studied the situation. No one could sneak up on them from behind. A belt of trees grew along the base of the limestone, and that was it. Unless an entire war party hid in the shelter, they faced one old woman, and maybe the young girl who'd killed so quickly after they raped her.

"Stop there, warriors of the People!" The feeble cry wavered in the air.

"She's one of the People?" Left Hand asked.

"Who are you?"

"I am White Calf. Come no closer or you'll die!"

"The witch!" Straight Wood gasped, thoughts going back to that day when White Calf had appeared and taken the berdache and the boy from under Heavy Beaver's very nose.

"Witch?" Left Hand laughed. "Are you a witch?"

"No. But go away. You have this chance. Otherwise you'll die."

Left Hand's arm shot back. Human lightning, his body bent, putting weight behind the cast of the dart. Straight Wood stared, watching the slim projectile glinting in the sun. It could have been a hawk, so smoothly did it fall from the blue sky, lancing down to transfix the old woman's gut with a soft slap.

"Come on!" Left Hand yelled. "Let's find the girl!" And they charged forward.

Straight Wood straggled along behind, eyes fixed on the old woman where she still sat, fragile fingers tracing the shaft of the dart that stuck up from her guts.

He didn't see Left Hand take the dart that killed him, but the warrior stumbled and went down, whimpering horribly.

"The girl!" Firm Dart shrieked, pointing, changing the direction of his charge, oblivious to the plight of Left Hand. The others sprinted after her. She ducked through the trees with the grace of a deer in flight.

Straight Wood hesitated, and finally walked up the gradual slope, looking down at the old woman. Yes, this was White Calf. She stared up at him, black eyes flashing.

"So," she croaked. "You killed White Calf? Fool, you just bought the death of the People."

"Heavy Beaver's warriors are everywhere, witch. Anit'ah flee from us. Most don't even stand and fight. Heavy Beaver's Dreamed their destruction."

She chuckled and winced at the pain. "With my death you've spat upon Power for the last time."

"What do you mean, witch? What would you know of Power?"

White Calf grinned happily, fingers clenched around the dart shaft. "Where's your war party? Eh? Look down where they ran. What do you see?"

Straight Wood tore his gaze from the old woman's sparkling eyes and stared down the valley under the shade of his hand. He looked just in time to see Firm Dart charge full tilt into a cast missile. The warrior shrieked, falling face forward. Quick Fall, the last on his feet, slid to a stop, frantically turning, sprinting for the far timber. The dart caught him before he'd even started, penetrating the small of his back. He pitched on his face and slid in the grass, trying to crawl painfully away.

"You're the last. Run now. Run like you've never run before, boy. And tell Heavy Beaver that a new leader has risen among the Anit'ah. Her name is Tanager. And tell Heavy Beaver the Dreamer . . . *and the Wolf Bundle* are coming for him. Tell him, and all the People . . . they'll have to Dance with fire!"

Straight Wood barely heard the last. He turned on his heel, pounding back across the meadow, back tingling as his prickling skin anticipated the bite of a keen point.

He paused only long enough to throw a look over his shoulder when he reached the trees. The sight left him stunned. From out of the clear blue morning, a whirlwind had formed before the shelter. It whipped the grass angrily, sucking debris and dust high, twirling it all into the clear, still air. Then it moved up the slope, centering over the old woman, tossing her hair this way and that, flapping her clothing about. Finally, it rose, lifting over the cliff face.

Straight Wood cried out, and ran as he'd never run in his life.

How long? Three days? Four? The pattern of sunrise and sunset had blurred in his fevered mind. A continual pain shot up Little Dancer's burning leg, powered with each beat of his heart.

"Wolf Dreamer?" he croaked yet again.

Only the faint whisper of the wind accompanied his pleas. Sometimes, when the delirium came on him, he thought it spoke in familiar voices, but he couldn't distinguish the words. In those moments, he talked back, hearing Elk Charm and Hungry Bull, or perhaps the rattling cackle of White Calf's dry laugh.

Uneasily, he slept, and the Dreaming came on him. He'd be one with the eagle soaring high overhead, feeling the precise control of the wing muscles and tail. What freedom to enjoy the subtle changes in attitude or the tensing of feathers that traced the currents of air.

Other times, he jumped with the rats in the night, listening carefully for the faint hiss of owl wings in the darkness. His keen nose sought for the rich sweetness of ripening grass spikes.

"I'm dying," he mumbled to himself, curled in a fetal ball as the sun sweated the last of his body water from him. Pain had driven him mostly mad. All it would take would be to drag himself to the edge, to let his tired body tumble over the side and down into the forbidding rocks below.

Wearily, he raised his head to look down at his leg; the sight of the swollen member sickened him. The skin had puffed out under pressure, nearly twice the size of his other leg. The color had become ghastly. When he touched the skin, it felt fit to burst, like a bladder under pressure. Nausea swept him.

"I'm dying."

"You are."

He looked up, squinting into the sunlight, seeing the features of Wolf Dreamer forming out of the very gold-spun rays of the sun. He stood, tall, glistening, bathed in the golden light, skin traced by the patterns of the Spirit World.

Wolf Dreamer settled himself on the rock with no more sound than a feather on dust. He crossed his legs gracefully and sat serenely, back straight, hands in his lap. The beauty of his face, the sympathy and concern expressed in his sad eyes, melted Little Dancer's soul. The confusion, the worry and despair, drained away, replaced by a warm breeze that caressed him.

Little Dancer smiled, splitting his cracked lips in the process. The cutting burden of what he had to say lost its keen edge—no matter that the consequences would condemn him.

"I can't be your Dreamer. I can't leave Elk Charm . . . or my girls. I love them too much." he sighed, emotions blunted by the throbbing agony in his leg. "I should apologize, but I don't think I really can, not for loving my wife and children. That's not something to be ashamed of. You see, when you asked me if I'd live and be your Dreamer, I didn't know how much I'd—"

"I don't need your explanations."

Little Dancer stared, eyesight wavering from the burning fever. "No? But I . . . Well, I thought that when a person made a promise to a spirit and then didn't follow through . . . well, things happened. You know, like the story about the woman who wished to have the Power to heal. Then when she got it, she used it to help her win at gambling games and the spirits crippled her legs in punishment."

"It's not the same," Wolf Dreamer added in a gentle voice. "I knew you'd come to love your wife so. I knew your love for your children would overwhelm you."

"You did?" Little Dancer struggled, mind whirling with the giddiness of fever. "I don't understand. Then why let me live? Why send me wolf to take care of me? Why did he drag me to his den when I couldn't go further? He curled up, warming me with his body. Why did you do all that when you knew I'd eventually fail you?"

The smile warmed him, shooting like bars of golden sunshine through the darkness of regret and suffering.

The words came like balm: "Perhaps it will take a while for you to understand, but I needed your humanity. From Clear Water you got the ability to Dream. From Blood Bear you got strength. Two Smokes taught you endurance. From Hungry Bull you got vulnerability. From White Calf you got wisdom. But the most precious gift of all came from Sage Root; she taught you humanity, that common identity with your peoples. She gave unselfishly of herself, knowing what was coming."

"And it destroyed her."

"So it will destroy you, too—in the end."

"Wait. You don't understand. *I'm not the one!* I'm dying. And I wouldn't leave my people. Not Elk Charm, or my girls, or Hungry Bull, or Rattling Hooves, or—"

"Or the rest of humanity which needs you?" Wolf Dreamer laughed and clapped his hands together. "Yes, that's right. And family and friends, they all love you, but that's what I need. A lovable Dreamer who's strong and charismatic and vulnerable. You'll do fine, Fire Dancer, just fine."

"My name's Little Dancer."

"You never took a man's name."

He stared down at the rock beneath him. The stone had been stained by his sweat. He rubbed a finger absently in the pecked groove of the Spiral. "After everything I'd seen, taking a different name didn't seem that important."

"I'm renaming you now. You're a man, more so than the greatest warrior or the most cunning hunter."

"But I'm dying. The poison's deep in me. I've seen snakebite. I know the signs, the blackness in the blood, the swelling as the tissue dies."

"Tell me, Fire Dancer, why did you climb up here?"

"To find you."

"And why did you do that?"

"To tell you I couldn't leave my family. That I'd come to love them too much. That I couldn't leave them alone."

"But you could have simply stayed at camp. You didn't need to seek me out at all."

"Wolf was there, watching."

"Did he ever threaten you? Did he ever act to remind you of your duty?"

Little Dancer clamped his eyes shut, trying to think, remembering only the level stare wolf had given him the night the Wolf Bundle had called to him. "No. But I thought—"

"I told you the first time we met that free will couldn't be denied. Did I ever imply that you'd be punished if you failed me?"

"No."

"So you could have run. But you came, knowing even as you did that I might destroy you for saying you wouldn't—"

"But I owed you!" Little Dancer tried to sit up and gasped at the pain in his throbbing leg. "I couldn't just pretend nothing happened up there in the snow."

"You are a man who accepts responsibility." Wolf Dreamer lifted his face to the sun above, closing his eyes, seeming to enjoy the warmth.

"It doesn't matter," Little Dancer whispered. "My first responsibility is to my wife . . . my children. Now, it seems the rattlesnake has used his own free will. I guess it's all without point anyway. I would ask one last thing of you. Please, if you could make things easier on Elk Charm and my daughters, I'd—"

"I have no intention of letting you die, Fire Dancer. Less now than I might have before."

Again, his vision seemed to swim, and his eyes had trouble focusing. "What?"

Wolf Dreamer stood, rising like smoke, and walked closer, settling next to Little Dancer's fevered body. "Oh, you're quite in the right condition. Your mind is wandering, shifting from real to unreal. For four days you've been without food and water. That's the sacred number. Snake venom has lowered your resistance even further. The gates of your mind are open, the thresholds dropped. You're teetering on the verge of losing yourself, ready to touch the One. Once, I had to use mushrooms—as you will one day use another poison. Now is the time to teach you to Dream with the One."

"Even if I've told you I can't abandon my family?"

Wolf Dreamer's smile might have been everything good in the universe. Little Dancer's soul would have sung to see it again.

"I know you love them, Fire Dancer, but I'm going to give you something more powerful. I'm giving you the Dream. I'm giving you the One. With it, you'll Dance the Spiral back into balance. You'll be One with the fire, air, and water . . . with the very Earth Mother. Everything has ties to the One. Even your family.

"Come, take my hand. Together, we'll Dance the poison, and you'll learn it's only illusion."

"Then White Calf was right?"

"More than she could ever know."

Little Dancer winced at the pain, gulping for air, seeking to quiet his reeling reality. He reached for the man of light, fingers grasping into a brilliant flash. . . .

He awoke, flat on his back, staring up into the night sky. A terrible thirst burned with the intensity of fever. In his mouth, his tongue rasped like dry leather.

He whimpered and forced himself to sit up, looking about owlishly, trying to place where he was. A solitary spire of rock supported his back.

"What?" The sound of his voice frightened him.

He blinked, remembering. He'd climbed to find Wolf

Dreamer. The snake had bitten him. Frantic fingers clawed at his leg, feeling familiar firm flesh. He stared around, seeing nothing out of order in the darkness

The memory of Wolf Dreamer settled warm in his mind. He'd Danced with the Wolf Dreamer; together, they'd been the Oneness, floating like the wind, Dancing with the pulse of the universe, singing and chanting in harmony with the beat of the Creator. In that manner, they'd felt the twirling beauty of the spinning stars, heard the songs of distant suns, and felt the pulse of life. He had known freedom then. His soul had become light. The memory clung to him with the rich sweetness of warm honey.

That bit of flesh that made up Little Dancer had been left behind, a bit of matter, a composite of tissue that deluded. The glory of the One shimmered in his memory, absorbing his thoughts until he realized the sun had climbed into the sky.

Could he do it again? Could he Dance the One, Dream it out of thin air without Wolf Dreamer? He felt the call, desperate, yearning. Like a melody on the wind, it came to him.

"The Wolf Bundle."

He crawled to the edge of the pinnacle and looked over the side. The spirit of the rocks hummed beneath him. Without a worry, he lowered himself, seeking a foothold.

His muscles quivered from the strain, irritating pain shot up his fingers as the rock dug into his skin.

First he had to recover the Wolf Bundle. In the depths of his mind, he could feel it as he'd always known he could. The long wait had come to an end. So little time remained. He had to get the Wolf Bundle, restore its Power—and he had so much to learn.

Two Smokes hitched his painful way up the side of the drainage, wincing at the pain in his knee. The older he got, the worse it seemed to hurt. In his hand he clutched a delicate shock of ricegrass. The seed pods, full and ready to burst, bobbed as he walked.

He stopped for a moment to get his breath and stumped over to a large flat boulder. There, he gratefully lowered himself and pulled the leather roll of his grass collection from where it traveled securely in his belt. He unrolled the long leather strip, staring at the various grasses he'd collected through the years. He had lots of ricegrass, of course, and now stared at it, admiring the fragile beauty.

Overhead a raven cawed and clucked, wheeling about as if to give him a casual inspection. A grasshopper rose on clicking wings, silver glinting off its shimmering flight. The summer stretched around him, alive with the sounds of insects and birdsong.

Two Smokes let the sun burn into his face. To live on a day like this made everything worthwhile. The warmth paid him back for the storms that rolled across the land and made his bad knee ache. This day rewarded him for the long blizzards, the times he'd shivered in rain-soaked clothing or huddled under frost-stiff hides.

Absently, he picked up a rounded sandstone cobble and used it to smash a seed pod of the ricegrass, staring at the flattened seed and the tiny hairs. He mashed another and another with increasing excitement.

"You stupid old fool!" He blinked, feeling the pieces of his long quest coming together. Here lay the answer, after all the years of chewing individual seeds, of grinding grass stems, and pulling the shoots apart by the hour to nibble the sweet stalks of the grass. No, people couldn't eat the body of the grass, but the seeds—yes, the seeds—could be eaten!

His heart felt fit to burst and a tear trickled down his weathered cheek. He'd never thought to collect the seeds— they were the smallest part of the plant. But how many times he had plucked a stem, just to have the seeds fall out and scatter? And no matter that seeds were small, there were so many. Grass grew everywhere!

He looked about, seeing the nodding heads of grass going to seed everywhere. As he did so, movement caught his eye. The black wolf walked out of the juniper, followed by Little Dancer.

Two Smokes chuckled to himself. "Hey, come here! I found it! I found the secret of the grasses! Come look! It's the seeds! *It's the seeds!*" Two Smokes whooped and waved his hands.

Little Dancer wound around the stands of rabbitbrush, a

weary stumbling to his walk. Like a man in a dream, he made his way. The wolf trotted swiftly to one side, panting in the heat.

Not until he stood before Two Smokes did the old berdache realize the difference. The ecstasy stilled in his heart as he looked up. "Little Dancer?"

That familiar face had changed; even the scar on his cheek seemed to stand out, lit from within.

"You've found the secret?"

Two Smokes nodded, aware of the strange glow in the young man's eyes, like he lived a Dream. "It's the seeds." He paused. "We can collect the seeds. In a basket like we do berries and . . . Little Dancer, what happened?"

"I Dreamed with the First Man." Little Dancer's voice sounded faraway. "He came, found me on the top of the rock. Together we Dreamed . . . and, Two Smokes, it was so beautiful . . . so beautiful." He smiled, lost in the memory.

So it had happened after all? Little Dancer had found his Power? "And Elk Charm? What about her?"

Little Dancer smiled, lighting a part of the old man's soul. "Wolf Dreamer will protect her. I asked . . . asked that you all be protected."

"What about you?"

Little Dancer reached out to place both hands on his shoulders. Two Smokes started at the touch, a tingling shooting through him. He lost himself in the depths of the brown eyes staring so thoughtfully into his. "Two Smokes, I see now. You've given so much, and no one has ever understood. You've found the secret of the grass?"

"Yes. You have to collect the seeds. They're little—but they're everywhere. It's not the stems, you see, but the *seeds* that are important. I—I never thought to grind them! That's the difference. And—and it's been right before my eyes the whole time! Grind the seeds into a paste like we do with biscuit root."

"And you've tasted this?"

"Well, not yet, but I can. I will, I'll bet it's wonderful!"

Little Dancer closed his eyes, tilting his head back. "Would you collect some? Make it for me? The first . . . to take with me?''

The heart almost stopped in Two Smokes' chest. ''Take with you? You're going Dreaming?''

Little Dancer's face pained slightly, dimming the Power in his eyes. ''I have to go. The Wolf Bundle needs me. It's time, old friend. The Spiral has come around. But I just don't know how I—''

''But there's a *war* going on up there!''

Little Dancer smiled nervously. ''And maybe it will end now. Maybe I can Dream it away.''

''You can't Dream all those Short Buffalo People away, and Blood Bear—''

''Is my father. Circles, Two Smokes, everything runs in Circles—even the Spiral.'' The touch, so light on the old man's shoulders, lifted. ''Make me your grass secret. Despite the worry I see in your eyes, Two Smokes, your heart is near to bursting over this. Your happiness glows around you like a warm fire on a cold night.''

Little Dancer's smile wavered and he looked away, lost within himself.

''What has happened to you?'' asked Two Smokes. ''You're different. Is it the Power?''

Little Dancer seemed to hesitate, unsure. ''I . . . I don't know what to say anymore. People . . . Elk Charm . . . they don't . . .'' He offered his hands, a pleading expression twisting his face. ''Two Smokes, I Dreamed with the First Man. I saw the illusion of all this.'' He gestured at the world around them. He lifted his hands, staring at them in awe. ''We touched, He and I, and we Danced and Dreamed and Sang. Together, we shared the One . . . the harmony of . . . of . . . everything.''

Two Smokes listened, nodding. ''Go on.''

Little Dancer dropped to his knees, heedless of the sharp rocks. ''But I . . . The One, it's a whole wondrous . . . Your soul Sings, and Dances, and . . . and . . .'' He stuttered to a stop, a glow reflecting the experience in his mind. ''It's . . .''

Two Smokes reached down, taking the young man's hands,

pulling to lift him. "Tell me. Tell me about Wolf Dreamer and the One. Tell me about it."

The anguished look returned. "It's beautiful, like the wheeling of the stars and joy of the light and the heart of a snowflake and the drifting of a bit of down. And your soul pulses with the Power, is One with it. Breathes with it." His eyes cleared. "Do you understand?"

Two Smokes frowned, holding Little Dancer's hands tightly. "Sort of. At least, I think I do. The Wolf Bundle used to send a tingle of something like that through me. It was as if I could sense the presence of a huge cavern. My fingertips could only explore the edge."

"I fell through it, and back again, inside out in the light." Little Dancer's fingers flexed and straightened. "But I . . . I . . ."

"Yes?"

"I can't tell you. Not in words that make sense. I can't say what it is to become lost in the Great Mystery, in the Creator's Dream. Words don't tell what it's like." He gestured passionately. "Like . . . like explain orgasm to a rock."

Two Smokes chuckled at Little Dancer's analogy as well as the panicked expression contorting his face.

"Don't laugh," Little Dancer protested, jumping to his feet, stalking back and forth, the panic deepening. "How do I tell people? How do I make them understand?" He whirled, pounding fists against the side of his head. "Two Smokes, I don't fit anymore. I've been beyond this world, Dreamed the One, heard the song of the stars. I've felt, *felt* the soul of God! Don't you understand? How can I sit down and talk about hunting . . . or how big the sego lily is this year . . . or laugh at a meaningless joke or . . ." He shook his head frantically. "None of it means anything to me. Don't you see? I feel like an adult—and the world around me is full of children. None of their problems are important." He dropped his head. "But they are, of course. Only, it's all illusion. Existence here, on this earth . . . the reality is so different for everyone. We all make it up. Only how do I tell them?"

Two Smokes sighed and clapped his hands on his knees. "I understand."

"No, you couldn't. Not unless you Dreamed the One, Danced with—"

"Not your Dream. That's not what I mean."

Little Dancer stared at him, a hollow look in his passionate eyes.

Two Smokes filled his lungs, enjoying the feeling of life, of understanding for the first time. "I always wondered why I was chosen. Why I, a berdache, was tied to your life."

"I don't understand."

"No, I don't suppose you do. It's too new for you. You're lost, floundering in a swollen river of new experiences that's rushing you along so fast you think you're drowning. But among the Red Hand a berdache is prized. We are called mediators, living in the worlds of man and woman. But we live in two other worlds, that of Power and earth. Clear Water came to me at first because I could understand her Dreams. She could tell me what it meant and I could help her understand.

"I remember when the Dreams of Blood Bear first began to bother her. She couldn't see the sense in letting him couple with her. Even then he was a violent man. He needed to hurt her to enjoy sex, to release his seed. I couldn't understand either, but it was Power and I wouldn't ridicule her. Then when his seed caught, the Dreams changed. Clear Water came to me, telling me about how she needed to steal the Wolf Bundle, how the two of us had to run away."

Two Smokes smiled up at Little Dancer, remembering. "It was Power, and I'd come to love her by then. Of course I went with her. I could feel the edge—as I told you earlier. Ah, those days, Little Dancer. She and I walked alone—but together—and Power ebbed and flowed around us. The Wolf Bundle practically hummed with Power.

"Then you were born and we were so glad. That was the first time I used the Wolf Bundle for a birth. That was the first time I felt it pulsing in *my* hand, and I could sense the cavern, the One, lying just beyond the ends of my reach. What a wondrous thing that was. So you can imagine my horror when the buffalo gored your mother and left me crippled in the dirt. What purpose could that tragedy have had?

Why take me all that way to be broken and cast down in the dirt and pain?

"Then, one night after White Calf rescued me, I swore to protect you—and I foolishly swore over the Wolf Bundle—which bound me forever."

"And you took very good care of me. I've never thanked you."

"Nor am I finished. For now, at this time of your life, I have finally become useful." He smiled, feeling the rightness. Awed, he experienced the sense of Power, of the cavern, just beyond his reach.

Little Dancer licked his lips, the question in his eyes.

"A berdache lives between the Circles—man and woman, earth and Power. For this, I have been prepared. You've seen beyond. If a man is worried about his wife coupling with another man, do you care about his dilemma? Such a concern is foolish in your eyes. You see only that the One is true. You've been beyond the difference, the I and you, the this and that of this world. The Power kept me for this moment. I am your bridge, Little Dancer. Through me, you can touch this world you call illusion. I can ease the way for you, teach you, and understand you at the same time I understand the people around you. That's why I was chosen. Only now do I understand. Only now do I see why I was led to this place to sit on this rock. Perhaps, that's why the secret of the grass evaded me until this moment. The Circle had to come full."

"But what do I do?"

"Dream, Little Dancer. That's what you do. You Dream the real new way for the People. You Dream the Spiral back. Leave the rest to me. I've been shaped for this just as a horn bowl is shaped and carved by a craftsman. Fool that I was, I'll be serving you until the end—and through it, I'll get my wish. I'll get to touch the One." He smiled up into the morning sun, raising his hands. "Thank you for this day, Wise One Above. Thank you for the wonder. Thank you for the light of understanding. I, Two Smokes, thank you for letting me finally see."

Elk Charm sat at the top of the trail staring up toward the peaks where Little Dancer had gone. How long would it take?

As she sat, she rubbed long sections of the juniper bark back and forth between her callused palms. She'd peeled the lengths earlier, using a large quartzite flake to strip the bark from mature trees. By working the hairy bark vigorously, she could shred it into fibers and crush them to make an absorbent for her infant's bottom. And infants can go through an incredible amount of absorbent.

She chewed fretfully at her lip, taking a quick look to see that the baby slept peacefully in the cradle board. A bluebird shot past, landing on an overturned stump, trilling to the warm air of the morning.

She saw Two Smokes hobbling along in his swinging walk before she made out Little Dancer and the lean shape of the black wolf darting through the sage. Something about the way Little Dancer walked, that curious looseness so uncharacteristic of him, reminded her of a man in a daze. Getting to her feet, she ran for him.

Two Smokes called out, trying to get her attention, but she could see the slackness that filled Little Dancer's expression. A glaze lay behind his eyes.

She twisted past Two Smokes' reaching fingers and threw herself into his arms. He held her awkwardly, but her frantic worry hid that fact from her in the beginning. Only when she felt him stiffen and draw back did she look up, searching his face for some indication of the problem.

"Little Dancer? Are you all right?"

"I'm fine," he told her uneasily; the familiar light of love in his eyes warred with something else, something powerful and frightening. "I've Dreamed, you see . . . touched the One."

"Elk Charm?" Two Smokes put his hand on her shoulder, warm and firm. "Elk Charm, he's been in the Spirit World. He Dreamed with the First Man."

She stared up at him, wondering at his detached smile. "Little Dancer?"

He reached out, placing hands on either side of her face. For that moment, he smiled for only her, and her soul leapt. "Elk Charm, my wonderful Elk Charm." Tears ran down his face as he hugged her tight, crushing her to his breast. "I understand. You, too, have taught me. That's why you came to me. I couldn't have ever understood all the ways of love without you. I couldn't have understood so much about people, and why they are the way they are.''

She shook her head, confused, happy that he held her. If only she didn't have the dread that something precious had begun to slip away from her life.

"Come," Little Dancer told her, backing away, reaching for her hand as well as Two Smokes'. "I have to prepare. There isn't much time."

"Time for what?" she demanded. But Little Dancer had already continued his way, stopping only to place his hands on the baby's face before walking down the trail. As she unhitched the cradle board from the tree, she noticed that Two Smokes studied her thoughtfully, worry mixed with anguish.

"It's time," he said gently. "He must go now."

Chapter 23 ◎

Tanager ran, exalting in the rush of air from her lungs as her leg muscles pumped. The feeling of smooth power, of balanced stride and reserves untapped, thrilled her. For the first time in her life, she'd found her place. Where once she'd been teased for her odd ways, for her desire to hunt and trace the paths of the animals, now she would prove her worth.

She twisted around trees, vaulting rocks and deadfall where it lay in the trail. She'd always enjoyed running through the timber, meeting the challenge of the cool green ways, ducking and dodging branches. Like the elk, she'd prided herself on the ability to pass rapidly, quietly. And like the wind, no one could keep up with Tanager when she shot through the trees like a dancing dart. Not even the most powerful men could match her fleet steps and avoid tangling in branches or crashing through like a buffalo who'd lost the trail. Here, the heart of the mountains, was Tanager's element.

As she ran, the darts clacked hollowly in her hand. White Calf's darts—a legacy of Power and courage.

"So it's done," the old woman had whispered as Tanager lifted her old head from the ground. White Calf's skin had sunk, going sallow, exposing the lines of the skull.

"White Calf?"

"Hush!" The old woman had tried to wave it away. "I don't have long. My Power will be with you, girl. Use it well. Just promise me you'll follow the Dreamer. He's coming. I can feel him. Feel him with the edges of my mind. Power's calling."

"I was afraid when I saw the whirlwind."

"Pretty good, eh? Wish I knew if I'd done that . . . or if it was just chance. Wish I could see their faces when that fool warrior tells . . . tells . . ."

"Easy. Rest easy, White Calf."

"Dreamer's coming. Dreamer . . ." And the old woman's eyes had stopped, staring in the glazed look of death as her body sagged in Tanager's arms.

Now she ran, powered by anger, driven by a will to see her darts driven through as many Short Buffalo People as she could find. Not until the last had choked to death on his blood, not until the mountains were rid of their foul feet, would she rest. Nor would she smile again until the sun set on the last of their raven-picked, coyote-ravaged flesh.

"So a Dreamer's coming?" She glared down the trail. "So is death, Short Buffalo People. And I'm bringing it."

The shouts drifted faintly through the trees. Tanager slowed, catching her breath, moving with the silence of a midnight shadow as she threaded her way through the thick stands of fir. Louder now—she placed their location.

She skirted a meadow, catching a glimpse of men moving across the grass. Before her rose a knob of rock defended by only a few, while a circling band of warriors shouted and shook fists, Dancing to their Power before they cast darts up into the rocks above.

Through the clear air, Never Sweat's voice carried as he stood resolute on the top of the outcrop. "Come and die,

Short Buffalo! You may kill us, but we'll chase the souls of your dead on past the Starweb!''

A roar of shouted insults erupted from the surrounding warriors as the attackers launched slivers of death.

Tanager's anger broke loose as she charged heedlessly into the open, sprinting across the grass, a dart already nocked in the balanced atlatl. White Calf's soul seemed to pulse through the spear thrower, throbbing, vibrant. Power ran through her, thrilling her heart as she burst into the midst of the enemy, driving a dart through a man's back as he prepared to cast at the defenders.

From the depths of her enraged soul, Tanager shouted and whirled, close enough to physically drive a dart through another. A song burst from within, echoing the anger and Power of her soul. Spirit took her, possessing her, Dancing her through the darts, making her a whirlwind of death.

As if in a haze, she fought, wheeling, releasing her darts one by one, Singing them into the bodies of her enemies. A man charged, his dart seeming to slip harmlessly past as she plucked the heavy Short Buffalo man's atlatl from her belt and cracked his skull. The rest milled around now, one cast dart missing her by a whisper to drive into another charging warrior.

The Power coursed through her veins, giving her the strength and agility to Dance away from deadly darts and close with her enemy. Her jabs and thrusts seemed to slip by their guard, bringing blood before she skipped lightly away. Pandemonium broke loose as they charged her, unable to cast their deadly missiles lest they impale their friends.

Around and through them, Tanager Danced death, her Song ringing in her ears, drowning their shouts and confusion.

Then the enemy broke, running, scattering as she pursued, aware of Never Sweat and other Red Hand following, plucking up dropped darts to cast at the backs of the Short Buffalo warriors.

Her band pursued, chasing stragglers down the trails and into the maze of timber, where they died one by one. When they ran out of darts, they smacked skulls with their atlatls.

Tanager paused, aware that the last of her victims lay groaning at her feet. She struggled for breath, trembling, as she bent to wrench an angular rock from the resisting ground. She grunted as she lifted it. The man turned, looking up, a low moan breaking his lips as he shook his head, a pleading in his eyes.

The stone cracked bone as she drove it down on his face.

In silence she stood, the forest eerily quiet, not even broken by the chirr of a squirrel. A soft wind began to sigh through the trees as she stared at the dead warrior.

Drained, she turned, lungs laboring, and slowly retraced her way. In the meadow, she stopped to pull darts from the dead, driving the keen points into the hearts of the wounded despite their whimpers and pleas for mercy.

She stood on the thick summer grass, watching Never Sweat's warriors walking out of the trees, laughing, jumping, slapping each other on the back. They went quiet as they approached, staring around at the dead, nervous, awed glances returning to her.

Where she stood over the body of a dead warrior, she reached down, placing her hand in his blood. She met their eyes, one by one, as she straightened, lifting her bloody hand to the sun.

"Once we were the Red Hand. We lost the right to that name under Blood Bear's leadership." At that, she clapped her bloody hand to her chest, letting the clotted liquid seep into Two Smokes' carefully tanned leather. "Now we are again!"

Elk Charm slashed the grass with her digging stick. The seeds shot every which way, most missing the collecting basket.

Hungry Bull saw her anger and straightened before walking over.

She crouched on her knees, head down. Mourning-shorn hair tickled at the nape of her neck. The dullness in her heart pounded against an empty soul. She barely felt Hungry Bull's hand on her shoulder.

"We've always known," he said kindly.

She shook her head. "Not like this. I never thought it would be like this." Frustrated tears burned at the corners of her eyes, flooding across to shimmer her vision. "Last night. In the robes. He wouldn't even touch me. He pushed me away. Said he couldn't . . . not with the Dream.''

She wiped at her drippy nose, and sniffed. "I don't know him anymore. I can't reach him. He's a stranger to me."

Hungry Bull settled beside her, hugging her tightly. "He's found Power. It's something beyond us. Two Smokes was telling me—''

"Two Smokes! *Two Smokes!* That's all I ever hear anymore! Two Smokes is the only one who can talk to him? I . . . I hate him! I hate it all. Maybe he'd better go with his berdache! Share his robes with *him*!''

"Hush. You don't mean that." Hungry Bull's soft voice reflected his own disquiet. "You're angry right now. Upset. Two Smokes has never been anything but kind to us all. He's showed us all how to live. When you had your babies, it was Two Smokes who sat with you all night, feeling your pain. It was Two Smokes who nursed you when you were sick that time. He loves you with all his heart. And if he'd heard you say that, you would have killed part of his soul. It's not his fault.''

She glared up at him, made more miserable by the knowledge he was right.

"There, now, this will all be over one day."

She shook her head. "I'm glad you believe so. I can feel the change. It's all through him. Like pus in a wounded deer.''

Hungry Bull sighed. "Perhaps. But he was born for it. I guess I never really thought it would be like that. I always tried to avoid Power. I never understood it. Maybe that's why White Calf left him with me. Maybe he needed to live like that.''

She looked up at him, resenting the extra time Hungry Bull had had with his son. Time she'd been excluded from. The thought shamed her. She turned her head away.

"I know. But I love him, too." Hungry Bull gestured futilely. "I've got my own sorrow. When I should have been there for him, I was locked away in my own heart. I spent too long mourning Sage Root. Drowning myself in pity when I should have been listening to his needs, helping him come to terms with the Dreams. Instead, I ran away, kept to myself." A pause. "You gave him the happiest moments of his life, you know."

"Why doesn't it feel that way?"

"Because the hurt is new. And you're making yourself suffer for what might come in the future."

"I don't see anything getting better. All he does is sit up on the ridge with that cursed wolf. When I go to talk to him, he's locked away in his head . . . Dreaming during the day. He barely eats. He won't talk except to Two Smokes. It's making me crazy."

"Two Smokes says they're going after the Wolf Bundle."

"I know."

"It's Power, Elk Charm. It's just the way it is. We can't control it. If a tree falls in the forest, it's beyond your power to set it upright again. Power is like that with Little Dancer. Power is part of the world, like the wind that blows over trees. Once it's come, it won't go back again."

"When a tree blows over, it's dead."

"Then that's one of the better things about Power. He's not dead."

"He might just as well be."

Hungry Bull lifted her chin with a callused finger, searching her eyes. "Tell me, if you could drive the Power out, and you knew it would ruin his life—like cutting off his leg—would you?"

She stared at him, the dullness spreading. "No."

"Wouldn't you be grateful he's happy? Isn't that the real meaning of love? No matter what, you've got the girls. You've had his smile and all of his love. Now he has to belong to the world and spread what he knows around. Two Smokes thinks Little Dancer can change things, stop the war. Isn't that worth something?"

For a long time she hesitated, knowing she remained powerless to stop the turmoil her life had been pitched into. "I suppose." *And I know he has to do this. To stop him would kill him. I just didn't know how badly I'd hurt.*

He smiled and winked at her. "Then come on. Let's fill these baskets and see if this scheme to make food out of grass is any good."

* * *

"Someone comes!"

The cry drew Heavy Beaver's attention from the bits of feather and bone he'd laid out on the finely tanned buffalo-cow hide before him. Across the way, Seven Suns watched curiously, massaging his wrist where the joints had started to stiffen and bite.

"I think this bodes well. The Anit'ah will be moving, trying to hide in the timber."

Seven Suns narrowed old eyes. "I think it doesn't take a Spirit Dreamer to know that. If I put myself in the Anit'ah's place, what would I do with an entire people swarming over my country?"

Heavy Beaver allowed himself a casual smile. *You dare not challenge my power now, Seven Suns. It's gone too far for that.* "You may place yourself in anyone's position you want, old friend. But remember yours." He enjoyed the stiffening of Seven Suns' lined features. The old man could have turned to stone. Only the knowing eyes remained expressive—and, of course, Seven Suns knew the reality of his situation.

Voices broke out in a babble.

"Perhaps I should see to this new disturbance?" Heavy Beaver pulled himself to his feet, irritated by the extra bulk he'd put on. A Spirit Dreamer should look prosperous, but perhaps he should move about more, watch his diet. Too much fat would be just as detrimental as too little.

He ducked through the lodge flap and straightened, watching the evening sunset falling bloodred over the mountains that rose above him. The cottonwoods rattled and chattered with the breeze while the thick stand of juniper and tall sagebrush behind the camp whispered. The Red Wall burned crimson—the color almost painful to the eye as it reflected the sunset. The broad green valley of the Red Wall stretched north and south in a delightful emerald vista of lush grass. Blocking the entire western horizon, the mountains rose as if the earth had been turned up. Limber pine and juniper dotted the slopes, leading one to believe their seed had been cast randomly by the Wise One Above. A narrow slit in the rising slope marked the sheer canyon of the middle fork of the Clear River.

Here, where once the Anit'ah had camped, the packed

lodges of the People now pointed their tops toward the sere vault of the summer-scorched sky. The dense forest of juniper and tall sage rising behind the camp crackled with drought.

The babble of voices rose. Dogs barked and yipped; the high tones of crying women added to the confusion.

Heavy Beaver turned his steps toward the commotion, rounding a lodge to find a knot of people bearing a warrior. Straight Wood! He recognized the young man the crowd supported. The warrior's head hung low, one leg hitched up painfully as he hobbled.

"What has happened?" Heavy Beaver stopped, shrugging so his white buffalo-hide cape would sit regally on his shoulders.

Straight Wood swallowed hard, raising his head. Pain racked his pale face. Sweat streaked his clothing and glistened in a sheen on his pallid skin. Looking closely, Heavy Beaver could make out the bloodstains on the young man's legs. Despite the crowd of anxious people supporting his weight, flies seemed to home in on the wound.

"Spirit Dreamer." Straight Wood gulped at his dry throat and shivered.

"Get him some water. Place him on a robe so he can relax. Someone get him food."

Heavy Beaver watched while the others led Straight Wood to a lodge and placed him on a hurriedly provided robe. After food and water were provided, the People crowded around until Heavy Beaver ordered them back, the word "Dreamer" still echoing in his mind.

"Now you're safe. Tell us what's happening."

Straight Wood looked up, a crazy light in his eyes. "We captured an Anit'ah woman. She escaped and killed Two Blue Moons and Tiny Ant. We tracked her and came to a rock overhang like the Anit'ah live in. An old woman sat out front. She told us to leave or die. Left Hand darted her and the woman we'd captured ran. I went to see about the old woman. She wasn't dead. It was . . ."

"Yes, yes, go on."

"It was the old witch . . . White Calf."

A gasp went up from the people.

Heavy Beaver grimaced, waving them down. "This isn't trouble. I Cursed her to die long ago. She was Powerful. It took warriors I had personally blessed to kill her." He smiled sleepily as he turned. "You see, my people. Not even a Powerful witch can stand before the Dreaming of Heavy Beaver."

"Then you'd better Dream harder," Straight Wood gasped.

"She didn't die?" Heavy Beaver turned, glaring down at the youth, putting all his malice into the expression.

Straight Wood glared back. "She died . . . I think."

"You *think*?"

Straight Wood swallowed hard, sweat-shiny throat working. "I didn't stay long enough to find out. The Anit'ah woman killed Left Hand, Quick Fall, Firm Dart, and all the others. The old woman sat there, looking like she'd triumphed. She told me that we'd brought about the death of the People. She said, 'Fool! With my death you've spat upon Power for the last time.' "

People gasped again, some taking a step back, hands over their mouths.

Heavy Beaver chuckled. "So, you'll have us believe that one woman killed all these brave warriors?" He laughed again, reading the effect of his scorn on the rest of the People. He had their attention now. "*Fool* is right!" He shook his head. "Straight Wood, tell us the truth now. You fought a party of Anit'ah warriors, didn't you? You became frightened and ran, didn't you?"

A burning hatred rose in a bile to charge Straight Wood's eyes. "You call *me* a coward? Then listen, Heavy Beaver. Listen good, all of you!"

"Enough of this." Heavy Beaver stifled a forced yawn. "I think we know the full truth of it."

"You listen, Heavy Beaver! *Listen!*" Straight Wood struggled up, almost falling as fresh blood broke out to leak down his leg.

This was really too much. Heavy Beaver motioned to two of the old men. "Get him to rest. He's fevered."

"White Calf told me, 'You're the last. Run now. Run like you've never run before, boy. Tell Heavy Beaver that a new leader has risen among the Anit'ah. *Her* name is Tanager. And tell Heavy Beaver that a Dreamer . . . and the Wolf Bundle are coming for him. Tell him, and all the People, they'll have to Dance with Fire!'"

Heavy Beaver had made two steps before stopping and laughing. "What's this? A woman? *A woman?* You expect me . . . and all the People to believe that a woman will drive my warriors out of the mountains?"

Straight Wood extended trembling hands, eyes pleading. "You refuse to hear me out. You accuse *me* of cowardice. Then know this. I ran from White's Calf's. But I thought I'd been foolish. I found Has Strength where he'd trapped a party of Anit'ah in the rocks. There I proved myself. I killed one of the Anit'ah and started to charge their position when this same woman appeared in the middle of our warriors. She killed right and left. Darts wouldn't touch her. She Danced and Sang with a strange smile while—"

"Enough!" Heavy Beaver roared, waving his hands. "We'll hear the rest of this when Has Strength's warriors—"

"You'll wait a long time," Straight Wood cried. "He's dead! So's most of his war party. She gave heart to the Anit'ah and they charged down from the rocks. We couldn't stop them! They came and came and came until we ran. You hear that, Heavy Beaver? *We all ran!"*

Heavy Beaver shook his head. "Routed by a woman?" He smacked his lips, adopting a pained expression. "Take him away. He's out of his mind. Delirious with pain."

Straight Wood lifted his bloody shirt, exposing the wounds in his side. "You know so much, Heavy Beaver. You've seen wounds. You look. You know the difference in how a dart goes in and comes out. I took this facing a man."

"You see?" Heavy Beaver pointed. "No wonder he's delirious. Poor man. Take him away. I'll come Sing over him later, try and bring him back to his right mind."

Straight Wood snorted disgust, sinking slowly to the ground, lungs working. "And I'll tell you another thing I saw. I saw White Calf's ghost rise into the air. You've all heard the stories. Her ghost called a whirlwind and rode into the sky.

"And maybe I was a coward." Straight Wood worked his dry mouth. "But after what I've seen, Heavy Beaver, you'd better hope you can Dance with Fire. I know truth. I saw it in White Calf's eyes."

Heavy Beaver's eyes slitted. "You'd better be right, boy,

because lying simply to scare the People and cover your own cowardice will bring down a more terrible fate than an An-it'ah dart!''

And he stomped away, breaking through the ring of surrounding people who watched him, intently.

The fires glowed with reddened eyes in the night. A thin sandstone slab had been placed over each glowing pit of coals. On the surface of the rock, grass seeds had been milled into a paste and turned into patties and roasted on the dry heat. Faint wraiths of steam rose in the ruby light of the hearths, filling the air with a delicious aroma. Two Smokes shifted his attention from one fire to another. Here, at last, he could feel the solution to the problem that had preoccupied him for years. At the same time, he tried to absorb what Cricket and the others related.

The people had begun arriving the morning before, talking of the war in the mountains. They came in ones and twos or strings of up to five, walking with their dogs and packs. Women and children, elders, and youths too young to fight. Each had a similar story about surprised camps, of token resistance and flight.

Now they sat, talking in low voices to Rattling Hooves and Hungry Bull. Meadowlark and Black Crow listened on one side while Three Toes and Makes Fun hovered over another fire pit, lifting boiling stones to drop into the water, heating an elk-paunch boiling bag full of root stew.

Firelight danced on tired faces, some of the fugitives simply staring into the flames, the weariness and despair of their souls reflected in the slack expressions. Some fumbled with uneasy fingers, legs crossed, looking around at the camp, at the overhanging rock wall that caught the light or out into the darkness, minds disengaged. Throughout the assemblage, worry and defeat seemed the constant thread. He saw a people undone, lost, unable to understand.

Two Smokes cast a quick look at Little Dancer. The Dreamer sat, half listening, eyes focused on a point out beyond the fire, as if wonderful forms wove themselves from the very night. The big black wolf sat at his side, ears pricked as he watched the dogs snuffling around the perimeter of the camp. Even the dogs seemed cowed, unwilling to challenge the wolf, their canine natures as baffled as those of their masters.

Elk Charm looked miserable where she cradled the youngest baby to her breast. Her stare slipped to the refugees, to Cricket who'd been her friend, and to the others with whom she'd lived, and inevitably back to her husband. Through the atmosphere of gloom, Two Smokes could sense her preoccupation and frustration.

Rattling Hooves saw to distributing the stew among the hungry visitors. Hungry Bull continued to listen, waiting politely while his guests ate, a pensive look on his lean face. Preoccupied, he stroked his chin.

Finally, Cricket laid her bowl to the side and belched loud and long to demonstrate her appreciation for the food. She clasped her hands in her lap, looking at Rattling Hooves and then, with some suspicion, at Hungry Bull. "We have come here. Tanager suggested it. What do we do?"

Hungry Bull stood, taking the center of attention. "I've heard your words. I've also read the suspicion in your eyes. I would tell you that you are welcome with us. I think we can feed most of you for as long as you stay. Two Smokes has found the secret of the grass, which will give us a new food. The grass is everywhere."

"And what about your ties with the Short Buffalo People?" One Cast rose from where he sat at the edge of the camp. His old eyes glittered in the firelight; grief still marked his face.

Hungry Bull gestured resignation. "We are no longer Short Buffalo. We are something else, a different band . . . neither Short Buffalo nor Red Hand. We, too, have fled Heavy Beaver and his Dreams."

"He is no Dreamer," Little Dancer whispered from the side. "He isn't of the One. He has perverted the Spiral."

People glanced at him, curiosity mixed with wariness.

"As I was saying, One Cast, we are different. We have no ties with those who were once our relatives. You are all welcome with us. Our camp is yours for as long as you wish. Already your children and ours are playing, enjoying each other's company. I think there is a lesson to be learned from our children.''

One Cast bowed his head, steely eyes on Hungry Bull's. "And if the Short Buffalo come down the mountain?"

Hungry Bull gestured to the west. "We'll leave. The Fish Eaters live across the basin and only—"

"Short Buffalo have been known to hunt in the basin."

"But the buffalo have left," Hungry Bull countered. "Only one or two small herds live down there now. With the drought, they've moved down along the Mountain Sheep River. I hunted out there once as a young boy. I know that the grass Two Smokes has made food from is thick out there. And to the south lies the Warm Wind Basin. More mountains are beyond those. Somewhere we will find a place for our people.''

"My grandfather's bones are here," One Cast added. "You ask me to leave this place?"

Hungry Bull shook his head. "No. I only tell you what our people will do if Heavy Beaver brings his war here. We're not warriors. We're hunters and collectors of plants. That's all.''

Little Dancer stood. "You will not leave the mountains. Tomorrow I go to reclaim the Wolf Bundle. The time of Fire has come. The Spiral has come full. I go to Dance the One, to restore the Circles. To do so will set the Spiral back. Heavy Beaver must be faced by a more powerful Dream. Fire must have its way. The time has come.''

He smiled at something inside his head and walked through the firelit center of the camp, raising his hands to the night sky.

People watched silently, eyes wide. Wolf rose and followed Little Dancer into the darkness, taking the path to the rimrock.

"Ah!" One Cast exhaled with amazement. "Then it's true. He *is* a Dreamer?"

Elk Charm wilted, biting her lower lip. She fled from her spot, ducking through the hangings and into her shelter. Cricket got quickly to her feet, parting the hangings and stepping inside.

Two Smokes sighed and stood. "He is a Dreamer. He's a Dreamer like the Red Hand haven't seen for many years." He filled his lungs, then told the story of Clear Water and the Wolf Bundle. With great deliberation, he recited the whole story of Little Dancer's life, of the Curse of Heavy Beaver, of White Calf's attempts to train him, of the Dreams and frustrations. Finally he told of the vision.

"Little Dancer climbed the mountain to find a high place. There a snake bit him and his leg swelled. For four days, he waited, dying, until Wolf Dreamer appeared from sunlight."

"You know this?" One Cast asked.

Two Smokes nodded. "I am berdache. I felt the Power in his words. Together, Little Dancer and First Man Dreamed the poison from his leg. You can see the punctures still red and inflamed on his ankle. I myself have heard the Wolf Bundle calling. Little Dancer was changed. He Dreamed the Dance. He has told me a new leader has arisen among the Red Hand—a warrior who will break the strength of the Short Buffalo People. And when that happens, Little Dancer will meet Heavy Beaver and Dream the Spirals back so the world doesn't end in drought and our brothers, the buffalo and antelope, won't be hunted to extinction as our ancestors hunted the monsters."

"Then"—Hungry Bull's face worked—"you'll leave with my son?"

Two Smokes turned, placing a hand on Hungry Bull's shoulder, knowing intuitively the man's sudden worry and pain, and nodded. "Soon we will go."

"Then I'll put my pack together tonight. I'll go with you."

"No."

"But he's my son!"

"Hungry Bull, my longtime friend. He's not your son. You only raised him and loved him. He's the child of Power. Power will guide him now." Two Smokes gestured to the people. "You have never wished to meddle with Power and its ways. Here, before you, is your responsibility. These people need a leader. These people need you. Camps must be prepared. Food must be gathered. More Red Hand will be coming in the next weeks. This winter, you must feed them all."

Hungry Bull shook his head, baffled. "But if the Short Buffalo are going to be broken, if Heavy Beaver will be . . . I don't understand."

"Yes, you do, old friend. During this war, no food has been cached. Camps have been destroyed. Little Dancer didn't tell me the whole of it, but I know enough of his words to tell you the Red Hand would starve in the high camps this year. They must move lower. Power has its ways. We came here for a reason. The secret of the grass came to me when it did for a reason. Trust your old friend, Two Smokes."

Hungry Bull licked his lips, a desperate frown on his forehead.

"But my son . . ."

"*I* will care for him. All my life, I've been prepared for this journey. We'll do what we can."

Hungry Bull fought to find the words, and only stared.

"Come, let us try these cakes we've made of milled seed. From the grass, we now take life."

Hungry Bull knotted his fists and remained standing, a stunned expression on his face.

He sat still, eyes closed, seeking. A subtle panic built and swelled within. The One lay there, just beyond reach.

The night pulsed with life, with the feeling of the One that twined around and through. Insect wings beat the air, a coyote yipped in the distance. A soft sound came from the night breezes through the juniper. Air drifted coolly across his hot face. The rock bit angrily into his flesh. A gurgle of hunger churned in his gut. Memories of voices clamored for recognition. Faces around the fire hovered new and exciting at the edges of his mind.

Fire Dancer stilled his thoughts, battling with the words and images that crept up to distract him. The Wolf Bundle beckoned, its Power drifting away like water from a punctured bag, one drip at a time.

I'm coming! Fire Dancer called, seeking to trace a way through his jumbled emotions. Elk Charm's face formed before him. The look of anguish she gave him shattered the serenity he sought.

I'm hurting her. It's my fault that she's miserable. How can I bring so much pain to someone I love? Hurting her only hurts me worse. WHY AM I DOING THIS TO MYSELF . . . TO THE ONES I LOVE?

The link he sought popped away, vanished like mist in the sun. The One beckoned, its Power shining, alluring, irresistible. Frantic, he reached out, and grasped nothing. The One remained, hovering, elusive as a spiral of smoke that can be smelled but never felt.

The way had been so easy when Wolf Dreamer had taken him to Dance. He'd experienced the thundering silence, the unity and disharmony. He'd gloried—and felt nothing. The call strengthened, drawing him on, like a man suffering of thirst while the river retreated just beyond his fingertips.

It was so easy! I just took Wolf Dreamer's hand and crossed. Why can't I do that now? Why do I get so close— only to lose it to illusion?

He settled himself again, blanking his mind, driving the deceptions of illusion from his concentration. Stillness, quiet, he stretched his mind and soul, forgetting the world around him. The One hovered closer, the sweetness of it caressing his very soul like the radiant warmth of a fire on a cold night. He sought the flames, extending himself in an effort to encompass.

Laughter drifted up on the still air, carrying the emotions of the people. The image burst.

The panic within him spread. The One lay so close—yet so far away.

To drop the thresholds was so easy. I did it. I can do it again. Just let go, drift around the One. He imagined Wolf Dreamer's hand in his. His fingers tightened on nothingness until his muscles trembled, pain eating into his concentration. *No, not that way. That's a false trial. Another illusion to trap you.*

In the back of his mind, a voice reminded. "The time is now. You must go and Dream. You must. You must. . . ."

He clamped his eyes closed, desperation bottled within his burning breast. "What if I can't?"

Panic burned free until he collapsed in tears.

* * *

Morning had begun to cast a muddy yellow haze across the implacable wall of the mountains to the east. The mighty crags of rock stood resolute, impervious to the light. A giant black wall, it rose, irregular and jagged, to block the coming of the sun.

Like my soul, Elk Charm thought.

She climbed the last bit of steep trail, stepping out onto the cap rock in the chill morning air. A robin called plaintively in the predawn. Already a knot of people stood uncomfortably, their forms contrasting with the puffy shapes of the juniper and rabbitbrush. To one side, Little Dancer sat crosslegged, staring out to the east, hands in his lap, eyes closed, face expressionless.

Gravel grated on the rock underfoot. She forced her muscles to work, walking awkwardly as if to spite her natural grace. Cricket's feet scuffed the rock behind her. She hadn't slept that night. Instead, they'd talked of love and life and pain. Did anything else exist in this world?

Her heart beat dully in her chest as she stopped, staring at her husband. Memories of his smiles, his jokes and uncertainties whirled through her mind. And it had all come to this?

He's the hope of the people—Red Hand and Short Buffalo. He's got to go. He's got to. He's a Power warrior, fighting for his world. She shook her head, remembering how Two Smokes had warned her. Cricket's tales of fear and death only strengthened the knowledge that his time had come. *I must let go. I have to free him. But why does it hurt so much?*

As if he heard, Little Dancer opened his eyes, turning his head to look at her. He rose to his feet. Wolf appeared magically at his side, following as he approached. The others might not have existed as he came to stand before her. The sight of his tortured features, of the desperation, sliced her composure with the keenness of sharp obsidian.

What tormented him so? What terror gave him that look of anguish? The curb on her emotions broke and she threw her arms around him, hugging him tightly. His arms went around her.

"I'm sorry," he whispered in her ear. "You'll understand one day."

"Maybe I understand now. Go, Little Dancer. Dream the world back to normal. I'll Sing for you. Chant. Do anything I . . . by the Wise One, I'm so proud of you it hurts."

"I love you. I'll never stop loving you. Maybe, well, it's my strength in the Dream. I had to know love, be willing to give up everything for it. You've given me the greatest of gifts."

"We'll be waiting. Your girls, all of us. Come back."

"If I can."

And he pulled away.

Dry-eyed, she stared up at him, seeing the pain in his eyes. Slowly she shook her head. "I'll be waiting for you. For as long as it takes. Forever."

His smile warmed her soul despite the chill.

He stepped back, turning to Cricket, who held his youngest daughter. He reached where the child slept in Cricket's arms, and touched the little girl's forehead, the caress as tender as a spring breeze on a fawn's hide. A delighted smile curled his daughter's lips and a gurgle erupted.

Next, Little Dancer settled where their oldest daughter stood, an uncertain thumb in her mouth.

"You will be good? You will mind your mother and grow to be as beautiful?"

She nodded curtly and rushed into his arms. "Don' go. Don' leave me!"

"I must, little one. The Power calls." He bent to kiss her on the top of the head and her tears dried, lit by a smile.

"Tha's good."

"That's the Power, little one. Take it with you."

And he stood, a tear leaving a trail along his cheek. "This is so hard."

Elk Charm's stomach knotted as if she'd been kicked.

"Come," Two Smokes said gently, stepping out of the crowd. "We've a long way to go."

Elk Charm's protests died in her throat. Silently, she watched as Two Smokes and Little Dancer took the trail to the east.

"As long as it takes," she whispered.

She barely realized her daughter had clutched her hand, hugging her leg. A wailing rose within. Despite the promises, her eyes swelled with tears, shimmering her vision so he walked away in a silver mist.

Chapter 24 ◎

Tanager watched the sunset, gazing at the magnificent swell of blaze-orange cloud that glowed with the dying day's light. The sky overhead had turned a forever shade of cerulean blue in contrast to the gaudy colors of the sky. The land below her position might have been touched by fire as the crimson rays of light diffused from the spectacular sky.

"A world aflame," she mused, before forcing herself to tear her eyes away from the marvel and make another inspection of the surrounding country. Enemy war parties might be anywhere, skulking through the trees. Prior to the fading of last light, any dangerous parties of warriors must be located. Tanager couldn't allow another surprise attack. In the intervening weeks, she'd led her growing band successfully. They'd tracked enemy parties, ambushing them, scattering the prowling Short Buffalo warriors as more and more of the Red Hand retreated to Rattling Hooves and the camps there.

Below her in the rocks, her warriors settled in for the night, cookfires carefully screened, smoke rising on the still night air so as not to alert raiders. This camp couldn't be surprised. Scouts lay out, pending the night along the trails to raise the alarm.

As she turned her attention to the remarkable sky again, she couldn't banish the thought that they'd already lost. Despite her courage and the will she instilled in her warriors, they remained so few against so many.

"Then here I'll die," she promised as she had so many times before. "This land is mine. Given to us by First Man."

So she'd resigned herself. Absently, she ran long fingers over the atlatl, feeling the Power of it, knowing White Calf's soul had truly gone into the weapon. When she fought, she Danced and Sang, and called that Power forth. With it, she remained invincible. Her daring feats had broken more than one heated fight. Where she Danced inviolate, her warriors followed, stirring their own courage to a raging heat.

Darts ghosted by her, leaving her untouched. The enemy stood dumbfounded, refusing to believe a woman would kill them as she bashed their skulls or drove her darts into their bodies. She'd chosen carefully, finding a rock, shaping it, and binding it to the atlatl shaft she'd taken from Two Blue Moons to fashion a war club just right for her balance and strength.

Already her fame had spread as Red Hand warriors came seeking her camp.

As she watched, the burning clouds reddened, enraged by the setting sun. "So is my world maddened. Like fire, my anger pushes me. So the Short Buffalo People feel my heat— the burning of Tanager's soul."

Without thinking, she raised her hands to the towering clouds that shot flame through the sky. Did her eyes deceive her, or did she see the form of a man staring at her with blazing eyes?

"Give me the anger and strength to drive the Short Buffalo from my lands. Hear me, First Man. Hear the plea of Tanager. Give me the weapon to drive these beasts from the lands of your Red Hand!"

A low rumble of thunder rolled across the land.

As quickly, the color in the clouds faded, going dark and drab.

She lowered her hands, wondering. Turning, she scrutinized the timber again, searching the meadows and the fringes of forest. So dry. No matter that the clouds had piled high, no rain had fallen. Where she could look over the basins, they remained sere and dry, a land parched. Even here, high in the Buffalo Mountains, the timber was desiccated, and the few night fires they allowed themselves guarded carefully lest the sparks fall upon the dry grass or settle in the branches of the desperate trees.

"A land that cries," she whispered, lowering herself amid crumbling grasses. "And the Red Hand cry with the land."

The buffalo had become more numerous, climbing from

the heat-cracked basins, seeking the water and grass of the high country. So the Short Buffalo lived off the land, as did her warriors. But what of winter? What of the food that men and women should even now be caching? Who could prepare when warfare raged and parties fought in the shadows of the trees?

She shook her head, a gloom settling with the fall of darkness.

Wiggling around the rocks, she wrapped her hide tight against the dry chill of the night. She'd seen no movement. The scouts had made no report. This night, they should rest secure before sending more parties out in the morning, blood and anger in their hearts as they cut for tracks. Where they should have been hunting balsam and sego lily, now they hunted men.

Weary, she allowed the tension and anger to drain from her fatigued muscles. Heat lightning flickered in the tall mass of clouds to the west.

She huddled in her robe, willing her eyes to close, willing sleep to come.

And with it, the Dream . . .

Blood Bear led the way. Behind him, the remains of his band ducked through the tinder-dry timber, stepping cautiously over deadfall, moccasins crackling on the dry needles. Dusk loomed overhead, lit only by the striking sunset they could catch a glimpse of through the somber trees.

Snaps Horn and the others followed him blindly, led by the knowledge that he carried the Wolf Bundle. Even through so many setbacks, so many deaths and defeats, their spirit remained loyal to the tiny bundle of hide.

Fools! Couldn't they see the silly thing had no Power? Blood Bear clutched the Bundle to his sweaty chest. Nevertheless, without it, his hold over the Red Hand would have eroded long ago. Even though he was Keeper of the Bundle, men and women had begun to look sideways at him, skepticism in their eyes.

He, the greatest warrior of the Red Hand, remained powerless to stop the advance of the Short Buffalo People. Even with the Bundle in his possession, more and more of his warriors trickled away into the timber, following the path south to this new leader, this Tanager.

Tanager? That skinny girl who haunted the canyons and ran wild through the meadows? What could she possibly know of war? Of the men who'd bedded her, most said she remained aloof, and none had planted a child in her muscular loins. Granted, for a woman, she had strength and balance. None could Dance as well as Tanager. But she'd been so odd. Even the charms of her body had eluded Blood Bear. Around her, he'd been uneasy, as if she knew too much. Who wanted a woman who could move through the trees with more craft than he, who could throw a dart with such accuracy?

He grunted to himself. And perhaps that was her secret in warfare? That she never missed?

The challenge of her rising status simply couldn't be ignored. Blood Bear's resentment had been stirred when talk centered around her, and a curious light began to fill the people's eyes. The Red Hand could afford no other leader than he when it came to this war with the Short Buffalo. Who better to lead them than Blood Bear, who'd survived for years alone in the land of the enemy? Who understood their ways better?

No matter. He knew where Tanager operated, cutting off the trails available to the enemy. He had only to confront her, perhaps bed her to show her his mastery, and her following would fly apart like cattail down in the wind.

He smiled to himself, thumping the Wolf Bundle with his thumb as he walked.

Heavy Beaver stalked the camp, hearing the subtle talk of the People, muffled now by the lodges. What could he do? He batted at a mosquito that hummed eerily about his head. The bones of the Clear River stood out in the channel where the crystal water wound around the rocks. Behind him, the Red Wall glared gaudy in the light of the burning clouds high above the Buffalo Mountains. Like fire, they reflected the sunset. Shades of pink, red, yellow, and orange glared against the incredible blue of the sky.

The lush valley they'd entered had withered brown under the lack of rain—as if by camping here, they'd condemned the grasses and plants. Only for a moment did Heavy Beaver let the thought bother him.

"Is that fire up there?" someone asked, stepping out of a lodge and staring west.

"Only the sunset of the Anit'ah," another called—but the joke didn't carry any humor.

And there lay the crux of his problem. Straight Wood had taken two days to die, during the last of which he lay in delirium, spouting on about White Calf the witch and her unsettling prophecy.

Heavy Beaver had Sung over his fevered body, nauseated by the pus that dribbled from the man's side. The smell had been terrible, that of punctured gut and putrefaction. No matter that he'd been locked away in a lodge at the edge of camp, Straight Wood's shrieks and dire warnings could be heard all through the night.

"White Calf," Heavy Beaver whispered under his breath. "Still trouble, even in death."

He swatted another mosquito, wishing he could so easily crush the rumors that circulated, undermining his authority. Viciously, he ground the dead insect between his fingers.

No matter that he'd claimed that Straight Wood was possessed by an evil spirit, the people still doubted. The news of a terrible female warrior had been carried down from the mountains. And with it came stories of his warriors being cut to pieces, routed by her ferocity and Power. Already some of the women had developed a spark in their eyes, a resentment in their actions. More than one had been beaten bloody because of their flippant remarks.

So how did he regain mastery of the situation?

"Mother?" He looked up at the sky. "What would you do? What would you tell me?"

In the still air, nothing came to him.

Memories of the Blessing returned to stalk his mind. When the drums boomed and the people Sang, he could almost hear. If only the words didn't elude him. But that had been a different time—the Power of the People unchallenged. When he walked among them now, he could still see respect in their eyes, but another feeling now lay hidden in their thoughts: doubt.

Why now? Meat came down the trail in a constant stream. More than enough had been dried, cured for winter by the women and youths. His warriors continued to loot the prize lands of the Anit'ah. He could have recalled his men and sent small camps out to kill those last herds of buffalo along the major rivers. He could rest assured in his Power, in the vision his mother had dreamed.

The buffalo would come back. He'd cleansed the People of the taint of women. Buffalo Above would see their humility and lift the drought, bringing his children to fertility. The buffalo would continue so long as the People remained untainted. Mother had told him that as a young boy.

So why keep whittling away at the Anit'ah? the voice of reason demanded.

"Because they stood before us. Denied us the land which is ours. Because they *defied* me!" He raised a clenched fist to the mountain wall.

The drums of the Blessing remained in his memory, pounding their message of unity and the Power of the People. They'd been together then, untainted by the evil prophecy of a dying witch.

He stopped, staring up at the fire in the clouds, remembering the way the huge bonfires of the Blessing had even masked the light of the Starweb.

"Yes. A Blessing. A way to purify the taint of Straight Wood's possessed soul."

He smiled blandly at the sky, thankful for the sign his mother had sent him. He could reaffirm the Power of the People, make them one again. Together they'd Dance away the taint of Straight Wood's prophecy—and the witch White Calf at the same time.

He smacked a pudgy fist into a palm before slapping another mosquito. Already he could hear the drums, feel the Power of the Dancing People. The women could be shown their place.

The Power of Heavy Beaver would be renewed. And maybe, just perhaps, he could understand his mother's words this time if he purified himself, sweated and fasted.

"Thank you, Mother," he whispered to the dying hues in the clouds. He'd need some time for preparation, of course.

He couldn't recall the war parties from the mountain and leave their back exposed. To do so might give heart to the Anit'ah. But if runners went up to tell them the People Danced a Blessing, perhaps they at last might see the end of the Anit'ah.

Fire Dancer led the way up the rocky trail behind White Calf's shelter, called by something beyond. The huge black wolf whined softly, warning. Muscles rippled along the animal's flanks as it fixed piercing eyes on Fire Dancer. Why? What did it know?

The western horizon blazed in a glory of light as the sunset illuminated the clouds. The color stopped them as they reached the crest of the trail. Was it imagination, or did a man's form stare at them out of the packed thunderhead? A shiver played down Two Smokes' spine; a feeling of Power filled the air about them. Some terrible worry betrayed itself in Fire Dancer's posture as he looked up at the radiant clouds, eyes on the shining face that had formed from the cloud mass.

The anxiety had been growing as they climbed the trails and cut through the valleys. Fire Dancer rarely spoke, locked away in his preoccupation and worry.

Then to have found White Calf's shelter empty, and a bloodstain in the soil, had added to the premonition.

Two Smokes hobbled up and stopped, following Fire Dancer's gaze. The old woman lay on her back, illuminated by the vermilion tones cast by the enflamed clouds. Already the coyotes and ravens had been at work. White splotches streaked her clothing where the ravens had evacuated. The flesh had been eaten from her face and feet. Despite the ravaging of her gut, the fatal dart shaft still stuck up to the sky.

"No!" The cry tore from Fire Dancer's throat.

An aching hollowness yawned within as Two Smokes hitched his way forward—pain forgotten in his tortured knee. He stopped at the edge of the stone circle, seeing how someone had propped White Calf's head on the central cairn, facing her to the west so her soul could watch the setting sun. Wisps of gray hair fluttered around the wreckage of her skull.

She'd been dead for some days. Now her exposed teeth

glinted in the bloody light. The empty sockets of her eyes gaped at the sunset. Her death rictus mocked the dying day.

Two Smokes wavered on his feet, catching the odor of decay and raven feces. He seemed to hang over an abyss, a portion of his soul torn away to disappear with the wind.

Fire Dancer walked up to stand beside him, the strength of his grief buffeting Two Smokes' already tortured soul. The black wolf whimpered, a keening note in its plaintive voice.

"I thought the People didn't believe in killing their own through violence." The thought surfaced and Two Smokes had to say something.

"They've lost their way," Fire Dancer whispered. "Others must pay."

"They'll pay," Two Smokes gritted. "They'll pay in the end. You'll Dream them all away, into the ground, to be locked forever in blackness."

Two Smokes shuddered at the weight of Fire Dancer's hand on his shoulder. The soft voice soothed something in his rent soul.

"Do you kill children for foolishness? Do you destroy them because they've no parent?"

Two Smokes clamped his eyes shut, trying to block the memory, to ignore the scent of death in his nostrils. "Is that what we are? Parents?"

"Perhaps. Maybe a better word is teacher."

Two Smokes blinked to clear his vision and looked at Fire Dancer, awed at the feeling of loss. The man stood, staring, an incredible sorrow in his anguished expression. Had so much of Fire Dancer died with White Calf?

"I wanted to come talk to her, to see if she knew a way for me. I . . ." He shook his head. "The path to the One is so difficult, Two Smokes. Illusion is real to us. It's powerful—so hard to deny. Once I lay dying in the snow, and I freed myself. Then I lay dying of snakebite, and the barriers in the soul lowered to let me Dream the One. I had a guide each time. Don't you understand? *I had a guide!*"

Fire Dancer swallowed and lowered his eyes, a sag to his shoulders. "What if I can't Dream it? What if the illusion blinds me? I'm . . . so unsure."

"You counted on White Calf?"

"She knew so much."

"When her soul went free, something wonderful left the world." The knot in Two Smokes' throat tightened. "She was my friend. She, of all the people I've known, understood me best."

"Grief is an illusion," Fire Dancer repeated under his breath. "Only illusion."

"And if it fills you when you try to Dream?"

"Then it may kill us all." He turned away then, walking wearily back toward the trail that led down to the valley, and suddenly collapsed, sinking to his knees. He cupped his face in his hands. "I feel so lost."

"But you've Dreamed the One."

Fire Dancer hunched as if against a blow. "I've Dreamed. Yes, I've Dreamed the One. But, Two Smokes, why do you think I sat up on the ridge? I've tried, and tried and tried. I can't do it on my own. Don't you see?

"Imagine a mountain in front of you, and you can see a fire at the top. You stand in darkness, bathed only by the light of the fire, but you can't see the trails. The mountain is illusion, and you don't know the paths through it. So you start up, and find your way blocked by rock. You go back, and start again, and that way is blocked by deadfall, but you get higher, closer to the light. Each time you go back and retrace, finding your way around dead ends, and each time you get farther—but I've never found the path to the top, and each of the dead ends is always there, ready to block you again if you forget the way around it.

"Worst of all, it's cold at the bottom of the mountain. I want to feel the fire, experience the warmth. That drives me, makes me more desperate. The more I want it, the farther light is away, the more impossible to reach the summit. People think to Dance the One you just spread your wings and fly—but you have to walk, take each step up the path of illusion.

"And I haven't found the way yet by myself. At the camp, Elk Charm, or my daughters, or Hungry Bull . . . something blocked me. Even my own doubts."

"But you Dreamed the One!"

"Yes!" he cried. "Wolf Dreamer came to me. I almost

had to die to reach that threshold! Can't you see? I'm my own worst enemy! It's not Heavy Beaver or Blood Bear . . . it's *me* that I have to defeat!''

"Maybe Wolf Dreamer will come to you when you need. Power can't just throw its tools away like a silly old woman does a flake after she's cut—"

"But it can." With fevered eyes he glanced at Two Smokes. "I don't know, call it a feeling, but it's not just Wolf Dreamer, or Power, or what they'd wish. It's me. *I'm* important. *I* have to dream the Spiral back. And I can feel it, like that sensation you get when a grizzly bear is watching. I have to make it to the One on my own. It's within me. My free will—if you want to think of it that way.''

"There's also the Wolf Bundle."

"How do I use it? I can feel it, but it's like the One. It hovers out there, locked in Spirit Power, and it's dying. Ever since that day Heavy Beaver threw it into the dark, it's been dying. What if so much of the Power has drifted away that it's like an old man, incapable of casting a dart?''

Two Smokes ripped his attention from the gruesome corpse. "And if the Wolf Bundle can't help?"

Fire Dancer's shoulders rose and fell. "Then I don't know what I'll do.'' He stared up at the garish sunset. "These past days, I've been haunted—seeing the love in Elk Charm's eyes. I long to hold my daughters, to see them play. I want to hear Hungry Bull laugh at Black Crow's jokes, enjoy Three Toes whistling like a bird.

"Now, when I close my eyes, I'll see White Calf's corpse, feel the grief twisting inside like a rabbit on a stick. Do you know what that means? What if I can't control my will? What if I can't find the path by the time I need it? What then? I only know I can do it. I can touch the One. Once I'm there, I can Dance the world without getting lost. But can I climb the mountain when I need to? *I need more time!*''

Tanager woke before sunrise. She lay curled in her hide, body stiff as if she'd run and fought all through the long night. Desperately thirsty, she worked her tongue around the dryness of her mouth, grimacing at the sour taste.

Flames. The image of the Dream stayed with her. Spirit

Power had come and she couldn't forget her appeal to the clouds at sunset the night before.

She sat up, stiff muscles twinging, and looked out at the predawn light graying the east. Yes, it would work. The Dream had shown her the way. Hunger gnawed at the pit of her stomach. She ran a fist across her rheumy eyes and stood, shaking out her hide before pulling it over her shoulder and picking up her pouch.

For the moment, she sat on one of the rocks, watching as the morning broke clear and cool. The dry air massaged her as the breeze rose up the canyon. Hunters knew that breeze. Rising in morning, falling back down the canyons with the night. She sniffed, enjoying the odor of the firs and dry grass.

"Only someone driven by anger could do what I must." She relived the images of the Dream, seeing the way. She needed only to revive those terrible memories of Short Buffalo warriors throwing themselves on her to rekindle the burning rage.

She watched as the sun rose to crest the peaks, illuminating the meadows with golden light. Already cookfires burned dry wood, the faint smoke dissipating through the trees.

Confident that no enemy lurked near, Tanager started down the steep slope, hesitating only long enough to strip a bit of fir bark and a handful of needles. With a thumbnail, she pressed the inside of the bark, learning what she needed to know. In one fist, she crumbled the needles.

Walking into camp, she greeted her warriors with jokes and spirit. A feeling of freedom blew through her soul with the biting freshness of a spring storm.

"Ramshorn? I want you and Hanging Rock to do something for me. You'll have to move fast. Each of you takes a different direction."

"How many people do we need?" Ramshorn trotted over to hunker down on his haunches.

"As few as possible. Last night, up on the mountain, I had a Dream. I know a way for us to survive."

She grinned at the sparkle that lit his eyes. "A Dream? A Power Dream?"

She nodded, feeling the certainty bursting within. "A Power Dream. A message from the Spirit World."

Ramshorn pulled at his ear and nodded. "What do you need?"

With swift fingers, she cleared a spot in the dirt and began lining out her strategy.

"Blood Bear!"

The call came from his right. He turned, seeing Warm Wind rise from behind a deadfall, darts in hand, another nocked in his atlatl.

"Warm Wind? What are you doing hiding like that?"

The young man walked carefully out of the timber, grinning. "You've brought the Wolf Bundle. We're whole again! But you ask what I do? I guard the trail. If you had been a party of enemies, I would have killed the last man in line and run back through the trees. There's an elk trail back there. Then I would have run to warn the camp. By the time the enemy quit thrashing around in the timber looking for my shadow, we'd have an ambush for them at the mouth of the canyon up there."

Blood Bear smiled humorlessly. "Then I take it Tanager's camp lies ahead?" He stared around, noting the narrow path through the trees. Afternoon light slanted down through the branches of the densely packed firs.

Warm Wind nodded. "It's the best place. From here, we can control the trails north. You go any farther east and you get all snarled up in those vertical canyons where One Cast had that bighorn-sheep trap. Too much farther west and you've got all those peaks to climb. This way, we've got the enemy in a bottleneck. They've got to go through us to get north."

"What about south?"

Warm Wind shrugged an insolent shoulder. "Most of those camps have been raided and the people have fled to Rattling Hooves and that bunch she lives with."

"Those Short Buffalo People, you mean?"

"White Calf liked them. Two Smokes went with them. Tanager's been sending everyone who can't fight there. But they're living on the west side—on the other side of the peaks."

Blood Bear nodded. "Then I can't miss Tanager's camp?"

"No, go right straight ahead. When you come out of the canyon, you'll see the big rocky knob. That's it. From there we can see most everything. Tanager sent two men out this morning on some plan or other. She won't tell us what, just that we'll know in four days. I do know that she had a Spirit Dream last night up in the rocks. I've never seen her this happy before."

"I see."

"And Never Sweat took another bunch out to drive off a bunch of Short Buffalo warriors who had the nerve to try and hunt buffalo where we could see them. They ought to be back soon. We saw only six or seven. Never Sweat took ten men and women with him."

"Women?"

Warm Wind grinned. "Maybe you forget, Tanager leads us. Women fight well. They can't run as fast as men, or maybe cast darts as far, but they'd rather be dead than dragged off as Short Buffalo captives. You'd be surprised what a woman can do with a club when she gets mad. Try being a sheep in a trap—or a wounded enemy warrior."

"Tanager leads you?" Blood Bear's anger stirred.

Warm Wind squinted slightly, changing his posture as the others behind Blood Bear shifted uneasily. "You'll have to take that up with Tanager."

"You're not coming with us?"

"No. Not and leave this trail unguarded. People die that way."

Blood Bear stared at the man through narrowed eyes, seeing no hesitation in the hard gaze that met his. Things had gotten farther out of hand than he'd anticipated. Rather than scoff, he should have come at the first rumor of Tanager's rise in status. But who would have thought that skinny girl had it in her?

"Then guard the trail. I'll speak with you later."

Warm Wind nodded, then added, "I wouldn't push too hard, Blood Bear. You're the Keeper of the Bundle, but some of us would urge you to think clearly and not let your emotions lead you to trouble."

"Oh?" Blood Bear wheeled in the trail, a deadly quiet settling around his heart.

Warm Wind saw and kept his neutral posture. "You heard me. Keep in mind that Tanager has saved more than one of our lives—the one most dear to me being my own. She's kept us together, and at least shown us a way to stop the raiders for the moment. If you go to cause trouble, you'll be splitting the Red Hand down the middle at a time we all need to stand together.

"Tanager's said nothing against you. When the subject of your leadership comes up, she steers us away from it, leading us to other subjects with the admonition that we shouldn't quarrel among ourselves. Keep that in mind as you deal with her and the people in the camp."

Blood Bear couldn't keep the sarcasm from his voice. "Thank you for your care and concern for the people, Warm Wind. I'll cherish and respect your advice." And he pushed on down the trail, the mutters of those following burning in his ears.

Didn't they remember who rescued the Wolf Bundle from the Short Buffalo camp in the first place? He was Blood Bear, the greatest of their warriors, the man who'd driven the Short Buffalo People from the mountains time and time again! He had been the one to reunite the Red Hand through the Wolf Bundle. It had been his leadership that kept Three Rattles and his Traders returning to the mountains with goods from the western ocean. Had his leadership been so bad?

With an angry thumb, he batted at the Wolf Bundle, a feeling of trouble growing within.

They found the camp as the sun sank below the horizon, shadows stretching across the land. Blood Bear walked self-consciously across the open meadow. Grasses gone dry swished on his moccasined legs. He stopped, hands on hips, before the rising pile of rock. Even through his anger, he could see that Tanager had chosen well. No doubt if the camp were rushed, the defenders could hold off the worst of the attack while the rest scattered through the rocks. A faint memory of hunting in the area hinted of trails leading down the other side. A perfect spot. Tanager couldn't be surrounded and cut off.

As he neared the camp, warriors—men and women—appeared to rise out of the ground, calling greetings, smiles on their faces.

The irritation grew. These didn't look like desperate defenders. But where would they be when the cruel fist of winter closed on the mountains and they had no caches of food?

He climbed the base of the rock to find a sheltered camp, the fires screened from view. Cracked Rock lay to one side, a poultice on a bad thigh wound.

Tanager stepped out on one of the boulders above. "Blood Bear! We're happy to see you. Make yourself welcome and rest. For the moment, only one foolish band of Short Buffalo has decided to try us today. Never Sweat just chased them away and killed at least one in the process. They're probably still running."

Blood Bear squinted up at her where she stood in the cool shadow, realizing she had the position of authority up where her words could carry. Everyone would know he'd been welcomed.

"Come down, Tanager. You and I must talk."

"You've brought a way to kill more enemy? We're happy to have you. More darts to drink enemy blood!" Like a flash she disappeared, leaving him off balance again.

Brooding, he waited while others crowded around, asking for news, hearing of relatives and who'd been wounded. When he looked behind him, his little band had been absorbed, hearing stories of battles fought and won. The animation in the eyes of Tanager's warriors seemed infectious. He missed her arrival, preoccupied by the sound of cheers that grated on his very soul.

Someone stirred up the fire, dropping rocks in the blaze to heat stew. Someone else arrived with a paunchful of spring water, hanging it on a tripod. Glaring, he turned, seeing her standing there, lithe and powerful, wearing a finely worked dress. She cocked her head, a grin on her lips.

"With the Wolf Bundle, we can't lose. Thank you for coming and swelling our ranks. Within a couple of days I want you to take a band of warriors to the south. You'll know by the—"

"You don't give me orders." He leveled a finger. "I lead the Red Hand."

She tensed, eyes slitting in the sudden silence. Looking around at the silent people, she nodded. "Then come, let's settle our differences. We have too much to lose by bickering among ourselves. Be seated and I'll present our options as I now see them. You can give me yours. I wouldn't force a man to assume anything his spirit rebelled at.''

People nodded assent around the fire.

Blood Bear's anger rose. Still, some warning tripped in his mind.

"We can't afford trouble," Tanager said reasonably. "It's enough to fight the enemy. You, Blood Bear, must follow your own path as you will."

He filled his lungs, glancing about, seeing all eyes upon him. "I am the rightful leader of the Red Hand. I am the Keeper of the Wolf Bundle!" He lifted it high to be seen. "I've come now. I will direct the fighting against the enemy."

Tanager lifted her arms and let them slap to her sides. "That's fine. Only I will continue to lead those who follow me in my own way. As I wouldn't expect you to accept my orders, I cannot in turn accept yours."

"But you will."

She shook her head, a muttering rising among the warriors. "No, Blood Bear. I've received my own Power. White Calf told me—"

"That Short Buffalo witch? *She* told you what?"

"That I would become the new leader of the Red Hand." She stood before him, arms crossed, no give in her expression.

"Perhaps you've forgotten the Wolf Bundle."

She shook her head. "I've never forgotten the Wolf Bundle. Suppose I told you a Dreamer was coming?"

"Dreamer?" Blood Bear laughed from deep in his belly. "What Dreamer?"

"I don't know." She walked up to him, looking up at the Wolf Bundle. "He's a man."

"And that bothers you?"

"That bothers me." The anger burned bright in her eyes. "I don't serve any man. That day—if it ever existed—is done. I know my way."

Blood Bear reached for her, catching her hand in his, squeezing with all his might as she grunted. Looking into her blazing eyes, he added, "Perhaps we'll discuss this in the trees, eh? Perhaps you'll bed me tonight?" He increased the pressure on her fingers.

"Don't be a fool," she hissed through clamped teeth. "You'll anger every person here."

Already men and women had begun to stand, uncertainty in their eyes as they fingered their darts.

In a low voice, he added, "Is it so important to keep from dividing the people? Then walk out into the trees with me."

Already his mind had begun to put the pieces together. He still held the Wolf Bundle. All she had to do was say yes. Then, when he took her, no one could call it rape. He could demonstrate his strength.

A panic vied with the pain in her eyes. Slowly, she shook her head. "I'll see you dead first."

He laughed and cast her down, his strength overpowering her. "And you call yourself a warrior, woman?"

She glared up at him, massaging her fingers, taking time to wave the warriors back. "How many camps have you saved, Blood Bear?"

He looked around, meeting the angry eyes of his people. In that moment, he understood that she'd won. Or had she? He smiled around. "It has long been the policy of the Red Hand that the Keeper of the Bundle has certain prerogatives. You know me. You know that I've married only once. I would now take this woman, Tanager, as my wife."

"You *what*?" Tanager sprang to her feet again.

"What I just did—though some might have wondered— was test your dedication to the Red Hand. Yes, I want you as my wife."

"That's insane! First you challenge me? Then . . ." Her face reflected confusion.

"Name another woman as worthy as you, Tanager?" He patted the Wolf Bundle. "Together you and I will—"

"Never!"

"Let's ask the people here." He turned before she could reply. "How about it? Would you rather have us working together? Would you rather have the leadership united in—"

"Never!" she insisted, stepping up to him. "You'll never touch me! Never take me to your bed!"

"And *that's* how you lead the people? Cut the Keeper out from under them? Perhaps, Tanager, you've let your emotions betray you after all. I've asked to marry you, to make you a successor to the Wolf Bundle. And you'd turn down that honor? Drag the trust of the people through the dirt?"

She looked around, frantic, trying to figure how she'd lost the advantage, seeing confusion in the faces of her people. To them, the request couldn't seem to be the underlying threat it was.

With hatred in her eyes, she returned her hot stare to his. He relished her sudden confusion. Yes, through this, he'd broken her hold. How delicious! He hadn't lost his power to manipulate the people. She'd refuse—he could see it in her eyes—and it would erode her position. Granted, his wouldn't be strengthened, but he'd saved himself from disaster.

"You know"—her voice came almost wistfully—"you've succeeded in dividing the Red Hand again, breaking up what I've worked so hard to make one."

He spread his hands innocently. "I only came to ask a woman I thought was worthy of the Wolf Bundle to take her share. True, I had to test you in the beginning, see if you were strong enough. You passed that test. To turn your back on the people now, well, I just can't imagine you—"

"You . . . *you maggot!*"

Taking a foolish risk, he slapped her, hearing cries from the people. No dart landed in his broad back, assuring him for the moment that he'd carried the argument.

Careful, you fool! Some of these idiots owe her their lives. Push it now, before she recovers. Use the Wolf Bundle against them!

"So that's what you *really* think? The Keeper of the Wolf Bundle is a maggot?" He looked around, seeing that for the moment he'd shocked Tanager beyond responding. She stared at her hand, pulling it back from a bloody lip.

"You see, my people. She's given you spirit. She's been cunning, yes. But anyone who insults the Power of the Wolf Bundle like she just did—well, can we allow ourselves to be led by her likes?" *That's it, play on their foolish attachment to the Wolf Bundle. Build on it!* He held it up, waving it back and forth in the firelight as night deepened.

The resistance in people's eyes drained away as they looked up at the Wolf Bundle. For this moment, he should have cleaned it up a little. Maybe put some new paint on the scuffed and worn hide. Still, some hesitated, staring back and forth between Tanager and the Bundle he held high.

"Don't be fooled!" Tanager cried.

"If you would hesitate," Blood Bear continued, "think about this. Why has the Wolf Bundle stayed with me through the years? Hmm? Bundles have Power." *Or so you fools think.* "Are there any of you who would betray your loyalty to the Bundle in favor of Tanager's claims?"

And he *had* them! The last holdouts licked their lips or lowered their eyes in confusion.

"Think!" Tanager cried. "Think about what we've done! You, Fat Elk, you, Tall Fir, or you, Green Snake, remember the times I've changed the course of a fight? Who Dances her Power as she drives the Short Buffalo from the land? Will you turn your back on that?" She wheeled, fire in her eye. "I ask you, Blood Bear, how many of the Short Buffalo People *you've* driven from the land this last year! Count them!"

"More than you can imagine," he told her smugly. "Tell me, Tanager. Who do you think Dreamed your Power? Hmm? Did it just come out of the air?"

"White Calf!" she cried, raising an old atlatl in a defiant fist.

"White Calf?" He laughed yet again and slapped his side. "Did it ever occur to you that maybe the reason you drove all those enemy away, Danced your fight so well, was because I—yes, *I* was using the Wolf Bundle to *give* you that Power?"

Her mouth opened as she shook her head in disbelief.

Use it! Use it now! He turned, lifting the Wolf Bundle high. "Yes! *I* did it! Her Power, her strength, comes from the Wolf Bundle! Think, people! Think hard! What is the Power our fathers left us? What's the Power of First Man? *This is!*" He shook the Wolf Bundle in a clenched fist. "And with it, I've Dreamed *all* of your courage."

He turned, seeing reason leaving Tanager's eyes. Good, goad her just a little more, and she'd attack him. Then he'd have justification to break her once and for all. Drive her insane with anger, loose that uncontrolled emotion, and she'd condemn herself.

"So I've come, people, because I could see that Tanager wasn't capable of leading you. She's too involved with her own delusions of Power—without the control a war leader should possess. The Wolf Bundle told me she'd fooled herself with the image of Power. She was *false* to the Wolf Bundle! She refused to recognize the source of her Power and gave credit instead to some witch—who came from the *enemy in the first place*!

"Yet I thought I could help, come to test her and offer to make her my wife that I might teach her the true Power of her people! That's what I came here to do!

"Now she spits on the will of the Wolf Bundle! But I've seen. I've heard the voice of the Wolf Bundle. It's told me to save the Red Hand before it's too late!"

Tanager gathered herself to spring, an insane rage glittering in her eyes as slim fingers knotted on the handle of a war club.

Have to time this just right. Have to duck so she hits the Wolf Bundle. Then she's destroyed herself. No one will challenge me after that! He glared victory down into her eyes, seeing the last of her sanity crumble in rage.

"Yes, that's what the Wolf Bundle told me! I hear its voice now!" He raised the Wolf Bundle, placing just so.

"Liar!" a voice called from the darkness.

Tanager froze at the start of her leap, eyes going to the evening shadows.

Chapter 25 ◎

Tanager watched them come, unable to move, knowing she should launch into Blood Bear. An elderly woman—no, a berdache—limped into the light of the fire. A nervous young man—Elk Charm's Short Buffalo husband—followed, a stricken look on his face. He had eyes only for the Wolf Bundle. A faint sweat sheen glazed the young man's skin, heightening the anguish in his eyes. Behind them all walked a huge black wolf, deadly yellow eyes taking each person's measure. The animal stopped to stare at Blood Bear, ears going back.

"Liar!" the young man repeated, voice strained. *"Don't you know what you've done?* How many times have you lied on the Wolf Bundle? How many times have you—"

"Little Dancer." Blood Bear swelled his chest, walking out to meet him. "And, of course, Two Smokes. This time, you've finished yourselves. What's this? Come to spy on us? Is that it? You're here to find out how many we are? To take information to the Short Buffalo?"

Two Smokes looked as if he'd eaten something rotten. "The only thing I'll never understand is why the Bundle hasn't killed you yet."

"Give it to me." Little Dancer extended trembling hands. "Give it to me, and maybe you'll have saved your life. Can't you feel the Power swelling, growing?"

Blood Bear guffawed and bounced from foot to foot. "Saved my life? You arrogant little fool! The Wolf Bundle is *the* Power of the Red Hand! Or maybe you forgot where I found it? In *your* lodge in *Heavy Beaver*'s camp?"

"And you almost killed it—and the Red Hand—the night you slapped it off the tripod. It's only been waiting. Waiting for me."

"Slapped?" someone whispered incredulously. People shifted nervously around Tanager.

"And why would it wait for you?" Blood Bear sneered, stepping back and hugging the Wolf Bundle. He winced slightly, rubbing the stump of a short little finger on the front of his shirt.

"Because he's your son, Blood Bear," Two Smokes added in the shocked silence. "Your son . . . and Clear Water's."

"My . . ." Blood Bear gaped.

"You never asked. You never wondered if I might have kept the child alive. It was easier to pass the story that he'd died. White Calf knew. Hungry Bull knows, as does Rattling Hooves and Elk Charm and all the rest of them by now. Look at him." Two Smokes turned away, pointing. His sad eyes took in the stunned faces of the people. "And the sorrow is that he'll have to kill his father this night."

"This young pup? Kill me? Why?" Blood Bear demanded.

"Because you won't give him what is rightfully his."

"Can't you see what you've done?" A glimmer of tears had formed in Little Dancer's eyes. "You've almost driven the Power from it! Feel it! It's calling! Power can't be abused forever. Not even the Power of the Wolf Bundle can take what you and Heavy Beaver have done to it!"

"You're no son of mine." Blood Bear chuckled. "No son of mine comes crying to take the Wolf Bundle. You're an enemy. The blood of Short Buffalo People runs in your veins, boy."

"I have to take it . . . save it." Little Dancer glanced around, bending to pluck up Tanager's war club. "You must give it to me now. I *have* to restore it—to save the Power and Dream the Spirals."

"Drop the club, boy, or you'll regret it." Blood Bear's eyes gleamed as he crouched.

The big black wolf hunkered down on its belly, fur rising as it pinned Blood Bear. Lips drew back to expose flashing canines. The muscles bunched under that sleek hide, firelight gleaming in the rippling coat.

"He'll kill you, Blood Bear." Two Smokes sighed and shook his head. "The Power's against you."

"Don't!" Little Dancer pleaded, blinking suddenly. "Feel it? Can't you feel it? The anger, it's building."

A low nervous growl issued from the wolf's throat.

"Don't try to play games with me, boy!" Blood Bear's face twitched.

The club dropped from Little Dancer's nerveless fingers as he cried out and staggered forward.

Two Smokes grabbed his head, collapsing as he pressed his hands to his ears.

"What's this?" Blood Bear cried. "Games? You'd play games?" He viciously kicked Two Smokes in the bad knee, and got a scream.

"Your last chance!" Little Dancer pleaded, dropping to his knees.

From where she watched, Tanager felt the beginning of a throbbing headache. She looked up, wincing at the pain. Blood Bear stood, a curious look on his face. He grunted softly to himself, sinking slowly, as if he'd lost control of his muscles. Surprise mixed with fear to glaze his eyes.

The wolf yipped softly, as if in pain.

Little Dancer reached out as he scrambled forward, grabbing the Bundle from Blood Bear's trembling hands, cuddling it close to his chest, a radiant look on his face.

Squinting at the after effects of her headache, Tanager blinked hard and stood up, walking forward on unsteady feet.

"I . . ." The words choked in Blood Bear's throat where he lay staring up into the sky. *"I . . . can't . . . move."*

Two Smokes moaned softly, sitting up, grabbing his damaged knee before rubbing a shaking hand over his eyes.

"I can't help you," Little Dancer whispered where he held the Wolf Bundle. "You did it. All these years, the Power's waited for me. I—I came prepared to kill you, if I had to, to take it back and restore it. I hated that thought—even if you'd never been a father to me like Hungry Bull. A son shouldn't have to kill a father over Power. Clear Water knew that. The Wolf Dreamer knew that. I see now. They had to take me to the Short Buffalo People. I had to grow with the Wolf Bundle. I had to see the way Heavy Beaver has changed the Spirals. I had to be the way I am to become Fire Dancer."

He licked his lips, talking absently, an odd glow in his

eyes. "You'd never have let Clear Water keep the Bundle. You would have stolen it—or killed her. And I would have had to kill you. I would have been just as wrong as you, Blood Bear."

"Why can't I move?" Blood Bear's scream rent the night.

"Paralyzed," the man who now called himself Fire Dancer whispered, eyes going vacant. A blank look possessed him as he sat and swayed. The corners of his lips quivered as his muscles tensed.

Blood Bear's eyes lost focus and he whispered, "The Wolf Bundle, it's . . ."

Fire Dancer's jaw trembled before he spoke slowly, the words not his. *"Now you'll live as I. Feel as I did, human. Through each moment of your life, you'll know what it felt like to be used like a toy to mislead the People. And you should know that Wolf Dreamer, the First Man, still has the tip of your finger. A promise made . . . especially to Power . . . must be respected, human. So live the life you've made for yourself. Feel the Power around you. Feel my Power, growing now, in your son's hands. Every abuse you gave me will be paid back. Now you'll feel every insult, every slap and bruise. Not until the day you're as worn, scuffed, and cracked as I, will you die, Blood Bear."*

Fire Dancer made a whimpering sound, a shiver shooting through his body.

"What?" Tanager wondered, staring at the empty look in Fire Dancer's eyes.

Two Smokes stared, awestruck, hands up with his fingers spread wide. "The Wolf Bundle speaks through him! We're hearing the Wolf Bundle."

Fire Dancer swallowed hard. He sagged, coming to, looking up with bleary eyes. "I don't feel very good. I think I need to sleep now."

Tanager glanced around, aware that everyone had frozen in place, terrified stares locked on Fire Dancer. "Someone make a bed for him. Hurry."

"What about the Wolf Bundle?" Green Snake asked as she came to place a hide over Fire Dancer's trembling shoulders. Her gaze locked with the suspicious wolf's and she froze.

Tanager stumbled, trying to decide, when Two Smokes said, "It's his. Leave it with him. The wolf won't hurt you."

Green Snake paused and shot a glance at Tanager.

"Or would you risk what happened to Blood Bear?" Two Smokes continued.

Green Snake might have held cactus the way her fingers worked tenderly to settle Fire Dancer and the clutched Wolf Bundle into the bedding. The huge black wolf moved silently to curl around him, yellow glare missing nothing.

Tanager sighed with relief, turning to Two Smokes. "How do you know all this?"

"I am berdache. I live between the worlds. This"—he gestured at Fire Dancer—"has been a long time in coming. And now it's only begun."

"Why can't I move?" Blood Bear cried out again. His face worked, tears leaking from shining eyes to streak his cheeks. "My finger! It's on fire! Like it's burning."

Tanager swallowed, looking at his amputated member. The stub seemed to wiggle. She tore her eyes away. "Tall Fir, Fat Elk, take him down by Cracked Rock. Feed him and get him something to drink. Then make sure he's warm for the night. Someone stay with him, talk to him. Keep him calm. Maybe . . . maybe it'll pass."

The look Two Smokes gave her didn't reassure.

Blood Bear whimpered as they picked him up, Tall Fir obviously nervous at touching the man.

"And *don't drop him!*" Tanager ordered, seeing the hesitation. She turned to Two Smokes. "White Calf said a Dreamer was coming."

Two Smokes nodded toward Fire Dancer where he huddled under the covers. "He's come."

She steeled herself as the guardian wolf turned attention to her. "But he seems so young."

Two Smokes took a breath and sighed. "And so incredibly old."

"You said something about the Spirals. So did White Calf. What did that mean?"

Two Smokes almost cried out, holding the knee Blood Bear had kicked, as he resettled himself against the rising wall of rock. "Look around you. The world's changing. We're in the last refuge from the drought. Even here it's come. This is an age of Fire. You wonder why Heavy Beaver could gain such Power? His people were starving. The buffalo have been dying off, their numbers ever fewer. When a man arises who has answers, the people will listen. And worse, they'll believe. By controlling the mountains, Heavy Beaver will have a supply of meat while his hunters continue to kill the last of the plains herds.''

''And what can we do about that?'' a woman asked.

''Nothing. Nothing but fight them off.''

''Then there's no hope?'' Tanager asked, propping her chin on a callused palm. An eerie sense of premonition haunted her. The remains of the headache slowly ebbed. Yes, she'd felt Power, awesome Power unlike anything she'd Danced during a fight. The after effects left a shiver in her soul.

''I didn't say that,'' Two Smokes continued wearily. ''The rest is up to him. Up to the Fire Dancer . . . and the Wolf Bundle, if it isn't too late.''

''Explain.''

Two Smokes looked up through bloodshot eyes. ''He, Fire Dancer, has to Dance the Spirals back. He has to go and face Heavy Beaver and Dance a new way for the Short Buffalo People.''

She laughed. ''And he's going to just walk in and do it?''

Two Smokes lifted helpless hands. ''I don't know how he'll do it. I don't even know if he can. He's the Dreamer.''

''So? Isn't that enough?''

His lips trembled. ''Not even a Dreamer is proof against a dart in the back—and he's got to walk right into the middle of their camp to Dance and Dream. And he's going to take the Wolf Bundle with him.''

Tanager could only stare, feeling her heart beat soddenly in her chest. The piercing stare of the wolf affected her soul like coals on bare skin.

White Calf's dying request echoed in her mind.

The Dreams wove and meshed, tightening until they became a knot. One by one the strands broke, parting again to weave into a new image. Hungry Bull laughed. Sage Root scolded him for touching one of his father's hunting darts.

Chokecherry slapped her leg and cried out at some imagined outrage. Heavy Beaver smiled, the flat features of his face going ever wider, dominated by that curl of lips that mocked and scorned and dared. The image split, tearing down the middle while Three Toes manufactured a stone point, his baton clicking rhythmically as it drove thin flakes from the stone. Throws Rocks grabbed his arm. Terror throttled his outcry as a heavy stone hammer rose over his skull.

Fire Dancer tried to pull away, struggling with the Dream that possessed him. Again he felt the Wolf Bundle ripped away from Two Smokes' grasp, pinched cruelly in strong fingers and thrown, the sensation sickening as the Bundle sailed through the air. Earth and water bruised when it landed in the grass.

Stunned, he lay aware of the soil, of the soul of the grass as it throbbed around him. The Spiral bent and quivered. Anger! Driving passionate anger filled the world, tremors spreading like ripples on a broad pond.

Elk Charm's voice called, urging him to come back. His daughters squalled from terror and loneliness. White Calf whispered from beyond the haze surrounding him. Love twisted within him like a bull snake choking on prickly pear, each spine burning with a powerful intensity. He whimpered, knowing he loved too much. "Come back to me . . . back to me. . . ." Elk Charm's call beckoned, sweet as honey from a hidden comb.

"Fadder?" his daughter asked plaintively.

He cried out at the longing in her voice, hearing her need. "Let me go," he whimpered to the Dream. "She needs me."

Fire leapt up, a forest aflame burned around him, trees splitting in the heat. Branches torched, yellow-orange spires of flame tormenting the sky as reddish smoke rose in towering columns to threaten the clouds.

"An age of Fire."

"He's too young. His mind has no discipline. Feel the confusion? He can't free himself to reach the One. How do you expect him to Dance with Fire?"

"There's no more time. We have no other choice."

"Kill Heavy Beaver."

"His way won't die with him. It must be changed. People

*change only through the Power of the Dream. Ideas are that
way. They can only be replaced—never killed entirely. We
deal with the Power of the human soul.''*

''If he's strong enough.''

''Yes, if he's strong enough. We've given him all we can.''

Fire Dancer suffered the feeling of falling the way he had
when he almost died in the snow; haze settled over him,
vanquishing the burning forest, dropping around him like fog
on a frosty winter morning.

He waited, seeing the cloud around him whirl and twist,
images forming from the billowing mass. Struggling, he
sought to identify them, making a face from one, a tree from
another. Finally, he managed to conjure Elk Charm's warm
features from the drifting chaos. Crying out, he reached for
her, only to have the changing mist reorganize, his youngest
daughter's baby face appearing in the mist.

''Illusion.''

And the baby's face disappeared.

White Calf beamed at him from the patterns of cloud. He
called as she shifted into the gray haze.

''Illusion,'' the voice repeated. *''As all life is illusion. As
earth, stone, water, and air are hollow, a thin web of illusion
which defies their real natures.''*

''Elk Charm?'' he cried out, soul wrung like a twisted
piece of damp leather.

''You must break the pattern of illusion.''

One after another images formed, his mind jumping to
identify them before they shifted in the madness of the mist.
He watched, feverishly attempting to see.

''Too young,'' the second voice affirmed.

Fire Dancer closed his eyes, curling into a fetal ball, ignoring it all, lost, unable to comprehend. He could feel the
mist, swirling, changing. All of it mist. Formless, featureless, the reality remained.

''There.''

His body came to rest. As he opened his eyes, he saw the
Wolf Bundle lying before him.

''I must be restored, smoked, Blessed, and made whole,''
it told him. *''Cleanse me. Renew me. Two Smokes has the
skill to make a new cover. The contents must be purified and*

made whole. You have little time. Restore the Power. Breathe your soul into mine. Wolf has been with you for a long time. His life is my life. You are First Man. When the time comes, he gives himself to you. You are the Fire Dancer.

"Listen to me. You must take Two Smokes and renew the Wolf Bundle. This is what you must do. . . ."

Scene by scene, a Dream unfolded. Fire Dancer cried out in horror, feeling what must happen, living it in the experience of the Dream.

"The damage must be undone . . . in the manner we have shown you. Do not fail. Believe in yourself . . . in your Power."

Fire Dancer's heart continued to throb. Only the curling mist remained, trying to form images in his mind. Bit by bit, it hovered closer, bathing his flesh as he dropped into a deep sleep, illusion swirling endlessly about him. In the background, he could hear Elk Charm whispering her love, hear his daughters crying out in fear. Somewhere, somewhere just beyond . . .

Two Smokes enjoyed the sunlight, feeling it sink into his flesh, warming his blood. No one had slept much the night before, only Fire Dancer, the wolf watching protectively, lifting a threatening lip if anyone stepped too close.

This morning, the light seemed clearer, no haze over the mountains. Each crag in the gray peaks could be made out in detail, so clear that if he reached, he might touch them. The endless vault of blue remained unmarred by a single cloud.

Two Smokes looked across, seeing Fire Dancer sleeping soundly. How curious. What Power had coursed through him that he might speak for the Wolf Bundle? What Power had they all experienced that laid haughty Blood Bear low? At the memory, Two Smokes felt his soul chill. That moment would live with him forever.

Tanager climbed up the rock from where she'd been talking with her warriors. Several of the young men had turned, trotting off across the meadow while sunlight glinted and leapt from their polished weapons.

The young woman seated herself beside Two Smokes,

looking back at the sleeping figure of Fire Dancer. "We'll have to put a sunshade over him soon. Will the wolf let us?"

"I suppose. To be a black wolf in the sun must not be much fun."

Tanager called, ordering her people to see to it. None appeared to appreciate the job, but wolf didn't react as they fixed a hide shelter.

"When will you go do this Dreaming?" She gave him a curious look.

Two Smokes shrugged. "He's the Dreamer, ask him. Any change in Blood Bear?"

"No." She leaned back on locked elbows, stretching her long legs out before her. "And I wouldn't have expected he'd be so quiet. I thought he'd be hollering for this and that, driving people crazy. Something seems to have settled into him. He simply lies there with a terrible expression on his face, staring. Always just staring. Everyone's frightened."

"With reason." Two Smokes reached into his pouch, removing the pieces he'd been working on to sew into moccasins. "Everything Fire Dancer said last night was true. Power's been abused."

She studied him. "And do you think he can do this thing? Dream these Spirals?"

Two Smokes raised his eyebrows. "I don't know. White Calf dedicated all of her life to the study of Power. Her mind was very keen, so why did Power choose the boy? Why not someone used to Dreaming, who had a whole lifetime of it? I don't know."

Tanager hesitated. "My warriors have been reporting. The Short Buffalo are hunting. That's why we've had so few raids. They've been making meat. When they make a kill, they strip it and dry it, and carry it down to the main camp on Clear River at the Red Wall."

Two Smokes gave her a questioning glance. She looked away, avoiding his eyes.

"What do you think, Tanager?"

"I think they're having a ceremony." She considered for a moment, frown lines deepening. "If it looks like they're going to leave in the next day or so, I'm going to have to hit them hard, keep them up in the mountains."

"And this could affect Fire Dancer?"

She continued to hesitate and nodded. "It could." Her cool stare probed. "I, too, had a Power Dream. You know how the wind comes up in the afternoon, blowing from the west?"

Two Smokes nodded.

"In two days, several of my warriors will start fires in the thick timber. Part of holding the enemy here is to trap them in the flames. The Red Hand are used to fires. We live with them. These plains people?" She lifted a shoulder. "If we can get them to panic, perhaps some may be trapped in the black timber. Others will be scattered, easy to destroy."

"You know how dry the trees are? The brush? Everything?"

She nodded. "That's why I think it will work. The Dream told me. Wait four days and light the fires. If the enemy starts to leave, we've got to attack, keep them up here in the right place. At the last minute, we'll have to pull out, leaving them to the flames. I've already set up decoy parties to lead them into the thick timber and get them lost. There are places where the deadfall is piled pretty thick."

Two Smokes experienced a flutter in his heart. "Of course! He's the Fire Dancer."

"What?"

"His Dreams. Especially the one where the forests are burning. We . . . well, we don't have much time."

She placed a hand on his arm. "Only a very few know of this. I've kept it secret. Power Dreams are not to be shared freely."

He nodded and placed a hand on hers. "I am berdache. I understand."

At that moment, wolf walked out from the sunshade. Fire Dancer, hollow-eyed and haunted, crawled out on trembling hands and knees. His features appeared pale in the light.

"Two Smokes? We need sweetgrass. We have a lot to do."

A tightness formed in Two Smokes' gut. "I think things are beginning to happen."

Tanager swallowed and nodded.

The place consisted of nothing more than a cove in the rock. On each of three sides, the walls of the mountain rose.

Pinkish-gray granite reflected the light of the setting sun. The sky streaked in tinges of reddish orange. A small spring surrounded by willows seeped into the boggy soil, draining the hollow. Aspens rattled where the slight breeze touched them. A tangle of fir masked the bottom of the rock while thick grass swished around their legs.

Two Smokes grunted, drawing Fire Dancer's attention. The old berdache's expression looked strained and rivulets of sweat streaked his lined face. Gratefully, Two Smokes settled with a grunt, rubbing hands on his knee. He winced and looked up.

"I'm not sure I can make it down the trail. That last kick Blood Bear gave me . . . well, it's never hurt so badly."

The black wolf made a circle of the spot, sniffing here and there, marking territory.

Worry settled around Fire Dancer's heart. He worked his lips, looking around. "Maybe it'll heal. We have a little time yet." Then the rushing pull of the Power filled him, driving him, prodding at his mind with pointed urgency.

"You sit. I'll make us a sweat lodge." So saying, Fire Dancer set his pack down, making sure the Wolf Bundle rested on top, unencumbered. Anxiety shot through him. How could Blood Bear have been such a fool?

With a flake taken from his pouch, Fire Dancer waded into the muck around the seep, hearing his feet squish in the soft moss. Using the sharp edge of the flake, he cut willow stems loose, Singing for the plant's soul. Sloshing out, he began stripping the leaves, driving the sharpened ends of the willow into the soft ground, bending them over in a large cross set east to west and north to south. These he tied in the middle to support the weight of the hides they'd carried. The framework created a low dome.

Next he unrolled the thin hides, settling them in place to make a sealed shelter. From the rubble below the slope, he collected rocks and cut more willow to make hearth sticks with which to handle hot rocks. Next he pulled fire sticks from his pack, expertly spinning them to create fire. This he fed until he had a crackling blaze and piled rocks on the coals to heat.

Wolf sat, tail around his legs, watching.

"We haven't eaten," Two Smokes pointed out.

"Not for days." Fire Dancer smiled. His appetite had vanished at the sight of White Calf's corpse. So much had happened. So little time remained—and so many doubts.

Reverently he picked up the Wolf Bundle, placing it where it would be safe. He dumped the contents of his pack on the ground, slogging once more through the muck to fill the pouch with water. Drips formed along the tight seams Two Smokes had sewn with such care; nevertheless, the bag held water. This he hung from a tripod made of dead aspen that he placed inside the sweat lodge.

Finally, he raised his hands to the filtered sunlight and stripped his clothing off. Two Smokes stood, shucking out of his berdache's dress. He, too, raised his hands, eyes closed as he offered a prayer to the air.

Fire Dancer used the sticks to carry hot rocks into the sweat lodge. Two Smokes ducked through the door, favoring his maimed leg. As he settled the hanging over the door, the interior of the lodge went black.

"We must purify ourselves, clear any taint from our minds and bodies." So saying, Fire Dancer Sang to the Power of the Wolf Bundle, to spirits of earth and air and water, and reached into the hanging bag. With the end of his prayer, he cast the water onto the stones, hearing the sizzle as steam rose to fill the lodge.

In one corner of his mind, Elk Charm called. Frantically, he blocked it out, willing himself to forget. The old battle began again. Sights and sounds, memories, it all rushed to clog his brain while he began to sweat. His stomach growled, longing for a warm stew. One by one, Fire Dancer forced the images from his mind, trying to clear the confusion.

Two Smokes' chanting soothed, creating a link from which Fire Dancer could expand. He let himself drift with the chant, repeating the words, feeling the Song massage his soul. Four times he cast water on the hot rocks until his skin tingled and his lungs cried out.

Time seemed to drift away in the heat and purity of the lodge. Each of his muscles slipped into a lax feeling of unity.

Around him, the earth pulsed. Through the lodge, he could feel the Power of the Wolf Bundle.

When that unity flowed through him, around him, he sighed and let the moment exist.

He crawled from the lodge, almost staggering as he stood and sucked the clean night air into his fevered lungs. His skin prickled with the feel of the breeze on his body.

Wolf stood waiting, a shadow in the darkness.

Two Smokes crawled out and lay still in the grass, breathing deeply.

Fire Dancer raised his eyes to the heavens, lifting his arms to beseech the Starweb above. "Hear us. We come to renew the Wolf Bundle, to make whole what has almost died. Help us, Wise One Above. Help us, Wolf Dreamer. We seek to make new what has been abused."

He waited, eyes to the sky, a terrible worry pressing down on him. *Can I do it? Am I strong enough? What if I fail?* He could feel the Power, waiting. Unbidden, the memory of Blood Bear sinking to the ground, the powerful body gone numb, settled in his mind. *I'm not the one to be meddling with things like the Wolf Bundle. White Calf should be here. I'm lost.*

"Help me," he croaked. A dread feeling spread.

Wolf padded up to stand before him, those terrible yellow eyes locking on his. The animal grunted, prodding him with a hard nose before backing off and snorting. Wolf lifted his muzzle, eyes closed as if in prayer.

Fire Dancer winced, picking up the one dart he'd brought with him. How could he do this? Wolf's presence loomed in the night, waiting. The Dream had been explicit. He'd seen, felt, and now he must do. He turned, driving the dart through wolf's side. The big black animal staggered, sidestepping before it fell. Blood pooled under the muzzle as the lungs drowned in the rush from severed arteries. The wolf's sides ceased to labor. The yellow eyes stared sightlessly.

Fire Dancer's breath caught at the feeling of the animal's soul as it flinched and lifted free from the body. He dropped to his knees, remembering wolf's warmth during the blizzard. He ran fingers over the sleek coat, feeling the warm flesh beneath. He'd owed his life to wolf—to the Watcher. A twist of grief formed to ache in his soul.

Forgive me. It's the way. You knew. Like a betrayer, he stared at the convulsing animal—pierced by a pain as acute as if he'd driven the dart into his own flesh. A Dream image flashed through his mind, replaying the scene of a sheep netted in a trap, the club rising. He shook himself, forcing it away, knowing the way of death, of the floating freedom.

Two Smokes began to Sing and together they chanted, feeling the rightness, feeling wolf's soul rising into the air, an old animal whose life had come to the end of the Circle.

With trembling hands, Fire Dancer used the sharp dart point to cut the body open and remove the heart. This he lifted to his lips and drank, hot blood salty on his tongue. "I am the Wolf Dreamer . . . *and I am not.*"

Like morning rays, warmth flowed through him, wolf's strength adding confidence to his fearful mind.

"What next?" Two Smokes asked, voice intruding on Fire Dancer's concentration. As if he lived the Dream, Fire Dancer looked at the dark bundle where it rested on his clothing.

"A new Wolf Bundle must be made." He bent and began skinning the thick coat from the hot carcass. The very air seemed to stifle him, as if he sat under a huge teetering rock, ready to fall.

The pelt he handed to Two Smokes. "No one among the Red Hand has more talent than you. You must sew it, fit it around the bundle."

Fire Dancer took the carefully collected sweetgrass and wet it, adding more wood to the fire before he placed a knot of sweetgrass on the flames. Yes, he lived the Dream. Four times he passed his body through the billowing smoke, feeling the purification.

With his own clothing for a rest, he utilized an obsidian flake, frowning in the light of the fire. Chanting the rightness, Power shifted around him, reeking of the night, of the stars above. Tension brought sweat to his forehead. His mouth had gone dry, making it a labor to swallow. His gut roiled as he gripped the flake, hesitating. From the darkness, unseen eyes watched, sending shivers up his back. Taking a deep breath to steady himself, he severed the worn bindings on the bundle, opening it to the night.

Was that thunder? Or the imaginings of his quivering mind?

Power played along his fingers, rippling the muscles of his arms and chest. His heart danced, a terrible thrill in the depths of his soul. He felt like of a man who'd outrun a flash flood.

One by one he laid out the contents, fingers trembling, while sweat beaded on his body. A large bear claw with a bit of snow-white fur attached. A piece of carved ivory bearing the effigy of a monster. A large stone dart point of a workmanship Three Toes would have envied. The point was long and lanceolate, fluted at the base—a monster-hunter's point. A raven's head came next, wound in sweetgrass. An ancient stain, like that of blood, caked the feathers and beak. A seashell gleamed opal in the firelight. His fingers encountered a string of wolf's teeth hung on a cracked and stiff thong that he dared not try to unwrap. These he placed on the sweetgrass, Singing and Praying to the Power to make them whole again.

The night shifted, ebbed and flowed. Fire Dancer tried to take a breath, lungs oddly starved of oxygen. He blinked and looked up into the night, awed at the way the stars appeared to shimmer erratically.

With agile fingers, Two Smokes worked, using a flake to cut the raw wolf hide to form, using the old as his model. At Fire Dancer's direction, he smoked the piece in sweetgrass, rubbing it clean of blood with the sacred leaves of sage which gave life and luck. The pungent scent rose as he worked.

One by one, Little Dancer continued to smoke the relics, cleansing them, renewing the Power that ebbed and flowed. Night pressed down—a physical presence.

Two Smokes punched his awl through the wolf hide, taking care to keep it from touching the ground, blessing the gut thread he stripped from wolf's corpse, purifying and working the material until it seemed perfect. Laboriously, he began the double stitch that bound the new Bundle together.

Fire Dancer waited, watching the path of the stars across

the night sky, Singing, feeling his soul drift, floating in the night.

Are we right? He lifted his face to the cool breeze, wishing he could breathe normally. Beside him, Two Smokes continued his labors. They sat, two figures hunched against the night.

Have I done it right? Fire Dancer closed his eyes, a desperation aching within. *What if it's not? Will I be horribly maimed like Blood Bear?*

Where they rose on all sides, the rocks seemed to hang over him with a ponderous weight. A curious blackness dimmed the stars.

Tendrils of Power, like fingers of mist, snaked through the night. Heavy Beaver dreamed he stood in the middle of his camp. Around him, men and women chanted and clapped their hands as they Danced. Each turned adoring eyes on him, smiling their warm wishes, worship in their eyes.

"You see, Mother. You see what your son has done?" He raised his hands, hearing his People whoop and holler. "I've given them the new way. Look at them, strong, powerful. Not even the mighty Anit'ah stand against us. I've remade the world, as you would have wanted it."

The camp seemed to shine, new hides on the lodges. Even the dogs looked fat and lazy. Parfleches had been stacked about, each brimming with dried meat. The clothes the People wore had been perfectly tanned, stained with white clay, and worked to a supple softness by the unceasing labors of the women. Young men paraded, Dancing his glory.

"This I've done! This is my new Power! Buffalo Above, look down on your children, purified from the taint. I, Heavy Beaver, have cleansed the People. I have made this happen."

He lifted his hands to the sky, reveling in the blue depths, knowing the Sun Man watched, feeling the warmth of his life-giving rays.

He could feel his mother's spirit rising above, looking down in approval. About the line of swaying chanting Dancers, children ran and played, young boys giggling and throwing mock darts made of grass at each other. About them on the hills, buffalo grazed in clusters. The whole place seemed to glow with a light as bright as the sun itself.

"Your Dream, Mother. I showed them. Those who ridiculed are gone, vanquished by the People's war darts. This I have done. They mocked me. They allowed women to soil their ways. I won."

He spread his arms, a joy almost bursting his breast.

Already Fat Dog, of the Cut Hair, had begun to fail. Among those camps, the young men talked of Heavy Beaver and the Power of the Short Buffalo People. To the east, the Fire Buffalo People had been reduced to rags, seeking to raid the camps of the River peoples for wild rice and the plants they gathered there. In the north, the White Crane pushed ever farther from the Big River, their will eroded by the virility of his warriors.

"I control the plains! I control the buffalo. The Spirit World has blessed me. So do I bless my People."

The Dancers continued to beam at him, a radiant glow in their faces. Yet, through the merriment, a wail arose from behind the line of Dancers. At first, they seemed not to notice, their adoration for him alone.

The keening grew, leading Heavy Beaver to frown. "What is the meaning of this wailing?"

As suddenly, a gust of wind tore through the camp, flapping the lodge covers, whipping dust from the packed ground. The Dancers hesitated, trying to cover their faces against the flying grains of sand.

A woman shrieked, the Dancers looking away from him, cowering back from some horror only they could see.

"Dance!" he ordered, crossing his arms despite the wind that swept the camp. As the first gusts passed, the gale blew hot, withering like the heat off a thick bed of coals.

The Dancers cowered, their attention riveting on the wailing.

Daring the blistering wind, Heavy Beaver craned his neck to see. The line of Dancers had stopped now, and as suddenly as it had come, the wind stopped, leaving the camp in silence.

"Dance!" he bellowed, ignored as the People watched, spellbound.

"What is this? Dance! *Dance for me!*" He raised a fist, voice booming in the silence. For the first time, he noticed the sky had gone leaden, ominously gray.

The wail carried on the air again and the People screamed, backing away, fleeing this way and that.

"Stay and Dance!"

A low rumbling rolled across the sky, the sound of muted thunder before the storm.

Where the People had fled, a lone individual walked forward from the empty plain. Heavy Beaver swallowed. Another and another came, as if their figures appeared out of the shimmering mirage that rippled the air. Where buffalo had once packed the hills, only sunburned and twisted grasses remained. The silence on the land could have been felt if he could but force himself to reach out and pluck at it with his fingers.

The figures hobbled closer, worn clothing hanging in tatters about their bodies.

"Dance!"

The wretches remained on his Blessing ground, and came closer and closer.

"Go away!" He waved his arms. "I am the Dreamer, Heavy Beaver! Go away or I'll Curse you all!"

And still they came as he stood his ground, the unfamiliar sensation of fear clutching in his chest. He blinked, hating the suffocating heat around him.

"Dancing Doe!" the cry tore from his throat. The first of the figures could be distinguished now; the cruel shaft of a dart stuck out from her gut at an odd angle. A glitter filled her eyes. A baby's voice cried out—and was silenced, as if dashed against rock.

Behind her, Sage Root walked, horrible gaping wounds in her wrists as the flies buzzed about her. Even in death, her figure tantalized, a sexual sway to her hips. Chokecherry hobbled along, materializing out of the mirage. White Calf came behind her, a promising grin on her ancient lips.

Heavy Beaver raised his arms. "Go back! This is *my* Blessing. Go Back! *Back!*"

They wouldn't stop. A panicked voice in the back of his mind urged, *Run! RUN!*

Sage Root's voice rumbled in the still air, a cross between thunder and Dream. *"We touched the Wolf Bundle, shared souls. Now Power is loose, Heavy Beaver. Black Power, changed Power. What have you wrought? We're coming . . . coming for you. Powered by the Wolf Bundle. It hasn't forgotten . . . and the time is soon."*

Whimpering, he turned, sprinting through the desolate lodges, crying out. No one answered—only the scorching wind whistling through the empty lodges.

And behind, he could feel them coming, *feel* them reaching for him.

He jerked awake, crying out, and sat up. Blood rushed in his veins as Red Chert blinked awake, staring at him through dull eyes.

He ripped the covers off, stumbling to his feet, pulling on his ceremonial shirt. Desperately, he jerked the hanging aside and stumbled out into the cool air. From the faint graying of the eastern horizon, dawn lay at hand.

He stared at the lodges, at the parched trees overhead. Cool, peaceful. It had only been a Dream. A terrible Dream. Yes, a *real* Power Dream.

They would start the Blessing today. All would be as it should. He gasped and wiped at the fear-sweat beaded on his fleshy forehead. Panting, he walked around, enjoying the mangy dogs that came to sniff and scampered away as he kicked at them.

"It's all right. It's all going to be fine."

Then why did a fist seem to grip his heart?

Chapter 26 @

A hot, brassy day. Another in a long pattern of hot days. The morning breezes rose up the canyons, bringing the smells of dry grass and suffering pine. Tanager ran fingers through her hair, braiding it. She needed this fight. Her blood fairly pulsed for it.

What had it been? What Power had the Dreamer wrought? Her sleep had been tortured, flashes of the rape filling her with dread. The images of men dying on her darts replayed over and over again. She'd listened to the wet smack time after time as she crushed an enemy's face with a heavy stone. Each time, she'd reveled in the anger set free, feeding her hatred for the men who'd come to brutalize her and her people.

The memory stirred the anger. Not long now, only the slight movement of a shadow or two and she'd let loose her wrath, vent the stirring rage that burned within. After that, she'd lead attack after attack, bunching the enemy, assuring their destruction. A warm anticipation vied with the soul thirst for revenge.

The Short Buffalo would rue the day they'd climbed the trails. Warriors would sing for many generations of Tanager, who trapped and killed the Short Buffalo People.

A grim smile curled her lips.

She squinted at the trap. Scouts reported the Short Buffalo warriors climbed even now. Steep rocks lined either side of the trap while her warriors waited in the tangle of serviceberry, screened from view. The enemy would walk out into the small open space, winded from the long climb. In that moment, she'd have them, her warriors cutting off retreat back down the trail. Only one avenue would be left open for their escape—into the black timber. There, she'd hound them, driving them deeper into the trees, leaving them to their fate. Her heart raced with the high fever of a hunter who has his quarry.

Each time she killed, it fed that desperate need within her to hurt them as she had been hurt. Each time, she paid them back for that wretched evening in the camp when they'd hurt her so deeply. The body had mended, but the mind continued to cry out, in haunting Dreams like she'd had last night.

White Calf's ghost had walked the land, that knowing squint in the old woman's eyes.

"Help the Dreamer . . . the Dreamer. . . ." White Calf's words echoed.

Help him how? What did she know about Dreamers? She jumped at the feel of tiny feet running up her arm, looking down, expecting an insect. White Calf's atlatl lay in her hand, a deadly dart nocked for release.

"Why me?" she wondered, licking her lips.

"You must listen to the Dreamer."

"The last man I listened to was Blood Bear." Anger rose again as she remembered the way he'd undercut her, forced her to lose herself. And if she'd struck? She closed her eyes, trying to rid herself of the image. Not even Fire Dancer's arrival could have saved her from that.

No, she'd stay here, ensure her people got out in time— and kill more of the enemy at the same time. What business of hers was it what the Dreamer did with Two Smokes up in the high country?

"Are you strong enough?" White Calf's question left an uneasiness in her mind.

"I'm strong enough—and the Short Buffalo People will prove it."

"That's passion." White Calf's words came from the depths of her memory. *"Can you force yourself to look beyond your rage?"*

"Trust the Dreamer?" she whispered to herself.

Suddenly she remembered Two Smokes' words about a dart in the back. No, not even a Dreamer could counter that. But what mad scheme could possess him? Alone, Two Smokes and Fire Dancer would walk into the middle of Heavy

Beaver's camp simply to Dream? Who'd watch their back for that deadly dart?

She wiped unconsciously at the prickle on her arm, realizing again that nothing crawled there.

"It's insanity." Then she stood, hastening to where Snaps Horn waited in hiding. "Snaps Horn, do you know what to do?"

The young man looked at her and grinned. "Kill as many as possible and chase them into the black timber."

"There's more," she added desperately. "You've got to keep together, drive them in until they get confused, split up. Keep them there. Watch the skies."

"In the black timber?" He cocked his head.

"You'll know." She glanced toward the trail head. "When you see the sign, run! Get everyone out. Follow the winter elk trail and run like the wind. The Short Buffalo will be taken care of. You can do that?"

"Yes, but what about—"

"I have to help the Dreamer! Trust me." And she was running, knowing now the path Two Smokes had taken.

Under her breath, she added, "Curse you, White Calf, you'd better be right!"

Ramshorn stepped out on the point, looking down over the sprawling basin that stretched west of the Buffalo Mountains. The land reflected stripes of brown mixed with clots of tan and light gray. The eye could lose itself out there, while beyond, the Stinking Water Mountains lay where the earth bubbled and boiling water shot high into the air. A land of ghosts, some said. The distance drew him, appealed to something in his soul. Even an eagle would be hard pressed to fly across that in a span of days.

But Tanager had Dreamed, and while he might come back here someday, more than ghosts lay behind him. Tanager had picked this place with unerring accuracy. From here, the fire would spread, bringing destruction to the Short Buffalo People.

Ramshorn squinted into the distance one last time. Turning his back, he walked down from the point and began pulling up the dry brush. He worked until a fine sweat coated his body. Already the west winds had begun to blow hot across the basin behind him.

He studied the trees, the wonderful trees whose branches waved in the wind.

"I'm saving the world," he told them. "Forgive me for this."

He bent down, reaching for his fire sticks where they lay in his pack.

Two Smokes led the way carefully, gritting his teeth every time he stepped over a deadfall and his bad leg took his weight. Despite his clamped teeth, a groan escaped his lips as agony shot up his leg.

"Should we rest a bit?" Fire Dancer asked.

Two Smokes swallowed at the pain. "At that rate you'd never get to the People. Heavy Beaver would have died of old age. Go on. If Power calls, you can't wait for an old berdache."

Fire Dancer smiled thinly, the detached look in his eyes unfocused. "No, old friend. Here, sit."

Two Smokes gratefully lowered himself on a log, panting his relief.

Fire Dancer reached into the pouch, producing the Wolf Bundle where it lay wrapped in the black wolf pelt. Two Smokes dug worried fingers into the rotten bark underneath him. "What are you thinking?"

Fire Dancer unwrapped the bundle, resplendent where lines of wolf blood had been copied meticulously on the smoothly stretched hide.

"We've restored the Wolf Bundle."

"We *think* we've restored the Wolf Bundle," Two Smokes corrected, a tingling of premonition charging his veins. "We did what we could."

"And that counts with Power," Fire Dancer said. "Let me Sing over your knee."

"And if it doesn't work? If the Power's not right yet? Let's not be hasty. Maybe a little pain's not a bad thing. You just watch, I'll . . ."

But Fire Dancer had closed his eyes, lifting the Wolf Bundle to the sky. He chanted a Spirit Song, calling to the Power, a benign expression modeling his face.

Two Smokes gulped as the Bundle lowered to his knee. He quivered at the feel of it, the old sensations returning, drawing him.

And if we turned the Power? He didn't have time for more. The world seemed to pitch on its side. Searing fire shot up Two Smokes' leg.

Tanager burst into the cove, a rush of relief bottling her throat as she walked up to the sweat lodge. "Two Smokes? Fire Dancer?"

Silence.

She lifted the flap, finding nothing but a tripod and rocks inside. She bent down and felt of the rocks, cold. Moving to the fire, she rubbed the ashes in her fingers, detecting the heat. Not gone long.

She looked around, starting at the sight of the wolf. Skinned, the animal rested on a platform, face to the west. Suddenly unsure, she walked carefully around it, noting the dart wound, seeing how the entrails had been carefully repacked in the body and the gut sewn closed with infinite care.

A pool of blood marked the animal's spot of death.

A knot formed in the back of her throat as she backed away. "Forgive me, Spirits," she called, fearing to raise her voice. "I came only to help the Dreamer and the Spirals. In your presence, I pledge to do this."

Step-by-step, she retraced her way, careful to disturb nothing. Beyond the cove, she waited for her heart to stop throbbing. She, Tanager, warrior of the Red Hand, quivered.

She turned, cutting for tracks until she found Two Smokes' hobbling trail. A smile of relief lit her lips for a brief instant. As she looked up, she caught the rising pall of yellow-brown smoke, bent by the winds, blowing east across the timber. It moved so gently, looking as if barely pushed. Any Red Hand could tell you the lie of that—especially in a year this dry.

Looking frantically to the north, she noted yet another plume of smoke. She had to hurry.

* * *

Fire At Night trotted down the trail, careful of turning an ankle on a rock. Curious how that worked—going up was so hard, but going down proved ever so much more dangerous.

Behind him, Throws Stones slid on unstable footing.

"Hey, watch that. You fall and break a leg and you'll miss the Blessing. I sure won't carry you."

"Uh-huh, and I'll tell Heavy Beaver you left on your own and I was chasing you."

"We've been through that."

Throws Stones grunted. "I know. He can't do much to his two best warriors. Beats hanging around up there, waiting for an Anit'ah dart. I don't know, I've been spooked ever since Straight Wood told us that witch tale."

"So, we stick with the story that we came down to check and see if the meat made it safe. I don't trust those boys who carried it down."

"You think Heavy Beaver will swallow that?"

"If your courage was going to fail, it should have done it up there." Fire At Night jerked a thumb back over his shoulder at the bulk of the mountain. "This *was* your idea."

Throws Stones gave a laugh he didn't feel. "So, how long have we been up here chasing through the trees, huh? Two moons, maybe three? And what's happened? We raided a couple of camps, killed a couple of people, and took some women. Then the Anit'ah disappeared. I think Left Hand was right. They ran over on the west side of the mountain."

"I sleep better at night knowing we chased them away, and wonder why we Sing over more of our friends every day."

"We keep learning the trails."

"But we can't hold them. I don't know. This isn't like the plains. You can't get them to stand up, fight one-on-one. They don't have a warrior's honor. They're like coyotes, sneaking around everywhere. You never know when one will get brave and sneak in to nip your butt."

"They can't last this winter. When have we given them time to cache their stupid seeds? They don't even have time to hunt. All we have to do is keep the pressure on them, then let them starve this winter."

"Then where are the old men and women? Gathering food,

I'll bet.'' Fire At Night slowed to a stop, muscular chest heaving. "I don't know, I tell you. I think that old stories about mad dogs and larkspur-eating fools being the only ones to fight Anit'ah is right.''

"Their cousins, the White Crane, weren't so much.''

"Their cousins didn't have that Wolf Bundle. And they didn't have that she-bitch of a warrior either! You can say what you want about them in a stand-up fight, but that last time I cast three darts at her, and I'd swear they bent out of the way each time.''

"Heavy Beaver will kill her with his Power one of these days.''

"Like Two Blue Moons thought he would? I almost didn't get away last time I fought her. Fortunately, I was near the trail. The rest got chased into the trees and you know what happens then.''

Throws Stones lifted his lip. "Maybe she gets her strength from men, huh? Milks their semen before a fight? You know what Heavy Beaver says about women, how they rob a man's strength, drain him.''

Fire At Night chuckled. "I could be drained like that more often. That's one of the reasons I decided to come. Three moons without my wives is too long.''

"You know, the more I think about this, the less I like the excuse about the meat.''

"So?''

"So we tell him we need to talk about strategy, about how to beat this woman. What's a tanager anyway?''

"That red, yellow, and black bird that lives up in the tops of the trees.'' Throws Stones thought about it and grinned. "Yes, I like that. A war strategy. Heavy Beaver will go for that. If we stroke that fat ego he keeps in that fat body, he'll do a special Sing for us, Bless us so we can kill that woman. After that, the Anit'ah will fall apart like a cattail tuft in the late fall.''

"Then we'd better quit standing here like perching ravens and get down there.''

"A change of heart?''

"No, just a better story for Heavy Beaver. After all these years, I still don't underestimate him. I remember what he

id to Sage Root and the others. I don't mess with a man like
aat.''

"I think it's this way."
Fire Dancer looked down the steep trail. "I don't know.
What if it's a dead end? We'd have to climb back up that."
Two Smokes puffed out his cheeks and exhaled. "I don't
now either. It's been a long long time. I was young then."
"How's your knee doing?"
Two Smokes smiled. "I don't think it's ever felt this good
ince the buffalo stepped on it."
Fire Dancer rubbed the back of his neck. "I didn't know.
When you almost passed out, I thought . . . well, I'm lost. I
on't trust myself."
"Then trust an old berdache and let's take this trail."
"And if you're wrong?"
Two Smokes looked over the edge, seeing the winding track
isappearing into a thick stand of lodgepole. To either side,
heer walls of the mountain dropped off in cliffs impossible
or them to descend. Before them, all of the basin lay exposed
nd sere under the burning sun.
"This other trail doesn't look any better. And if we try the
nain trail, you're going to be Dreaming on the end of a
varrior's dart."
Fire Dancer bit his lip, lost in thought.
"Can't you sense which path is right? Dream something."
And the second Two Smokes said it, he wished he hadn't.
Fire Dancer's face twitched. "I—I don't know. I'm so con-
used." He shook his head. "All I can feel is the Power.
You don't just talk to it unless . . . well, you're Dreaming."
Two Smokes rubbed his sweaty face. "Then let's go this
vay. There are fewer rocks." He gestured toward the lodge-
ole.
"Not only that, look. Tanager's plan is working." Fire
Dancer pointed up.
Two Smokes shaded his eyes against the blaze of the sun.
A faint haze of smoke dulled the sky. "Then we'd better get
•ff the mountain. Dry as it is, it'll burn fast. My father
old me about the first coming of the drought. His father told
im. It was like the whole world burned."

"Not like in my Dream, I pray. Not that." Fire Dancer swallowed nervously and finally nodded. "All right, down down."

Two Smokes started over the edge, suddenly uneasy. Power wouldn't protect him from a broken leg. And without him who'd hold the Wolf Bundle while Fire Dancer Dreamed and Danced with Fire? . . . If they lived that long.

"Hey!" The cry came from above as if in answer to his fears.

Two Smokes turned to see Tanager waving as she jumped down the steep trail in a cascade of rock.

Wearily, Two Smokes hitched himself back up to the restricted shoulder of the mountain they stood on.

Tanager came puffing down the slope. She looked disheveled, legs trembling as she gasped for air. Apparently, she'd run a long way.

"Not . . . that way," she panted, pointing. "You'll be in a dead end. That trail ends in a sheer cliff. Only the deer use that trail to go up and down to get the brush that's there for winter feed. It would have cost you a half a day."

Fire Dancer closed his eyes and nodded, a subtle panic hidden behind worried eyes.

"Why have you come?" Two Smokes asked.

Tanager looked away, breasts heaving as she sought to catch her breath. "Something White Calf said. I don't know the why of it. Power. She said if I did this, maybe I could save the Red Hand."

"Another Dreamer following a Dreamer," Fire Dancer added softly. "And this other trail?"

"It's rough, but I don't think we'll find Short Buffalo People on it." She rattled her darts. "And if we do, you can Dream them to the Starweb."

"But why?" Two Smokes insisted. "Why you?"

She looked out over the basin. "White Calf said something about balance, and Spirals, and things I don't understand. I've been given part of her Power. I think she wanted me to use it." She swallowed. "And I swore I would. I promised the Spirits back where you had your sweat and killed the wolf. I didn't know it was a sacred place until too late. Maybe this way I won't offend Power."

Fire Dancer smiled absently, eyes gone out of focus. "Then let us hope none of us offend. Time is short. Which way?"

She shook off a shiver and pointed with the darts. "This way."

Red Chert brought Heavy Beaver a roasted piece of buffalo backstrap skewered on green willow. The meat had been wrapped in balsam leaves with yarrow sprigs and sage inserted into the tender meat. Then the whole had been deep-pit roasted until it simmered in its own juices. Now the flesh barely clung to the skewer, cooked to perfection.

"Bring me a bowl, woman." He scowled as rich juices ran down his arm, staining his best ceremonial clothing. He flicked the droplets away, checking to make sure none had spotted his white buffalo hide.

Elk Whistle, Seven Suns, and Two Stones sat in the places of honor beside him, waiting their turns. The huge fire burning in the center of the camp kept the herd of children scampering to collect more wood as the women who'd been punished for this and that levered deadfall between tree trunks to break it into sections.

To waste so much wood in the middle of summer seemed almost profligate, but they'd move camp by the time winter set in. The few warriors that remained to guard the camp had taken a break from their Dance, sitting in the shade of the cottonwoods, laughing and joking among themselves as they looked to their decorations and repainted their bodies where sweat had run.

For the moment the Singers continued to chant, thumping the pot drum, voices rising and falling in a Song for the Girl's Dance. On a tall pole a buffalo head had been hung and Blessed to watch over the Dancers. Eagle feathers had been woven into the matted hair to flutter with the breeze.

A group of girls circled the fire, following the pattern of the sun, twirling and jumping to the beat and chant of the old men.

Heavy Beaver watched, noting their athletic grace and boundless energy. For a wistful moment, his memory drifted back to when he'd been a boy—and never a good Dancer by any means. Boys had their own Dance that called for exuberant jumping and hopping. Why hadn't he ever had energy like that? All his life he'd tended toward fat and much preferred lying in the shade to running and playing.

Because I've always been different, always in my head. Mother saw that in me. She knew. He shook the sudden melancholy off and grunted to himself. That terrible Dream had left him irritable these last few days.

"It's only because you're finally removing the last of the threats," he reassured himself.

"What was that?" Elk Whistle asked.

"Nothing." He tilted his head back, chewing thoughtfully and savoring the flavor of the lean meat. "When we're finally coming to the end of our labors, a man must take time for reflection. Remember where he's been and what he's accomplished. This Blessing renews our spirit. At the same time we pay respects to Buffalo Above and the Wise One for giving us the strength to do what we've had to."

"We had better hope the rains come," Seven Suns reminded him. "There can't be enough buffalo up in the mountains to support so many people up there. Even the Anit'ah had to split when they grew too many. That's when the White Crane moved to the plains."

Heavy Beaver shot a hard look at the old man. Would he always be like a thorn in a moccasin sole? "Perhaps you misread the signs, old friend. The drought came upon us to remind us our work wasn't done. The Anit'ah continue to offend the Spirit World with their way. When we've broken them forever and taken their mountains, the drought will break. Just as it did when we cleansed the People and pushed our enemies away."

Seven Suns said nothing, a pensive look in his old eyes.

"Look!" One of the warriors pointed from where he sat in the shade, a horn of pigment in his hand.

All eyes craned to the rising puff of haze over the mountains.

Heavy Beaver squinted into the sun, shading his eyes with a greasy hand, instantly wishing he'd wiped it. It would be foolish looking if it streaked his forehead.

"Clouds," he decided, looking back at the old men. "You see, as my words mentioned it, so did—"

"Not clouds," Elk Whistle corrected. "Smoke."

Smoke? Heavy Beaver stared again, seeing what he'd missed the first time. The yellowish tinges couldn't be mistaken.

"Perhaps some party let their campfire get out of control."

"Or it's an Anit'ah trick. This woman of theirs, this Tanager, might have found some way—"

"Stop this foolish talk!" Heavy Beaver clapped his hands to ensure their attention. "No woman outside of my mother could think up a trick that clever. No, this is a sign. Our warriors probably started it. It's some way to make an end of the Anit'ah. Do you think the Anit'ah would burn their own lands? Already they've been prevented from collecting food for the winter. When have they had time to hunt?"

"They eat plants, too," Two Stones reminded him.

"And plants burn."

"Or they know something about winter up there that we don't. Maybe the bighorn ranges don't burn like the forests? They're crafty people, clever," Elk Whistle reminded.

"And you're fools." Heavy Beaver glared up at the smoke, a worry tickling his fears. The Dancing had stopped. People stood around, looking, muttering nervously to each other.

I have to stop this or the silly fools will all be running in circles crying doom. He struggled to his feet, walking out into the Dance ground, hands raised.

"My people! Observe the Power of Heavy Beaver! Already the Anit'ah are breaking! Buffalo Above has sent us an ally in our fight! Look whose lands are burning! See the justice of Buffalo Above against those who stand in his way! Dance! Everyone Dance! Feel the Spirit as you Dance and Pray! Cry your thanks to Buffalo Above! This is the turning! This is the way of our victory!"

The warriors screamed their delight, charging into the Dance circle and whooping as they jumped and brandished their darts. The pot drum began booming as the old men raised their voices.

Around him, the People began to Sing and Dance, hands raised to the pall of smoke over the Buffalo Mountains.

The sheer Power of it leapt like fire in Heavy Beaver's breast. Yes, this was the way! This was the Dream. They

Danced for him, raising their arms over their heads in time with his, screaming and cheering. He stepped back, watching, joy about to burst in his chest.

They Danced for him!

Elk Charm carried a basketful of infant-soiled juniper bark up the trail, knowing the way by feel now. She reached the cap rock and walked over to cast the litter onto the rock. By the next morning, the breezes would have carried it away.

That's when her gaze caught the glow high on the mountain. She stopped, frozen, staring up. The intervening ridges stood starkly outlined in the reddish tinge. Where the smoke rose high, gaudy flames lit the whole of the eastern sky. Never had she seen a fire like this.

An age of Fire. The words whispered through her mind. *And Little Dancer is up there!*

"Elk Charm?"

She jumped, clutching one hand to her chest. "Cricket? You frightened me."

Her friend materialized out of the night, standing by her to stare up at the mountain wall. "Snaps Horn is up there, fighting the enemy."

"And so is Little Dancer. Gone to find his Dream." How much more of this could she stand?

"Let him be safe." Cricket shook her head. "I should have stayed. I should have fought with him."

"And who would have cared for your baby?"

"I could have left him. I could have brought him down and left him. My grandmother is here. Perhaps Rattling Hooves or you would have taken him. Then I could have gone back. With a lighter dart, I'm just as deadly as a man when I cast. Just have to be closer is all."

Elk Charm bit her lip. "I couldn't have done anything for Little Dancer. A wife can fight, can use a club, a dart, but I can't Dream for him."

Cricket's arm went around her shoulders. "Won't this ever end? Maybe Tanager's as Powerful as they say. She always saw things differently. Maybe she's the one. Maybe she can save them. She knows the timber better than anyone. She should have been a man."

Without thinking, Elk Charm supplied, "Maybe it takes both. Little Dancer's Power and . . . hers." And a part of her whimpered, *Why couldn't I be the one to help him?*

"Black Rock came today. He says that Tanager has become a powerful warrior. That no one can touch her in a fight, that he has Power she got from White Calf."

Elk Charm's gaze remained riveted to the blaze. "He was supposed to Dance with Fire." She swallowed, falling to her knees, arms lifted to the night sky. "Take him if you will, but give him strength! Hear me! Help him Dance the Fire. Even if I never see him again, you must help him!" She blinked at the tears. "For all of us."

She glanced again at the raging inferno on the top of the mountain. Could even a Dreamer Dance with that?

"Anything, take anything from me. But help him."

Fire Dancer awoke, blinking, staring up into the night. He lay exposed on his back, the stagnant air too hot for covers. Above him, the Starweb looked fuzzy, shrouded by the smoke, while over the mountains, the night glared crimson. Tanager slept to one side, barely distinguishable as a dark lump. Two Smokes lay on the other side.

Dreams had haunted him, scattered images refusing to come together as a whole. Troubled Dreams for troubled sleep. He'd walked again through the burning forest. Now the reality raged above him.

Have I missed it? Was that trial only a warning in case I might have failed?

He stood quietly, missing the ghostly presence of wolf. Always aloof, the animal had nevertheless become a companion in loneliness. What choice had there been? Wolf knew. His soul had been in tune with the need, become part of the Wolf Bundle. It had taken wolf to restore the Power, make it new.

Wolf and man, their paths had twined from the distant past. Brothers, predators, who ate not only buffalo and elk and deer, but berries and rodents and mice. Like men, wolves lived in their own societies. Like men, they sang to the stars and loved and raised their families. But, unlike most men, they shared souls with the One, perhaps less distracted by illusion.

He climbed up on one of the boulders, eyes to the reddened sky. "Fire Dancer."

They'd come down a tributary of Clear River along the northern end of the Red Wall. Less than a day's walk to the south lay Heavy Beaver's camp. This time tomorrow, he would have Danced Fire with Heavy Beaver—or he'd be lying dead somewhere, his soul drifting back to the One. Memories of the sensations of death, of the settling of the soul, clung like tufts of marten fur in the back of his mind.

With a pang, he realized the finality of it. Elk Charm would be left behind along with the daughters he'd never see grow to adulthood. He'd never know their joys and sorrows, see the expressions of delight on their faces, or dry their tears.

"Why?" he asked the night sky. "Why did you ever allow me to love? It hurts so much to give it up."

Hungry Bull would grow old, hair shot with white as his face lined. He'd die without his son to care for him, to Sing him to the Starweb where he could find Sage Root.

"Did you have to pick me?" A stirring resentment rose. Like a hoop in a child's game, he'd been rolled about this way and that. Callous spirits, like the children in the game, had cast their darts at him, some striking, others quivering as they landed in the dirt in his path. While they laughed and gamboled, none had cared about the bruises and cuts the hoop of his life had endured.

Yet through his resentment, the bliss of the One permeated, drawing him like an aster drew a bee. No matter what, he'd have to taste that nectar. He'd have to immerse himself in the sweetness. And therein lay the pain, knowing he couldn't back away from the colors of the flower and the rich feast it contained. No, not even love could make him retreat.

Power had pulled him with an addiction stronger than Hungry Bull's adoration of the hunt. To seek the One had become his single purpose.

He closed his eyes, taking a deep breath, stilling his thoughts. Again he tried to cross the threshold, searching for the One. Bit by bit, he channeled his mind, seeking the silver touch of it just beyond his reach. Harder and harder, he tried, forcing himself.

Finally, in futility, he opened pained eyes, glaring angrily up at the night. "How? Tomorrow is the day . . . and I can't."

A rustling in the night breeze whispered through the brush around him, ruffling the dry grasses.

He cocked his head, listening, the sound that of a rattlesnake. A rattlesnake?

A swell of Power pressed the air around him. The strange voice chanted in his imagination:

> *Monster Creatures on bellies crawl.*
> *Legless, armless, hair of scale.*
> *Shakes a rattle on his tail.*
> *Teeth of poison, hollow flail,*
> *Makes the blood black and frail.*

The threshold.

Chapter 27 ◎

Tanager cried, "Here!"

Two Smokes turned from where he peered under the sagebrush to see Fire Dancer rushing over. As he hobbled closer, he watched Fire Dancer bend down on his knees, facing the buzzing reptile.

"So now we catch it?" Tanager asked uncertainly.

Fire Dancer wet his lips and looked up. An unfamiliar expression, part awe, part worry, met Two Smokes' questioning look.

"Yes, we catch it."

"Wait!" Tanager started forward, too late, as Fire Dancer extended his open palm. His hand trembled as he gritted his teeth, determination on his face.

Two Smokes cried out, watching as the coiled rattlesnake drove fangs into Fire Dancer's hand.

"No!" Tanager reached for him, stricken, only to have Fire Dancer shrug her off, reaching around to grasp the snake behind the head.

Fire Dancer inspected the wounds. Meanwhile, the snake twisted around his arm, straining, the *shishhh* of its angry rattle loud in the air.

"What?" Tanager drew back, shaking her head. "You're out of your mind!" She turned away, staring back up at the smoke-capped mountain. Already, ash fell from the still air like some perverted snow.

Two Smokes stared, undone at the two beads of blood that formed where the fangs had sunk into Fire Dancer's living flesh.

"This is it," Tanager added firmly. "I'm going back."

"You can't," Two Smokes pleaded.

She whirled, sparks in her eyes. "I didn't come down here to walk into Heavy Beaver's camp of warriors with a delirious madman!"

Out of the jumble of confusion, Two Smokes tried to form some argument. "But . . . you said—"

"White Calf told me to trust the Dreamer, to set aside my anger for the Red Hand. She didn't tell me to . . . to take care of a crazy fool!"

"The threshold," Fire Dancer murmured to himself. "It stings, burns . . . all illusion. Seek the gray mist, feel it swirl . . . illusion."

Tanager shook her head and stared. "A *mad* fool!"

"Come with us. I don't know why, but we need you. I can feel it."

Tanager stamped back and forth. "Need me? For what? To carry *him* when he starts falling over?"

Two Smokes raised his hands in a soothing motion. "Trust him. He knows what he's doing."

"What he's doing? *He just stuck his hand in a rattlesnake's mouth!*"

Two Smokes gestured frantically. "Yes . . . yes, he's done it before. I don't know why. *He's* the Dreamer! Trust me. I can feel the Power of it!"

"The Power of lunacy." She gripped her darts and started back the way she'd come, shaking her head.

"Wait!" Two Smokes pleaded. "Didn't you say you'd promised? That you'd been to the place we renewed the Wolf Bundle?"

She stopped short and lowered her head, hesitating for a moment before nodding. Wind tugged at her braid, her fine dress looking shabby in the smoke-filtered sunlight. She stared up at the streaked sky, seeing where the light shone evilly through the shadows of a flaming world. She turned, glaring at him from the corner of her eye.

"I guess I'm committed. One way or another."

Two Smokes took a deep breath, the odor of smoke in his nostrils. "Yes, I guess we all are. This is the road of Power. All we can do is walk it."

Tanager turned. "And pray like mad we know what we're doing."

Fire Dancer had raised his eyes to the turbid sky. "The threshold. Please make this be the threshold. Where is the gray mist? The mist of illusion?"

"Come on," Tanager ordered, shouldering past them, a disdainful glance cast at the Dreamer.

Two Smokes pulled Fire Dancer to his feet, staying well clear of the writhing rattlesnake.

Already they could hear the faint boom of Heavy Beaver's pot drum. *A mad fool?*

Make it not be so.

Beyond the confines of his lodge, Heavy Beaver could hear the Dance, Singing, drumming, the chants of the People. Dusk fell about the camp like the drifting ash, murky, somehow lessening the Power of the occasion. He'd come here, not wanting others to overhear.

"Why don't I trust your motives?"

Throws Stones shot a quick glance at Fire At Night before stating, "This Anit'ah woman, this Tanager, has Power. We knew you were holding a Blessing. None of your warriors has more courage than we. Fire At Night and I have taken a vow to kill this Tanager."

Heavy Beaver watched through slitted eyes. He heard the half lie. "Tell me more."

Fire At Night cleared his throat nervously. "She Dances and Sings as she fights. I myself have seen men set themselves, take aim, and have their darts sail harmlessly past her. Straight Wood told us—"

"I've heard *enough* of Straight Wood and his stories!" Heavy Beaver clapped his hands to signify the subject closed.

"So we came to be Blessed, to have *you* Sing special Power for us. We had the Red Hand beaten before she rose to take the leadership from Blood Bear and his pathetic Wolf Bundle."

"There is no Power in the Wolf Bundle," Heavy Beaver stated calmly. "It is a pollution. If it comes my way again, I intend on burning it. I should have in the beginning."

And now what? He watched his warriors sitting nervously before him. If these two could have grown tired of the ceaseless war with the Anit'ah, how many more felt the same but didn't have the status to challenge him?

"What of the fire on the mountain? What caused it?"

Fire At Night shook his head. "We don't know. It started after we were almost down the trail."

"Could it be our fire?"

"Possibly." Throws Stones resettled himself as if he were uncomfortable. "Some of our men have been careless with fire before. Firm Dart almost set things on fire one night but got the coals stamped out."

The solution came. "Very well, I will make you special Power. Come." He rocked back and forth to get his weight moving and got to his feet. He led them out into the camp, into the middle of the Dance circle.

Raising his hands, he called, "People! Tonight we will make special Power! These two men come bearing tidings of a *woman*! Yes, an Anit'ah woman who claims to have Power! In the tongue of the Anit'ah, her name is Tanager—a little yellow bird!"

Someone laughed. Throws Stones shifted uneasily behind him.

"So I call you to witness. Someone bring a sharp knife."

Heavy Beaver turned slightly, seeing Fire At Night's features go ashen. An old man waddled forward, a hafted chert knife in his hand.

Heavy Beaver walked over to the roaring bonfire and extended his hand to the two warriors. "Before all the People, I Bless you!" He reached for Throws Stones' hand, taking the blade and slashing the man's arm. Blood welled. In turn he made a similar cut in Fire At Night's.

To the People who watched solemnly, he explained. "Now I mingle their blood!" And he pressed the wounds together. "So they are bound by this oath. The next time they see this Tanager, they must kill her!" He forced their arms over the fire, letting a few drops of blood drip onto the coals to hiss and spatter.

"It is done! Their word of honor is sent to the sky as smoke, proof to Buffalo Above of their worth!" And in a low voice he added, "And if you don't kill her when you see her, you're both Cursed with the sticks as I did to Sage Root so long ago. You know my Power."

For long moments he stared into their eyes, seeing the effect of his words shrivel their souls. "Now, *Dance*! Dance like you've never Danced before!"

And he turned, walking back to his seat of honor as the gathering dusk darkened the sky around him and the mountain flamed redly above. Heat lightning lit the skies to the north and south and east.

Yes, now they knew his Power. He gazed angrily up at the burning mountain. Flames had crossed the summits, flickering in yellow tongues along the slopes. The People glanced up, awed by the sight.

Heavy Beaver experienced that flutter of his heart. Power roamed loose on the land. *Mother? Where are you?*

"Are we ready?" Two Smokes asked quietly as they came within sight of the camp. A huge fire lit the place. There would be no stealthy approach.

Fire Dancer had begun to stagger, his bitten arm swollen, the other clamped tight on the snake so that Two Smokes thought more than once the animal might have suffocated.

Tanager lifted a shoulder in a pointless shrug. "I'm already dead. I can't be more ready than this."

"The threshold," Fire Dancer whimpered. "Where is the threshold? Gray mist . . . gray . . . illusion."

"Then we wait for a while," Two Smokes decided. "Fire Dancer, your time has come. Dream, boy. *Dream*!"

The sacred datura pulsed within him. As it began to leach its power along his veins, Heavy Beaver started to hear the whispers of Power. Perhaps it had been foolish to take the last of the plant, but he *had* to hear his mother's voice in this moment of triumph.

He walked out in the center of the Dance circle, feeling detached, and silhouetted himself in the light of the fire. He raised his hands, gesturing to the People. He blinked, knowing the swirling of Power around him.

Watch me, Mother. Then speak to me.

"You see my Power!" Lightning flickered again in the inky sky, illuminating the clouds, backed by the inferno swelling from the Buffalo Mountains.

The cheer entered like a breath and grew within, filling him fit to bursting.

"We are the People! We are the new way!" As they cheered, pride pulsed up and down his soul. *Mother, see me! See what I have done with your Dream!*

"Look, people! Look and see that I have burned the An-it'ah!"

Firelight danced off the buffalo head hanging from the pole. "We, the People, have renewed you, brother Buffalo! Make your herds grow and know you feed your brothers.

"No one can change our way! The taint of weak women is cleaned from us."

The warriors whooped and jumped, rattling their darts. Their gleaming eyes were for him alone, ignoring the fire where their comrades now fought for their lives. Even the women watched, cowed, accepting their lot.

"Who would challenge Heavy Beaver's Power?"

"I would."

Heavy Beaver froze, refusing to believe. "Who?" he demanded hotly. "Know that you are Cursed as you speak."

Images from the terrible Dream replayed as the People backed away, clearing a path. Three people—a young man, a crippled old woman, and a tall thin young woman—walked through the ranks.

"Who are you?"

"Have I changed so much, Heavy Beaver?" The old hobbling woman spoke with a man's voice.

"Two Smokes!" The knowledge came through the shimmering sweetness of the datura rushing along his veins. "You bring the vileness of berdache here on this day? You have the nerve?" And the young man, why did he look so familiar?

"A Dreamer has come," Two Smokes said firmly. "He's come to Dream the Spiral—which you've forgotten."

"And this . . . this *woman*?" He gestured.

"Her name is Tanager. The greatest warrior of the Red Hand. She has come as our escort."

"A brief escort."

The young man stepped forward, lifting a rattlesnake high in a swollen hand. Something about his eyes caught Heavy Beaver's attention. Even through the years, he knew. "Ah— Little Dancer? Came for the same fate as your mother? Or have the Anit'ah thrown you out?"

Fire Dancer's voice carried, eerie in the night as he lifted a bundle in his good hand. *The Wolf Bundle!* "I have come to Dream with you, Heavy Beaver. Together we'll Dance the Power." And he lifted the snake high, a smile on his face. "Come and Dance with me, Heavy Beaver."

People gasped, eyes lit with wonder. Fire Dancer held their attention. With that, he handed the Wolf Bundle to Two Smokes, a chant on his lips. In the firelight, it seemed like a Dream. Chanting, the young man Danced up to Heavy Beaver. The People remained rooted, too shocked to move.

The world began to pulse with Fire Dancer's steps, shifting and shimmering. Or was it the datura? Heavy Beaver blinked, a curious chill in his flesh.

"If you're a true Dreamer, Heavy Beaver, you can Dance the venom. Prove as I have proved, that it's nothing but illusion." The People cried out as the rattlesnake bit Fire Dancer on the breast.

Heavy Beaver swallowed, staring with wide eyes at the serpent.

"No, you're evil."

Fire Dancer laughed, cavorting and leaping. "Feel the One! Feel it running through us. Feel the Spirals! This is a night of Power."

He extended the snake again. Frantically, Heavy Beaver batted the serpent away, grateful that it landed writhing and hissing in the flames.

"Is that your response to the Dance?" Fire Dancer whirled away, Singing and Dancing.

Heavy Beaver raised his hands, calling on his strength, on everything he believed. The datura swelled and rippled along his soul.

"Little Dancer, I declare you a foulness. You and your berdache are Cursed. You will die . . . die in agony!"

"See the Power of the One!" Fire Dancer pointed to the sky.

Heavy Beaver followed his pointing finger to the night sky. There, on the western horizon, a whirlwind rose above the flames, flickers of light showered out of the night sky, falling, drifting here and there, lighting the darkness.

The voice mocked in Heavy Beaver's mind, *"I am the Wolf Bundle. Feel my Power!"*

Horrible things spiraled down out of the night sky, reaching for Heavy Beaver.

Tanager never let her eyes wander. Fear pumped bright with her blood. So she'd condemned herself to death? Here they could rush her, take her alive, rape her, make a slave of her.

"Never again," she promised under her breath. What kind of lunatic followed another? Her place was fighting with her people against the invaders. Still, she'd vowed a dart would drink Heavy Beaver's blood before her own ceased to pump.

The two men advanced carefully, nervously. She caught their movement as Heavy Beaver's voice rolled out in some terrible threat. A prickling ran up her arm. At least White Calf's soul hadn't deserted her.

She watched, poised on balanced feet. They planned to

cast at the same time. A dart apiece for the berdache and Fire Dancer. She'd have to be fast—fast like she'd never been before.

Not even a Dreamer can guard against a dart in the back.

The war chant burst from her lips as she moved into the Dance. Not even Cougar had her swiftness. The enemy charged and cast. She planted a foot, slapping aside the first dart, spinning and batting the second from its mark. The Dance filled her as she whirled, nocking her own deadly missile. She whipped her arm forward, sending it to its mark, driving it deep into the man's chest even as he nocked a second dart. She shifted, batting a third dart from the air, body surging in the trance of the Dance and Power.

She thrilled, bracing for that brief instant, casting with all the muscle of her whip-thin body, knowing the cast had been good. Then she turned on nimble feet, covering the Dreamer where he Danced his own Power. She grinned at the shocked enemy, who stood unmoving, as if planted in the ground.

Yes, she'd been meant for this. None of the other warriors so much as quivered. Through wide eyes, they watched, gaudy in their paint, courage thin as water as they stared at the two dying warriors who whimpered and moaned on the ground, one bleeding at the mouth, the other staring horrified at the dart shaft that stuck from the hollow under his ribs.

Tanager whooped as fire rained down from above.

Two Smokes heard the snapping rattle of darts. Shooting a quick glance over his shoulder, he caught sight of Throws Stones and Fire At Night where they lay, watched by the circle of faces.

He sighed, lifting the Wolf Bundle high, ecstatic at the Power that ran through it. He lifted it, drifting, a wonderful floating sensation filling him.

"I CURSE YOU!" Heavy Beaver shrieked, glazed eyes on his dying warriors.

"You Curse no one," Fire Dancer Sang, stepping to the bonfire. "Your Power is illusion, Heavy Beaver. Learn with me. Dream with me."

And he Danced, Singing with a Power that swayed souls.

"I am Fire Dancer, come to Dream the new way. Feel the Spirals, feel the One, changing now, becoming whole!"

Heavy Beaver gaped, mouth open, disbelief large in his eyes. He swatted at something in the air, crying out, as if things reached for him.

"No! Leave me alone! I Curse you, Wolf Bundle. *I Curse you!*"

Fire Dancer stepped around the fat man, a detached light in his eyes, fixing Heavy Beaver in his stare like a snake did a bird. Behind him, flames crackled up in the juniper as hot sparks fell red and glowing from the ink-shot sky.

"Feel the Power, Heavy Beaver, feel the Wolf Bundle. That's what possesses you now. Take the coals. Dance with them. Dance the One."

"No! Leave me alone!" Tears squeezed from clamped eyes, running jaggedly down his contorting face.

"*Feel the Power!*" Fire Dancer Sang. He whirled before the People. "Dance! Dance with me! Dance the Spirals! A new way has come. A new way!"

Heavy Beaver shrieked, voice twisted with terror. He slashed at the air with futile fists, beating away things only he could see. Screaming, he lurched to his feet, fleeing toward the edge of camp, dashing into the burning juniper, heedless of the flames.

One by one, more people began to move their feet, learning the Song from Fire Dancer, following the Dance.

Where he stood in the center, Two Smokes held the Wolf Bundle high, tears falling from his cheeks as his soul drifted with the One. The Blessed, Blessed One.

Heavy Beaver crashed madly through the brittle juniper. He tripped and fell, stumbling over a twisted sagebrush. Whimpering, he thrashed at the darting things swooping about him. He covered his head, feeling the earth seething beneath him. Or was it only the datura?

Crying, he looked up. Around him the trees burned, fire leaping orange and yellow, searing, crackling, and roaring as entire junipers and giant sage exploded in waves of flame. Blinding tongues of light leapt for the night-black sky, illuminating the cloudlike masses of tumbling smoke in an eerie

eddish tint that receded into charcoal smudges of ruby and
maroon as they rolled higher and higher into the flame-
treaked sky.

The air roared and rushed to feed the tremendous inferno.
Entire trees cracked like thunder as the trunks split, steaming
and whooshing into the wall of racing flame.

The heat of it beat into him like a fist, crushing him into
the parched soil, grinding him down flat as the world burned
around him.

"Mother?"

In the heart of the roaring incineration a figure moved,
stalking the white ash like a shadow.

Heart pounding, Heavy Beaver watched as Little Dancer
walked through the flames, tongues of it licking around
him.

"Why don't you burn? *What are you?"*

"I'm the Dreamer of the People." And the figure blurred
as a wall of flame swept past, searing an afterimage on the
back of Heavy Beaver's eyes.

Shielding his gaze with an uplifted arm, Heavy Beaver
squinted, expecting Little Dancer to have been charred to
sizzling grease and blackened bone. Instead, he stood there,
tall, handsome, the gaudy light of the burning world reflecting on his smooth skin.

"What . . . who *are* you?"

"I'm you, Heavy Beaver . . . and not you. I'm the Dream
and the reality. I've led you here . . . and followed you. I'm
that which is . . . and is not. I'm the Dream you denied!"

Heavy Beaver blinked, feeling his skin blister. In horror,
he watched fire swirling around Little Dancer, watched him
Dance with it. Little Dancer reached down to sear Heavy
Beaver's fat flesh.

Panicked, Heavy Beaver jumped to his feet, charging head-
long into the fire, feeling his flesh sear. His lungs scorched
as he drew a breath to scream. He beat at his burning hair,
stumbling, rolling in the fire as pain crackled his charring
skin.

A final gust from the Wolf Bundle scattered the bits of his
soul.

* * *

"The Spiral is glowing, changing," the Wolf Dreamer called from the golden mist.

"We have our Dreamer," the Wolf Bundle Sang, its voice echoing the stars.

"And we are One." Fire Dancer whirled in the Dance.

By ones and twos they came down the trails. Some limped, some carried others burned too badly to walk on their own. As they came in to the camp, Two Smokes bandaged them, sending women and children for specific plants to make a poultice. Warriors sat stunned, vacant looks on their faces. Soot-grimed, with hair singed here and there, they stared at the smoldering mountain with empty eyes.

Tanager watched, impassive, as she guarded the Dreamer's lodge.

Two Smokes finally hitched his way over and settled next to Tanager. "I've asked many people. They say that as the fire began, the Anit'ah disappeared like a raindrop on a hot rock."

She nodded, a grim smile on her lips. "We *are* the Red Hand. The mountains are ours."

"Yes, the mountains are ours."

"I've been keeping my guard up for Heavy Beaver. What's happened to him?"

Two Smokes studied his callused hands. "They found him over there. Where the fire burned up the juniper. I still don't know why it didn't take the whole camp."

"Many things happened that night."

"But why did he run into the middle of the fire? Why?"

She gave him a hard glance. "He abused the Wolf Bundle once, didn't he?"

Two Smokes averted his eyes and nodded.

"You'd better be very careful of it."

"How's Fire Dancer?"

"He woke up a while ago."

"And you could bring me food," a weak voice called from within. Fire Dancer crawled from the lodge, gazing up at the mountain. He looked wasted, thin, but his eyes glittered as though not of this world.

Two Smokes sighed. "I thought hunger was only illusion."

"It is. Only I must live this illusion a while longer yet. You and I, my friend, together we must teach these people a new way. They must learn the secret of the grass from you. I must Dream for them, and you must be the bridge."

Two Smokes nodded, knowing the way of it. "And where will you do this?"

"I've been thinking of the Warm Wind Basin. There are no people who live there. And your grass grows everywhere. At least, that's what Three Rattles said last time he was through."

"And that will take the pressure off the buffalo for a while."

"Like men," Tanager said, pointing to the exhausted warriors, "buffalo need time to recover."

Two Smokes laughed. "It could be more difficult than that. One of the warriors started to beat his wife. She took after him with his own war darts. When he threatened to kill her, she told him Tanager would get him. You should hear it. There are arguments all over. One of the women insists on sitting in council. Seven Suns and Elk Whistle agreed. I think the warriors have missed the women."

Fire Dancer smiled weakly. "It hurts to miss a woman." He looked away.

"Your time will come. The People are quick, they'll—"

Fire Dancer shook his head. "You've Danced with the One. You can't go back, Two Smokes. It would . . . well, hurt worse. She'd never understand. I'd only make her miserable. My way is different now. You're berdache, you understand."

A silence passed.

"What of the Wolf Bundle?"

He gestured at Tanager. "She is the leader of the Red Band. It must go with her."

"And us? What do we do?"

Fire Dancer smiled, eyes focused on the distance. "You and I have the One. We Dance with Fire."

Epilogue ◎

Beyond the hangings, wind wailed down the canyon as
snow fell in twirling wraiths. Even the dogs had come sneaking in, cowering, fearful of being thrown out into the storm.
In the center, the fire crackled, lighting the faces of the young
children who listened raptly as the Trader talked.

". . . So the Spirit Helpers came down and gave Fire
Dancer a Spirit Dream. They told him that Heavy Beaver had
no Dream, that only his greed and ambition made him claim
Power. But the People didn't know the difference. The world
was changing and whose word should they believe?

"Wolf came and told Fire Dancer to renew the Wolf Bun-
dle. And he did this. And they Danced and Sang and made
Power together. In the midst of this, First Man came and
Danced with them.

" 'Go to the People,' First Man said. 'Take them the new
way and Dance the Spirals back the way they were before the
badness was let loose by Heavy Beaver.'

"And Fire Dancer did this. He walked down from the high
place and met Heavy Beaver. For four days they Danced and
fought. And once, Fire Dancer grabbed a handful of fire and
threw it up on the mountain, setting it all on fire. And they
continued to Dance while Heavy Beaver threw Curse after
Curse on Fire Dancer. But each time a Curse was thrown at
him, he picked up fire and washed it away. You know, like
you rub soot off your skin.

"Finally, Heavy Beaver sent all his warriors to kill Fire
Dancer, but Fire Dancer had his own warrior, Tanager, a
woman from the mountains. He Sang Power into her and she
killed all Heavy Beaver's warriors one by one.

"Fire Dancer had about had enough of Heavy Beaver and
his Curses, so he Danced them up to the burning mountain

and when they were in the middle of the fire, he left Heavy Beaver to burn up. And Heavy Beaver did. You know why?''

"Because he didn't have Power!" little White Stones answered seriously.

The children giggled.

"That's right," the Trader told them, spreading his hands. "That's why now all people are told to go to the high places and Dream. Everyone must do that to keep the Spirals like the Wise One Above made them. Heavy Beaver wanted the One all to himself. But if everyone seeks his own way to Power, no evil man will ever take it for his own again.''

"And what happened to Fire Dancer?" asked Busy Boy, talking around the finger in his mouth as he stared with big brown eyes.

"Fire Dancer saw that the way of the People had been returned to right. That Buffalo Above and all the spirits were happy, and then he rose to a high place and rode to the Starweb on lightning. And that's the way it was.''

From where she sat in the back, Elk Charm blinked her sightless eyes. The arthritis had knotted in her hands, making them ache when the weather turned this way. She'd suffered through each of her teeth abscessing and falling out; and after the time she'd fractured her arm, it had never worked right.

As long as it takes . . . That pain so long ago had never healed either. His laughter, the glint in his eyes, remained forever fresh in the sunlit memories in her mind—no matter that her eyes had gone dark.

"So that's the story they tell nowadays," she whispered to herself, remembering. "Maybe it's better so.''

She curled into her robes, feeling the dull ache in her joints. Snow always did that anymore. Tonight she would Dream of a big black wolf and a Dream-ridden young man, and of the young woman who loved him. And this time, maybe, just maybe, she'd let her soul go to the Power that called her.

In the background her great-great-grandchildren laughed.

BESTSELLING BOOKS FROM TOR